HALO

HALO

Paul Cook

an imprint of

ARC
MANOR
Rockville, Maryland

ISBN: 978-1-61242-003-5

www.PhoenixPick.com

Great Science Fiction & Fantasy

SIGN UP FOR FREE EBOOKS

Published by Phoenix Pick
an imprint of Arc Manor
P. O. Box 10339
Rockville, MD 20849-0339

www.ArcManor.com

How easily the blown banners change to wings...
Things dark on the horizons of perception
Become accompaniments of fortune...

From "TO AN OLD PHILOSOPHER IN ROME,"
by WALLACE STEVENS

CONTENTS

PROLOGUE

It seems to be one of the great ironies of history that just when the prospects of expanding Mankind's domain and cultural reach had come within his grasp, the Halo made its untimely visitation. This sense of irony is exacerbated by the fact that the promise of a more efficient system of space flight had seemed virtually imminent through the mathematical genius of Dr. Annette Sayles-Trenton at UCLA. Her quantum-field equations on Longjump space-bending seemed to be just on the verge of being confirmed experimentally when the Halo put an end to all earthbound research—as it had put an end to just about everything else Mankind had going for it at the time.

Had we not established our corporate colonies in space and on the moon and faraway Mars with the use of the Shortjump, the Halo's work might have been thorough. As it is, we are left with only an incomplete corpus of study that promises so much, but as yet offers so little. If we can actually locate Dr. Sayles-Trenton—even salvage what remains of her notes—then Mankind might have an opportunity to regain some of its lost ground.

Since the Halo itself has long since passed beyond the confines of the solar system, all we can do is speculate as to its true purpose. The Seeds—the so-called "pacifiers" which the Halo left in its wake—might have been enough to halt the growth of civilization; but there are those of us not living in the Hoovervilles of earth who feel that given the right effort and support, all of Mankind can benefit from any attempt to fight back.

We therefore fully recommend Operation Cakewalk as described and out-lined by former Lunar President Dr. Ross Trenton and his Moon Men. The risks, both politically and diplomatically, are worth the possible consequences. Otherwise, we hold to our original projections: without a solution to the Longjump and a way to nullify the Seeds, earthbound civilization will not endure beyond the end of the twenty-first century.

—concluding chapter from the
RAND CORPORATION'S FEASIBILITY
Study #231 as recommended to President Ralph Scanlon,
September 9, A.D. 2039.

ONE

SHORTJUMP

—— 1 ——

"I don't care what that report says," the President of the United States growled aside to his aide. "If this doesn't work, we're not even going to make it to the end of the next *year*, let alone the end of the century."

Ralph Scanlon's aide-de-camp, James Guthrie, stood quietly beside the great man in tacit agreement.

"Besides," the President continued, "I don't like the idea of the first President of the Moon leading the expedition." Scanlon sneered. "Those Moon People. How the hell do they know what's good for us anyway?"

"Moon Men, sir," the diminutive James Guthrie returned with. "And the Rand Corporation is here on the earth. They are the only people we now think can do this thing."

President Ralph Scanlon *harumphed* and squinted off into the misty gray sunlight of the western Atlantic sky.

The President was busy fussing with the thread of a nylon fishing line, trying to get it around a multicolored lure. "Moon Men, my ass. We should have let them tackle the Halo in the first place when it came by in '33. They think they're so smart…"

It was hard to imagine that the passing of the alien artifact known to them as the Halo in the autumn of a.d. 2033 was still affecting Mankind six years later. For the huge, greathearted Ralph Scanlon, all he wanted to do was to continue fishing off the East Portico of the Floating White House. After all, the Moon Men were a quarter of a million miles away and here he was, stuck out in the middle of the Atlantic Ocean on a makeshift barge—as he called it—now that Washington, D.C., was a series of Hoovervilles. The East Portico of the White House was really a porch with a cheery canvas overhang that fronted an infinite meadow of ocean called the Sargasso Sea.

Ralph Scanlon stood a precise six feet six, big as a tree, dwarfing just about anybody who came within a half mile of him. His aide, James Guthrie, was a mousy five feet seven and could have been Robin to Scanlon's Batman.

Ralph Scanlon's ruddy complexion and reddish-blond hair gave him the look of one of Ireland's original Nordic conquerors. But it was hard to say just who James Guthrie's people were. Small, innocuous, they seemed bred purely for bureaucratic service. However, this far out in the Atlantic it didn't seem to matter. Water was definitely *not* their element.

Like the President, Guthrie wore khaki shorts and a light cotton short-sleeved shirt. The weather was persistently balmy where the temporary center of the United States government now floated, but both men knew that the weather was about to change for them.

Guthrie adjusted the glasses on his nose and held up his aluminum clipboard as Scanlon struggled with his lure, oblivious of everything.

"These are the details of the Cakewalk, telefaxed this morning, sir," Guthrie announced. The communications building was directly opposite them on the floating platform that was the temporary White House. The platform was a two-mile-square hinged invention that boasted administration buildings, two runways for aircraft of various kinds, and a small port for boatcraft. At the opposite end, away from all the hustle and bustle, was the White House itself: a series of Quonset huts thrust against the water like insect husks.

Presently, as the platform floated aimlessly, they were in the western fringes of the Sargasso about two hundred and thirty statute miles north of Grand Bahama. Each time a swell nudged the platform, vast, sophisticated hinges took out some of the sickening surge. Scanlon, however, didn't like it, and yearned for the day when he could return to Washington and take up residence in the real White House—which currently had a Seed, surrounded by an impoverished Hooverville, on its disheveled front lawn.

Scanlon looked up momentarily. "It's so goddamn depressing. Why don't you tell me some *good* news?"

"The good news is, sir," Guthrie piped, "that they think they can actually pull it off."

"Fish a Seed out of Lake Tahoe?" Scanlon concentrated on his lure.

"The only one like it, sir. The Moon Men think they now have the resources to take it apart."

"*If* they can get at it," Scanlon countered.

"Yes, sir."

Today the platform of the Floating White House drifted calmly, moored in the midst of a lime-green carpet of kelp. Occasionally bits of debris—mostly unidentifiable gnarls of plastic—floated within range, trapped by the Sargasso's currents, but none of this interested Scanlon. These days, very little did.

However, since most of the cities of the earth—including those of the United States—had been made very difficult to live in, the only safe places now were deserts, the oceans, and polar regions. As President, he had the option of where he wanted to locate the White House.

This was his third year of regretting his initial decision.

He stood up on the lip of the portico. Deep within him, he knew that he'd much rather be participating in something, *anything*, such as Operation Cakewalk, than trying to snag a fish in the Sargasso Sea. However, out here there was little else to do but fish. The only excitement came when a STOL soared in from the mainland or a hovercraft hissed up onto the White House landing platform with an assortment of scientists or dignitaries.

Life could be worse, though. Scanlon held the antenna box of his electric reel and adjusted the dial as he flung out his gaudy hook. The thing sailed high into the air, then plunged into the faceless kelp with a gentle *ploop!*

Scanlon turned to Guthrie. Guthrie's thinning brown hair, slicked to his skull, shone in the sunlight. "Are all of Trenton's Moon Men in on this?" he asked distractedly.

Guthrie brightened, deferential, glad to be of use. "Yes, sir. The President will be leading it himself."

"*I'm* the President," Scanlon thundered.

"Yes, sir. Dr. Trenton's also a psychologist and has coordinated the whole—"

Scanlon cut him off. "I'd spot a Moon Man a mile away. Those Tahoe people'll know something's up."

"Our experts trust Dr. Trenton. After what he did when the *Jaguar Skies* fell out of lunar orbit into Copernicus—"

Scanlon glared at Guthrie. "That was a cheap way to win a presidency."

"He was nearly killed, sir. And they lost the *Jaguar Skies*."

Nothing moved out in the kelp. From behind them, out on the landing strip, the blades of a Navy jumpcopter began whining. Scanlon pondered the line, which resembled a gossamer spiderweb. He gave it an impatient, if impotent, tug.

"This thing better work," he snarled.

"The fishing reel?" Guthrie stared out to sea.

"No," the President snapped. "Operation Cakewalk! I don't want to spend another four years floating on this barge. I'm a president of a country. That means *land*. Not some point of latitude and longitude out in the ocean."

"Yes, sir," Guthrie said, sympathizing. Scanlon scowled blackly at his aide.

Then something gurgled out in the kelp and the antenna box began singing its little song of recognition. The line went suddenly taut.

"There!" Scanlon said happily. "First goddamn catch of the day!"

But then the chiming from the box ceased and the jewellike monitoring lights went dead.

Scanlon sulked. "Damn!" He handed the reel to Guthrie. "Goddamn fish swallowed it whole. Bit right through the line."

From far behind them, on one of the runways, a stubby-winged STOL roared into the bright Atlantic sky, gulping air voraciously. The President and his aide watched it escape, its afterburners gasping hotly, giving it the extra lift it needed.

"At least *some* things still work," Scanlon said, indicating the sleek STOL.

James Guthrie said nothing.

2

The man from the moon walked the quiet, autumn shores of Lake Tahoe. *Walking* was hardly the word, though. At times he wobbled; at times he tripped. Yet, he persisted.

He had to.

Mostly he was just glad to be there. His heart soared, being on the earth once more—even if the lake reminded him of happier times when he and his wife had honeymooned there. It had been a time when the mountain lake seemed to sink into itself, when the clamor of the summer's tourist population had dwindled down to a few stragglers whose campfires in the woods ringing the large lake bobbed like Japanese lanterns in the dusk.

Dr. Ross Trenton breathed deeply the smell of earth, his Stively-built heart shuddering almost rapturously in his chest. The calm wings of twilight had wrapped themselves around the landscape, but it was nothing like what passed for calm on the moon. *This* was life preparing for a night of sleep. Not a night of cold and impersonal lunar silence.

Lake Tahoe was proof that, even after the Seeding of '33, there was still life to be found, even if it resided in only the sounds of a few night birds and an insect or two along the shores.

Ross Trenton, Ph.D., walked out onto an abandoned fishing pier and pondered the evening lights of Tahoe City just up the shore road. To him, they seemed lonely and reclusive, withdrawn into their own protectiveness.

Trenton could understand the need for such withdrawal. That's what they had done on the moon after the Seeding; here on earth it was no different. The world had become dangerous. The creaking of the pier's aged wood seemed to echo that fact as it tried to bear up under his considerable weight. Trenton was a large man, though a mere six feet tall. Only up close could anyone assess his true physical strength. His bright blue eyes sparkled in the light of Tahoe City's few remaining business establishments; however, his eyes were full of caution and diligence rather than humor and playfulness. His dark hair, threaded with incipient gray, lay beneath a felt Stetson and he knew just how predatory he could look to an outsider who didn't know him.

And at the moment he was feeling quite predatory.

He listened to the thick waters of the lake gently nudge against the gunwales of abandoned boats tied to the collapsing pier. The rowboats hadn't been used all summer long and decay was prevalent, as if decay and disuse had become the most common lakeshore residents.

The road up from South Lake Tahoe had been utterly deserted, itself showing signs of wear. South Lake Tahoe—which Trenton had skirted in his walk up to Tahoe City—was now a Hooverville, with one alien Seed dead center in the town. The road between the two villages clearly was being used less and less as time went by.

The Halo, Trenton thought. Even though it had slung itself out of the solar system years ago, it had affected nearly everything and everyone. Even the shores of this ordinary lake had been graced by its touch.

The chill Trenton felt as he considered the lake came more from the rainstorm—autumn's first—of that afternoon. The constant presence of the emptiness caused by the Halo only added to the brooding presence of the water. Though he was happy to be back on the earth, he still perceived the insensitive clutch the alien manufacturers of the deadly Seeds had spread about the earth. *Even here*, he thought. *Especially here.*

"Damn," he said aloud. "What a waste."

He turned and walked back up the pier, getting the kinks, of which there were many, out of his legs. But he wasn't about to be taken for a hoofer. Not in these backwoods. It was too dangerous.

Still, he almost felt like running. In Yancy City beneath the rugged Carpathian Mountains on the moon, the air filtration system never gave them the smells of a recent rain, the humus of fallen leaves, the aromas of autumn.

He strode out onto the dark, tree-lined lakeshore road. He knew that someday he was going to have to bring his twin daughters down here. Bring them down, he reminded himself, to the place where they had been conceived.

But he quickly put that thought from his mind, for it compelled him to think of Annette—and the place where she was trapped. *If* she was even still alive. He couldn't think about it. *Too much emptiness…too much heartache…*

Disguised as an average forty-two-year-old cowboy of the Sierra Nevada, Trenton pulled his Stetson down tighter around his ears, digging his gloved hands deeper into his coat pockets, and walked briskly toward Tahoe City. His Stively-built heart pumped blood down into his legs, adding adrenaline to assist him through the strange gravity.

Cabins along the way, he soon noticed, were thoroughly deserted. So were the residences of Tahoe City—most of them at any rate. Again, he realized, it was the work of the Halo and its swift passage. Their dark windows in the fading twilight were the eyes of skulls, surprised at their own sudden demise.

The Halo had been the Fifth Horseman of the Apocalypse. Eight years ago, in the summer of a.d. 2032, it had been sighted just inside the orbit of Jupiter. Japanese astronomers at Tsutsumida Station on the moon's farside had seen it: a toroid like a golden halo, forty miles in diameter, came plunging toward the sun at an impossible twenty percent lightspeed. Before the earth or any community on the moon could mount an expedition to catch it, it was gone. Though it did not respond to human communications of any kind, it was at least proof enough for Mankind that intelligent life existed elsewhere in the galaxy. And even though its apparent source of origin was in the Centauri system four light-years away, further attempts at probing Alpha and Proxima Centauri with radio-telescopes and gravity-wave detectors yielded no responses of any kind. There followed a spate of head-scratching and puzzled questions, but it was only a year later when everyone—more or less—realized what the Halo's true purpose had been.

On the night of November 12, A.D. 2033, the earth was peppered with objects left in the wake of the Halo's passing. The Seeds glided into the earth's cushioning atmosphere on parasails and drew themselves like magnets to all the large cities of the earth. No city, no country, was spared. More than a million Seeds fell into the earth's ecosphere during that awful night.

Trenton at the time was in Yancy City, a practicing trans-personal psychologist, having finished his historic term as first Lunar President. His wife, Annette, was living down in the San Fernando Valley of Los Angeles conducting a physics seminar when it happened, when the Seeds changed all of their lives.

The Seeds, upon landing in the centers of cities, began emitting powerful alpha-waves. Though the Seeds themselves were merely the size of basketballs, they were dynamic enough to calm enormous masses of people—pacify them, bedevil them, entrance them. Speak to them hypnotically the way a lover would, the way a mother would to a child nursing at her breast. Speak to them the way the Lord might to a lonely mendicant.

The Seeds effectively shut down civilization in the autumn of '33.

Even now, Ross Trenton could feel the slight pull of the one Seed residing in South Lake Tahoe, miles behind him down the road. It made him shudder to think of it. People were drawn to their stultifying alpha-waves, circling the mighty Seeds, living in tents, basking in the soothing alpha-rhythms as they abandoned jobs, families, hopes, and dreams. It all depended upon what one envisioned in the Seed. And everyone envisioned something—if they got close enough.

And South Lake Tahoe got one Seed. Reno, Nevada, to the north, had gotten six. Carson City to the east, got three.

However, Tahoe City, in the quiet pines on the west shore of Lake Tahoe, had gotten none.

But only the Moon Men knew the reason, having just recently discovered why.

Trenton made his way into town, his boots casting out small wings of water from the puddles on the empty sidewalk. He hadn't been the only person to lose a loved one to a Seed—if, indeed, even after all these years, Annette was truly gone—but he certainly wasn't going to take the Halo's invasion lying down, now that there was something they could do about it. They needed Annette, and the Moon Men now believed they could reach her.

All they required was a Seed to examine up close—and eventually learn to nullify.

And whether they knew it or not, the people of Tahoe City were going to be part of Mankind's resurrection, and Trenton was there to see that they cooperated.

A Seed lay in the deep waters of Lake Tahoe that no one apparently knew about, and Operation Cakewalk was there to snatch it up. Unfortunately, it was like stealing candy from a baby—with the mother, father, and several beefy uncles standing nearby grasping baseball bats. Seeds made people feel good. And Hoovervilles tended to protect their exposed Seeds.

Trenton took a deep breath, swallowed nervously, and headed on into town.

3

Trenton reached the center of the lakeside community just as the velvet sable coat of night had draped itself over the lake. What few streetlights burned did so with a somnolence that was almost palpable. The houses were mostly mausoleums, unravaged by time, waiting for the return of their owners. Everything was quiet.

Trenton, alert to these things, noticed how looters hadn't touched the town. *Western Confederates*, he realized. *Someone's holding up this countryside, protecting it....*

Two motels, a Best Western and a Motel 6, still functioned for the few tourists who'd managed to come up either from the Bay Area or out of Nevada deserts. A single saloon winked its pink neon sign at him: the waystation.

Trenton felt completely exercised as he threaded through the cars and trucks out in front of the Waystation, none of which, he noted, were any younger than the Seeding—Detroit and Tokyo had long since become ramshackled by Hoovervilles. Ghost flags of mist steamed off the truck hoods from the afternoon's rain.

Trenton heard the jukebox inside twang a ditty about someone's cinnamon girl as he eased himself cautiously—but rather confidently—through the door.

The incursion of the Seeds had changed little in the lives of the smaller outlying American towns, and Tahoe City was no exception. Proof lay in the Waystation. His eyes already adjusted to the dark, Trenton's heart leapt when he caught the long-forgotten aura of a bar: cigarette smoke, beer, and the low rumble of idle conversation filled the air and he fairly reeled from it all.

"I'm home," he suddenly said to himself with uncontrolled vigor. He took off his hat and without losing stride made for the first empty table. He did not remove his gloves.

A waitress wearing Levi's, cowboy shirt, and Acme boots sauntered by. Her engraved belt said: Zola.

"Grab a seat, hon." She smiled, snapping chewing gum.

Passed the first test, Trenton said to himself, breathing easier. He'd almost forgotten what *real* life was like.

The folks at the bar could have been out of any era in America's past. A tourist couple or two inhabited booths along the far wall, with perhaps twenty people in all in attendance. A television over the bar hovered like a blue-faced angel.

The men along the bar seemed to be regulars, and they seemed to be holding court.

"One TV station for *all* northern California," one man said with a drunken slur. No one commented either way; perhaps, by their silence, assenting. He continued. "Six years since the Seeds fell and they *still* can't get the government working!" He belched noisily at the screen, his eyes blurred with indignation.

Zola came over to Trenton holding a plastic tray out before her. Her blond hair was tied up in a severe bun, as if to discourage her more aggressive patrons.

"What'll it be, hon?" She looked as if she'd been poured into her pants.

"Beer." Trenton smiled. "Any brand that's cold."

Zola peered at him as she snapped her gum. "Haven't I seen you before? You look like somebody I know." She penciled Trenton's order on a napkin as she spoke. She smiled rather pleasantly.

"I don't think so—" Shaving the thick beard before Operation Cakewalk had been a good idea. Everyone knew who the first President of the Moon had been, even if it had been six years ago....

Trenton looked back at the television and the bar as a signal that Zola was to leave; she took it with a smile and a sharp click of her gum.

The loud man at the bar still held forth. To the individual next to him he said, "Dammit, Sam, what do we pay taxes for? You pay as much as I do."

"More," Sam huffed from beneath his cowboy hat. Sam looked to be fiftyish, strong as a moose, visibly bitter with the way his life had turned. They were *all* bitter.

The bartender adjusted the picture's reception.

Sam's friend persisted. "*Now* we get word that Fightin' Jack wants to raise our taxes. He says if we're to beat Scanlon we gotta raise an army. Bull*shit!*"

The bartender faced the loudmouth. "Bevis, keep quiet. Nobody's gonna fight you tonight on *no* account. Fightin' Jack only runs California. When he secedes, we go with him and you'll find all the fightin' you can handle."

Trenton sipped on a rare bottle of Coors—paid with an unused ten-dollar bill. *These men*, he realized, *had been robbed. Robbed, each one, by the Halo.*

A newscast came on the screen. Everyone had apparently been waiting for it. A pretaped scene displayed a city in collapse as a correspondent's voice spoke over: "...as the Mexican census bureau's statistics confirm. Five-point-three million citizens have been mysteriously consumed by the Seeds within the past eighteen months. With more and more homeless migrating to the Hoovervilles in Mexico City, government officials are requesting support from the United States. Jo Ann Weismann, Secretary-General of the United Nations, has called upon everyone to..."

The bartender irritably reached up and turned down the sound.

Bevis punched Sam lightly. "You see that, Sam? *That's* what I'm talking about. Half of L.A. swallowed up by Seeds, and now they want us to feed *Mexico!*" He was drunk with outrage. Bevis' rugged complexion glowed angrily. "You're our mayor, Sam. You got connections with Fightin' Jack. You gonna let us feed Mexico?"

A gauntlet had been laid; Trenton tugged at his frosty Coors, taking it all in as his hand-crafted heart thundered in his chest. He checked his watch.

Sam growled at Bevis. They could've been friends or enemies; Trenton couldn't tell.

"What're you so wound up for, Bevis?" The mayor demanded. "It's the same story all over. There are Seeds everywhere. Ain't nothing anyone can do about it, even Fightin' Jack."

Bevis' eyes seemed to go askew, so drunk was he. "Fightin' Jack says us little towns are important. Big government's falling apart." He gave the mayor a desperate look. "Sooner or later the government'll come after us, make us keep the cities going."

Sam hunched over his drink. "Bevis, nobody's gonna fool with us here. We're too small. Fightin' Jack wants it that way."

"But we're on the way from east to west!" Bevis insisted. "Tahoe's strategic!"

The bartender, looking to defuse the situation, said, "Hey, Bevis's learned a new word."

"But he's right," Ross Trenton said from his table in a loud, commanding voice. He checked his watch. It was time.

Everyone swung around and stared at him. Zola brightened proudly. Bevis teetered on his barstool and took a few seconds to focus on the large stranger.

"So who asked you anyway? You're just passing through," he snapped.

Trenton, still wearing his coat, rose with the beer bottle held in his gloved hands. Behind him he heard someone's panicked whisper: *"Damn, but he's big! He'll tear the place apart!"* It was like the voice of a ghostly Greek chorus offstage.

"You are important," Trenton said in a controlled doctor-to-patient tone. He tried to appear casual.

But Bevis, not interested in anyone's opinion, slid from the barstool hostilely.

Sam tugged his arm. "Hold on, Harold," he said to Bevis. "Man's right. We got to stick together. Let him say his piece."

Bevis' eyes went weasellike and beady. "Nobody comes in here and tells us what to think."

"I'm not telling you what to think." Trenton set his beer on the long bar top, walking over. "I'm agreeing with you, that's all."

The whole tavern went silent, closing in like a crypt. But Trenton had to know more about them for the Operation.

"I'd imagine anyone passing through would benefit your community," Trenton said in a mollifying manner.

Bevis breathed heavily. "Outsiders are full of trouble!"

Zola, at her waitress station, blanched. "Harold, now you don't know…"

"Say, I've seen you before," he grumbled. Sam tried to hold him back. "I bet you're from the government!" A smattering of intelligence twinkled in Bevis' eyes and Trenton knew he now had a situation on his hands.

Bevis, consumed by his own fires, charged him, his right fist swinging out swiftly.

To everyone's astonishment, Trenton's gloved hand shot up and clung to Bevis' wrist like a vise. The glove glittered a crimson-flecked gold in the bar's amber light as if it were indeed made of metal.

"*Hey!*" Bevis shouted as Trenton stood up fully, raising the redneck off the floor.

Eyes went wide and chairs scraped backward.

Trenton, using both his politician's voice and the one he was most trained for, that of a therapist, said, "Your mayor said there's no need to get excited. No one's going to hurt you."

Bevis swung around his other fist, enraged. "Sonofabitch!" It thumped ineffectually off Trenton's other arm. "Put me down!"

"Not until you listen to me."

There were a lot of giggles from the offstage Greek chorus, as well as many fearful gasps.

No one saw a little creature of a man in the darkness near the jukebox lift up a wooden chair and rush toward Trenton.

The small man shouted, "Hit 'im, Bevis! *Now!*"

The chair unshaped itself loudly across Trenton's back even as he ducked. Sam, the mayor, fell backward as women screamed.

Bevis, momentarily free, brought up a tight fist into Trenton's stomach and encountered the same thing the chair had: solid muscle. Bevis seemed stunned.

Trenton rose, unharmed. He held up his gloved hands and spoke quickly. "Now, people, you don't have to get excited. I've got something to tell you—"

The little man who previously wielded the chair stared incredulously at what was left of it in his hands. Bevis, meanwhile, clutched his broken hand as other interested parties became further interested. And very quickly.

Two of them flung themselves through the shadows, just waiting for something like this, propelled by the screams of frantic women, and they knocked Trenton onto the floor. With their knees on his huge chest, they each grappled with an arm.

"Hey, what's this guy made of, anyway?" one shouted.

The other made ready to pommel Trenton's face with his fist.

Trenton said, "Shit!"

And immediately sat up.

One man was flung against the brass footrail, his head clunking there musically. The other man found himself pin-wheeling into the tables and chairs.

Trenton jumped up and whirled around, his fists clenched, his back to the bar.

That was when the bartender gracefully hopped up onto the bar with a thirty-six-inch Roger Maris baseball bat and pirouetted like a ballet dancer, despite his girth, putting all his weight behind it, aiming right for Trenton's skull.

"*All right, friend,*" he said. "*Party's over!*"

Trenton pivoted just as gracefully and saw the bat approach the vicinity of his head. With a motion nearly inhuman, he simply reached up and plucked it out of the sky. The bartender, thrown off balance, somersaulted out onto the floor, slamming into a table. The needle in the jukebox scraped its way to another song.

They ringed Trenton and watched, utterly astonished, as he held the bat before them—a bat of the finest processed pine—and broke the thing in half. Just like that.

They couldn't have been more surprised.

"People," Trenton began. "Let's be reasonable."

Bevis, still on the floor, scrabbled like a polecat suddenly and wrapped himself around Trenton's leg.

"Take him, somebody! *Do something!*"

But no one was moving.

Except for the little rodent of a man who'd just scurried from a back room with an ancient twelve-gauge mountain of a shotgun.

"*Watch it!*" someone shouted in the wings.

The gun came up as Trenton tried to shake Harold Bevis from his leg. Everyone instinctively ducked.

The gun's barrel roared with a dragon's fiery breath, filling the tavern with thunder and light.

The blast caught Trenton on his upper chest, punching him around horribly, shearing off in tatters the upper part of his coat at his shoulder as if each pellet of buckshot was one in a nasty row of shark's teeth.

Trenton crashed into the tables behind him, falling like a clipped fullback, flat on his face. Blood dolloped the floor and nearby booths.

After a few seconds, when their ears cleared, Zola, nearly faint with fright, said, "First decent man in town, and you have to go and kill him."

Then she bent closer in the shadows and saw something she hadn't seen before, dangling from Ross Trenton's ear to his collar.

"Jesus Christ," she said. "The guy even had a hearing aid. You animals!"

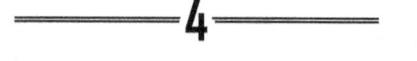

A voice whispered to him in the rapt blackness. It was the Sheriar, Trenton realized vaguely. It meant that he wasn't dead. At least not yet.

You never learn, it spoke softly, yet scoldingly, for it was programmed to do so in times like these. *Men with rifles, crossbows, or spears. They always mean violence.*

The micro-comp's voice intoning from the jack behind his ear swam beneath the layers of his preconscious mind, being his own therapist this time around, grounding him, reassuring him that he was truly alive.

And it, indeed, never stopped. The nonsense. The violence. The Sheriar dredged up an image of a past life, amplified it—as it was designed to do—and thrust it at his mind rudely, as if to say: Let this be *another* lesson for you.

As sulfurous fumes curled from the nostrils of the assassin's shotgun, filling the already smoke-filled saloon, Trenton knew the Sheriar was right. Tapping into his brain—merely to keep him from slipping over death's precipice—it found the right *sanskara*, an impression of a former life. And the vision came from deep out of his past....

It is a.d. 1453. Given the tilt of the indifferent sun, Trenton imagines it to be late afternoon. Far beyond the ramparts upon which he stands in this life stretches an undulating field of Ottoman troops, the fiercest warriors the Holy Roman Empire has ever faced. They are laying siege to the pitted walls of Constantinople. They are led by the fanatical Mehmed II, black-caped and furious. His sword curves in the air above his forward line of cavalry like a wraithful last-quarter moon.

In this life Trenton is an emissary from Rome who has, perhaps foolishly, accompanied the Pope here. The Vicar of Christ had that morning presided over a half-full congregation in the Hagia Sophia, praying to the merciful Lord that Christians be saved—even as Allah's revengers were fording the artificial moats beyond the city's walls.

Trenton knows it is of no use. The Sheriar is bringing it back as it had occurred *in that life.*

He is a Crusader, equally adept with sword and miter, and he sees himself running out across the flaming ramparts, now shorn of his priestly garb. There are barely eight thousand soldiers of Christ to defend this last bastion of Eastern Christendom, and he is one of those eight thousand. Just one.

Goblins of smoke dance around him; his chain-mail vest is exposed at the shoulder where a glancing blow from a catapult's firebrand had knocked him temporarily unconscious.

Trenton, at the walls, stares out across the green fields. The largest cannon the world has yet seen is being positioned for the attack. Behind it, sixty oxen struggle beneath the whip, hauling carts of explosive shells.

Around him are many screaming men and women. This is the death wail of a great city, as arrows sing through the air. Rome seems so far away that it might as well be on the moon.

Suddenly he is struck in the chest with an arrow of native oakwood. He kneels to the rampart's bloody edge: a sacrifice before Allah. All is dark....

"Bloody Christ," someone cursed in the Waystation. "You didn't have to do that, Morris. We *had* him."

One woman wept openly. Zola, the waitress, announced, "I'm gonna be sick," and stumbled quickly to the ladies' room.

The bartender snatched the gun away from ferret-sized Morris.

Someone else observed, "Not much blood for a guy that big."

"Wonder who he was?" someone else said. "Anybody see him drive up?"

"Tourist, I guess," another man said. He turned to Sam. "You seen him before, Sam?"

Sam shook his head. "He did seem familiar. Been some strange folks through town lately."

Harold Bevis, hair straggling down his forehead, found his hat and some of his pride. "Maybe he's with those three soldiers who we—"

Sam's eyes went black. "We don't talk about them, Bevis. Just keep your goddamn mouth shut. You've caused us enough trouble tonight."

Harold Bevis, drunk and riddled with fear, said, "What if the government's closing in, Sam? They say Fightin' Jack can take over most of California and Oregon—"

"Just shut up, Bevis!" Sam snapped. His clenched fists were all the authority he needed. Everyone shut up as Sam pondered Trenton's prone form. Behind them, in the ladies' room, a toilet flushed. Sobbing could be heard.

Sam turned to the little, energetic Morris, who was crouching by the jukebox. "Morris, you send Fightin' Jack word what's going on."

Morris, wretched and beady-eyed, nodded unsmilingly.

Sam pointed a roughened finger at him. "But goddammit don't you lie or say anything crazy. I'll tear your head off if you do."

Morris whisked around and was gone like a rat out of a cellar window.

The bartender, though, was quite concerned. "Sam, there might be more of them. Maybe he's got friends."

"Maybe he doesn't," someone else said. "No one's been looking for those three Marines we iced in June—"

"Damn!" Sam shouted, glaring at everyone around him. "Doesn't anybody know how to take orders? I said not to talk about those guys, and I meant it."

Zola, her blond hair let down now, eyes rimmed with tears, came out into the saloon. "So what're you gonna do this time, Sam? Chop him up? We could use the meat."

"This isn't funny, Zola," Sam said, still pondering Trenton's hulk—which was now draped with a tarp someone had brought from a back room.

One man, dressed in sport coat and casual shoes, clearly a businessman in the community, said, "Sam, we better notify Sheriff Danbury about this before we dump him."

The bartender said, "Jake's right, Sam. Danbury's got to be on top of this. He's got to know."

Jake, the businessman, had a confident air about him, though his eyes seemed full of ready shortcuts and evil deeds. He pursed his lips and turned to Sam.

"You know, before I closed up this afternoon, I heard something from one of the Fallon boys. They'd been hunting just west of town when the rainstorm struck."

"And?" Sam's interest was now back, sharp as ever. The electricity rose in the Waystation.

Jake pointed offhandedly at Trenton's blood-spidered tarpaulin shroud. "I didn't think much about it at the time, but Rich Fallon swears he heard a bunch of noise going on in the hills. Like thunder. And lightning too."

Bevis, a bit wobbly in his cowboy boots, said, "Wasn't no thunder with the rainstorm. It just rained, that's all." He turned to the mayor. "Sam, what's going on?"

One man said, "We haven't had any campers west of town in years. There's nothing out there."

Another man got up from his barstool, pulled on his brown felt cowboy hat, and announced, "My guns are in my truck. I'll call up the boys."

A number of men hastily exited the Waystation as the city elders pondered the mayor and the body on the floor.

Jake's pale blue eyes glowered with paranoia. "It's way past tourist season, Sam. This guy's trouble. We'd better dump him, and fast."

Sam nudged Trenton's body with the pointed toe of his boot. He turned to Jake. "Why didn't you tell me about what Rich Fallon saw?"

"Didn't think it was important."

Sam, caught up in it now, breathed heavily with resolve. "Okay. First thing is, we unload this guy. Then we find Sheriff Danbury and his men."

"Then what?" Harold Bevis said, also breathing rapidly, as if resurrecting the specter of excitement he'd felt the previous June and what they'd done to the three Marines they'd caught snooping around the marina.

"Then we figure out what's going on, that's what!" Sam fairly shouted at Harold Bevis, who was the cause of all this mayhem.

Quickly they rolled Trenton's body in the tarp—and it took four of them to do it.

No one heard the Sheriar jack as it persisted speaking its soothing words into the socket behind Ross Trenton's ear.

5

ut into the cool autumn night they trundled the shrouded form of Ross Trenton into the open bed of the mayor's waiting truck. October stars punched holes in the night sky overhead as the survivalists of the Waystation and Tahoe City breathed foggy plumes of air. They ran for their trucks and cars....and guns.

Jake Bremser, the natty businessman, joined Sam Taylor, the mayor. Together they chain-smoked anxiously and waited for the funeral procession to begin. Behind them various cars began snarling to life.

Jake said, "I still can't figure what the government wants with us, Sam. Except taxes, maybe."

Sam was watching the entourage assemble itself beyond the dark glass of his cab. "Maybe they know something about those three Marines..."

Jake then countered with: "Yeah, but what were they doing here in the first place?"

The bloody canvas cocoon in the rear of the truck rocked awkwardly as Sam pulled out slowly into the rain-spattered street.

Behind them Harold Bevis was being driven by a surly woodsman named George Seigler, who had lugged along a bottle, like a dark gem, of Jack Daniel's—a pre-Halo relic. This they kissed for more than just comfort.

Over the open channel of their CB, Sam Taylor's voice crackled. "George, you there?"

"Right behind you, Sam," Seigler said gravely into the microphone. His cauliflower-size hands gripped the steering wheel firmly as Harold Bevis swilled the whiskey, gaining strength.

Sam Taylor came back. "We're going by Sheriff Danbury's first. I've got a funny feeling about this."

"God *damn*," George Seigler breathed. Harold Bevis laughed, both men sitting like huge drunk bears in the cab of the truck.

The cortege snaked through the rain-dappled streets, past homes which were either boarded up or glowed dully from within, their inhabitants quiet in their own lives, accepting what the Halo had delivered to them years ago.

The sheriff's station, crouched low amid the larger buildings of downtown Tahoe City, burned its one light like a beacon of the last bastion of law and order. Sam pulled up in front of the station, waving the rest of the procession to a halt.

The office was empty except for the back room, which held the dispatcher's radio. Ellen Drake, a doughy woman in her late forties, turned from her headset, seeing Sam enter.

"Sam," she called out. "What's going on? I've been trying to reach—"

Sam held his hand up authoritatively. "We shot us a government agent in the Waystation. You better let Danbury know we're heading for the lake."

Ellen Drake's eyes, dried almost yellow from constant cigarette smoke, twitched. She said, "Sam, I can't raise him."

"What do you mean?"

She swallowed and lifted her half-burned cigarette from the littered ashtray. "He and Deputy Griff got a call to Lake Forest about a half hour ago, but he hasn't checked back in. I tried about ten minutes ago, but he didn't call back."

Sam's eyes narrowed. "What did they want up in Lake Forest?"

"That was the funny part, " Mrs. Drake said, sucking desperately on her cigarette. "The caller didn't say."

Sam pointed directly at her, almost shaking. "We're going to Gordon's Cove." Her face instantly registered the implications. "Tell Danbury when he gets back."

Ellen Drake's pallid face seemed to flash with alarm. "Maybe we should contact Fightin' Jack's people."

"Morris Bly's doing that right now," Sam said. "You just stay put."

Her gray eyes filled with panic. "Sam! This have anything to do with what them Fallon boys saw this afternoon?"

"Maybe," Sam Taylor breathed. "Just maybe."

He turned and thundered out the door. He was in a hurry. A *big* hurry.

A different voice—an override—came into the jack-plate behind Trenton's ear. It wasn't the Sheriar this time.

It said: *I knew you shouldn't have gone by yourself. What an asshole. Hey, Ross, you there? This is Torque. Snap out of it!*

A pause filled with whisperings in the background filtered through the Sheriar, then Toquero came back.

We're in orbit just above you. The main Sheriar on board says you just went back to a.d. 1453. Some homecoming, huh? How about that time off the coast of Norway in a.d. 912? Remember? We were Vikings. Moon Men of the Middle Ages....

The voice whispered aside to someone else: *He isn't responding. Damn.* The voice faded.

Sam Taylor bent over the steering wheel as he led the procession out onto the lakeshore drive. The lake to their left was a meadow of solitude, gone steel-colored in the calm clutch of the night. Rain hissed beneath the wheels of their trucks. A few leaves already tainted by autumn danced in their headlights.

"Sam, I've been thinking," Jake Bremser announced suddenly.

"About what?" Sam was busy checking the dark corridor of the forest road as they raced south.

"That man's gloves and boots. I don't think he was from the government."

"Why's that?"

"Hell, they were expensive. Fightin' Jack says the government's within a year of losing control. They're not going to send agents out dressed like that."

"We still killed him," Sam pointed out. "And the sooner we dump him, the better. We'll find out later who he was."

Sam picked up his CB microphone and barked: "All right, everyone. We gotta do this quick, then get back into town. Lights out, and nobody make *any* noise!"

Sam wheeled his pickup into a campground that had once been called Gordon's Cove—back before the Halo strangled the tourist trade. Fans of brittle autumn weeds brushed beneath the truck like claws of the dead reaching up out of the earth. Everyone followed Sam's truck, lights extinguished, down toward the cove.

The cove was a circular gathering of picnic tables and sites for campfires, now fallen into ruin through rough winters and disregard. Against the invisible shore rocks, water gurgled in soft, lapping waves.

Sam backed his truck down to the shore, slogging through mud and weeds to a spot where he, and all of the others, knew a small aluminum-hulled rowboat lay buried in fragile cattails and reeds. That boat had previously ferried three murdered Marines to a haunted spot in the lake just south of the cove.

But none of them liked the cove. Or the lake. Or what they knew they now had to do.

Harold Bevis fell out of his end of the truck as he and George Seigler ran up to the mayor and dapper Jake Bremser.

"Sure is quiet," the massive Seigler said from beneath his hunter's hat.

"Don't talk so loud," Sam cautioned. "They can hear us clear across the lake."

Harold Bevis, fishing around in his pants, finally found what he was looking for and began pissing in the weeds. They crackled loudly and the rest of the men and women of the entourage laughed. But it was a nervous, mirthless laugh.

Sam and Jake began grappling with the body in the back of the truck, lurching it into position. Behind them in the gloom of the pines, gun cartridges jerked into place as everyone else took up positions as a precaution.

Harold Bevis, zipping up his fly, staggered. "Hey, Sam." He boomed. "We going to need any rocks? I thought we used up the big ones the last time—"

Seigler shouted, "Bevis, shut up! You're like a goddamn bullhorn!"

Bevis waddled over, belching.

Sam meanwhile struggled with the camouflaged tarp that covered the aluminum canoe, whipping it back. Normally he could expect some small animal, perhaps a squirrel, to have made its summer home there. But nothing seemed to live comfortably along the lake anymore. He rolled the canoe over.

Cigarettes glowed in the dark of the cove like crimson will-o'-the-wisps. Feet shuffled uneasily in the weeds.

Sam ran up to the truck. "Use those cinder blocks. My snow chains are in that box there. They should be heavy enough."

George Seigler, the strongest of them, hefted the body toward the edge of the tailgate.

Seigler said, "I used to fish out here when I could get away from the wife. Now this place just spooks me, you know?"

Jake Bremser said nothing, not used to so much physical labor.

"The boat's ready," Sam announced. "Let's do it."

Then one of the others standing guard in the cove called out suddenly, "Hey, Sam! I think I hear something."

They froze. A woman—one of the wives—chimed in, "I heard it too."

Gun bolts clicked, cigarettes were extinguished. Sam came around the truck.

"Sam?" Jake Bremser whispered hoarsely.

"Shhh!" the mayor commanded.

That same woman, now down behind a protective tree, called out, "There's something moving on the other side of the lakeshore road. I can hear it. In the woods!"

It broke the quiet of the cove like a rock smashing through the ice of a pond. An enormous crashing resounded in the dark green of the forest as if something *very* large was chopping its way through. And it was getting louder and louder.

"*Oh, shit!*" someone cried.

Lights thirty feet up, like a row of spiders' eyes, burst into luminance and the entire area around the cove flooded with a light which blinded them.

And the lights began moving, coming directly at them.

"Jesus Christ!" Jake Bremser shouted, dropping a cinder block on the lip of the tailgate. "*Look!*"

Plowing through the woods, pushing aside bushes and tree limbs, a vehicle came at them.

"*It's one of them space machines!*" George Seigler yelled. "*A terrain crawler!*"

As big as a walking house, the terrain crawler fully exposed itself as it stepped out onto the lakeshore drive.

Then another appeared behind it—and another. Rather suddenly, there were six of them bearing down on the cove.

"*Fire!*" one of the survivalists screamed, and a dozen guns coughed knives of flame.

Bullets and buckshot sang along the impervious metal of the oncoming insectoid machines. George Seigler stood erect and yanked out his .357 Magnum, and its cannonlike concussions deafened them all.

"*Where'd they come from? How'd they get here?*" someone wailed above the thunder of his own weapon.

They began running for their trucks and cars as the machines came at them like spiders stalking their prey.

A man with a pump-action shotgun pumped wildly. When the gun was empty, his wife handed him another one fully loaded. Others, remaining, kept at it with manic desperation, light and fire crisping the air.

Sam Taylor drew out his own nickel-plated .22 Colt Python as George Seigler hastily reloaded. The mayor began firing.

"Sam," Seigler shouted at him. "Those things Shortjumped here! It *is* the goddamn government! I knew it! I just knew it!"

He lifted his gun once again at the approaching assault vehicles.

Then, just as suddenly, he fell over.

He was knocked off his feet by a flying cinder block and a long snaking strand of broken tire chain.

From beneath the tarpaulin came the sounds of shoulder joints amplified by very tiny motors as Ross Trenton sat up, the tatters of his coat revealing the armor of his protective Moonsuit. The cuts on his face and neck were only superficial, but the anger deep within him was real.

Very real.

His power-enhanced arms threw aside the tarp, the cinder blocks, and the chains. He sat up and announced, "You guys are all under arrest."

And he came up with metal fists swinging.

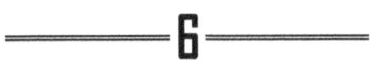

Dr. Ross Trenton, normally a kind and gentle man, had sense enough to know when to take control of certain situations. This came from being a political leader as well as a transpersonal psychologist and therapist.

However, his faith in human nature often inhibited necessary actions. It took the goading of Roderigo Toquero high in earth-orbit through the Sheriar mini-comp lodged in his Moonsuit collar to bring him to his senses.

Brought thusly around, Trenton slammed a machine-amplified glove into Jake Bremser's pretty face, feeling several bones crumple. Trenton's super-alloyed Moonsuit, the invention of one of his aides to assist the continuous-flow Stively-built heart, glowed like the steel of a knight's armor as he leapt to the ground.

"*He's alive!*" shouted one of the would-be assassins, seeing Trenton. The man lunged around, bringing his rifle to bear.

Sam Taylor shouted to everyone else, "*Run for it!*" as the man fired in the chaos.

Trenton turned his head away; it was the only exposed part of his body—all else was Moonsuit underneath his borrowed earth apparel.

The rifle barked an ugly sound, but its projectile skimmed off happily into the forest, having met the impenetrable surface of the Moon Man's armor.

Trenton's amplified hip joints and leg muscles dug into the mud, propelling him forward. He plunged a powered hand into the assassin's chest, knocking him backward into another of the Waystation's motley crew.

Trenton then grabbed the rifle and stood fully erect. With the same easy motion he had gone through with the bartender's bat in the saloon, he snapped the rifle in half; its metal screamed. Trenton sailed it like a boomerang far out into the lake.

As the huge lunar terrain crawlers stepped out of the gloom of the forest, Trenton scrambled amid the staunch citizens of Tahoe City. Searchlights and gunfire danced everywhere.

Thick punches—followed instantaneously by booming explosions—pommeled themselves up and down his back. He turned and saw George Seigler and his .357 Magnum trying to kill him in the bright lights of the oncoming assault vehicles.

His gun emptied, Seigler's face blanched as Trenton faced him. "Just hold it right there!" Trenton ordered.

Seigler reared back and flung the useless weapon at him with all the strength he could muster. Trenton caught it with lighting speed—then crushed the handgun as if it had been made of soft clay. Seigler took off through the brush of the cove.

"*Dr. Trenton!*" an amplified voice hailed him from the terrain crawler in the lead, which straddled the lakeshore road. "*Are you all right?*"

Bullets needled the air from the remaining Western Confederates— and Trenton knew now that was *exactly* what they were—who had been cut off.

He shouted, hands cupped to his mouth, "Yes! Block the road back to town! We've got to stop the mayor!"

All around him came the crashing of terrain crawlers making their way toward the cove, as well as the sounds of car and truck motors growling to life.

One crawler heaved itself out of the thick woods just in time to bring down a gargantuan foreleg into the open end of a pickup which was peeling out of the campsite's gravelly drive. One step, and the truck's back was broken and the two cowboys inside rattled around like stones in a medicine man's gourd. The Space Marine guiding the terrain crawler grinned from the safety of the control station. Indeed, the terrain crawlers looked like cakes on stilts, thick-bodied insects able to ford lunar potholes, ply the sands of Mars. Operation Cakewalk was Trenton's baby, and Trenton glanced around him as the "cakes" literally walked into the area of the cove, scattering the citizens of Tahoe City like bees from a broken hive.

Quickly Trenton tore away his remaining clothing. It was too cumbersome and his Moonsuit needed more room within which to move.

From hatches underneath the terrain crawlers, heavily armed Space Marines spun themselves out into the fracas, some with laser rifles, others with standard-issue M-30 machine guns.

Trenton raced for the lakeshore drive amid the specters of headlights, claps of gunfire, the screams and shouts.

Darting between a cluster of saplings, Trenton gained the road and intercepted a truck fishtailing in a desperate getaway.

With a rapid motion, Trenton snapped the controls at his belt and his Moonsuit went rigid. The truck's lights widened, came at him, and he leaned in to take the impact. Not quite up to full acceleration, the truck nevertheless struck with considerable force.

But not enough to knock him over.

The truck was using its front-wheel drive, and Trenton, knowing this, dug his metaled fingers into the grille and lifted mightily. The wheels spun, splattering mud out around him in great galaxy swirls.

Inside the truck were George Seigler and Harold Bevis, both of whom braced themselves as Trenton's eyes narrowed above the bloodied abrasions of his neck and face. Trenton threw his shoulders into gear and rotated. The truck rolled over, back into the brush and trees.

The terrain crawlers had by then come out of their hiding places and blocked off both ends of the road to the campsite. Soldiers rounded up the remaining tag ends of the Confederates—those who were still alive, for several had perished.

Harold Bevis wormed out of his end of the truck and vomited heavily onto an innocent bush. George Seigler appeared with a starfish of blood painted on the side of his face.

"Damn!" Trenton said to himself, looking around. The mayor—the man who could potentially cause the most trouble—was nowhere to be found.

A figure in a metallic green Moonsuit dropped out of one of the terrain crawlers. Unarmed, he walked up to Trenton. Glenn Thorpe's thin blond hair and hawklike facial features made him seem more hawklike than he really was. Among the Moon Men, he was their inventor and resident pacifist.

"You look awful," Thorpe said, his lips narrowing. "Torque thought you were dead."

"I thought I was too," Trenton commented, his gauntleted hand coming away from his jaw with a trace of crusted blood.

"You knew something like this would happen, didn't you," Thorpe told him. It wasn't a question.

Trenton pondered the campsite. "We had to find the center of authority. Someone had to check the place out."

Glenn Thorpe touched Trenton's upper chest, examining the impact of Morris Bly's shotgun volley. He smiled to himself. Moonsuits were *his* baby.

"At least it held up. Worse could have happened, Ross. These people mean business."

Trenton nodded. "So do we."

George Seigler blinked in the lights of a terrain crawler aimed right at them. A Space Marine contingent came up with guns ready.

"You won't get away with this," Seigler snarled at them. "Wait till Sam gets back into town. This is *our* country!"

"It's ours, too," Trenton retorted. "Sort of."

Harold Bevis, hair matted to his forehead, bile dribbling down his cowboy shirt, gave them a perplexed look.

"What do you mean, 'sort of'?" Seigler queried.

Glenn Thorpe said, "We're from Yancy City on the moon. We're Moon Men and this is President Trenton."

Seigler's eyes widened with recognition, but Harold Bevis was too sick to let anything of such import register.

"You Shortjumped here," Seigler breathed raggedly, the real truth of the matter finally settling in. "That's illegal! The Russians will kill us—"

Trenton motioned for the Marines to take them. He said, "The Russians won't know if nobody tells them."

"Wait until Fightin' Jack finds out," Seigler protested. "He's tougher than you think!"

Trenton smiled wryly, having felt the effects of the toughness belonging to the Confederates of Tahoe City.

"You've got no business here!" Seigler shouted as two Space Marines wrestled him away from the truck's wreckage.

"Actually we do," Trenton said. "And one of these days you're going to thank us."

"What the hell are you talking about?" Seigler snarled.

Trenton gestured to a Marine guard to take him. He said, "There's a Seed no one's known about at the bottom of your lake. We're going to take it apart and see how it works."

Both Seigler and Bevis stared incredulously at the two famous Moon Men, for clearly they now recognized the men for what they were: Glenn Thorpe, that century's equivalent of Thomas Alva Edison, and Dr. Ross Trenton, the first Lunar President, both survivors of the fall of the *Jaguar Skies*.

"*What?* A Seed? Here?" George Seigler couldn't have been any more surprised. "Hey, there's no Seed in the lake."

The Marines took hold of him firmly.

"There sure is," Trenton told him, as the Marines roughly escorted him back to the confines of one of the terrain crawlers now at rest. "And we're going to dredge it up."

Harold Bevis, hardly coherent, managed to utter, "Why?" He teetered like a wayward gyroscope.

"Because," Trenton said, pointing to the crystal horseshoe of the moon hung in the western sky, "there's another Halo on its way and we need a Seed to help us figure out a way to stop it."

Harold Bevis, finally understanding, did something rather loud and unpleasant in his pants. The Marines hustled him off anyway.

7

The dawn out on the mid-Atlantic had come up stormy, but by noon the President of the United States was ready for some amusement. The early-morning squall had left footprints of mirrored rain puddles all up and down the concourse of the Floating White House complex, but that wasn't going to deter the President. James Guthrie could tell.

Guthrie sighed, adjusted his glasses, and cradled his clipboard, as great-hearted Ralph Scanlon drew out a driver from his golf bag and a sacrificial golf ball. Guthrie sighed heavily from beneath his sou'wester: he expected more stormy weather.

Thwack!

The pebbled globe sailed out into the Atlantic and lost itself in the Sargasso's senseless kelp.

Scanlon mused upon the ball's trajectory. Then to his aide he said, "I hear we're stuck for a while."

"Only until the engineers untangle our sea anchors, sir," Guthrie informed him.

The President set another ball upon the tee, which was wedged in a crack in the metal surface of the concourse.

"Well," he said mightily, "if it isn't one thing, it's another. Right?"

"I suppose so, sir."

Thwack!

Born to golf, Guthrie thought remotely.

"Beautiful," Scanlon muttered as he watched the ball fly off into the carpet of kelp. "Two hundred eighty yards, maybe more I bet."

He seemed happy with himself.

"I'd say two hundred, sir," Guthrie informed him. He cleared his throat. "I think you'd better look at these reports on Operation Cakewalk, sir." He held up the clipboard, ignoring Scanlon's disapproving frown.

"It's those Moon Men, isn't it," he wheezed, bending over. "I knew they'd blow it. We should've gotten our own people." However, his interest in the golf ball was a bit more consuming at the moment.

Guthrie lowered the clipboard. "The Moon Men are the only people who *can* do it. Our military is too busy policing the cities, keeping law and order where they can around the Hoovervilles."

Scanlon's bushy blond eyebrows came together like two serious caterpillars. "Seems to me," he said with a touch of suspicion, "that this Cakewalk is a ploy by the House of Toquero to gain influence back here on the earth."

Guthrie pushed his glasses back up on his nose. "I don't believe so, sir. The Moon Men may get their wealth from the Toquero mining concerns in space, but they want to keep their own shop, especially President Trenton."

Scanlon glowered forcefully. "*I'm* the President, remember?"

He gripped his nine iron like a weapon.

"Yes, sir," Guthrie responded, knowing full well that the President perpetually needed to be reinformed of certain situations. "The Moon Men were the ones who took those new pictures of the Hoovervilles from space, sir. Emmett Shea, the mayor of Yancy City, now thinks it's possible to find Dr. Sayles-Trenton. With their equipment for the Shortjump and with Glenn Thorpe's expertise, they can probably do it."

Thwack! went another innocent ball.

"They're in *my* territory, though," Scanlon said, fingering another ball.

"Sir, if they can nullify even one Seed, that's part of a city *you* get back—and all those people who haven't voted in six or seven years."

Scanlon turned and faced his aide. "Sometimes you surprise me, Guthrie." He fumbled for another ball from his cumbersome leather bag. "But I want it known that Trenton is to clear out when the Operation is over. There are rumors he might run for President down here."

"That's hardly likely, sir. The Moon Men probably won't let him. They're...bonded in some way."

Scanlon was in the middle of a swing when he stopped. "What? Don't be ridiculous. A man with that much charisma's a fool to waste it on the moon. He'll be back down here."

"I don't think so, sir. Dr. Trenton's needed up there. He's a transpersonal psychologist and works with every leader on the moon almost weekly. They need him."

Thwack!

Scanlon watched the ball this time take a mean curve to the right. In the rough, as it were.

"He's their shrink?" he said to his aide.

"That's about the size of it, sir. After the lunar settlements in Yancy, Gambart City, and Macondo, where the House of Toquero is located, all incorporated in late '25, they needed someone to help with lunar solitude and other—"

"Lunar *what?*"

"Lunar solitude, sir. It's a recognized psychological phenomenon akin to cabin fever."

"Like out here, right?" Scanlon directed Guthrie's attention to the magnificent Atlantic on all four sides of them.

"It's a bit more serious, from what I understand. But Ross Trenton uses a special machine called a Sheriar which enhances past-life impressions to help him understand his patients' current mental problems."

Scanlon was eyeing him skeptically. Guthrie continued. "It turns out, sir, at least according to our reports on Dr. Trenton, that all of the Moon Men had been together before at some other point in history."

Scanlon huffed with a faint hint of righteous indignation. Scanlon's people came from proud American Christians, who claimed to be reasonably intelligent yet insisted on ignoring anything new or different.

"So," Guthrie went on, "when the lunar cities banded in '25 and separated themselves from the earth, they elected Trenton as their first President."

"They elected their *therapist?* Is that what you're saying?"

"They're quite close up there. That's why I don't think Dr. Trenton has any designs on your administration, sir. Besides, he's not a Republican."

Scanlon, bending over to try a different iron, looked up suddenly at his aide. "You say that like it's a dirty word, Guthrie."

Guthrie, shielded in raincoat and sou'wester, held out his clipboard instead, and moved on to more pressing issues.

"Perhaps we should talk about the Russians, sir."

Scanlon turned his back on Guthrie, addressed the tee, waddled in an exaggerated fashion, and struck. Guthrie could sense something more forceful in this particular shot.

"*That's* two-eighty, sir."

Scanlon, angry at having to even *think* about the Russians, faced his aide.

"So what's with the Russians now?"

"As you know, sir, they've been having their problems with New Moscow on Lake Seliger. Since Moscow itself has twenty-one Hoovervilles, they've decided to abandon the city to the pilgrims and seekers."

"So why is this our problem? Every government capital has had to move. We just did it sooner and faster." He snorted, staring at the mindless Atlantic. "Although we might've chosen a better spot than this." He waved his arm around like a showman indicating one ring of a three-ring circus.

"Sir, they've apparently gotten word about our use of the Shortjump for Operation Cakewalk."

"That's impossible," Scanlon grumbled, trying his best to be uninterested. "I was assured that—"

"Everyone was assured, sir, but it has something to do with gravity waves being generated by the Shortjump's power surge."

"Technicalities."

"It would break the Shortjump Prohibition Treaty of 2020. If the Russians knew we were using the Shortjump within ten thousand miles of earth's surface, they just might start using it too. Only with what's left of their nuclear stockpile."

Scanlon closed his eyes and leaned on his club as if for support.

"Moon Men," he wheezed. "Those idiots. I was specifically told that there'd be no way, if done right, that anybody could detect a Shortjump from lunar orbit."

"Yes, sir. But our agents in New Moscow are fairly certain they've picked up something. The situation there is still unsettled, so the Russians might not be able to operate on their information. It could give us time, sir."

"Oh, *sure*," Scanlon said, towering over him. "And in that time they might decide to Shortjump a warhead right *here*. That's all I need to think about."

Guthrie leafed through the memos attached to his clipboard.

"Speaking of that, sir, it says here that your wife is coming in tomorrow, or perhaps later today if the weather holds. I guess she's done doing whatever she wanted to do in Outer New York."

Scanlon addressed another ball as Guthrie folded up the clipboard.

"Sir?"

Thwack!

The tiny, helpless golf ball disappeared into the gunmetal-gray sky. Guthrie never did see it land.

8

Deep underneath the lunar surface, following a burbling stream down one of Yancy City's secure corridors, two men walked. One was a Moon Man, the other wasn't.

Emmett Shea, the mayor of Yancy, strode briskly alongside the creek which sported its own garden-variety of Moon-fish and White Marsh Marigolds blooming in the artificial illumination of the hall. He was happy, and Lloyd Bramlett, the non-Moon Man, wasn't and didn't like it.

Dr. Emmett Shea and Lloyd Bramlett were equal in height, but Shea's decisive lunar pallor and pale blond hair gave him a smaller appearance. Bramlett, newly shunted up from Cape Key in Key West, where the nation's launch facilities had been moved after the Seeding of '33, was tanned, trim, and seemingly full of power—power which Emmett wouldn't acknowledge. He also reeked of tobacco, a substance which was prohibited in their delicate environment.

Bramlett's dark eyes stormed with potent fury. He was there in Yancy to assist in coordinating Operation Cakewalk for the government at home. But it was clear to all involved that the small team of highly skilled Moon Men, led by Dr. Trenton on the earth and Dr. Emmett Shea on the moon, had matters under control.

Bramlett had voiced disapproval of Trenton's sally into Tahoe City, where it had been rumored the Western Confederacy had a toehold. They had lost contact with the three young Marines sent in earlier that summer, and Bramlett—along with the New Pentagon authorities—didn't see the need for Trenton to wander in. He told Shea so, but Shea, in his usual manner, seemed unwilling to be affected by Bramlett's politics.

"Hey," Emmett said as they walked, "Ross and Annette honeymooned there. He wanted to see if it had changed."

Bramlett fussed, having a hard time with the joints of his new Moonsuit, which all newcomers were required to don during their first weeks on the moon. He said, "The man could've been killed."

"Ross knows what he's doing," Emmett stated.

Bramlett sneered. "Shea, *nobody* knows what they're doing on this! It's a dangerous operation all the way around. You ought to know. It's your machine that sighted the Seed in Tahoe in the first place. You know how powerful those things are. If you ask me, this whole project is foolish."

They came to an intersection. Emmett slapped him on the super-alloy of his shoulder. "No one's asking you, Lloyd. We're just glad you're here." He smiled at him as they waited for an electric tram pulling Blue Collars off-shift to pass by.

"It's almost morning down there now," Bramlett said, looking up at a row of international, lunar, and martian clocks. "Lieutenant Mac-Readie tight-beamed that they think the mayor made it back into town. If he did, you bet your bottom dollar he'll be doing something about it. We're losing whole sections of the nation to secessionists. Europe's one big mess, in case you haven't heard."

They turned down a corridor which had another stream choked with watercress and green whorls of bedstraw plants. Emmett always did like the smells and sounds which they'd managed to plant permanently on the moon.

"That's why we're doing this," Emmett told him as they approached their destination.

Bramlett huffed, still very much loyal to America and America's particular security concerns. Like most earthbound folk, Bramlett couldn't accept lunar independence, especially since an entrepreneurial firm—the House of Toquero—had allowed it to happen back in '15 with the free use of their money, ships, and engineers. Bramlett was of the old school of thought: the moon belonged to America and its military. As Emmett knew all too well, Bramlett and his kind—particularly the President of the United States—had conveniently forgotten how many Canadian firms and Japanese firms had contributed to the colonizing of the moon. Bramlett believed in Manifest Destiny; Emmett believed in Moon Men. And the Moon Men had to stick together, regardless of their country of origin, mostly because of the severe environment.

But mostly they knew that they were free of Seeds. And for the last six and a half years they'd all been working on various solutions to the problems besetting the bright blue globe that filled a good portion of their pitch-black sky.

Only a select handful of lunar inhabitants knew directly of Operation Cakewalk. The current President of the three lunar cities was in Macondo in the gray wastes of Mare Vaporum just south of Yancy City. President Dubie, presently in the middle of his five-year term, resided in Macondo and knew every step of Operation Cakewalk, since the

House of Toquero was providing the transportation and backup. Only the Space Marines were from the outside: they belonged to the United States government. This was Bramlett's only trump card.

Emmett had called a meeting of the Moon Men that morning, and as he and Bramlett entered the small auditorium, he could see that most of the vital personnel were assembled.

Lisa Palazetti jumped up from her seat between her two assistants and ran up to Emmett in her sterling-white physician's tunic and red caduceus badge.

"Emmett," she whispered. "We got word there was a fight down there."

Dr. Palazetti was nearly Emmett's age of thirty-nine, but her long black hair had silvery strands of gray from years of concern and worry. One of their chief physicians, Lisa Palazetti was a full-fledged Moon Man—or Moon *Person,* as she was wont to call herself—and had been quite close to Emmett ever since they met during the fall of the *Jaguar Skies* years ago. Her dark brown eyes met his as the whispering in the auditorium ceased; everyone wanted to know what was going on "down there."

"It's all right," he said gently. He gave her an honest, reassuring smile—not one of his car-salesman smiles, which he had to use on Bramlett and other earthly authorities. "Ross has everything under control."

Bramlett, seating himself in one of the two plush chairs on the stage, gave him a disagreeable look that suggested otherwise.

"I guess we can begin," Emmett said, scanning the darkened auditorium. He then frowned and looked at his watch. "I don't see Torque anywhere. Anyone contact Toquero? We need him."

Heads turned, voices buzzed, then in through the door appeared a flamboyant figure boasting two female Blue Collars, one on each arm. Roderigo Xavier "Torque" Toquero strutted in wearing a purple Moonsuit with the Toquero coat-of-arms embossed on his chest. All he needed, Emmett thought, was a purple cape, a sword, and a pair of pirate's boots. The handsome scion of the House of Toquero also wore a nonregulation goatee—and a black eye patch. He'd lost his left eye during the fall of the *Jaguar Skies,* and while such things were replaceable these days, Toquero opted for showmanship.

The young man, tall and debonair, escorted his two beauties to seats right in front. "Sorry I'm late, Emmett. I wanted to wait until I was darkside of Russian scanners before I Shortjumped. Just got here, in fact."

Bramlett disapproved of the thirty-three-year-old rake. "We appreciate your desire for secrecy, Toquero," he said with heavy sarcasm.

46

Toquero's one dark eye glittered impishly. "Actually, I had to pick up my two friends here. They're welders on the *Clark Savage, Jr.*" he said, cuddling each one around the shoulders. "Ross doesn't need me down there and I thought I'd have a little fun." He winked and continued to smile.

"You're always having fun, Toquero," Bramlett said impatiently. "Just keep it up."

Emmett Shea, holding a cluster of important papers, leapt upon the stage. "Okay, men. Let's get on with it. President Dubie wants a report from me by day's end and I mean to give it to him."

The lights on the stage dimmed and an image of the west coast of the United States flashed upon the white wall screen.

Reddish dots, like wretched cancers, peppered the regions of the cities of the west coast.

"These," Emmett began, "are coming to us from our orbiting alpha-wave scanners. These are the Hoovervilles."

Emmett turned aside to the crowd. "I called you here because in the past forty-eight hours I've had the time to analyze the object of our search."

At this juncture, the technician controlling the projection altered the image. An aerial scan of the Lake Tahoe region appeared, and off to the side of the lake—couched in a soft mauve color—glowed the fallen Seed.

"The color is not a computer enhancement," Emmett stated, rising from his chair. He commanded considerable respect. Despite his height and wan color, he was a Nobel laureate and knew whereof he spoke. "The Seed is actually weaker than any existing on the surface."

"Why?" Dr. Palazetti asked.

"We don't know why," he told her. "But we're going to find out. It might be because it's in water. Water might inhibit the transmission of its alpha-waves."

"And it's the only one like it?" Lisa asked. Her voice was nearly musical in the hall.

"Yes," Lloyd Bramlett interjected with his own tone of authority. "All of the other Seeds managed to aim themselves at cities and towns. This one must have been blown off course during the storm which was over the lake at the time."

"But South Lake Tahoe got a Seed," Dr. Palazetti pointed out.

"Right," Bramlett affirmed. "We're just lucky that the only Seed we can get access to is in our own country."

"I wouldn't call it luck," Toquero chided. His girlfriends smiled at him.

Emmett then said, "We know that the Seeds were *guided*. None landed in any other lake or ocean and none fell into areas with sparse human populations."

"They knew what they were doing," Bramlett added.

"Now all we have to do is figure out who 'they' are," Emmett said grimly, nodding to the technician in the rear.

Another vision appeared on the screen. A starscape shimmering in the lens of Tsutsumida Station's darkside telescope showed them a field of stars—with one golden exception dead center of the image.

Everyone gasped; they'd heard the rumors, but *this* was verification.

"I caught it on a gravity-wave scan of the nearest stars," Emmett told them in a somber voice. "It's about one light-year out. Its albedo is very low and we can't tell if it's another Halo or the invasion fleet the first Halo was meant to precede."

Toquero took his arms from around the shoulders of his shapely companions and leaned forward. "Is it coming from the Centauri system?"

"No," Bramlett intervened. "This one's coming from…Delta Pavonis." He had to check his notes.

Toquero sat up straight. "You mean we're *surrounded*?"

"It's hard to say what we are," Emmett confessed. "But whoever *they* are, they mean business. Delta Pavonis is in the same general quadrant with the Centauri stars, but it's about twenty light-years distant. Halos could be slinging themselves all over the place in our neighborhood. That's why we've got to figure out a way to nullify the Seeds."

"When will it get here?" Lisa began fearfully. "How much time do we have?"

"We've got about a calendar year," Bramlett volunteered.

"That's not much time," someone in the crowd voiced.

"Right," Emmett acknowledged. *And it was running out.*

A shot, again another aerial photograph, flashed up onto the screen.

Emmett was fully caught up in his thoughts, but knew he had to be careful with what he was about to reveal.

He said, "I'm concerned with two things." He pointed to a crisscross grid of north Los Angeles and the rings of Hoovervilles there. "If we can solve the solution to the Seeds, we might be able to figure out how those things generate so much power to back the alpha-waves. As you know, alpha-waves work on that part of the brain which stimulates transcendental mind-states. The closer you get to a Seed, the stronger the effects."

A close-up vertical shot of a particular Hooverville revealed itself next. Emmett continued.

"First thing is to tap into a Seed's power. Annette was very clear in her last notes as to the enormous energies a Longjump engine would need. That's the first goal of Operation Cakewalk. Capture a free Seed and sustain it. The second is to get at Annette's final equations, and if we're lucky, get Annette herself out of the Hooverville."

The close-up revealed a bulls-eye shot of a Hooverville, its concentric rings packed with torn-down houses, ragged tents, with dozens of people simply living out in the open.

But their attention was focused upon the glowing objects closest to the Seed itself.

"I've heard that they now call them saints," Lisa Palazetti said. "The ones trapped by a Seed."

Bramlett stood this time, the "expert" on earthly matters. "Yes," he said. "And they also say that the Seeds themselves are angels. I've never been close to one so I wouldn't know. However, as Emmett here will tell you, there is a lot of evidence to suggest that the Seeds actually swallow people up."

"Like a gravity-well or event-horizon around a black hole," Emmett said. "There's so much power pulling them in that thousands are disappearing into the Seeds each year."

"And we can get her out?" Lisa asked.

Emmett indicated a structure quite near the glowing, blurred image of the evil Seed. "We think this is her car. The Seed itself landed two hundred yards from where Ross and Annette had their apartment. She's either still there, caught up in the Seed's time-dilation, or she's gone. As you can see, there are literally hundreds of 'saints' surrounding the Seed. They've been caught there for years. That's why I suspect they're held in some kind of warp or suspension."

"Then she could be still alive," Lisa said hesitantly.

"Right," Emmett nodded, feeling a slight thrill at their closeness. They were a team, and for the first time in years there was a modicum of hope circulating among them.

Just then, over the intercom link at the arm of his chair, a concerned female voice broke in.

"Dr. Shea?"

"I'm here," he said into it. "What is it?"

"We seem to have misplaced a sandcrawler in exit bay number eight," the woman said.

Exit bay eight was near Yancy City's main apartment complex as well as the day-care center. Emmett didn't like the sound of that.

"Specifically, *which* sandcrawler?" he asked reluctantly.

The woman returned, almost frantic. "The one Cindy and Cheryl Trenton told me that you said they could play in."

"I didn't authorize—"

She cut him off. "We didn't think you did. But the girls have gone out in it anyway. We're sending out scouts right now. I thought you'd want to know."

"Oh, shit," Emmett muttered under his breath.

He looked down at Lisa Palazetti. One of these days he was going to find the time to marry her—or at least so he thought.

But Ross Trenton had left two nine-year-old twins behind for him to baby-sit, and they were just like their parents: smart and adventurous.

He turned to the gathering of Moon Men. "Mr. Bramlett will fill you in on the details of Ross's night in Tahoe City. I've got to check into this. Excuse me."

He jumped from the stage and crashed through the door out into the hallway beyond. *Time*, he thought, *there's never enough time....*

9

Trenton woke groggy, close to dawn, unrested and thick with vague dreams. His Nerzhin sleep-modifier indicated the time in lime-green letters: two hours, fifty-five minutes. Still, it wasn't real sleep.

Unity. The thought rang in his mind as he fumbled for coffee in the dark of the terrain crawler command center. *Bring everything together... bring Annette back...unify the family.*

His girls on the moon, Annette trapped....

Outside the protective windows of the crawler, fog haunted the lake surface. The cove and the Confederates had been secured during the night and not a discouraging word came down the lakeshore road at them from Tahoe City. Trenton's anxiety, though, remained unabated. He fingered the plasti-derm mold on his neck and cheek, flush with new blood and antibodies. He knew he would never be able to grow his beard back. Perhaps it was, he thought, time for a change.

The alpha-rhythms of the Nerzhin sleep-modifier should have soothed him during his rest period, but they hadn't. Instead, he used the micro-thin Sheriar—lodged in the collar of his Moonsuit, the size of a quarter—to help him revisit the kingdom Morpheus. The Russians—keen on long journeys to Mars—invented the Nerzhin to assist in stabilizing the psyches of their cosmonauts. The Sheriar, an invention out of western India, did much more and was much more compact, requiring the electrical energy provided by the patient's brain stem and a jack from the computer chip itself to its lock behind the ear.

Even so, acting as his own therapist rarely was effective. A *sanskaric* image of a past life as a nineteenth-century Polish Uhlan lancer—the one the Sheriar found closest to his preconscious mind at the time of his sleep—did not abolish, or explain, his obsessiveness for unification. He'd originally run for the lunar presidency having sensed a need from his patients—and Moon Men—that the lunar settlements needed a unifying vision. But now, back on earth with its seductive colors and sounds and smells, he felt the need in himself to get it all back again. His twin girls needed their mother, he needed his wife, and the earth-lunar community needed the Longjump, which, according to Emmett, only Annette could provide.

Beyond the murk of the windows of his terrain crawler, he could see the huge vehicles squatting like dormant insects in the blue mud of the cove. The crawlers, some martian red, others in khaki camouflage swirls, were spread out strategically, lights dimmed. Space Marines, though, were on guard, both out on the road and before each stilted crawler. Laser rifles with infrared scopes were constantly on the alert.

In the crawler next to his he saw a sliver of light appear in its port side. Fog intruded in the ghost-shadows and a Space Marine guard saluted the Moon Man who emerged and jumped to the ground a few feet below. Glenn Thorpe, newly risen from his own Nerzhin sleep-couch, approached Trenton's vehicle, easing through the white-flannel fog.

Moonboots clanging up the rungs of the short ladder preceded the small man's entrance.

"Coffee first," Thorpe said, sleep wrinkles still around his eyes.

The coffeepot chuckled to itself as Trenton gestured out toward the lake. "No birds, no fish. Not a peep. This place is dead."

Thorpe slurped his ersatz coffee. "How do you know about the fish? I thought you were asleep."

"MacReadie's scouts have given me a report." He indicated a sheaf of papers which were on the console when he had awoken. Trenton's crimson-gold Moonsuit seemed to glow with its own authority, despite the man within.

Thorpe considered the report. "Says here that two of the marinas might still be operational."

"But little used," Trenton added. "I saw one. All the boats are in dry dock. Just like everything else. The whole place is in decline."

"I didn't think earth was this bad," Thorpe confessed as the caffeine began to soar through his system.

Trenton stared grimly. "We all have been away for too long. I felt it walking into town last night. It was a shock." One window had been cracked open, letting the fingers of the night fog creep in. Trenton breathed deeply and managed a smile. "The smell of the pine trees just about knocked me over. I'd forgotten what this place was like."

And by *this place* he meant the whole planet.

Thorpe had also been thrilled by their landfall in the woods just west of the lake—which had been the "thunder and lightning" the Fallon boys had witnessed from the effects of the illegal Shortjump.

Lights in Thorpe's communications crawler came on and Trenton noticed them. "Are your men picking up anything from the town?"

The tomb of the predawn darkness was filled only with the sounds of the Marine guards lightly treading the moist ground of the campsite. The other terrain crawlers were now coming alive with the other remaining Space Marines as they withdrew from their Nerzhin sleep-couches.

"We've picked up nothing." Thorpe held his coffee cup to his lips. "No outgoing radio from the village, no sounds from the highway. If the mayor made it back, either he's done nothing or just kept on running."

Trenton touched the plasti-derm on his cheek and recalled his venture into the Waystation. "I don't know," he said. "Sam Taylor isn't one to head for the hills. My guess is that they've all been waiting for something like this."

Even as they spoke, the two Moon Men were considering several large blowups of photographs laid out before them. Marine activity outside increased.

"Too bad," Trenton said wryly, "our Seed didn't fall in some Canadian lake or in China. It would have made things a lot easier. It's going to be tough enough just to capture the Seed and contain it."

Thorpe waxed indignant at looking hurt, "Six years I've been working on a way to nullify a Seed, and now you don't think we can do it."

Trenton was staring, instead, at a recent aerial photograph of the Hooverville which had grown up close to his original apartment in Northridge, California—and the Seed which presumably had captured Annette.

His deep blue eyes glittered angrily. "It's like a basilisk, a voracious monster—"

The Seed shown on the photograph—which Emmett's new process had dimmed considerably—revealed the "saints" captured in its spell. As Emmett had made clear, the "saints" were moving in toward the Seed at an agonizingly slow rate. Those nearest the Seed would be those captured long, long ago. Trenton's veins, urged by the power of his Stively-built heart, seemed to swell with hope and excitement, now that they were back on the earth.

Thorpe took up a computer-scan of the lake bottom as Trenton stood beside him. Phase Two of Operation Cakewalk was near at hand. The photos helped.

"There it is." Thorpe's gauntleted finger hovered over the scan's fine lines. "Just sitting there having a good old time."

The scan was part of Emmett's original discovery: from Yancy City, using his refined gravity-wave scanner, he had decided to check out the gravity perturbations—if any—that the Seeds were making. Charting all of the Seeds as they lay consuming their Hoovervilles worldwide, he found one, apparently undiscovered, beneath the waters of Lake Tahoe. This particular readout showed the Moon Men in Gordon's Cove just exactly where on the lake bottom it lay.

The Seed resided in about six hundred feet of ice-cold water some three hundred yards due east of the campsite. Its outline was unobstructed, and it nested on a gently inclining slope.

Thorpe considered the Seed's contour. "It's still functioning, but water apparently curtails its driving force—whatever that is." Thorpe jerked a thumb over his shoulder. "We're picking up just the slightest alpha-rhythms from it, but nothing out of the ordinary. My guess is that anyone passing this way would just get sleepy or dreamy as they drove down the road."

"I felt a little of it," Trenton revealed. "But for me, it's hard to tell. I use the Sheriar every day. I'm just surprised no one in Tahoe City's noticed it before this."

Thorpe took up a thin yellow pencil and drew Trenton's attention to the computer's outline of the Seed.

"Notice this," he began excitedly. "It looks like the Seed is sitting on the para-glider that brought it in. Now, *that* would be a find in itself."

Trenton pondered the map, then the lake through the window. He felt the weight of the Seed's retrieval full upon his Moonsuited shoulders. He had more at stake here than merely the possible unification of his family. *This* was the first time in six years that anyone had even the remotest chance of reversing the damage done by the Halo. He felt its exciting call, but he was also aware of the inherent dangers.

A signal beeped on the console from the crawler thirty feet away—Glenn Thorpe's martian-red communications vehicle.

"Dr. Thorpe? Is President Trenton with you?" A technician's voice queried.

Thorpe toggled the contact. "He's here."

Trenton leapt to the console, hearing the hooves of bad news approach from beyond the horizon. "What is it?"

"Sir, this may sound strange, but we're picking up something coming from the lake."

"The lake? What are you talking about?" The two Moon Men looked at each other.

"It sounds like motorboats, sir."

Trenton switched off. He looked at Glenn gravely. He pointed to the computer scan and the image of the Seed.

"I've got some unfinished business with the mayor of our friendly little town."

He ran for the open port and swung out into the dark.

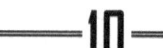

10

Ralph Scanlon, his blondish-red hair askew, bent over with great difficulty and laced up his Nike jogging shoes. A woolly ball the size of his brain filled his skull from the hangover the previous night's banquet had left him. James Guthrie, also dressed in white shorts and athletic shirt, could tell the mood the President was in. And it was foul.

The current Prince of Wales, with his touring party, had flown in after dusk the night before to pay them a state visit. Since the existing British crown had no practical use for the Prince, they often sent him abroad as a kind of roving emissary. Scanlon, gregarious and out of control, had tried to drink the boy under the table, thinking that a man of fifty-seven could squash a boy of nineteen. It naturally didn't work.

But the Prince had risen early, jetted off in a RAF jumpcopter, bound for more debauches in the Lesser Antilles, and Guthrie had to drag the President out of bed, hangover or no hangover.

The President gritted his teeth and finished his shoe-tying ordeal. "You hear what that little shit said last night?"

Guthrie, whose ears were as keen as his eyes, had heard much. "Specifically?"

Scanlon's eyes rolled upward like rusty ball bearings lodged in their sockets. "About those goddamn royal astronomers, or whoever they are. They think there's an invasion coming, or some such nonsense."

They walked out of the locker room on the west end of the make-shift White House, out onto the concourse. In the distance, men and women were busy at their duties, going and coming from the jumpcopters to the administration buildings. Clouds fleeced the midmorning sky, speckled with an occasional gull or two.

"They're right, sir," Guthrie said, fearful of the great man's moods. "The Japanese at Tsutsumida Station have confirmed Dr. Shea's data...."

"Swell," he snorted with disgust, leaning back, hands on his hips, stretching. A run around the whole concourse was an impossibility, but he and Guthrie would make a go of it.

"That's Theory One," Guthrie said, bending down in a forward stretch, touching his toes adroitly. Scanlon saw this and made a face. He had a midriff which eclipsed any view of his feet. Guthrie, however, was as lean as a whippet.

"I know, I know," Scanlon gruffed, now jogging in place. "That the Halo was sent in advance of an invasion, to dummy us up. Well, it did a damn good job."

Guthrie bounced on his toes as light as a ballet dancer. "There's always Theory Two."

"There is no Theory Two!" Scanlon snapped, then winced, hearing the echoes of his own voice in his head.

Guthrie pushed his big glasses back on the bridge of his nose; the moist air constantly made them slip. "Actually, there is, Ralph—"

"I told you not to call me Ralph! It's *Mister* President, remember?"

Guthrie, nonplussed, continued as he jogged in place. "A great many reports from our people say that the Seeds exude such good vibes that despite all the damage they've done, the victims believe that the Seeds *are* angels—"

"They shut down the whole goddamn planet!" Scanlon roared. "Is that Theory Two? If it is, somebody's made a mistake."

"There's a third theory circulating around that—"

"Oh, brother."

"Well, sir, some people now believe that the Halo was the colony ship itself and that the Seeds are the aliens."

Scanlon squinted while the sun cheerfully breached a hole in the mid-Atlantic clouds.

"That's absurd. The Seeds don't grow, they don't reproduce, they don't even get up and walk down to the store for groceries."

"In a way they do, sir."

Ralph Scanlon, his ham-size fists clenched, stood above his aide. "I was speaking figuratively, Guthrie."

"That's what I mean."

"What the hell are you talking about?"

"Well, Ralph, there's one thing we *do* know about the Seeds."

"What's that?"

"They definitely eat."

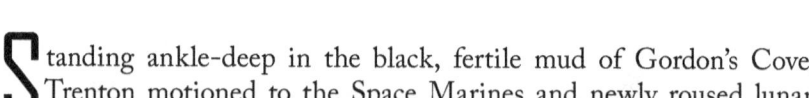

Standing ankle-deep in the black, fertile mud of Gordon's Cove, Trenton motioned to the Space Marines and newly roused lunar technicians. The insectoid terrain crawlers filled with life and light.

A blond-headed Space Marine lieutenant, wearing his own chitinous armor, slopped through the mud and grass through the dense, dark-morning fog. Somewhere to the east of them, beyond the lake, the sun was trying to hoist itself into the sky.

Lieutenant MacReadie, squadron leader, held his sleek M-30 machine gun. He saluted Trenton.

"Sir, we're positioning now." The twenty-eight-year-old lieutenant's eyes flickered excitedly, though his mouth was tight and grim.

Glenn Thorpe left the terrain crawler and bounded up behind them. He was in the process of fastening his green-tinted armored hood to the collar of his sturdy Moonsuit.

Trenton addressed the lieutenant. "We're picking up motion on the lake. Engines. They may be coming at us from that direction."

MacReadie squinted into the fog, which contained only the figures of scrambling Marines and solitary pine trees.

"It's still too dark," MacReadie said. "I'll send out a crew with infra-red scopes in a small boat—"

"No," Trenton said quickly, tightening the hooded cowl to his Moonsuit. "I don't want anything happening out where the Seed might be harmed."

MacReadie briefly considered the graveyard of fog which blanketed the lake—and what lay buried beneath.

"Yes, sir."

Thorpe announced, "Sun comes up in forty minutes. But in this fog, it'll be dark and hard to see."

Trenton touched the lieutenant on the arm. "Ian, have your squad use nightgoggles. We don't know what the Confederates have. Expect the worst."

"Sir!" Ian MacReadie said, spinning off into the ghost-fog of the cove.

Glenn Thorpe's face seemed tiny and compressed within the confines of his hood as it was anchored in place. "That seems to be the buzzword: Expect the worst."

Trenton nodded. "This may be the only chance we've got."

"Maybe someone should've told them that there's a Seed in their lake," Thorpe suggested as a terrain crawler came to life and began creeping toward the road to set itself up as a barricade.

"I believe we did," he said, reminding them both of the three missing Marines sent in the previous June.

Trenton could feel his heart kick into a higher gear, filling his body with an almost unnatural surge of power. He felt as if he was going to need it.

Squashing through the ruined coals of the campsite came a Moon-suited figure, leaping through the auspices of the amplified hip joints, as if the Moon Man within was purposefully testing their agility.

Glenn Thorpe, startled in the darkness, stepped back involuntarily. This newest Moon Man seemed to radiate a dangerous, quirky spontaneity.

"Hi, boss!" shouted the newcomer.

"Jesus, Roarke," Thorpe said cautiously. "This isn't a game of tag, you know."

Basil Roarke, aged thirty-four, was as tall as Glenn Thorpe, but much more solidly built, and the Moonsuit only added to his sense of strength. A former Space Marine, he was their resident wrangler, a space technician who spent most of his time in the wilds of space doing construction work and other risky chores. His brown eyes, black hair cut flat-top style, and rich tan seemed incongruous for any Moon Man. And no one knew him well, including Trenton, who had seen him in action during the fall of the *Jaguar Skies* when they had all come together as a unit. Basil Roarke was the only Moon Man who seemed to have no lunar or space phobias, or any sense of human limitations, which intrigued Trenton constantly.

Roarke held up his M-30 machine gun, smiling a toothy grin. "A guy back there says we're going to fight!"

Trenton snatched the machine gun away from the eager engineer. "The Marines are, *we* aren't."

"Aw, boss…"

Trenton's blue eyes, framed by the crimson-gold of his protective cowl, seemed like two admonishing demons. "Look, we may not have all the time we're going to need. I just want you ready for the scoop. And I don't need you dead right at the moment."

"I still think," Thorpe began in a cautious tenor, "that we should've tried reasoning with them."

Roarke's storm-cloud eyes challenged him. "That's just like you to back off from a fight when you've got one."

"Knock it off, you two," Trenton ordered. "We've got work to do." Privately he wondered if they were, each in his own way, beginning to show the strain of being on the earth after so long a period. Thorpe, possibly; Roarke, never.

The fog around them took on a waxy, spectral look as the predawn light tried to make its way through. Trenton strode through the campsite to the first barricade—a terrain crawler squatting across the road, flanked on either side by convenient bushes and thick-limbed trees.

MacReadie said, "We figure at least fifteen vehicles approaching down the road from the north, Mr. President."

One Marine technician was holding up a parabolic receiver, aimed at the road which disappeared into the fog. He nodded in agreement, silent beneath his earphones as he listened.

Then the technician went rigid with discovery.

"Lieutenant," he called out. "Something heavy. Not a truck."

MacReadie's eyes were trained upon Trenton.

"Heavy artillery?" MacReadie queried.

"Possibly," Trenton acknowledged.

"This is great!'" Basil Roarke said, running off into the bushes. "I gotta have a gun for this!"

Glenn Thorpe looked back at the young lieutenant.

"What about the road up from South Lake Tahoe?"

"Nothing, sir. Not a peep," the lieutenant reported. "That Hoover-ville's got them."

"It would do to keep an eye out, though," Trenton said.

"We're doing exactly that, sir."

The Marines positioned themselves throughout the woods. Trenton urged Glenn Thorpe down into a protective gaggle of new pines. There they found Roarke on his belly with a stolen machine gun, sighting it down the road.

They joined him in the moist leaves of the surrounding bushes.

"Hey, Basil," Thorpe pointed out suddenly. "Look."

Roarke turned and saw several small slugs, disturbed from their mulch, residing on the metallic brown armor of his Moonsuit.

"Slugs!" he cried, jerking suddenly. "I *hate* slugs!" He drew a gauntleted hand down his side, converting the slugs into long greasy streaks. "Ack!"

Trenton made a mental note of that, as they both crouched down into the bushes.

The convoy slowly appeared through the fog along the road, and out in front was an armored personnel carrier. The snout of a vicious-looking machine gun pointed right at the terrain crawler which blocked off the drive in the pines by the lake.

"Boy, will you look at that!" Roarke breathed as the campsite filled with the chirpings of machine-gun clips snapping into place among the waiting Marines.

"Glenn," Trenton said suddenly to his aide. "Better get back to the scoop. We might have to go fishing as they fight."

Roarke looked up, disappointed. "Aw, Ross. I want to see—"

"This isn't a playground. We're here to get the Seed, and the Seed only." He then snatched away the newly found machine gun from Roarke's gloved hands. "Maybe one of these days I'll let you fight three-legged aliens."

Roarke seemed to brighten.

Thorpe tapped Roarke. "Let's go, Basil."

"You guys are no fun," Roarke complained, but he did back off through the bushes with Thorpe.

Trenton watched as the Confederates—dressed in paramilitary khaki—climbed out of the convoy trucks and scrambled for position. *Professional*, he realized. *They've been waiting for this. Could Fightin' Jack be far behind?*

Lieutenant MacReadie stepped in front of his Marine barricade and held up a bullhorn. A hundred yards away the outraged Confederates of Tahoe City listened—briefly.

"All right, folks," MacReadie's baritone sailed out through the mist. "Stop where you are!"

From inside the distant personnel carrier, a man shouted into a microphone which blared: "Eat shit!"

And quite suddenly, the Western Confederates got down to the business of threading the air of Gordon's Cove with bullets which stitched and sewed themselves expertly through the pines and bushes.

Trenton ducked as a burst of heavy machine-gun fire chewed at the tree nearest him.

MacReadie toppled backward over the barricade, having absorbed a bullet in an unarmored right arm. The other Marines, though, brought their guns to bear and the peaceful, picturesque woods filled with unmitigated violence.

Out of the top of the terrain crawler across the road beamed a green rod of humming laser light which drew curlicues along the steel plating of the personnel carrier. Whoever was inside had been instantly fricasseed.

Trenton rushed to MacReadie's side. Two of his men had pulled their lieutenant out of harm's way and a medic was whirling a white tape around the gory wound.

"Lucky shot, sonofabitch..." MacReadie slurred.

Guns crackled and coughed around them as the Marines pushed through the woods toward the convoy. The plan was to take the offensive and push the Confederates back toward town and away from the cove and the sleeping Seed, rather than merely hold their ground. This, the Marines were now doing with resplendent skill.

"Are you okay?" Trenton said, bending over the lieutenant. Bullets tap-danced along the hull of the terrain crawler even as they spoke.

"Sure," the lieutenant drawled. But the medic had already gouged the man's arm with a hypodermic full of joy-juice. MacReadie was temporarily furloughed.

Behind him, Trenton suddenly heard a machine pistol barking out its single-shot call. No Marine would use a machine pistol.

"Damn," Trenton said, leaving the Marine. His mind was aswirl with all the loose ends of Operation Cakewalk, news of the approaching Halo, and worry about the possibility of finding his missing wife. And now *this*.

He found Basil Roarke not with Glenn Thorpe and the vital Scoop, but down on his ass, propping up a machine pistol taking potshots at goblinesque figures of the Confederates as they dodged in the trees beside the lake.

Roarke shouted at Trenton, who raced over to him beside a sheltering pine tree. "Hey, Ross, I think someone *is* out on the lake. Listen."

Trenton crouched as Roarke expertly reloaded the machine pistol. "That was the sound of the convoy coming down the lakeshore road, Basil," he informed the eager wrangler.

"No, it's not, Ross," Roarke said, fussing with the gun.

Ross Trenton bent an ear toward the fog-haunted lake. He could now make out a drowsy growl coming from the veil of gray drifting across the lake's flat surface.

They're militarists, he realized. *They wouldn't waste a chance of using the fog as cover....*

"Ross!" came an amplified voice from the communications crawler.

Trenton turned, keeping low. Bullets sang unpleasant ditties through the trees above him. A grenade exploded in the distance.

"What?" he shouted back.

"There's something real big out on the lake coming at us," the technician reported.

"*How* big?"

"A three-fifty-horsepower cruiser, fresh as the day it was born."

Several Marines, overhearing, shifted their positions and made for large rocks beside the shore, guns ready. One soldier wore night goggles and scanned the impenetrable fog for a sign of the big boat.

"I thought you and Emmett said this was going to be a piece of cake," Roarke chided, swiveling around on his seat.

Trenton ignored the wrangler and instead watched Glenn Thorpe, now in the communications crawler, who was using a pair of night goggles himself.

Into the microphone speaker, Glenn quickly shouted: "Ross, they're headed right over the Seed. I don't like it."

Roarke got up and headed into the water, wanting an open field of view for his machine pistol. Trenton followed as the Marines behind them watched.

"I wonder if old Sam is there?" he mused out loud. "I guess we're about to find out."

Trenton had been feeling the alpha-waves all morning long. But it could have been his imagination.

The flotilla eased out of the fog, almost in a line, and the moment they appeared—in boats of all sizes—the Confederates whooped and hollered and began firing at the exposed regiment at Gordon's Cove.

Roarke started shooting and Ross didn't even attempt to stop him.

He ceased—and so did the Space Marines—when a funny thing developed.

The boats suddenly began wandering around aimlessly as the Confederates on board went rigid with disbelief—and vanished from sight. Trenton gasped as he saw each of them—men and women alike—glow an unearthly blue, the blue of trapped Hooverville saints, and slip out of existence as the boats passed directly over the sunken Seed.

Within seconds, seventeen boatcraft churned this way and that, lumbering into themselves, engines sputtering and dying at the throttle.

Roarke gave Trenton a perplexed look.

"What happened?"

Trenton stared grimly out at the empty boats.

"We just found out what we're really up against out there, he said. "That Seed's very much alive."

12

Emmett Shea stood at the shielded window of his Watchtower, forty feet above the lunar surface, as he coordinated the search for Cheryl and Cindy Trenton. The Watchtower's steel aerie was one of the few structures still exposed to the cruel, torturous light of the bare sun. But within it, Emmett had access to all of Yancy City's computers and communications. Nothing would be served trying to hassle directly the scouts in exit bay eight. He could do it all here.

Instead, Emmett tinkered with one of the many wooden toys—this one of smooth oak—which he kept as a hobby. He'd finger them, rotate them, sometimes stare at them almost as if they were rosaries, objects of pure meditation. The Watchtower was full of them; so were his apartment and study below. They helped him think.

Unfortunately, he was also reminded of how much all the lunar children—Moon Babies, they were called—adored them. He set the big-wheeled truck down on the console and listened to the channel-chatter of the communications people as they attempted to locate the missing sandcrawler.

His stomach queased with a fist of guilt. He knew how important it was personally for Ross to oversee Operation Cakewalk. The former Lunar President might be the only stable Moon Man, but he did have his problems, not the least of which were two girls, aged nine, quickly approaching a precocious adolescence. They desperately needed a mother, as much as Ross needed a wife. Emmett loved the twins dearly, and the thought that they had somehow wandered out alone into the harsh lunar wilderness was suddenly strangling him.

Emmett stood hypnotized by the dull silver sea of Mare Vaporum. The lights of hidden Macondo shone like a goddess's jeweled brooch in the distance, and in between the two communities, the Sea of Vapors was crisscrossed by trails left from twenty-five years of surface vehicular traffic.

What made Emmett feel worse was the note the twins had left. It said that they were off in search of their mother. Emmett's heart felt for them; they were on their way to becoming true Moon Men, for everyone had to help everyone else where they lived. There was no other way.

The girls had been only three years old when the Seeding had occurred. Ross had been Lunar President living in Macondo when Annette had volunteered for a semester's teaching on the Shortjump at UCLA back upon the earth. Annette, Emmett knew, was barely remembered by the girls since the Seeding, existing only as a color image in various holos and video recordings in the Yancy City archives.

He nodded to himself, thinking back. *Ross must've told them how important it was for him to go back to the earth. The girls knew of the Cakewalk....*

Then, as he watched, the glittering diamond of the *Clark Savage, Jr.* slung itself into view as it passed in high lunar orbit. How he wanted to be on the *Savage* right now. No responsibilities! Ready to Longjump out of their trapped lives, off into the universe at large!

But there was no Longjump yet, and right now he had to find two missing girls or his ass would be in a sling when Ross got back. Even if Ross wouldn't do anything like that, he knew he'd do it to himself just to ease his guilty conscience.

Cindy and Cheryl Trenton sat in the comfort of their hidden sandcrawler and watched the *Clark Savage, Jr.* sail silently overhead.

South of Yancy City, the 'crawler idled quietly in the sheer blackness of one of the Copernican rills. They knew they were being looked for and both of them found excitement in it. The shadows comforted them. They were hiding.

Voices came over the console before them. *"Girls! Girls! Please respond if you can...use the emergency frequency...."*

The girls' faces were small pale moons in the light of the console, their short brown hair bobbed in lunar fashion. Their eyes were nebulinas of mischievous light.

"It's Lisa," Cheryl, the extroverted one, said in a low whisper. It had been her idea initially to sneak into the 'crawler and go off on a search.

Cindy smiled and said, "I think she's pretty." Cindy's mouth shaped itself into a cupid's bow, a feature the girls both had that was unique to their beautiful mother.

Lisa Palazetti's voice continued in its singsong way: "Girls, if you can hear me, please respond. We want to know if you're okay...."

In the silence of the 'crawler cockpit, Cheryl said, "If we call them, they'll find us."

Cindy stared at the console's lights, picturing the grownups back in Yancy City. She then turned to her sister.

"Where's the map?" she asked. "Where'd you put it?"

"Here it is," Cheryl said, pulling it from a door pouch. She then turned the voices down.

When she did, a certain background *ping...ping...ping!* became more audible. It hailed over a separate radio unit.

Cheryl noted it and said, "That's the transponder. We're close."

Cindy, the quiet one, nodded as she perused the map. She then pointed on the map. "This is where Daddy saved Mommy." Her voice came in an awed whisper, as if she were speaking the words of a special history.

And Cheryl knew as well. It *was* special.

The *pinging* that filled the small cabin of the sandcrawler came from the transponder, still under its own power, that lay buried in the gargantuan ruin of the downed *Jaguar Skies*. That part of the sloping rim of Copernicus was littered with the debris of scouting and mining surveys, but it was also the burial ground—quite unintentionally so—of the largest spacecraft anyone had ever built at the time, the *Jaguar Skies*, pride of the Toquero mining and metals consortium.

The girls knew that once upon a time the *Jaguar Skies* had been designed by their father's friends to mine the asteroids. But it took lots and lots of energy, and it was their mother who figured out how to make the Shortjump bend space. Their mother and Emmett Shea.

But even before it left lunar orbit, something went wrong. Maybe it was just too big, but the *Jaguar Skies* broke up and plummeted out of the black lunar sky. Their father, then only a psychologist but a good friend of the Toquero family, stayed behind with the Moon Men as everyone else was shuttled out in escape craft as the big ship was falling. Their father, Emmett, Mr. Toquero, Glenn Thorpe, and funny Mr. Roarke helped get their mother and many others away—but their daddy was almost killed when the shuttle craft came down alongside the *Skies*. They gave him a new heart and elected him president.

Or so the story went. It was a good story, but now Cindy and Cheryl wanted to help.

And as soon as the *Clark Savage, Jr.* eased out of sight they proceeded.

Cindy said, "It's over that way."

Cheryl, at the controls of the 'crawler, moved the surface vehicle out of the shadows. Ahead of them, the jungle of deformed super-alloy steel and twisted vanes lay like a broken dinosaur. Deep inside of it, the transponder sang its mausoleum song.

Each girl considered the other. Perhaps a clue lay within the skeleton of the *Jaguar Skies* or the smaller shuttle craft just beyond it that almost killed their father.

All they needed was a clue.

Back in his Watchtower Emmett sat and attended to whatever administrative duties remained to him as the reports came in from the scouting parties.

Nothing. No word, no trace of the sandcrawler. *Nada.*

His secretary came and went with various memos, but none of them seemed as urgent as finding the twins. Lloyd Bramlett rang to inform him of the status of the Cakewalk at Lake Tahoe, but he delivered it in such a way as to imply incompetence: *Something was going wrong.*

"Why is this happening to me?" he asked out loud, playing with a carved statue of an ancient Greek warrior on his desk. He didn't ask the question out of pity for himself—he just had too many issues to think about. As did Ross. As did every one of the Moon Men.

Perhaps it had been a mistake to run for mayor of Yancy years ago.

He stared over at a softly lit corner of his Watchtower. The Nerzhin sleep-couch was used only on rare occasions when he needed more time than he physically had—and sleep was a luxury.

But also attached to the couch, by way of a small jack, was the Sheriar. Trenton's main lunar Sheriar was in his offices several floors beneath the Watchtower administrative complex, and Trenton used it for his many patients even if they resided in the other lunar cities.

The Sheriar was the size of an ancient television set, its bulk taken up in the storage of individual memory engrams of Trenton's many patients. But Emmett knew that a Sheriar could be effective down to the size of a large coin. Its function was to simply find a memory of a past life, a *sanskara*, to amplify. But Trenton had to be there to use it and interpret the recreated scenario. And a transpersonal psychologist dealt exclusively with the impact of former lives. As such, the Sheriar was no toy.

However, all of the Moon Men had access to the Sheriar if they wanted to plug in and let the special computer record a past life for Ross to use later on.

Emmett kept staring at the couch and the Sheriar jack. In his own therapies with Ross he'd learned that he had joined the Moon Men ten years ago to escape a suffocating family environment back home in Boston. An oppressive father, an indifferent mother, two wastrel sisters now lost to the Boston Hoovervilles, had propelled him to leave the earth to find a new life among new friends.

But now one such friendship is endangered—only because he'd neglected his duties watching over the twins.

There *had* to be a reason. They were at a vital junction in history and even the smallest detail gone neglected could thwart their plans to regain the earth from the Seeds. And if an invasion fleet *was* approaching, then they were going to have to find Annette, for he could not, on his own, complete the Longjump equations.

Emmett got up, still clutching the toy soldier, and walked to the couch. He rerouted all incoming calls.

"Okay," he said. "Let's find some answers."

And the question he asked deep within himself was: *What's all this got to do with me?*

The Sheriar lead hums its alpha-waves through the jack attached to the communications plate behind Emmett's ear—a plate which all Moon Men wear. The vibrations calm him, soothe him, lull him to the edges of a dream from a time long, long ago. But his conscious mind is thinking of *here* and *now*, and the possibility of a Toquero Corporation sandcrawler stuck in the granular lunar soil where no one can find it.

Sand. Choking sand...

He dreams: It is 1300 B.C. The dust in the air beyond the palace windows is yellow, the yellow of locusts in flight, the yellow of spring waters treacherously poisoned.

He is—in this life—a female servant, and he...she...is scared. There is much shouting beyond the walls. Horses scream in their traces. Chariot wheels grind...Sandcrawler wheels...and the clatter of bronze swords fills the air.

She is running through the lamplit halls of the palace of Amon Re. Other concubines and guards as well are fleeing in every direction. The palace is being overrun!

She is holding something in her hand. A lamp which sloshes with palm oil leads her down a private corridor where she will be safe. She coughs in the darkness from the fumes of the lamp. No one will find her here. Not the besieging enemies of Amon Re. No one!

A secret panel gasps open, revealing a special passage into which she disappears.

Behind it, the sounds of the attack cannot be heard.

But there is another sound. A laugh of genuine surprise.

She turns and sees one of Amon Re's closest servants, the architect who designed this palace called Deir el-Balah. Of course he should be here! *she suddenly thinks.* He would know the places in which to hide his craven soul. The coward!

Her loathing of this beast is deep, for on many occasions has the architect been given her in the middle of the night to abate his sexual appetites.

But the palace is under siege and Amon Re is not here to see.

He cannot see, for example, the way Emmett Shea in this life as a woman takes out an obsidian dagger and swings wildly at the architect's fat throat—a fat man, a toad in the service of Amon Re.

The architect gasps as a tongue of blood appears in a slit that resembles a sick smile underneath the many layers of his chin.

She drops the knife suddenly, seeing the look in the man's eyes. She knows this man as something more *than just a tool for Amon Re. What is it? What is it?*

The eyes are pools of mountain water, clear and blue. The Sheriar modifies the image: the eyes of Annette Sayles-Trenton.

For Annette, too, had her Sheriar sessions engrammed into the computer's memory. And the computer—without the skillful intervention of Ross Trenton—shows Emmett Shea what he did to Annette Sayles-Trenton in the first of their lives together.

"No!" Emmett cries out with sudden recognition. He/she staggers backward in the secret room slipping in the warm blood that now graces the marble floor.

It is also that frightened cry which brings about Emmett's death in that life as well.

The invaders from the north have penetrated the walls of Deir el-Balah, and one of them in oxhide and studded leather has found the hidden door.

Emmett, as the servant girl, turns in the smoky darkness of the secret chamber. A sword, as long as the arm of the Hittite holding it, curves down at her.

The slice through her neck is as neat and quick as the break of the connection with the Sheriar—which knows, as any cruel god does not, just how much guilt from the past a man can take.

By ten o'clock that morning, the fog had burned off and the contingent of Moon Men hurriedly went about preparing the scoop. The Space Marines had secured the area, going so far as to chew a shallow trench across the lakeshore road, implant several concrete barricades, and make sure their thirty-seven prisoners—taken both from the night before at Gordon's Cove and that day from the morning assault—were comfortable in their own terrain crawler, now converted into a standing jail.

The boats of the doomed flotilla they let wander the placid surface of the lake. Trenton didn't want any of his men out where the same thing could befall them. Still, the Marines stood guard—and watched.

In the soft green grass of the cove, Trenton directed the main terrain crawler, with Glenn Thorpe inside at the controls. The giant six-legged machine lifted its bulky yellow armor in a whine of powerful engines, stepping into the thick water of the cove. It then leveled out, looking now like a house on stilts.

"Okay!" Trenton shouted to the technicians waiting behind the central crawler. "Bring the others out!"

It was like choreographing a ballet; everything had to be just right.

Trenton scanned the lake in all directions. The crawlers in their dinosaur colors *had* to have been noticed by now, he realized. An operation of this magnitude didn't go unobserved. Still, the communities surrounding the lake made no indication that anything was amiss. Trenton didn't like it.

A second terrain crawler, this one on four legs and rather squat, came out of the forest followed by several lunar technicians—Glenn's assistants—lugging long coils of cables like silver anacondas. This was the fusion reactor they were going to need to power the scoop. Trenton stood wary of it. The technology was virtually brand-new, and it was still a delicate piece of machinery.

In fact, everything they were doing was brand-new.

"Roarke!" Trenton called out to the third crawler behind the reactor. "Let's get going. We don't have all morning."

Roarke brought out a terrain crawler especially designed for Operation Cakewalk. The wrangler at the controls in a special Moonsuit waved behind the thick lens of the cockpit as he pranced the machine to the shoreline, where Glenn's assistants began running the power cables to it.

Trenton slopped through the mud of the cove to the scoop. The scoop itself, shielded and just big enough to snare a Seed, was hoisted above the cockpit. Roarke eased back the thick forward window.

"Look," Trenton admonished. "We don't know what's going to happen and I don't want to lose you. Anything funny and I want you to pull out."

Roarke flashed a row of brazenly white teeth. "If I don't vanish within a hundred yards of it, then it's not gonna get me, right?"

He slid the window shut and secured it tightly, not waiting for an answer. The man seemed hardly human to Trenton; he seemed to have as much courage as their reactor had the potential for power. Trenton backed off as Roarke bubbled the scoop down into the water, trailed by the snaking power coils.

Trenton made for the command crawler.

Inside, Glenn Thorpe's thin frame was hunched over an array of multicolored lights, each one flashing its urgent demands.

A technician in earphones and wearing a pinched, serious expression looked up at Trenton as he entered. "Sir," he said quickly, "gunshots in Tahoe City."

"We can't worry about that now," Trenton said. "Let the Marines handle it. You hear any planes, though, let me know."

"Yes, sir."

Trenton turned to Thorpe. "Is the reactor up to the power level?"

Thorpe's thin eyebrows knotted in worry. "We still don't know how much power we're going to need in the first place. I just hope Emmett's calculations are correct. If they aren't, we're going to be the first dwellers in the Gordon's Cove Hooverville."

Trenton seated himself before a special line of lights. He nodded grimly, watching Roarke's crawler submerge into the cold waters beyond the cove.

He said, "It's a wonder none of us thought of using beta-waves to counteract the alpha-waves of the Seed. We could have used a bunch of beta-guns during the Seeding."

Thorpe gave Trenton a look knowledged in the reflections of a painful past: Thorpe's father had been killed in a hunting accident when he was a boy, and his mother had been shot in a mugging incident in New York when he was away at college. As a Moon Man, he lived in a community where guns were outlawed. Space was the perfect place for a pacifist.

But he still knew the need to fight the Seeds, and Trenton had seen the preliminary sketches for beta-guns he'd come up with. It was something that just had to be done.

"Power's up, Dr. Thorpe," crackled the voice of a female technician—the one inside the fusion reactor of the crawler on the shore.

"Fine," Glenn said, turning to the blue go-lights of the board before him.

Trenton's Stively-built heart kicked in once more as nervous beads of sweat on his forehead suddenly appeared.

"Let's hope this works," he breathed.

The scoopcrawler disappeared beneath the gunmetal-colored waters of the lake.

Basil Roarke was in his element. Not water, but danger—even though the water made him feel as if he were at home in some inchoate way.

Trenton's voice came in over his earphones. "We're channeling the beta-waves directly into your suit and cabin, Basil."

Roarke, tight on the controls of the crawler as it made its way down the murky slope of the lake's interior, looked around him, feeling a gentle resonance fill the confined space of the cockpit.

"I don't feel anything, boss."

"You aren't supposed to feel anything," Trenton said. "It'll just keep you awake."

A forward television picture before the wrangler revealed a musky landscape devoid of life. Trenton and Glenn Thorpe were seeing it as well as the scoopcrawler stepped gingerly down the slope of the lake.

"No fish," he commented. "Strange to see a lake with no fish." He liked fish; they always seemed friendly.

Thorpe's tenor appeared. "The Seed will take out most higher forms of life."

The forward lights seemed to halt about thirty yards into the watery night. Roarke's heart pulsed with excitement.

"I love this," he said aloud.

"Just don't blow it," Trenton said. "You do and I'll break all six of your legs."

Roarke giggled, feeling slightly giddy. Was it the excitement? Or was it the conflicting brainwaves?

He brought the scoop down as the instruments before him revealed the enormous power now surging through the scoop cone itself.

"Fifty yards, Basil," Glenn Thorpe announced.

"No one's been this close to a Seed before," he suddenly said in a child's voice.

"It's an alien artifact, Basil," Thorpe told him. "Remember that."

"What if it's an *alien*?" Roarke stared hypnotized at the green corridors of light from the crawler's headlamps as seen on the television monitor. The scoop blocked a direct forward view—and he was now going on touch alone.

"Just calm down," Trenton cautioned. "You're almost on it."

And he *was* calm. Lost in the calm of the fall of angels from heaven. Cloud calm. The calm of space between the planets....

"Ross," he called out in a hesitant voice. "I'm starting to feel funny."

"Funny how?"

"Sleepy. Like I can hear a voice. A hypnotist, maybe."

It was the voice of a masseuse kneading the nodes of the hippocampal region of his brain. Wasn't that what Trenton told him to expect? *Mesmerizing him...*

Then he was suddenly back to normal as Thorpe sent more power to the beta-wave generator in Roarke's special Moonsuit.

"Wow," he breathed heavily, watching the controls. "That thing is strong, Ross. It's *real* strong."

Trenton said over the earphones, "You're coming up on it now, Basil."

On the television monitor a form seemed dead-ahead, snagged on the slope of the lake. It appeared shrouded in a broken-winged arrangement of tarnished silver.

"I see the para-sail!" he said with a burst of boyish discovery.

"We see it too." Trenton then said. "Now, go slow! We don't know what it'll do when disturbed."

And *that* sounded as if Trenton believed it to be a living creature. Roarke swallowed nervously and pushed the slow legs of the crawler down the slope.

He suddenly blinked.

Were the lights before him on the console wavering? Now, why would they do that? he wondered. It was as if the crawler was filling with whale oil....

He found himself almost automatically opening out the jaws of the toothed scoop—even as Glenn Thorpe topside was pushing as much power as possible into the beta-wave screen of the scoop itself. No human had *ever* been this close to a Seed and survived its event-horizon.

And how peaceful everything was! The scoop came down, and Roarke could feel the grit and grind as something was lifted from the mud out before the crawler. But what? What was so important out there, anyway?

He closed his tired eyes. Just for a moment. The surrounding cockpit was singing to him; even the water beyond the thick windows was singing to him. All of nature sang to him in voices of angels in a celestial choir.

"Hey, Roarke!" Glenn Thorpe shouted. "*Roarke!*"

Trenton cut in. "We're going on automatic, Basil! We're going to—"

That voice didn't interest Roarke, though. He liked the angel voices better.

And suddenly he is in church.

He is a boy with his mother and three older sisters. They are in St. Botolph's and a canted, cathedral light falls through the stained-glass kaleidoscope windows above him. Rich, Catholic, and Connecticut— and he is seven years old as Mother Angelica stalks the aisles like a shrouded bat, her face full of disapproval for the young boy he remembers being.

He knows he's in trouble. He can feel it. Mother Angelica, his own mother, and his sisters are all angry. But *what* has he done? All he remembers is cutting down some other boy's tree because the boys in the treehouse high above wouldn't let him in their club. His dad always did say he was good with machines for as young as he was. And, man, did that portable buzz saw sound neat....

Boys will be boys, Mother Angelica consoles his mother.

But the glare from the Reverend Mother could wither a petrified tree. *He's such a difficult child*, he hears his mother say. His own mother!

His gauntleted hands ease away from the controls of the crawler's scoop as the angel choir of St. Botolph's sings its song of sorrow.

But those are angel voices. Just out ahead of the scoop is something else.

He gasps deep within his fading consciousness.

It's the Lord himself, he realizes.

And what he is feeling from the Lord is nothing but complete and total acceptance of the *boy* he is and always will be.

Let go of your worldly troubles, my son, the Lord calls out to him. *Come to me.*

The alpha-rhythms around him are the flutterings of the wings of angels. Or is it his rapidly beating heart?

Suddenly the crawler lurches backward as some other force takes control. The growl of engines and the high-pitched wail of somebody's beta-wave generator fills the cockpit—even the thick armor of his very Moonsuit—and he is brought back.

"We got it, Basil," Trenton's calm, soothing voice announces. "And it's completely contained."

The vision of the Lord is gone, along with that of Mother Angelica. But an impression remains like the fossil of an echo: something still whispers at him and it isn't quite human.

It has power to it, and it is *definitely* not the Lord.

"*Get me out of here!*" he screams.

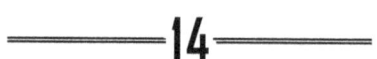

14

Exit bay eight was a Pandora's box of desperate activity. The giant hangar pulsed with technicians and rescue personnel as they prepped the remaining sandcrawlers. The two daughters of Ross Trenton had taken the only surface vehicle which was ready to go—but perhaps that was part of the plan.

Torque Toquero certainly thought so.

Over in an isolated quarter of the exit bay, on the Shortjump pad, sat the bulbous form of the *Lady Nelia Sealing,* one of five research vessels that berthed with the mother ship—now in high earth-orbit—the *Clark Savage, Jr.* Presently it was undergoing its regular servicing, but since the Blue Collars were busy getting the sandcrawlers ready, Toquero had his lady all to himself.

He didn't mind, though. It was, after all, *his* vessel.

Moreover, he knew the importance of keeping all aspects of the *Clark Savage, Jr.* shipshape. It had been a long ten years since the fall of his father's pride and joy, the *Jaguar Skies.* He felt that he had grown some since then, and he was resolved not to have the same thing occur to the House of Toquero's newest flagship.

Besides that, if something disastrous did befall the *Savage, Jr.*, he knew that his father would not trust him—or the Moon Men at large—with another craft so large and expensive.

But he was twenty-nine years old now—a big boy by his standards—and he wasn't about to lose what was rightfully his.

Unless someone interfered.

Almost the instant he ran that thought through his mind, he heard the clumping of environment boots on the ramp beneath the *Lady Nelia.* Someone was coming to call. He hoped it was one of his vivacious blond Blue Collars.

"*Toquero!*" barked a man's gruff voice.

The young rogue quickly sat back in his pilot's chair to give Lloyd Bramlett the impression that he was busy doing nothing.

"Stay away, Bramlett!" he shouted back down the hold to the research area below.

Shit, he said to himself as he heard Bramlett climb the ladder to the command compartment.

He swiveled around to see a fully suited Lloyd Bramlett. Only his environment helmet was missing.

Toquero sat up quickly, feigning amazement. "Hey, Lloyd, don't tell me they're putting you to work."

"Okay," he said flatly, catching his breath, not used to the suit's cumbersomeness. "I won't."

"What's the occasion?"

"We've been enlisted," the Pentagon liaison said. "Orders from earth. We're to help look for the Trenton twins, of all things."

Toquero sat back. "Oh, is *that* all?"

"It's enough!" he snapped. "We're moving out right now. The 'crawlers are ready and we're supposed to assist as best we can."

Toquero smiled through his natty beard, his one uncovered eye glowing. "Not me, Jack. I don't take orders from you."

"Look, Toquero." Bramlett leaned forward in his white suit, his breath harsh from too many cigarettes. "We've got our own experts, you know. As much as I hate to admit it, Trenton is important to this mission. He can't be told about his girls being missing. Now, if that irresponsible mayor of yours had done his job baby-sitting—"

Toquero punched him.

His purple-gloved fist came at Bramlett so fast that the liaison officer was on his backside in a corner with a bloody nose before he even knew what happened.

The twenty-nine-year-old scion of the House of Toquero towered over him, his fists clenched.

"This isn't Emmett's fault, you sonofabitch," he blasted. "It's a glitch no one expected. You can tell your experts down there that they can go hang themselves."

Bramlett's dark eyes swirled with thunderstorms of anger as his glove gingerly tweaked his nose to see if Toquero's Moonsuited glove had broken it. It hadn't. Blood, however, came away freely.

Bramlett cursed at him. "You people think you've got real power now. You think we need you—"

"You do, as a matter of fact."

Bramlett crawled up along the wall, keeping his distance. "This is battery, Toquero. Ill have you locked up when this is over."

"Battery and no witness will get you nowhere," Toquero said with a grin. "You're just pissed off because we're independent up here. The lunar cities *and* my family can do without you people quite nicely, and that just pisses you off...doesn't it?"

Bramlett stood his ground. "We have to stick together on this! Trenton said so himself!"

Toquero moved threateningly toward him. "I take my orders from Ross, not from you and *not* from that idiot President of yours."

Bramlett's head jerked back as if he'd been struck again. *That got him,* Toquero realized. *The man's a loyalist, just as Trenton briefed us. Interesting....*

"I don't want to go looking for those kids any more than you do," he started.

And Toquero cut him off. "Then don't, Bramlett. Go back to your quarters and let my Blue Collars handle it. This is their business. *Our business.* Let us take care of our own."

Bramlett's dark brown eyes went black as the blood from his nose stopped, crusting at his nostrils. He said, "I bet you *want* Operation Cakewalk to fail. I'll bet you want the Seeds to devour earth's population so that you guys can take control."

"Oh, brother..." Toquero said, rolling his eye with disgust. "You're really out of it, Bramlett. If there *is* another Halo coming in this time next year, then Yancy City, Gambart, maybe even Macondo will get Seeded. You just let us do our job."

Bramlett looked at the Spaniard—and Toquero knew what he was thinking: *What the hell does this kid know anyway?*

A deathbird of silence flew between them for a brief moment as their eyes met.

Then Toquero said, "I may be twenty years younger than you are, Bramlett, but I'm not stupid." Then he leaned over, his one eye glaring. "And I'll tell you this: insult Emmett Shea one more time and I'll kill you."

Bramlett's earthly tan went suddenly pale. He gripped the ladder to the level below with one uncertain hand. He prepared to descend.

A call sounded out just then over the console.

"Torque?"

It was Lisa Palazetti.

Damn, Toquero suddenly thought. *I don't want Bramlett to hear any of this....*

Lisa's musical voice filled the command module of the *Lady Nelia Sealing*.

"Torque," she began. "Can you look in on Emmett? I think something's wrong. I'm getting a reading here that he's using Ross's Sheriar all by himself."

Toquero eyed Bramlett as they both listened in.

"Is he at his Watchtower apartment?" Toquero queried in a calm tone, hoping that Lisa wouldn't spill too many beans.

"I tried to call him when one of my nurses pointed it out to me. But he's not answering. The last time I was with him, he said—"

Quickly Toquero cut her off. "Lisa, I'm not in a position to talk right now. I'll be there directly."

Bramlett wordlessly headed back down the ladder.

"Hold it, Bramlett!" Toquero called down.

He proceeded after him when the liaison officer did not slow. *How much did the man know about Emmett and Lisa?*

Bramlett's environment helmet was on the ramp and this he retrieved as he clattered down the metal ramp onto the floor of exit bay eight. The sandcrawlers were waiting, their bright lights like the eyes of huge insects.

Bramlett began attaching his helmet as two technicians came over to help him. They both noticed the blood.

Toquero pulled him aside. "You let us handle our affairs, Bramlett."

"*The man plays with toys!*" Bramlett fairly shouted. "You think Emmett Shea's going to crack the secret of the Seed? You think he's smart enough to get us the Longjump? *Hah!*"

He turned and waddled toward a waiting 'crawler.

Just then, high over them in the bay observation booth, several illuminated technicians began running about. One leaned over a microphone and gestured down to Toquero.

"Mr. Toquero! The girls are coming in! They're in the outer lock!"

From behind the giant lock which led to the outer surface of the moon, they could hear the leviathan wheezings of the air cycling itself back into the lock.

The technician continued as everyone's attention turned toward the still-sealed doors. He said, "One of our scout teams picked up their 'crawler coming in from the *Jaguar* ruins."

"Are they all right?" Toquero shouted up to the man above in the glowing booth.

"They *say* so. The sandcrawler's coming in under its own power, so they must be okay."

The hallway behind them which led back to the main arteries of Yancy City filled suddenly with the electric susurrations of a getabout, driven by Emmett Shea.

Emmett had donned his environment suit, complete with backpack, and brought the getabout to a halt.

Toquero noted the look of grim determination on the wiry physicist's face—or perhaps it was just basic pissed-offness.

"They're here, Emmett," Toquero said as Emmett climbed out of the electric car.

Bramlett, glowering from within his suit by his waiting sandcrawler, said nothing.

Everyone turned their attention to the large doors of the exit bay's airlock opening to reveal the missing 'crawler.

Toquero and Emmett ran up to the sandcrawler as its pleated wheels left fine tracks of lunar dust on the bay floor.

The girls, however, looked all right from where they stood.

Cheryl Trenton brought the 'crawler to its usual berth, but Cindy was struggling with something in the back of the vehicle. Toquero and Emmett both ran around to the rear of the 'crawler, where the equipment hatch opened out at Cheryl's command.

The loading ramp slid out from behind the surface craft like a corrugated aluminum tongue. Cindy's voice chimed merrily.

"Uncle Emmett, look what *we* found!"

The two mischievous nine-year-old imps rumbled out three dust-bitten gray-green Seeds, each just slightly larger than basketballs.

The suited grown-ups, to a person, gasped throughout the exit bay, staggering backward. The Seeds rolled among them like dice thrown from the Devil's clawed hand.

Cheryl Trenton stood beside her sister, arms full of rumpled silvery fabric. "We even found parachutes!" she announced proudly.

Cindy jumped down with a clump from the back end of the 'crawler. She pointed a moongloved hand at the three Seeds.

"But don't worry, Uncle Emmett," she said solemnly. "We think they're dead."

15

The machine at the far end of the uncovered tennis court coughed out fuzzy luminescent green tennis balls as the President of the United States huffed after them, swinging mightily his oversized Spaulding, missing every third one entirely.

The afternoon sun hovered at a point on the western horizon where Florida lay, but nothing beyond the usual sea of kelp could be seen. Only an incoming stevedore's diesel plume intervened upon its solitary beauty as James Guthrie watched Ralph Scanlon dash after the tennis balls, graceful as a toad.

Both men, dressed in tennis whites, were tired of the day's routine of holding together what remained of the government. Perhaps it was the soggy sea air which slowed everyone down. It certainly did Ralph

Scanlon as his racket sliced a silver streak, singing its song of incompetence and anger born of boredom.

Green tennis balls floated in the Sargasso Sea beyond the Floating White House like fruit in a child's bowl of cereal.

Scanlon leveled a freckled arm at the robot spitting balls out at him across the court.

"I want that thing fixed!" he ordered.

"It's on its lowest setting, sir," Guthrie reported, feeling slightly rejected because Scanlon refused him as an opponent, preferring a *real* workout from the robot.

Scanlon ducked as an ace sang inches from his ear.

"Sonofabitch!" he roared. He threw his four-hundred-dollar graphite racket at the robot. It bounced and warped off its senseless metal skull, falling like a question mark against the fence.

He turned his back away from the machine, but the robot witlessly shot a zinger at Scanlon's ample backside, placing a cherry where it'd take the President days to forget.

"Take the damn thing out and shoot it!"

Cowering White House assistants behind Guthrie did not make a move. They all could see his dark mood.

Guthrie interjected. "Perhaps we can now discuss the summit, sir," he began. Green balls rolled at their feet like affectionate kittens. Scanlon kicked them out of his way.

"We just had a summit, remember?" the President snorted from deep within a cotton towel, in the process of wiping his face.

"That was your predecessor, Ralph. Not you."

"Ms. Bresnahan should've been a Republican! A Republican knows how to handle the Russians!"

More cactoid tennis balls found their way in Scanlon's direction and the President turned on a Secret Service agent nearby. "Maiden! Find that clown, Motzenbacker, and have him throw that machine in the water!"

Mr. Maiden, corpulent and planted on the spot, stared back at the President. In his sunglasses, the agent looked as if all he needed for his disguise was a hat full of pencils and a red-tipped cane.

"Are you talking to me?" Maiden asked.

Scanlon's fists became little red hogs of wrath. "You're goddamn right, I'm talking to you! *Move!*"

Maiden moved.

Guthrie cleared his throat. "Sir, Ms. Bresnahan *was* a Republican and she handled the Russians rather efficiently. They say she prevented a third world war by convincing them that the Halo wasn't sent by one of our expeditions to Mars."

"I know my history, Guthrie," Scanlon said, snarling into the towel, blowing his nose with disapproval of anybody's political prowess but his own. He looked up. "What's Congress say about another summit?"

"Bipartisan agreement, sir. Given the circumstances, it seems like a good idea." The sun off Guthrie's glasses made it appear as if the small aide was wearing goggles.

"What circumstances? Operation Cakewalk?"

"The Russians have gotten word that we're up to something, or I should say the Moon Men."

Scanlon's pale blue eyes clouded with disgust. "I knew something would go wrong! If they find out we had to use the Shortjump..."

"We could use the summit to convince the Soviets that it's in both of our interests to neutralize the Seeds, sir. That's the idea behind the Cakewalk, at least from the way Dr. Trenton outlined it originally."

"Trenton!" Scanlon said, staring irately at the robot opposite them on the court, now out of balls to cough.

It coughed anyway.

He said, "You know our people say Trenton might oppose me in the next election."

Guthrie painted a wry smile across his face. "*If* there's an electorate in three years and *if* Trenton wants to reenter politics. Which, at this point, seems unlikely."

Scanlon leveled a mighty finger at Guthrie's face. "Nothing's unlikely in this world, Guthrie. That stupid Halo and those Seeds should prove that!"

"But the Russians think that something is—"

"I know, I know!"

Clearly the President wasn't in the mood to banter international policy at the moment.

Guthrie watched the great man ponder the issue before them, listening to the squeak of the squirrel cage in the President's brain as Ralph Scanlon ruminated.

"Does Jack Wheeler have anything to do with this?" he then asked.

Guthrie nodded. "It's possible. If he found out that the Moon Men Shortjumped into his territory—"

"It's *our* territory!"

"Yes, sir. They say, though, that he might have gotten word to the Soviets of their illegal use of the Shortjump."

"Why would he do a thing like that? What an idiot."

"Actually, sir, it's not so stupid as you think," Guthrie pointed out.

"What?"

"Certainly, sir. Jack Wheeler's got a broad constituency throughout that part of the country. If he can discredit you, then *he* might oppose you in the next election. He's virtually got Oregon and California right now."

"He's a secessionist! He wants to be a dictator, not a president!"

"He'll probably go for what he can get, sir," Guthrie said, trying not to imply that the President would do the same.

Scanlon, though, used to his aide's insolent barbs, glowered at him as if the words had been telepathically sent.

"We're going to have to do something about those Moon Men when they're done capturing that Seed."

"Like what, sir?"

"Like put them out of business! Keep them on the moon! Anything! They've got too much freedom..." He trailed off, thinking.

"They also don't have any Seeds, and for the last twenty or so years they've had full environmental closure, *and* thanks to the Toquero family, their mining and industrial enterprises actually make money for them."

"Don't remind me! I know what they can do!"

At that moment Agent Maiden appeared from the side of the gym building with a tall, skinny rail of a man pushing a contraption on three wheels.

"What's that?" Scanlon said with a studied expression.

Agent Maiden pointed to the man behind the wheeled device. "Mr. Motzenbacker said you wanted to try the Bull today."

Motzenbacker, in greasy overalls, cigarette dangling from his lip, jumped back as the Bull came to life.

"Here, sir! It works best with a cape!" Motzenbacker shouted, tossing Scanlon a red silk cloth about a yard square.

The Bull, the size of a minicar from Japan, with two acute heat-sensitive eyes, snapped out a pair of rubberized horns as long as a man's forearm as it came to life.

Motzenbacker and Maiden dived for cover as the Bull rushed the President and his stunned aide with more speed than they thought mechanically possible.

16

Technicians, daubed to the waist in gray mud, removed a hysterical Basil Roarke from the scoop's cockpit almost before the modified crawler had lifted itself upon the shore.

Thorpe was out of the command crawler and running up to the scoop. Trenton, directing traffic, waved his Moonsuited arms about.

"Can you feel it?" Trenton turned and faced his eager aide. "That thing's *alive!*"

Thorpe nodded, his pale eyes riveted on the locked bulb of the scoop and what it contained within.

The small, moveable fusion reactor in its special terrain crawler hummed audibly, sending all the power it could muster through the python-thick cables that snaked into the rear end of the scoop.

"This is what we came for," Trenton shouted to the techs as they guided the scoop, which was now on remote, into the gouged earth and broken serenity of Gordon's Cove. The scoop's foreleg pulverized a picnic table, itself gone to ruin.

"If that thing falls out—" Glenn began fearfully.

Trenton nodded, feeling his heart struggle to control his adrenaline level. *Delicately, boys, delicately...*

The scoopcrawler walked past them, bound for the lakeshore road. The fusion generator, piloted by a sober female tech at the helm followed, the tech's eyes never leaving the power-gradient instrument. One slip and it would be instant Hooverville.

Thorpe pointed at the muddied machine and its bridal train of lunar technicians. "I want to know where that thing gets so much *power.* Ross, we're running all the juice our baby can create."

Trenton pondered the scoop's treasure. He said, "tight-beam everything up to Emmett, pronto. If we go into a Hooverville, I want him to at least know what kind of power we're dealing with this close."

"And it's all coming out in alpha-waves," Thorpe said, ankle-deep in mud and mush. "No heat, no radiation of any kind. Whoever built that thing is way out in front of us. *Way* out."

From the command crawler they could hear Basil Roarke thrashing around in his Moonsuit, delirious and enraged. His eyes were focused upon some ethereal phantom no one could see as the techs fought the powerful Moon Man into the crawler.

"We'd better sedate Basil," Trenton told the inventor beside him. "He's too dangerous the way he is. I didn't think he'd have this kind of reaction."

"No one did," Thorpe returned.

Trenton rubbed his eyes. "There's just too much to think about. Too many variables."

"We got this far, Ross. We got what we came for, didn't we?"

"Barely," he responded, gently fingering the plasti-derm mold upon the side of his face.

"Now all we have to do is figure out how it works," Thorpe mused happily, feeling better the further the Seed got from them. The alpha-waves soothed them both—but not to the point of removing them from reality.

"Dr. Trenton!" the com-officer hailed from the communications crawler squatting several yards away.

Trenton looked up quickly. *Now what?* he wondered.

"There's an open-channel conversation out of South Lake Tahoe," the officer continued. "Jumpcopters have landed outside of town. Fightin' Jack's here."

"What?"

Trenton looked at Thorpe with great alarm. The cat was out of the bag. Just how big a cat, they were about to find out.

Glenn said, "I'll attend to the Scoop. This is your show now." The Moon Man took off toward the lakeshore road, along with several technicians and a couple of Space Marines.

Trenton dashed over to the thick legs of the crawler and peered upward to the com-officer. "How do you know it's Fightin' Jack?"

"It's his voiceprint, sir. Checks out. He's been up in Reno and someone must've gotten word to him. We picked up five jumpcopters ten minutes ago."

Trenton thought for a few seconds. They knew that Fightin' Jack had a vast armory, considering that California boasted some of the most complete Air Force bases in the country. But the Seeding of '33 left many of them in various states of disrepair—or literal Hoovervilles—and their weaponry had long gone abandoned. Jumpcopters—or STOL's—would bring the militia in behind tree cover and away from the Marines' lasers.

Pretty tricky, Trenton mused. *No wonder Scanlon's afraid of Jack Wheeler.* Americans hadn't seen a dictator since Franklin Roosevelt. Now they had one.

But the one thing America didn't need right now was someone to impede what progress the nation had made in the last six years. And Trenton knew all about power: the more you had, the more you felt you needed. He'd seen it time and again through his Sheriar, and he'd known it personally during his stint as Lunar President. Fightin' Jack wouldn't give up without a fight.

Trenton shouted up to the com-officer, "Pull out! Give the order! Cakewalk's over! *Everyone back to the platforms!*"

Lieutenant MacReadie, arm in a sling, one hand gripping a service revolver, came up to Dr. Trenton.

"Sir, we're picking up a recon drone." The athletic young man pointed with his gun out across the sleeping lake. A boat or two from the flotilla could be seen lolling out in the morning sunlight.

"I hear it now," Trenton acknowledged.

A buzz-sawing rattled out over the silver-blue surface of Lake Tahoe. MacReadie, angry with his own pain, turned to a Marine nearby. "Stamets!"

"Sir!"

Stamets, a Marine sergeant the size of a buffalo, leveled a laser rifle at a dark speck which was angling up from South Lake Tahoe.

A green needle of silent, deadly light sliced the robot drone in half, well short of its goal. It sputtered and splattered into the lake.

MacReadie turned to Trenton. "What if the drone had a warhead, Dr. Trenton? It could have, you know."

Trenton slapped him on his unhurt arm like a coach to his favorite split end. Trenton said, "Animals like Jack Wheeler like to play with their food before they eat it."

"Yes, sir." MacReadie turned and jogged for the other crawlers, shouting to his men.

Trenton stood alone in the cove as the huge machines surrounding him hoisted themselves up on their pistonlike legs and began their retreat into the woods. He thought back to the time of his honeymoon many years ago, when the world was whole and full of possibilities.

He shook his head. One thing at a time. He couldn't let his memories of Annette obscure his thinking. They still had a long way to go and he wasn't going to let a cluck like Jack Wheeler stop him. That was Ralph Scanlon's problem, ultimately.

On the other hand, he thought distantly, *I wouldn't mind tackling Wheeler myself....*

He abandoned the thought and the cove.

Jack Wheeler, a knotted muscle of power and righteousness, pulled his beret tighter over his shock of ash-gray hair as the wind tugged at him where he sat in his Jeep. The man's steely eyes pierced the sharp sunlight that fell through the pines which lined the lakeshore road north out of the Hooverville that South Lake Tahoe had become.

In the jeep sat a frightened Morris Bly, who'd spent a long night tearing through the woods, taking secret paths, all in an attempt to get out of Tahoe City and get word to Fightin' Jack. He'd been lucky, Morris Bly. He had gotten Jack Wheeler himself, who had personally jumpcoptered to the little town of Truckee on Interstate 80, where Bly had stopped in his exhaustion. The car he had stolen had also stopped as well. But Fightin' Jack had come anyway.

The fourth man in the jeep, other than the driver, was a thick-set man with a burly gray beard who continually wore a radio headset. His name was Thorgill and he was Jack Wheeler's right-hand man.

He tapped Fightin' Jack on the shoulder as the jeep—followed by the assault vehicles from the copters—made its hasty way through the woods.

"Jack! They shot down our drone. No gunshot. Probably lasers!" Thorgill shouted.

"They've got to be Marines," little Morris Bly squeaked, his thin hair ruffling like the hairs on the ass-end of a rat. "Sam always said they been watchin' us! It's a takeover, Jack!"

Fightin' Jack's eyes were like bullets, quieting the smarmy little man in the back seat.

"We'll put a stop to them right now," the large man bellowed above the wind. "Nobody Shortjumps in my backyard, that's for damn sure!"

Bly hunched in his seat, shivering. "But, Jack, what if the Russians find out? If they knew President Scanlon authorized a Shortjump—"

Fightin' Jack turned magnanimously in his seat to speak to the little man. "Use your brain, Bly! What the hell do Marines, or anybody, want with your scummy little town? *Huh?*"

Bly blanched visibly and swallowed.

"It's close to Reno—" he began, trying to counter their leader's argument any way he could.

"Horseshit!" shouted Jack Wheeler. "They'd Shortjump into Reno and grab me by the balls if they wanted to. No," he concluded, facing forward, "something mighty important's going on and I mean to find out."

Suddenly the driver swerved the jeep onto the side of the road. He pointed out ahead of him as the cadre of Confederates also ground to a halt.

"Something dead ahead, sir!" the driver shouted. "*Look!*"

Like a tall martian spider, two stories above the crumbling asphalt of the forest road, it came at them.

"Holy shit!" Jack Wheeler shouted, standing up in the jeep. "It's a terrain crawler!" He craned around and shouted to his troops. "Break off! Everybody into the woods! *Now!*" His arms waved in a desperate semaphore.

The Western Confederates, dressed in khaki, chest armor, and armed to the proverbial teeth, leapt out of their vehicles and clattered into the woods.

Thorgill tossed down his radio unit and yanked Morris Bly out of the jeep, as Fightin' Jack scrambled down off the road and into the protection of the trees.

Jack shouted in a gruff voice, "Space Marines will be right in behind it! Watch for laser fire!"

The forest filled with the insectlike clickings of deadly rifle bolts snicking into place as well as the legs of tripods for armor-piercing artillery being unlimbered behind bushes and trees. Rifle snouts leveled and took aim; all of them held their breath, their whole lives spent in anticipation of a moment like this.

The terrain crawler, a luminous cream color, new as the day it was forged on the moon, came at them, planting potholes with every step it took upon the road.

Jack Wheeler stood up bravely and commanded: "*Fire!*"

The forest exploded with the barks and hoots of gunfire in a chorus of deadly chatter. But the crawler came on.

"It's not stopping," Morris Bly cried. "*It's not stopping!*"

The Confederates dived farther back into the flanks of the woods, making for thicker cover, but never letting up as the crawler kept to its slow, steady canter, heading directly for the half-tracks, jeeps, and armored personnel carriers the jumpcopters had brought in.

It sounded like the Fourth of July, except for the metal slaps of ricocheting bullets off the crawler's alloyed skin.

They could now make out people in the forward cockpit of the crawler, as arrowheads of lead skimmed off the impermeable glass.

However, no other crawlers were following it, nor were there any Marines darting between the trees behind the behemoth.

"Wait, wait!" Fightin' Jack suddenly shouted, jumping out from the cover of the bushes beside the road.

Morris Bly gasped as the crawler came within closer view.

"Hey," he called out. "It's Bevis...and George Seigler!"

"Who are *those* people?" Fightin' Jack said, turning to little Bly. "They're not Space Marines!"

The Confederates ceased firing as Jack Wheeler and Morris Bly ran out onto the green-shadowed road.

The voices of the prisoners inside the crawler could not be heard—though clearly they were shouting to be let out, thumping their fists uselessly on the impenetrable windows.

However, the crawler was on automatic, stepping happily on down the road, oblivious of any concerns other than those locked in its computer memory. It traipsed past the jeeps and half-tracks, heading for South Lake Tahoe.

"God *damn!*" Fightin' Jack shouted, throwing down his blue beret, symbol of his authority.

And just as he did, they heard several thunderclaps from the area known as Gordon's Cove. Fightin' Jack knew the sound for what it was: air rushing to fill the void formerly occupied by Space Marines, Moon Men, and whatever it was that had brought them there in the first place.

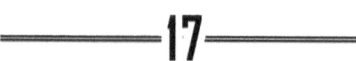

17

"I feel like Aladdin, who's just found his magic lamp, Emmett Shea said. Still encased in his environment suit—minus the helmet—he stood before a thick window with Lisa Palazetti and two naughty little girls, watching a bevy of lunar technicians examine the three dead Seeds.

Lisa Palazetti turned her doe's eyes to him. "Why's that?"

"I'm afraid if I rub it too hard, a big genie will pop up and give me all of my wishes." It was a child's thought with an adult's recognition of the Way the World Works. Still, Emmett wouldn't let go: an alpha-wave-generating yo-yo was at work in his hand, humming its soothing tune.

The Trenton twins, in their soft blue Moonsuits, perched upon stools and guzzled Cokes from the Coke machine in the outer hallway. They smiled at their father's closest friends, feeling invincible and proud of what they had done.

Lisa, in her physician's white tunic, held close to Emmett. "You shouldn't worry so much," she said quietly.

The yo-yo dipped and weaved; anyone within ten feet could feel its effects. He and Glenn Thorpe had engineered it that way as part of their attempts to understand alpha-wave generation.

He glanced sideways at the otherwise well-behaved nine-year-olds. He said, "I knew I shouldn't have let Ross talk me into running for mayor. I've got too much to think about." The yo-yo went down; came up.

"And no one knew you'd find that lost Seed in Lake Tahoe, either," Lisa told him, her own voice soft with a kindness Emmett wouldn't allow for himself.

Cheryl pointed to one Seed upon which two lunar techs were doing the equivalent of a CAT scan.

"I found that one," she said. "That's mine."

Lisa gave the nine-year-old a bright, though slightly admonishing look. "Just who taught you to operate a sandcrawler?"

Cindy spoke out. "It was Mr. Roarke! He taught us a lot!"

Slurping noises came from the two cans of Coke, then Cheryl said, "We were helping Daddy look for Mommy."

"Looking for clues," Cindy added.

Emmett helped the twins off their stools and gave Cheryl his yo-yo.

"Here, play with this for a while," he said. "Uncle Emmett has to check out your Seeds."

He gave Lisa a knowing look and she took Cindy's hand. "Girls, come along. We'd better take you home. It's getting close to suppertime. And I think you've done enough for one day."

"'Bye!" both girls said simultaneously waving to Uncle Emmett as Lisa led them away.

Emmett sighed deeply, then walked in through the pressurized doors to the examining room to get a closer look at his three new toys.

***

Emmett's chief assistant, Dr. Ticia Rhodes, was already at work, bent over one of the Seeds, when Emmett in sterile coveralls and white mask walked into the examination center.

Ticia Rhodes was the oldest of the Moon Men, at fifty-one years of age. Her hair, though streaked with silver-gray, was long and wild and lush—leonine—and burst out from behind her face mask as she studied the alien artifact. Like Emmett and the others, she, too, had journeyed in the Sheriar with Ross Trenton on several occasions. They were bound, all of them, by more than just the fact of their physical location and Ticia Rhodes was no exception.

Lloyd Bramlett walked in minutes later, also in white coveralls and mask, and when Toquero entered in his usual purple Moonsuit without a mask, Emmett could feel the air electrify, almost smelling the ozone burning between the two men.

Ticia looked up at them. "Dead as just about anything could be," she reported in a muffled voice behind her mask.

She rotated the large Seed with one firm hand. "But I'll be damned if I can figure out what it's made of."

Emmett consulted a computer scanner. "No radiation of any kind. Very unusual."

Toquero picked up one of the Seeds and hefted it.

"Don't drop it, dammit!" Bramlett said suddenly.

Toquero's unpatched eye glared at the Pentagon liaison, and his small mouth smiled maliciously from behind his goatee. "Man, this thing fell from no telling how high up. I could drop this right here and nothing would happen to it."

Which he did.

It bounced with little resilience—but did not break or crack. It only deposited a fine circle of three-billion-year-old Moondust.

"Torque," Emmett said quickly. He retrieved it from the Moorish-looking young man. "We've still got to be careful."

Back it went onto the examining table.

Torque pointed with a purple-gloved hand. "Okay, question number one. With a million or so Seeds on the earth, why are these three *here*? And why aren't they working?"

"That's two questions." Bramlett sneered.

Torque's one eye went icy with seriousness.

"Good point," Ticia Rhodes said, ignoring their squabble. "But I think I know. It's the transponder."

Emmett looked at her. "In the *Jaguar Skies*?"

Dr. Rhodes nodded, her hair cascading out wildly from behind the straps of her mask. "Remember that the night of the Seeding, all of Yancy City was virtually shut down. Only the transponder in the *Skies* was operating."

"It drew the Seeds in somehow," Emmett said, nodding above one of the Seeds. *Alien*, he had to remind himself. *These dead things come from somewhere else and here we are talking about them as if they were snowballs....*

Toquero seemed suddenly taken with the idea of a lunar-wide Seeding. It had always baffled them because no Seeds had fallen on either the moon or on Mars, where there was a fledgling Soviet colony.

"No atmosphere to assist in their guidance systems," he commented, verbalizing his thoughts.

"Right," said a man over in a corner. Bob Stapely, a tall, soft-bodied black man, was finishing up his Ph.D. in physics under Ticia Rhodes's chairmanship at their small university. Stapely was in the midst of examining the para-gliders. He continued: "My guess is that the chutes opened out just within range of some source of intelligent life. A city, perhaps."

"Or a transponder that can be picked up as far away as earth," Bramlett said in a low, thoughtful voice.

Toquero went uncharacteristically somber. "We're lucky, then. Damn lucky."

"Right," Emmett agreed. "The *Jaguar Skies* fell only thirty miles from Yancy."

More information paraded itself across their computer screens. Ticia noted this and announced: "Each Seed weighs in at six pounds, five ounces. And they've each got a diameter of fifteen inches. Very light and very small."

Emmett did the math in his head. He looked at the gathering of Moon Men. He said, "With a million, two hundred thousand known Seeds at six pounds each—approximately—that comes to three thousand, six hundred tons. Not enough."

"That's assuming," Bob Stapely interjected, "that they don't weigh more when they're alive and well. Do we have any data on the Lake Tahoe Seed?"

"Not yet," Emmett told him.

Lloyd Bramlett was out in the cold. "What do you mean by 'not enough?' Enough for what?"

Ticia Rhodes indicated the mute Seed. "The Halo was incredibly massive. Thousands of times beyond what it would need to do the earth in."

"Maybe they all got lost," Bramlett countered. "A scattershot effect. Cover your bases."

"Maybe," Emmett muttered.

But he was thinking of his own calculations six years previously. The Halo came from the Alpha and Proxima Centauri system of stars, pregnant with Seeds. But when it slung itself on out of the solar system, it seemed bound—at twenty percent light speed—for Eta Cassiopeiae, more than eighteen light-years distant. He looked at Bramlett evenly.

"Some for us, and some for the folks around Eta Cassiopeiae. And no telling who after that."

Outside, beyond the glass window, a handful of Space Marines, in full armor, placed themselves ready. They bore standard-issue M-30's. Their only beta-wave generator was on the earth as part of Operation Cakewalk. *If the Seeds came up to power now,* Emmett thought, *Yancy City would become a Hooverville overnight. Just add water...*

The commander of the Marines saluted Emmett through the window and then the men leveled their M-30's at the Seeds—just in case.

Emmett turned to Bob Stapely and Ticia Rhodes. "Let's see what the CAT scanner shows."

"Right," Ticia said, sliding the Seed onto a different table.

A separate screen gave them a tintype image which startled them. Even the guards outside the windows watched with awe.

The Seed under the scope wasn't an intricate network of computer chips and generators, but instead was mostly a plastic matrix that held in suspension a long, slender object that resembled—more than anything else—an arrow a Sioux warrior might use, tapered at one end, finned at the other. On either side of the arrow-shaped rod were two completely spherical objects. *Marbles,* Emmett thought. *Marbles and arrows....*

"Is that it?" Toquero said, standing upright, away from the screen. He seemed disappointed. They *all* seemed disappointed.

"It's enough," Emmett told them. "More than enough."

As the electric getabout bearing Lisa and the two girls made its way efficiently toward the condos where the Moon Men and their families resided, the good doctor sat between them, holding each of them to reassure them.

"We were only trying to help," Cheryl said as they exited one tunnel and made for another—this one filled with light from glowing vines.

"Yes," Cindy added.

"You've got enough to worry about," Lisa said softly. "You let us grown-ups worry about finding your mother. We're all working on it."

Holding the Trenton twins brought up very deep feelings she had for her own mothering instincts. Her own inability to bear children had brought her to Ross Trenton's Sheriar and many months of fruitful therapy. But while her own body could not, as yet, yield up any children, she always hoped that someday she and Emmett might marry and start a family.

However, at thirty-nine, she was well within a time of fading fertility—and it agonized her. As the Sheriar suggested, her inability to have children might be a kind of punishment. Her most revealing past life was that of a famous gladiator in Rome, around a.d. iii. Hundreds had perished by the sword that particular gladiator had wielded, and, as Ross had then dug up in further Sheriar sessions, Lisa's following incarnations allowed her *atma*, her soul, to work off that accumulated violence. Her life now was devoted to healing—a natural outcome of so much accumulated negative karma.

But somewhere, back in some past life, was the reason why in *this* life she wasn't allowed to have children. And that still eluded her. Holding the Trenton girls near only reminded her of her emptiness.

The getabout eased into a wide, parklike area where many of Cindy and Cheryl's friends were playing under the supervision of their cache-keeper.

"Hi, Cindy! Hi, Cheryl!" shouted a spunky six-year-old. Glenn Thorpe's little girl, Terry, jumped up and waved at the getabout.

"Hi, Terry!" Cheryl waved back.

A little boy, brown as a chestnut, also waved. He was holding the hand of another, smaller child.

"Hi, Gopal!" Cheryl shouted triumphantly. "Hi, Patty!"

Gopal Govinda was nine years old, and Patty Brown, five. Both were lunar orphans, their parents killed in separate mining accidents. Lisa was quite fond of them both as were the Trenton twins.

The getabout left the sheltered park and made its way to their condo, and they were met at the door by Cindy and Cheryl's live-in baby-sitter, Robbie Rogers. A student at the university, she took her duties a little too seriously. Her prematurely gray hair—for a twenty-nine-year-old woman—was her reward.

"Dr. Palazetti!" Robbie cried out.

Lisa directed the girls into Ross Trenton's large condominium as Robbie fussed about them.

"I was almost sick with worry!" she announced with considerable relief.

"We found them before anything happened," Lisa said quickly and in a voice she hoped the little girls would hear.

But the twins missed it.

"Yes," Cheryl chirped. "And we found a bunch of—"

Lisa cut the tyke off. "I don't think we need to bore Robbie with our adventures right now. You girls get out of your Moonsuits and let Robbie fix you some supper."

Robbie Rogers, all flustered and mother-henning her way through the suite, herded the little girls into their room. She turned to Lisa when it was safe.

"Oh, Dr. Palazetti, I could've died. I didn't know *what* to do. Did you radio down to Dr. Trenton yet? Did you tell him we found them?"

Lisa smiled wryly. "We didn't tell him they were missing in the first place. He's got enough to worry about." She gave the baby-sitter a confidential look. "I think we'd better keep this one a secret for a while, don't you?"

Robbie didn't answer, but rushed off instead to tend to her wards.

In their room, after showers and a dinner with a calorie-loaded dessert, the girls secretively pulled out a remote radio-command from underneath Cheryl's bed.

"Anson!" Cheryl sang into the transmitter. "Come here!"

Robbie Rogers, doing homework in the living room, blissfully ignored the girls in their bedroom, happy that they were safe. And the girls knew this.

Anson McDonald, a mindless robot companion, had been with them in the sandcrawler, and had been slow in returning to the condo complex. Slow because the twins had intended it that way.

And now it had merely been waiting out in the hallway until the girls were ready for it.

The chubby little machine passed by Robbie Rogers on its rubber treads. It was always coming and going, and she didn't pay any attention to it. Yancy City was full of them.

Once inside their room, the robot halted. The girls leapt from their beds, wearing their bunny pajamas, all perfumed and clean from their showers.

"I hope they didn't search him," Cindy said, frowning.

"Open up, Anson," Cheryl ordered, tapping it on its rounded head.

The robot companion's chest slid open in an accordion roll and revealed what the girls had earlier hidden that day.

Cheryl's small hands reached inside. She then showed her sister *their* treasure.

Not only had they found three whole Seeds and the torn para-sails, but they had discovered many broken ones as well. However, what they found didn't seem broken—just old. Brittle. As if they had simply died after they had crash-landed near the *Jaguar Skies*.

"Oooo," Cindy said, eyes wide with wonder. In the strong light of the condo, the objects they'd found were much more exciting than they had originally thought.

In their hands were several arrow-shaped rods which were still coated with a fine lunar dust, and they had over nine round, marblelike balls. These were feather-light and funny to the touch, as if their molecules shimmered with life very, very gently.

"Hold one of these!" Cindy said to her sister, giving her one of the quarter-size balls.

Cheryl's pink fingers turned it over and over as her eyes stared rapturously at the treasure.

From the living room came the impatient rustle of the pages of a book and Robbie's bedtime voice. "Girls, lights out now."

"Yes, Robbie," Cheryl said quietly.

Cindy looked at her sister—not moving to dim the lights at all. She said, "Were these made on another *planet*?"

"Maybe a star," Cheryl breathed. "But Mommy would know. She knows all sorts of stuff."

The girls sank into a reverential, contemplative silence as they began thinking of their missing parents. But then after a few moments their minds slipped into a totally different realm of thought as they toyed with the marble-shaped objects. Something was happening.

"Can you feel it?" Cheryl suddenly looked at her sister.

"Voices," Cindy breathed excitedly, looking up.

The marbles seemed to resonate with pleasant sensations they couldn't describe, but could certainly feel. Images came to their minds, along with colors and sounds from very far away.

The girls looked at each other for a very long time.

—————=18=—————

For a dark moment, he did not know where he was. Lying on his back, Trenton floated in the predawn stillness, fighting sleep, fighting wakefulness. He felt his Stively-built heart increase ever so slightly as the Nerzhin sleep-couch—having registered that he was now awake—disconnected itself softly from his Sheriar disc-computer at his collar. The sound of the Nerzhin jack coiling back into the bed's headboard frightened him with its suddenness, waking him fully.

Is that coffee? he suddenly thought, his olfactory nerves coming alive. *Real coffee?*

He sat up in the dawn dark, listening as the Nerzhin computer kicked awake the coffeepot in the corner of the special room. *I'm back home*, Trenton suddenly realized. It was coffee, and real coffee comes from the *earth*.

"Good," came a voice from the intercom beside his bed. "You're awake. Take your time. I'll come up."

The voice cut off before Trenton could recognize it; he was still groggy.

Coffee cup in hand, Trenton made for the closed curtains at the opposite end of the room and drew them apart.

Los Angeles, like a bowl of pustulant soup, a valley of fetid vapors and thick skies, glowed with cooking fires as the injured city itself began wakening, even though the sun had still yet to be seen.

Now Trenton remembered. Vibrations prattled up through the alloy of the legs of his Moonsuit, speaking of the life within this very building.

He remembered to keep the lights of his room off, for the building he was in was supposed to have been deserted for six years. Gutted by the Halo. Abandoned by time.

Now filled with Moon Men, he thought, recalling their Shortjump away from the mess at Gordon's Cove the day before. And as he sipped at his coffee, he could distinctly feel the activity, albeit clandestine, coming from the basement of the building beneath him: a huge fusion reactor was pumping massive amounts of electricity which they were using to keep their stolen Seed from overpowering them all.

Still, his immediate attention was absorbed by a sinister amber haze, a Halolike aura, just a few miles north of the building within

96

which he was sipping his true Colombian coffee. Out in the haze of the San Fernando Valley, now peppered with constellations of breakfast fires, the Northridge Seed—the one imprisoning Annette—glowed obscurely. It was yet too gloomy to make much of anything out, but he knew that his condominium complex was out there, very close to where the Northridge Seed had 'chuted in. Yet what he was given in the darkness was a landscape lost to the ravishments of despair, with its abundant eucalyptus groves flourishing out of control where lawns and streets used to be, along with the hulks of abandoned buildings and automobiles. The Northridge Seed was a dome of light calling... calling...calling...

Even the San Diego Freeway was quiet. Every one hundred or so yards a single street light burned, attesting to the fragile stability that still existed, thanks to the Western Confederacy. Some services were available, such as petroleum refining and water treatment, but Trenton knew that these would not be able to maintain themselves for too very long. He didn't need Rand Corporation projections to tell him that cities such as Los Angeles were quickly deteriorating. He could see it with his own eyes.

"Not much of a sight," came a voice behind him. A darkened figure stood in the doorway of his room.

"Hello, Chuck," Trenton said, turning.

Chuck Sproule sauntered into the room, having been up for hours. Another Moon Man, he was a wrangler who'd been sent down to Los Angeles to make way for the second half of their operation. A broad-shouldered man, Sproule defied all contemporary custom by growing his sun-yellowed hair to the base of his spine. Tied ponytail fashion, he looked like a dishwater-blond samurai.

In the darkness, Chuck pointed to the Northridge Hooverville. "Is this the first time you've been this close to the 'ville?" he asked.

"It's the first time I've been in Los Angeles since the Seeding," he told the wrangler.

Chuck stood close to the window and looked over toward the south. "Over there you can barely see it, but that's the Encino 'ville. The San Diego freeway goes right by it and it gets pilgrims every day. The Northridge 'ville is more settled, established. It'll be a tough nut to crack, as they say."

"Whoever *they* are," Trenton said sardonically.

Chuck Sproule's light green eyes reflected the dull malevolent glow from the Northridge Seed. Like all zero-gravity engineers, he had a fair amount of derring-do and was always ready for a challenge. He smiled at Trenton.

"Well, *they* happen to be very formidable, if our scouting reports are reliable," he said.

Trenton put a gloved hand to his cheek, feeling the healing pulse of the plasti-derm. "I know all about the Confederates."

"Wait until you run into the fanatics," Sproule reported.

"Is that their term or ours?"

"Theirs. You'll know why they're fanatic when you get up close to one of their 'angels.'"

"The Seeds."

"Right." Sproule then looked at Trenton. "We picked up a tight-beam message that's being sent throughout all of the Confederacy."

"Fightin' Jack, I suppose." Trenton sipped his coffee, relishing the aroma. Even the mustiness of the building excited him. He had forgotten how much he missed the earth.

"All of their forces are on alert, but they still don't know why you were at Lake Tahoe. They're royally pissed off about it, though. All of the 'villes will be going on partial alert until they find out."

Trenton's own blue eyes sparked with life. "Perhaps we can give them a little bit of help."

The abandoned Honeywell Systems complex was perfect for the Moon Men's needs. In the fall of 2033, Honeywell technicians had finished work on their own fusion reactor, completed the security systems around the perimeters, and then the Halo sailed through the solar system, putting everyone out of work—everywhere. Honeywell, Hughes Aircraft, the lot.

But the Moon Men needed a place with enough generating facilities to store a Seed, and they needed a place close enough to the Northridge Hooverville where they would be able to make a quick attempt at rescuing Annette Sayles-Trenton from the "angels'" beneficent call.

Sproule led Trenton down an elevator into the basement, where all their activity was centered. The fusion reactor was in a subbasement inhabited by a round-the-clock force of technicians, but the main basement was where all the real action was.

At the far end, illuminated like players on a theater stage, technicians were gathered around the scoop and its terrain crawler, which was presently surrounded by a phalanx of monitors and controls.

All eyes seemed drawn to the scoop and the deadly alien artifact contained within it. Trenton knew this was because of the residual seepage of alpha-waves. He had felt it back at Gordon's Cove; the technicians, however, were only now getting used to it. Mostly, all they had to fight was sleep. That was the only effect the Seed had on them.

"Mr. President," a female tech said, saluting. "Over here, please."

The white-tunicked woman pointed to where Glenn Thorpe was hovering over a computer screen, the bony finger of the inventor's glove dancing over the keys of the console. Sproule and Trenton made their way across the floor of the basement.

"We're talking *power*, Ross," Glenn said with unabashed awe. "This guy's been coming up to full strength almost from the moment we fished him out of Tahoe."

Trenton stared at the crawler and the scoop container out in front, to which all of their monitors were attached.

"Is it going to hold?" he asked.

"I think so. But I'll be damned if I can figure out how such a small thing can generate so much power."

"Alpha-waves are simple to generate," Trenton said, bending over the console, feeling the song of the Seed just a few feet away. In the quiet of the basement, the Seed seemed like a living being.

"Well," Thorpe said, straightening his back, "if I had the time and equipment, I could probably build enough scoop crawlers to snatch all of the L.A. Seeds."

Sproule chortled. "*If* you could get through the army of pilgrims and fanatics that surround each Hooverville."

Thorpe said nothing to counter that argument.

Trenton, though, was now scanning a very large photograph hanging on the wall. It was an aerial view of the Northridge Seed.

Thorpe saw him and said, "That just came in. I wanted an updated shot just to make sure she's where we think she is."

Trenton's heart leapt with an unexpected twinge of excitement. "Which one is she?"

Thorpe pointed to a very indistinct blur. "Right there. That image next to her might be her car."

"We had a station wagon."

"Right," Thorpe said. "That's what it looks like to us."

Trenton then faced Chuck Sproule, whose arms were crossed calmly across his wide chest. "Have you been into the Northridge 'ville?"

Chuck nodded. "But not far enough to see any of the 'saints.' The Seed's glow is too bright to look at directly. But there are over a hundred people currently caught up in the event-horizon. I didn't want to linger. Didn't want to blow my cover." He smiled, drawing a tendoned hand through his hair.

Chuck Sproule had spent the previous day personally scouting out the surrounding area so that when Trenton and his team Shortjumped into the basement of the Honeywell Systems building there would be no reception committees waiting. Civil order was minimal these days, and while Trenton could depend upon the government's contingent of Space Marines for protection, he knew damn well that if the fanatics, Western Confederates, or anyone else wanted his hide bad enough, there'd be little they could do to stop them. There were only a few thousand "missing" tanks, artillery cannon, even tactical nuclear bombs from abandoned Army depots, naval storage stations, and Seeded Air Force bases. And most were currently in the hands of civil insurrectionists.

Trenton knew just how much of a fight the Hoovervilles would put up if threatened. But he wanted Annette back desperately, *and* he wanted a solution to the Seeds. He knew from his life upon the moon that he couldn't live with any honest sense of prosperity if his birth-nation was not prospering as well. He'd helped establish the government on the moon; now it was America's turn for help.

"Take a look at these," Glenn said, drawing out another set of photos, which, upon closer inspection, revealed themselves to be specialized computer scans.

The inventor said, "These were faxed to us while you were asleep. Ticia relayed them from Yancy City. They're *really* going to help."

Trenton felt his Stively-built heart thump in his chest. The photos were CAT scans of Seeds, and they showed what cryptically lay within them.

"Where'd she get these?" He sheafed through the compilation of scans.

Thorpe smiled thinly. "I'm afraid you'll have to talk to those girls of yours, Ross. And to Roarke. He's partially responsible, though I'll be damned if I know why. Ticia wouldn't elaborate."

Trenton didn't know what Glenn was referring to, but his attention was suddenly taken up by an eruption of activity by the elevators.

From the elevator emerged a Moon Man in a monk's tattered garb. Basil Roarke walked out into the basement, struggling with a man who was wiry, unwashed, and buck naked.

"You can't do this to me!" shouted the creature in Roarke's unshakable possession, his bare feet slapping almost obscenely on the basement floor.

"Can and did," Roarke told the man.

Two black-suited and heavily armed security guards came rushing over and scooped up the prisoner. Several of the interrupted female technicians blushed upon seeing the man's exposed condition.

"Roarke!" Trenton said, alarmed. "What are you *doing*?"

Roarke tightened the rope around his waist and pulled over the shroud of the monk's hood. All that showed was Roarke's idiot's grin.

"I found him lurking around the building when I went out for some fresh air." He crinkled his nose. "Wasn't any better out there. Anyway, I beaned him, but he followed me into the perimeter." He then held out his thick, capable arms to show Trenton the wonderfulness of the monk's robe. "Great disguise, huh?"

The man being escorted off shouted to them in a wail of outrage. "I have my rights! I can sleep wherever I want! *Where are the authorities!*" The door closed and the man's tirade ended abruptly.

Trenton stepped up to Roarke. "Did you actually yank that guy off the *sidewalk*?"

"Hey," Roarke said in mock-innocence. "How was I to know he wasn't a spy?"

"There aren't any spies at five-thirty in the morning around here." Trenton glowered at him.

Chuck Sproule, the tallest of all the Moon Men, stood between Roarke and Trenton. "He's right. But if he's part of a pilgrimage, then his friends are going to miss him. And nobody attacks mendicants or pilgrims. They're like postmen. They keep commerce up between the 'villes."

"There wasn't anybody else out there but that guy," Roarke protested, indicating the back room where the security team was no doubt making the former monk feel right at home.

"*Everyone* has friends in this town, Roarke." Sproule leaned over the shorter—but clearly more dangerous—man.

"Everybody but us," Trenton reminded them all.

The gentle humming of the Seed filled the basement area with its soothing alpha-waves...and Trenton could suddenly feel as if he didn't want to do what he *knew* was required of him.

It's that Seed, he said to himself. He didn't know how the others could stand being around it for so long.

He looked at Sproule. "Maybe it's time we see if Roarke's monk has any other friends in the vicinity."

"I want breakfast," Roarke suddenly announced.

"Later," Trenton said, walking around him, bound for the operations room, where his own disguise lay waiting.

─────── 19 ───────

The Seeds—or whoever made them—weren't entirely stupid.

In the full light of day, Trenton could see more clearly the precision with which the alien artifacts had deftly pared civilization, particularly L.A., as if each Seed had been a knife coring an apple *just so.*

Since most hydroelectric dams and nuclear-power plants lay outside of cities, society still had power and water facilities—but not much else. Those freeways not weaving near a Hooverville remained functional, but the means to keep them up or to build newer ones were just not available. As Trenton stepped out into the fetid dawn air of Los Angeles, he could see that his City of the Angels was now long past any point of recovery. It saddened him.

"Looks like a war zone," he said, his blue eyes taking in what he could from beneath his monk's cowl. Like Roarke, he and Chuck Sproule had donned the most ubiquitous manner of dress in the city.

"More like the aftereffects of a war," Sproule muttered, leading the other two Moon Men out onto a deserted Sepulveda Boulevard. "Until you get near a Seed, then you think everything's heaven."

Roarke snorted and clacked the brown metal of his gloves which were themselves underneath the pauper's gloves of his costume. They all opted for Moonsuits, since both Trenton and Roarke—being new to earth's gravity well—were hoofers and still wobbled slightly. And Sproule needed something underneath which he could coil his luxurious hair. Being monks of the New Light would do.

The San Diego Freeway was coming alive with an occasional gasoline-powered automobile, one of the few left in the region, and clearly belonging to some bureaucrat or leader. The other traffic consisted of horse-drawn Conestoga wagons and pedestrians. Trenton did note that the Western Confederacy provided a rudimentary police force, and this consisted of mounted patrols. Order was maintained, even if society was slipping back several centuries.

As they proceeded down the main avenue watching the city come alive, a small caravan of covered carts and wagons came rattling around a littered corner. Everything their owners possessed was hooked or tied to the carts, and two mangy dogs hobbled beside the horses. Above them, two bearded men, slunk beneath broad and beaten leather hats, nodded unsmilingly at the three monks of the New Light.

"Just smile and wave back," Sproule said. His wide lips parted with a friendly grin, and he and Trenton waved back. Roarke growled from deep inside, and Trenton elbowed him violently.

"Do it," he himself growled.

Roarke waved. One of the flea-gnawed mutts barked at the stocky wrangler, but scampered out of the way. The caravan moved on.

"Where are they headed?" Trenton asked.

Sproule looked back to the south. "Probably to the Encino Hooverville. They move from revelation to revelation. Just like they did here in the twentieth century," he quipped.

Basil Roarke's blackened, perilous eyes looked up at the tall Chuck Sproule. "What? That's ridiculous."

"Not really. They don't have much else to live for these days. They're mendicants, some of them, and pilgrims. They're looking for an angel to live with."

"Or die with," Roarke commented.

Trenton breathed in the sulfur-laden air. "You've been close to a Seed, Chuck."

Sproule nodded, eyes kept forward searchingly.

Trenton continued, "You think that whoever made the Seeds knows of our mythologies and religions?"

Sproule shrugged beneath the crude burlap of his monk's costume. "It's real hard to say. You know how alpha-waves work. That Sheriar of yours is the same way. Alpha-waves can make you imagine anything."

"Well," Trenton began quickly, "the Sheriar works on a slightly different principle. It just enhances images obscured by current brain activity."

"So the theory goes," Sproule said.

Trenton smiled, almost with a hint of condescension. The Sheriar caused worldwide controversy when its plans were found in the Meher Baba archives in Ahmednagar, India. Proven experimentally, the Sheriar Past Life Locator went on to become an effective tool for therapy of all kinds. Even Sproule, a confirmed agnostic, had an occasion for therapy in Yancy City. Though he wasn't willing to admit to himself that he'd become a Moon Man because of holdover desires from previous lives to explore different lands, he nonetheless acknowledged its usefulness. And he also liked goading Ross, who he felt sometimes took life a little too seriously.

Sproule nodded toward a high-rise condominium structure which seemed to boast several thriving families.

"However," he began, "you'll note that not everyone lives around the Hoovervilles. The city's basically split in its loyalties and interests. They want to be governed, but they don't want the fanatics to do it."

Roarke clacked his gloves like pincers. "I'll tell you what I'll do with those fanatics..."

Trenton nudged him again. "You'll do what you're told or I'll pull your arms and legs off."

Roarke only smiled, fairly skipping along like a child.

A walk of five blocks brought them to their first stop. It was a car lot, of sorts. Anything with wheels and marginally useful was being sold. Pathetic triangular flags made of cheap plastic fluttered in a lame ocean breeze that had made it this far inland, and out in front of the double-wide trailer that functioned as living quarters and office sat a huge man, gone to seed, in frayed overalls. A stubby cigar was lodged, permanently it seemed, between his teeth. A sign overhead said: "red sammy's used cars."

The fat guy squinted through the foggy morning light, seeing the monks approach, at first not recognizing them. He then saw Sproule.

"Hi, Sammy," Chuck said as he led the other two Moon Men around a battered pre-Halo Plymouth with its trellis of spiderwebs underneath it.

"You brought the boss with you this time," Red Sammy said, rising to shake Ross Trenton's hand. "Name's Sammy," he said happily. "Red Sam, the boy with the happy laugh."

"A veteran," Trenton said, now comprehending the man's cover.

The space above Roarke's head filled with question marks. "What's with you guys?"

Fat Sammy laughed at the powerful engineer. "You still have an aversion to books, Roarke?" Red Sammy seemed suddenly intelligent and crafty. "Never mind. You guys step on inside my office. Have I got a deal for you."

The trailer—at least the office part of it—was as shabby as Red Sammy. *A bachelor lives here*, the furniture spoke. Ashtrays were heaped with cigar butts, beer cans lay crumpled underfoot, and on the walls were out-of-date calendars with pictures of completely naked women that transcended human beauty. Roarke's eyes went wide seeing this and his mouth fell open.

Trenton, all business now, turned to Red Sammy. "You have any information for us, Sam?"

"Sure do," Red Sammy said, bending over a pile of tomato crates—each one stuffed with fresh tomatoes. "Have one of these, though. Can't leave L.A. without at least one pleasant memory."

The tomatoes were fire-engine red, plump, and thoroughly delicious. The three visitors took them eagerly.

The Moon Men bit into them, with Roarke making sure that Sproule got sprayed.

"Jesus, Roarke!" he said, jumping back. In his monk's costume, Sproule resembled a big bat.

Trenton savored the tomato. "These come from around here?" It was the size of a softball; perfect.

Sammy nodded. "North. From the San Joaquin Valley. A family of Mexican nationals made their way through here two days ago. They pay for everything with the food they've picked."

"Didn't think the nationals were allowed to take any of the harvest," Trenton asserted.

"Mr. President, they *own* most of San Joaquin. The majority of the Anglo farms have fallen through. Mexicans are feeding us now. Hell, they always have been."

"What's their relationship to the Confederacy?" Trenton then asked.

"Not much," Fat Sam said, crooking his fingers in the straps of his overalls. "But the news is that the Confederates are clamping down. Fightin' Jack's been talking about consolidating. The nationals don't like it, but he's promised not to take their farms away.

"Yeah, sure," Roarke said, finishing his tomato. He wiped his gloves messily down the side of his monk's robe.

"He's also getting chummy with the fanatics and the New Light people," Red Sam continued. "You'd better watch it. If word gets down here about the Shortjump, everyone'll be screaming for bodies of anyone associated with the government."

"It's *that* bad?" Trenton queried.

"I'm afraid so. President Scanlon couldn't get California back even if he bribed it. He'd be fighting the Confederates, the fanatics, he'd probably even get a fight from the Mexicans." Red Sammy sighed heavily, wheezing from too many choking cigars. "I'm afraid it's over in these parts. Even if Glenn Thorpe can bust the Seeds. It's the middle ages here."

Trenton went somber. "That's a hell of a note."

"You guys are welcome to anything on my lot, though," Sammy said, brightening. "New Light people come and go in all sorts of vehicles."

Trenton turned to Sproule, who'd been busy rewinding his long hair into a tight braid. "How far away is the perimeter of the Northridge 'ville?"

"Ten miles as the crow flies," Sproule said.

"That's twenty as the city's built," Sammy said. He tossed Trenton a pair of keys. "Take the Toyota. The Japanese might not be building cars now, but the ones they did build are still running." Sammy heaved himself up from the desk he'd been leaning on. "But don't wreck it. I don't want to see some horse pulling it downtown draped with pots and pans."

Sammy led them back out into the lot.

"Can you feel it?" Chuck Sproule said as he drove the open-air Toyota Landcruiser down Roscoe Boulevard.

"Feel what?" Basil Roarke blurted out.

But Trenton had been feeling it. "Alpha-waves," he reported to the space technician in the back seat. "It's that Northridge Seed."

The alpha-waves, however, were also making him feel depressed. The city was a shambles, the air a soupy, almond color from wood and coal fires. Trenton had barely known L.A. from the few weeks he had lived here with Annette. His duties, though, were back upon the moon and so he had not had the time to familiarize himself with the Valley. But what he was seeing now was enough. More than enough. Apartments abandoned, houses—most of them—utterly empty, glaring at them like bones picked clean.

"Where are all the *people*?" he said, astonished.

Sproule smiled without any mirth. "All gone into the Seeds. Or just living around the Hoovervilles. If Annette's still alive, she's right in there with the rest of them. The fanatics rarely leave the 'villes."

Trenton couldn't imagine Annette as a fanatic anything. Her only obsession had been her work, and the closer she and Emmett were getting to the Longjump, the more withdrawn she had become. But Ross hadn't thought there was anything wrong with that. He only regretted having left her on the earth when the Seeds fell.

But then they all by now had regretted where they were and what they were doing that autumn of 2033. To Trenton, it was as if a malevolent God had said: *Life's too good down where you are. Here. Have a few Seeds....*

"You'll note," Sproule was speaking, "that the closer we get to the Northridge 'ville, the more deserted the buildings become."

Trenton nodded, guessing. "They'd rather live close to a Seed."

"Right."

Roarke leveled a powerful arm between them, pointing out ahead of them. "Trouble, dead ahead, guys!"

"Let me handle this," Sproule said. "Just act reverential, and don't say anything. I've been through this before."

The outer fringe of the Hooverville—fully guarded—was just ahead.

The alpha-rhythms continued to soothe them, and if Trenton listened close enough, he was almost able to hear singing. *We're here*, he realized as they came up to a formal barricade. *This isn't like fishing an overlooked Seed from the waters of a sleepy lake. This is Serious Show Business....*

The boulevard ended abruptly at a building which had been erected right in the middle of the road. Here Trenton could feel the very limit of the Seed's pull. To either side of the barricade began the Hooverville's outer ring. Large tents had been erected, and above them weaved the plumes of cooking fires. Sounds of daily human commerce could now be heard.

"It's like a county fair," Roarke said.

"Quiet," Sproule admonished as he pulled the Toyota up to a wide parking facility to the left of the gate. Other vehicles, including freight trucks, had been parked because clearly no vehicles were allowed inside.

Three Confederates in khaki uniforms and blue berets stood chatting with two monks of the New Light, who appeared to be the official sentries.

"Sam was right," Trenton observed as he climbed out of the Toyota. "They're in tight with the pilgrims."

The two monks were dressed in white robes, and in their eyes was a beatific luminance. They seemed friendly; the Confederate guards did not. However, these men moved on and paid Trenton and his comrades no mind at all.

"Charles!" one of the monks hailed upon seeing Sproule walk up. He was an older man, clearly adjusted to his life of poverty and service.

"Good to see you again. Glad to see your friends." He gave them a nod of friendly acceptance.

"Yes," Chuck said companionably. "My friends are visiting from Long Beach. They've come up to commune with the angel."

"Ah," the older monk said, understanding. "Then enjoy. Let us know if we can be of service."

"I shall."

The tall Moon Man led them into a mixed crowd of mendicants, Hooverville citizens, pilgrims, and other assorted lost souls. Trenton was surprised at the level of camaraderie.

Trenton clutched Sproule's arm. "It was *that* easy?"

Sproule nodded. "I've been coming and going as a New Light monk for about four months now. And they seem to accept me." Sproule's keen eyes searched the crowd for blue berets. "But watch out for Confederates. They sometimes act as police here, though the alpha-waves tend to mitigate any violent urges."

"Sure," Roarke said, his fists clenched. Trenton noticed how much Basil was fighting the alpha-waves.

I've got to get that boy under the Sheriar, he then realized. But staring out into the ruins of Northridge, California, he also realized that he did have other priorities.

Seed-busting was the main priority at the moment.

Still, Trenton found himself sinking into a maelstrom of despair the further they explored the depths of the Hooverville. Some people sat entranced in front of their lean-tos or tar-paper shacks, oblivious of their destitution. Others eyed them suspiciously. It all looked like a used-car lot for people.

Trenton, on an impulse, reached up into his cowl and eased out the Sheriar jack. He locked it behind his right ear. He *had* to know where his compassion and his anger were coming from. This all seemed so familiar.

Though a mile away from the Seed's terrible center, Trenton felt the emptiness of it all. *Hooverville.* The mini-comp in his collar found the thought, amplified it, using alpha-rhythms of its own. Even as he walked with his companions, the *sanskaras* of a former life came back to him.

It is summer, 1933. Long grasslands are rushing by. He is a hobo on the soot-smeared slats of a boxcar roof. He's on a train bound for Chicago and a rumor of work. Other men are with him, each a shade of gray, each face a symbol of America's failure.

And he is hungry…he's had only two apples in two days and it is getting worse. Winter approaches.…

Trenton's nose picks up the cloistered aromas of the rag-tag bodies of the Northridge Hooverville even as he walks, half-hypnotized by the tiny Sheriar lodged in his collar.

An image of a campfire appears. A dozen men surround its fibrillating light. Behind, in the stygian dark, a lonely train wails its cry into the night. *The poor man Trenton spent the early part of the twentieth century as is now living in a Hooverville, spooning a tin of Mulligan stew. Greedily he eats, not asking what his friends have found to put in it. It may be his last meal for some time. There was no work to be found in Chicago.

He hears laughter. A joke was made about an old lady's cat. Trenton stares into his tin cup and pulls up something long and stringy. He swears that it looks like the whiskers.…

Roarke accidentally bumped into Trenton, startling him out of his brief trance-state. "This place gives me the creeps," the shorter Moon Man muttered.

Sproule nodded in complete agreement. "We won't be here long. I just wanted you both to see what we're up against. I wanted you to see how the place is run and what the Seed feels like. It gets worse, believe me."

Though the streets conformed to the usual southern California grid style, the Hooverville itself was completely concentric. As Trenton could see, the 'ville was a series of rings, each one closer in filled with those men and women more "lost" to the song of the "angel." Indeed, where the three Moon Men walked, the blue light of the Seed was constantly to their left as they followed the circle of clustered tents.

Sproule indicated a family in the midst of occupying a newer home— this one across the street and closer in. The family moved slowly, as if automatically driven. Even the children.

He said, "When an inner-ring hut gets vacated, those on the outside rush into it, until they themselves get called."

Trenton began thinking of Annette. How far out had she been six years ago when the Seed fell? Was she sucked into it within days? Or was she farther out, caught in the time-dilation effects of the event-horizon, as Emmett suggested. Trenton swallowed hard. He dared not think of all the ugly probabilities. *If only they had better photographs....*

Suddenly Roarke announced: "I'm not going any further. No more." He stood solidly, as if he'd locked the mechanical stays of his Moonsuit underneath his robe.

"Roarke," Trenton whispered. "People are staring at us."

"I can't stand it." Roarke was adamant. "You guys go without me." He spoke with teeth clenched and eyes alive with manic energy.

Sproule began looking around. "The Seed's behind your apartment, Ross. Dead ahead. If we can make it around—"

"I'm not going," Roarke insisted.

"Basil," Trenton said closely. "We've *got* to check the place out."

"Not with me, you don't."

"What if I order you to?"

Roarke glared at him challengingly. "Then you'll just have to break my arms and legs like you said."

The man does not respond to the usual alpha-wave stimulus, Trenton observed. *Something's wrong. Very wrong.*

"Okay," he acquiesced. "You stay here. We've got to find a place to bring the scoop in—"

Just then a flurry of activity parted a gathering of tatterdemalions beside one particular hut. Three different Confederates—all of them carrying weapons much against the creed of the Order of the New Light—began walking toward the three disguised Moon Men.

"Shit!" Roarke croaked. "I knew we couldn't get away with this!"

The Confederates all bore smiles as if they knew something the Moon Men did not. Which was probably true, Trenton guessed.

One of the pilgrims, indistinguishable from the rest of the 'ville's citizens, suddenly pointed the three Moon Men out. Trenton knew then that they'd been followed.

"That's them!" The pilgrim shouted.

The Confederates brought their rifles up, but not before the three Moon Men brought their clappers out.

Trenton went down on one knee as Sproule held his special gun out. Roarke locked into a firing stance, as all three guns snapped out massive bolts of energy, like thunderclaps, which fried the air before each of the Confederates into smelly ozone. Huge, concussive retorts knocked the three secessionists on their backsides into the mud and dirt and filth. They were instantly knocked unconscious.

"Run!" Sproule shouted. "This way!"

Pilgrims everywhere around them began screaming.

Trenton and Roarke bounded through a barrier of tents and fragile shacks, the armor of their Moonsuits nearly indestructible. They plunged like tailbacks through an offensive line on a blitz.

Only they were on the *defensive*, and they were pursued by screams and shouts, and the sounds of ramshackle buildings falling asunder as they made their frantic way through the weir of the destitute city.

The Moon Men followed Trenton around the side of an abandoned supermarket where surprised pilgrims sat up from their meditations and children stopped playing. A dog barked indignantly.

"I don't like this," Trenton confessed. He began snatching off his monk's robe, feeling inhibited by its cumbersome cloth. To Sproule, he said, "If I remember right, there's a park on the other side of this supermarket. It should get us out."

"If we can stay out of sight, the pilgrims won't bother us. They only want to protect their angel."

Trenton checked the charge on his clapper. "Right, let's do it."

They stampeded down the littered alleyway, jumping a creek leaking from an exposed cesspool. But where an exit was supposed to be, they instead found more makeshift homes and surprised faces of the religiously lost.

"Back!" Trenton shouted as Roarke, in his own panic, crashed into him.

They turned and quite suddenly the air filled with dancing and snapping balls of furious electricity.

From the top of a nearby building, a Confederate sentry, wearing radio headphones, crouched eagerly over a tripod with a clapper rifle big enough to quell a riot. He was in the midst of showering the Moon Men with ball lightning, enjoying every minute of it.

When Trenton stopped bouncing off the sidewalk and street, he was thoroughly unconscious. His last fading wish was that there wouldn't be any rain to go along with so much lightning and thunder and burnt air. He hadn't been rained on in such a long, long time....

—20—

"**P**ull!" shouted the President of the United States.

James Guthrie, cradling an important swaddle of papers, crouched behind a protective shield near the eastern edge of the Floating White House. A *cha-kunk!* blossomed not too far away and a twirling disk sliced through the radiant ocean air.

Ralph Scanlon spread his mighty legs and fired his shotgun vaguely in its direction.

The target, unscathed, made a hasty plunge into the placid waters of the Atlantic.

"Damn!" Scanlon snorted through anger-flared nostrils. He turned his frustration on the individual cowering behind the catapult. "Motzenbacker! Do it right this time. *Pull!*"

The Viking-like President leveled the shotgun, pulled the trigger, and the new disk soared through a harmless cloud of pellets, pursuing its companion safely into the Sargasso Sea.

"Sonofabitch!" Scanlon roared. In his ire, he suddenly began firing at the spot in the Atlantic where more than just two target disks had disappeared untouched that morning. Geysers of kelp brayed up into the air, only to spatter back peacefully. He emptied the pump-action gun of its noisy shells. But on those throw rugs of kelp which contained the unsunken—and unbroken—skeet disks, the cannonade did no good.

"*Motzenbacker!*" Scanlon turned and shouted. Guthrie ducked, fearing the rifle in the dangerous man's hands.

Motzenbacker, in coveralls and fearful expression, stood up from behind the trap machine. "*What!*"

Scanlon pointed out into the kelp. "Those traps! Get them!"

"Are you crazy?" the thin man shouted back.

Behind them, in the Quonsets of the White House offices, several men and women could be seen watching.

Guthrie took this as his cue and stood up from behind his own shield. The wind fluttered briskly at his yellow breaker.

Motzenbacker did not move.

"Sir, perhaps it's time to take a minute to talk about this morning's duties."

Scanlon's beef-brisket hands were white as he gripped the shotgun. He glared once out at the ocean, then over toward the White House structure, where the faces in the windows suddenly lowered out of sight.

"All right!" Scanlon huffed. "But I don't see why *I've* got to work, what with Congress being out of session."

"It's your job, sir."

"I suppose so," he surrendered momentarily, the wind luffing from his sails. He indicated Guthrie's papers. "So what's this I hear about Fightin' Jack Wheeler and them Russians?"

"*Those* Russians, sir. Evidently Dr. Trenton's men left a terrain crawler—" Guthrie bent his bird's neck down to his papers, his big glasses sliding a centimeter down his narrow nose. "A model TC-3, I believe. They left it on the outskirts of South Lake Tahoe."

"What?" Scanlon was incredulous.

"Yes, sir. Mr. Wheeler now knows that the only way the Moon Men could've gotten into the area was to Shortjump. The parachutes President Trenton left in Gordon's Cove apparently didn't fool them."

"Listen, Guthrie," Scanlon boomed, jabbing a rigid finger in his aide's chest. "Quit calling him President. *I'm* the President, got that?"

Guthrie considered the shotgun, then returned to his papers. He said, "Anyway, sir, Mr. Wheeler has let it be known that he intends to inform the Russians of our breach of the Shortjump Treaty of '20."

A cool, lugubrious breeze sauntered along the landing field between the White House and the administration buildings. Sleek blue-gray Navy jumpcopters sat like ocean crustaceans in the pale light.

"How's Wheeler gonna get to the Russians? He tell us that?"

"The Russians still maintain an embassy in both Sacramento and Los Angeles," Guthrie reported.

Scanlon began shoving shotgun shells back into his gun. He glanced over at the trap machine, noticing that Motzenbacker's eyes only were exposed from behind the catapult.

Scanlon said to his aide, "Wheeler's got as much clout as a bunny rabbit. The Russians won't listen to some backwoods nitwit."

"Jack Wheeler's a former attorney general of the state of California. Before the Seeding, he was widely influential. He's also *very* wealthy."

Scanlon cocked the shotgun. "You've got an answer for everything, don't you, Guthrie?"

Guthrie swallowed hard. "Perhaps, sir, we'd better discuss what the Russians are grumbling about lately."

Scanlon turned away from his diminutive aide and searched the ocean, hand above his eyes like an Indian.

"Those Russians are *always* complaining. If I was a Russian, I'd be complaining too."

"It's not that simple, sir."

Scanlon looked over his shoulder. "Is *anything*?"

"Someone, sir," Guthrie started haltingly, "has informed Soviet authorities that the *Clark Savage, Jr.* is being built more as a battleship than a research and mining vessel."

Scanlon went dark as a thundercloud. "What?"

The question fell as flat as a dead waffle on a cold kitchen floor.

"It could have been a Soviet Blue Collar on the moon, sir. Or one of the lunar scientists in Gambart or Macondo."

Scanlon's eyes narrowed. "Maybe it's President Dubie. He's in Macondo. Maybe *he* wants my job too."

"I don't think so, sir. He's happy as a clam up there. Writes poems all day, from what I hear."

"Well, who did it then?"

"We don't know. They might've figured it out for themselves. The *Savage*, as you know, sir, is the largest vessel ever built. And the Toquero family will hire anyone who's competent to work on it."

"Those Toqueros!" Scanlon complained. "Maybe *they* told the Russians."

Guthrie sighed heavily. It was like talking to a constipated bear who was way back in the hollows of his depressing cave.

Scanlon, though, wouldn't shake loose of the idea that the House of Toquero, especially old man Toquero in Macondo, was out to get him. Guthrie had been this route before.

"I always thought it was funny that it was Trenton and Toquero's father who thought up this whole Operation Cakewalk."

Guthrie watched as Scanlon's eyes filled to the rim with right-wing paranoia.

Scanlon continued: "I get it now! If they can get a Seed, figure out how it works, then nullify it—they can use the process to blackmail us!"

Scanlon threw out his chest, proud that he'd thought this one up all by himself.

"Sir," Guthrie began in a small voice. "It was Dr. Shea who detected the Seed, and it was Dr. Trenton who thought of the possibility of rescuing his wife. It just also happens to be true that the Toqueros are good friends of theirs. They *are* a team, sir. And the whole idea, Ralph, is to stop the invasion when it comes. The cities up there on the moon aren't going to be any good if the earth is overrun by aliens—especially if they use Seed technology."

Scanlon held his gun up before him like a real man. "I'll tell you what *I'll* do to an invasion!"

A deep-chested growling came in from the east over the Atlantic as a sleek STOL angled in underneath the sun. The STOL pulled in a tight bank and made for the main runway on the floating platform. Technicians rushed out to meet it, some of whom lugged the thick scroll of a red carpet.

Guthrie, noting this, said to the President, "Oh, yes. I was to tell you that Mrs. Scanlon's returning from Outer New York. That's her now."

Scanlon stared at Guthrie as if the little man had uttered the wrong words in the garden of Gethsemane.

Guthrie hastened to add. "She telefaxed that she was also bringing her mother along for a visit."

A frog of surprise lodged itself in Scanlon's throat. He staggered briefly—then leveled the shotgun at the STOL now screaming its engines above exposed landing gear on the runway.

"*Sir!*" Guthrie shouted in alarm.

But the STOL was several hundred yards away. The President lowered his shotgun.

"You're right," he conceded.

However, he turned and walked over to the other gun cases lying on the tarmac. He drew out a Remington 700-BDL thirty-odd-six with a Leupold 3.5 x 12.5 variable scope.

He then turned and faced the leery individual behind the trap catapult. "Motzenbacker!"

"*What!*" Only Motzenbacker's eyes showed above the machine.

Scanlon smiled with absolutely no glee. "Silver bullets! Bring me silver bullets!"

21

In the dark heart of the Watchtower suite, Emmett Shea lay upon his back pondering his antigravity mobile as it swirled in on itself in its perpetual dance above him. Lisa Palazetti made a delicious silhouette over against the open window. He felt his loins glow with a reaching warmth as her naked form gave him all its desirable angles.

Their lovemaking had left his Moonsuit scattered like the chitinous husk of a ravaged insect all over the Watchtower floor. Emmett didn't mind. Lisa's skin moving over his was a more pleasing garment to wear than his crimson Moonsuit. She had just gotten off duty, and like the efficient physician she was, she had also made proper use of her time off. For that, Emmett felt thankful.

However, he also felt guilty for his pleasures.

Lisa lifted her arm gracefully to brush away her long black hair, as the globe of her half-moon breast caught the afterlight of the earth in the window beyond.

Lisa saw him admiring her. She smiled in the twilight of the Watchtower. "I know what you're thinking. Ross is down there and Glenn is down there, and you're up here."

She came over to him where he lay fully disrobed and thoroughly sated. She slid on top of him, her breasts cushioning her lightly upon his chest.

His hands explored the small of her back where her sweat had already cooled.

"I'm thinking," he began, "about three dead Seeds, who made them, and what they're supposed to mean."

Lisa craned upward, her long hair feathering his face. A playful pout passed over her face. "I suppose the mess we made of your bed here doesn't count."

Very carefully, fearing to lose the moment, he sat up. She rolled onto her back in the dim light of the suite, and the sight of her began to arouse him once more.

He walked over to a small computer unit against one wall. He said, "It counts. It counts for a lot. I wish we could do it more often."

For a moment she was caught up in a silence that was by now familiar. But she said in a soft voice, "Anytime you're ready. Just say when."

"I'll say 'when,'" he told her from the console where he was punching in a special code, "when all of this is over and Ross doesn't need me as mayor and we get Annette back."

Lisa sat up and gathered Emmett's ermine robe around her. They had spoken of marriage quite often; they practically lived together. And certainly neither one went for too very long without sharing their beds with one another—when they could find the time.

"Ross once said that there is a time for everything," Emmett told her. Lights came on in the corner where a special hologram grew into lucency, a Christmas-tree arrangement of lights around a laser-artificed globe of the earth.

Lisa bundled up on the edge of the bed. "Ross didn't say that. His master at the Meher Baba Trust in India said that. What goes around comes around. It's called *karma*."

"Well"—Emmett smiled wanly—"Ross believes it anyway." He punched more buttons and keys as smaller lights blossomed across the surface of the hologrammed earth.

Lisa got down on her hands and knees and slid across the rug slowly, like a stalking feline. In a purrful voice she said, "When the sign lights up and says 'Marry Her,' let me know." His back was turned to her as she crept, and he didn't see her coming.

She bit him on the Achilles' tendon and he jumped.

Before he could come down, she was up and had him in her arms.

"The sign's on," she said, kissing him.

Emmett kissed her back, then held her out at arm's length, trying to ignore the modest contours of her upturned breasts.

"This is the sign that's been bothering me," he told her in a disquieting voice.

The hologram was that of the earth. It stood a meter off its platform and slowly rotated, as per its computer program. On it were the pustules of reddish lights where he and Lisa both knew all of the earth's major cities used to be: a growing, festering pox upon the earth.

"Seeds," he whispered in the preternatural shadows of the Watchtower.

Lisa gave him a perplexed look. "You've had this holo program for a month now. Why's it so important tonight?"

He turned and threw a switch and the room filled with a kind of modulated humming—more like a mysterious mantra being chanted by cave-dwelling lamas in Bhutan in the Himalayas. Lisa's dark eyes were beautiful even as they took on an unfathomable expression of confusion.

"What—"

"The Seeds," he told her, switching the hologram off, "are apparently singing to each other."

Lisa held him, looking deep into his distant eyes. "When did you find this out? How long have you known?"

Emmett began retrieving the bits of his discarded Moonsuit. "Since this afternoon. I don't have even the slightest notion of what the Seeds are saying, either. They're just singing."

She found her robe and pulled it tighter around her. "Are you going to let Ticia know about this?"

"You bet," he informed her.

"When?"

He looked at the bed and its lovemaking rumples; then he glanced at the toy hung from the ceiling going around and around and around.

"Now," he told her.

He was back into his Moonsuit and out the door with little complaint from the patient physician left alone in bed.

Ticia Rhodes, with her wild, witch's hair, was poring over a Seed in the workroom—but without any protective clothing. Bob Stapely, also unprotected, was standing opposite her across the examining table. But beyond the thick glass of the laboratory there remained a contingent of Marines who were ready to destroy any enthusiasm on the Seeds' part for gobbling up Yancy City. Emmett walked past them, saluting the captain of the guard.

Ticia looked up. "Glad you could make it."

"What do you have?" he asked eagerly.

Bob Stapely placed an open palm over the top of the Seed as if it truly were a basketball. His brown fingers caressed it, lifting it, then turning it slightly.

"They're still alive," he told Emmett. "Watch."

Bob Stapely rotated it and as it wobbled to a halt on the table, Ticia Rhodes brought up two electrodes. These she placed upon the Seed and nodded to Stapely.

A slight electric current rotated the Seed on its own.

"When did you find this out?" Emmett asked her.

"About an hour ago," she said, sitting back down, staring constantly at the thing as if by doing so it might yield up more secrets. "We did an amplified scan to see if it contained anything down on the cellular level, and the jolt it took somehow got it to move."

"But it doesn't move much," Emmett noticed. "It just seems to right itself."

"But that's not the only bit of news," Bob reported, pointing over to the CAT scanner nearby. "We ran a scan at the time it moved on us. Hell, we didn't know *what* to think."

"Sure made Captain Salerno out in the hall jump," Ticia said with a leer, glancing over her shoulder at the watchful guard beyond the glass.

Stapely continued, "It doesn't take much power to bring it around, considering the level of energy they emit down on the earth. At first we thought there might have been something upstairs"—here he indicated with a nod the upper floors of Yancy and the surface beyond—"but anything might be causing it to shift like that."

Emmett's mind swirled with notions of gravity wells, curved space, and megaenergies tucking the folds of the continuum—all part of the theorized Longjump.

Emmett stared up at the ceiling, then around the laboratory itself. He pointed to a blank spot on the ceiling as if it held significance to them.

"Earth," he said suddenly, tiny lights going on in his head. "Earth is in the lunar sky about *there*. I'm sure of it."

Ticia Rhodes looked at the dour-faced Stapely; Stapely shrugged. "It's possible," he affirmed.

Emmett's mind ran through the possibilities, the same scenarios they'd originally discussed weeks ago when they'd found the stray Seed—and six years ago as well, when the Halo passed by, trailblazing its way through space.

He said, "They've probably got some kind of compass mechanism within them. And it's pointing toward home."

Stapely's eyes were almost yellow with surprise. "Home?"

"Life," Emmett corrected himself.

"But these things aren't alive, Emmett," Ticia told her colleague. "Nothing could survive six years on the slopes of Copernicus fully exposed."

Emmett's thoughts were fixed on the unit in his Watchtower and the hologram of the infected earth with its harmonic Seeds.

However, in the corner of the laboratory was another hologram platform. The computer program they had for it was that of the nearest stars to the earth: a cloud forty light-years in diameter. He recalled the cloud and these stars within. *If cities could sing with their Seeds*, he reasoned, *then why not stars?*

He turned to Dr. Rhodes. "Ticia, call Toquero down here for me. Tell him no excuses." He made for the door.

"Where are you going?" she suddenly asked. "You just got here."

"It's about time I showed you my newest toy," he said with a boyish grin. He swept out into the corridor and disappeared.

Had an outside observer been watching the Trenton girls in the twenty-four-hour period since their return from Copernicus and the tomb of the *Jaguar Skies*, he would have noted their peculiar behavior.

Cheryl, the normally extroverted child, spent much of her time walking slowly around their large bedroom, almost hypnotized by the nodule she held in her hand. At times she'd bump into a wall and stop; other times she'd just sit beside her sister and listen as the tiny marble told her things.

Cindy Trenton, true to her own nature, stayed completely quiet and rooted in one spot. Propped up against a wall by a mound of fluffy pink pillows, she spent her time rubbing and fondling the nodule, listening to its voices as they spoke to her.

"Not voices," Cheryl told her sister after a while.

Cindy was silent, then agreed. "I guess. I see pictures, though. Pictures like movies—they're moving. Going way back too."

Cheryl knelt down, hugging her legs, holding tight to the special nodule. "Is this what Daddy does, d'you think?"

Cindy's brown eyes opened wide with recognition. "Yes," she breathed. She knew. They both knew.

Cheryl opened her hand and let the pictures slide through the misty curtains parting in the back of her mind. "Incarnations," she said, pronouncing the big word carefully.

There was no order to the images. Some looked like lifetimes spent during the Middle Ages. Long, dull lives spent in the South Seas, or lives on the American Plains as wandering Cherokee.

Then Cindy got an inspiration. "No," she said. "Daddy's machine is different."

Cheryl stared at her nodule. "Then what—"

It was almost a grown-up's voice coming out of the usually staid Cindy Trenton. She rose from her pillows and stuffed rabbits. "Daddy works on impressions in the mind. These are *our* lifetimes!"

Both girls' eyes were whirlwinds of mesmerizing fantasies as the alien nodules in their hands sent bursts of warm energy into their minds, freeing the impressions already contained there because *atmas* never forgot.

Their *atmas*, their souls, bundled their former lives around them like overcoats, one coat it seemed for each lifetime. Both girls could feel the weight of all their accumulated *sanskaras*, for the nodes were stimulating both sides of their brains for memories of those lives.

"They're like tiny computers searching out programs," Cheryl Trenton suddenly announced.

"Ooooo," Cindy breathed, staring at Cheryl but not seeing her quite. "We've been together lots!"

Cheryl nodded.

Then quite suddenly each girl seemed to *fill up*.

That was Cheryl's concept for it. Cindy's eyes almost exploded with recognition and Cheryl *knew*. Their minds were being freed from the biological and hormonal limits of mere nine-year-olds as the intelligences came flooding up from the past. Not factual knowledge, Cheryl realized, for that would be limited to the constraints of any one particular era. But this was sheer intelligence. *Smarts!*

"I was…an engineer…" Cindy began with tiny, almost grown-up tears in her eyes. Tears of recognition. "I was an engineer and I helped build zeppelins! You remember *zeppelins*?"

What roller-coastered through Cindy's mind was also in its own way passing through Cheryl's mind. She suddenly saw herself as a Portuguese sailor of the sixteenth century. But it was more than that. She saw what that man had *known:* how to build a ship, what kind of wood was best for hulls, forces and pressures on the masts, even the kind of glues and caulks that went best with shipmaking.

And Cindy knew about zeppelins.

The sisters were nearly eye-to-eye as each watched the other fill with her own flood of hyperattenuated intelligence.

And neither felt the alien quality of the tiny machines—for that was what they truly were—which they held in their tiny hands.

"We can help Daddy find Mommy," Cheryl suddenly announced as life after life of sailor, military tactician, scientist, and engineer raced behind her eyes.

"I know we can," she concluded.

They jumped up in their pink pajamas and thudded through their suite, heading for their father's private den. Everything about their mother was there, hidden away. But they'd find it.

They both had this sudden growing interest in mathematics and the way in which things could move through space....

Later that lunar "night," the Moon Men found themselves standing around a hologrammatic display that kept them in complete silence. The laboratory was darkened to heighten the effect of the holo, as Emmett had desired. It even amazed Lloyd Bramlett.

"Where are you getting the data for this?" Lloyd asked.

Emmett was busy over the computer at the opposite end of the room. He said, "On farside at Tsutsumida Station. They've got a gravity-wave detector there that's similar to the one we placed in high earth orbit to detect the Tahoe Seed. Only this time I'm aiming it outward, to the stars. What you're seeing here is a simulation of our galactic neighborhood done up the *same* way we did the hologram of the earth with its Seeds."

Emmett had already set up the holo of the earth and played for them the mournful symphony of the Seeds down upon their sorrowful mother planet. But to hear the same modulations coming over the speakers from the stars was something else. It confounded the usually unconfoundable Toquero.

"This is too weird for me, man," Toquero said to Emmett. "It sounds like we're all a big huge family of Hoovervilles."

The holo was a misty cloud of stars, with the sun represented in the center, made slightly larger for their purposes of observation. They had linked up their dead Seed to Emmett's gravity-wave detector, letting the detector itself resurrect the Seed's ability to home in toward life. And intelligence, Emmett had to remind himself.

"If we're correct here," Emmett said excitedly, "then all those stars out there have intelligence."

"You mean they've *all* been Seeded?" Lloyd Bramlett seemed to glow with horror. The Moon Men were, as a team, avoiding him for he reeked of cigarettes. But they felt he had to be in on Emmett's discovery.

"I think we can assume so," he told the Pentagon liaison.

Ticia Rhodes walked around the three-dimensional map of the galactic sector. She observed: "Forty light-years isn't much of an area, as the galaxy goes, but it's enough." She bent over, looking closer as the computer-enhanced laser program sparkled the air above the platform with the lights of nearby stars. "Look here, Emmett. Which star is that?"

She pointed to one in particular about halfway to the edge of the hologram. Emmett squinted through the luminescent dark; he turned back to the computer.

"Delta Pavonis," he announced.

Bramlett scowled at the scientist. "Not Alpha Centauri? I thought the Halo came from Alpha Centauri."

Bob Stapely, his long arms folded above his chest, spoke out. All this time he had kept quiet and listened to the sound of the stars "singing." He said, "That was where the Halo came from *last*. It didn't necessarily have to start there."

Ticia nodded. "If Delta Pavonis is right in the middle of the Seed vectors, then can we assume…?"

They looked at her, not wanting to answer. Then they stared at the star, nineteen light-years distant.

"But," Emmett said in a low whisper, "what I don't get is why Delta Pavonis is singing too."

Toquero looked at them all. "Then where the hell *did* the Halo come from, if it didn't come from Delta Pavonis?"

No one could answer that. The only answer they got was in the form of a monotone chant. Over twelve tiny stars were singing their song of death. It was a neighborhood being overrun by the local Mafia.

And, clearly, they were there to stay.

From somewhere back in the far reaches of his preconscious mind, Ross Trenton heard the dim whisperings of the Sheriar, jacked behind his ear. The tiny collar-bound computer kept saying: *Not thy will, but God's will be done....*

The crippling effects of the electric rain from the clapper the rooftop Confederate used upon him had amplified the already present alpha-waves coming from the Northridge Seed a few crowded blocks away. The Sheriar merely stimulated the neurological synapses in the hippocampal region of Trenton's brain to such a degree that a past life came to him instantly. The Confederate had only accelerated the process.

And the vision is clear:

He sees himself in another life, as real as any he's ever known. He doesn't know who he is or what he's done, but what is certain is that he's standing in a very large public square of carved marble and ornate architecture. It could be Bologna, his dream-mind suggests—the rational part, the part trying to hold on. It could even be Madrid. The sky overhead is the color of tallow-wick, a candle poured of ill-mixed wax into an arena of smoke.

Auto da fé, Trenton suddenly realizes.

Crusaders from the papal court of Pope Innocent III stand in holy righteousness watching, knowing that God is on their side, and not allied with those guilty men and women strapped to stakes being set aflame.

And one of those individuals, as Trenton can now see, is himself.

He is one of a hundred and eighty Albigensians, the so-called Cathari mystics, who had taken refuge in the castle Minerve in the south of France, much against the wishes of the Pope. They are all being put to the torch for their heresies.

Trenton feels the fire lick at his sandaled feet and begins to feel his skin bubble and melt as the very air is sucked from his lungs. Around him are the screams like flying eagles of his fellow ascetics.

The warrior-cardinals sent by Innocent III astride their adorned stallions watch with grim satisfaction, knowing that God can only speak to the few and that they are among those especially chosen. Trenton sees the fiery wrath of God in their eyes.

Those eyes are saying: The common man cannot know God. You must seek him through us.

The blackness of eternal damnation descends upon him as the hungry tongues of the burning reach up around his face, his hair, and further on up to consume the stake itself as if the Devil's breath surrounded him there in those last moments of Trenton's life in that incarnation. He hears someone say: God gave man free will to obey, not to seek his own happiness....

As the pain of the remembering became too intense, the Sheriar shut down automatically. And such was the shock of withdrawal from the soothing alpha-rhythms of the miniature regression computer that he became instantly awake and aware.

His Stively-built heart maintained a regular rhythm, its own mini-computer feeling the pulses of his mind as he came around. Even so, he jerked involuntarily with the sudden realization that the *sanskara* he'd just witnessed was in some way pertinent to his current situation.

God was nearby, ready to punish.

He tried to move, but discovered instantly that his powerful Moon-suit was bound securely in an upright position where he faced a long hallway in a deserted building of some kind. *A bank? An office suite?* Down the hallway was a set of double doors in moon-pearled glass, and Light burning beyond them that suggested ugly possibilities.

He attempted to burst out once more. Duraplastic strips held him in complete bondage on an automated forklift, a robot more commonly found in heavy-industry factories. The straps themselves were locked into place by electronic devices that needed special commands. Both his arms and legs were bound, and no amount of power in the Moonsuit seemed capable of breaking the straps or the locks.

He could feel the alpha-waves strongly from the Light just beyond the building and presumably not too far down the street. *God, he thought, that sonofabitch is powerful!* He knew the Tahoe Seed was strong, but they had contained it underwater where the water itself—for whatever unknown reason—had stifled its energies. But the one down the street, even after six years, was burning bright and strong.

He knew now where he was. A First Interstate Bank. It was where he and Annette shared an account when they both had an occasion to be on the earth together. Your friendly neighborhood bank....

And he also knew that their apartment complex was a few blocks away. And that meant that Annette herself was perhaps a few hundred yards distant, frozen beside their station wagon, caught in the event-horizon along with scores of other victims.

He had to continually tell himself that—that the Seed *was* evil, because the alpha-waves were soothing him, calming him, telling him that God was out there, not the Devil or anything else for that matter. Certainly not an alien artifact designed to cripple a world.

Yet as he glanced around him in the bank he noticed that the walls were covered with paintings—mostly crude, though obviously sincere—

of whatever visions their artists had seen in the Seed beyond. Some were of angels, others of Jesus, others of mere beings of haloed light.

He realized that this was no longer a deserted First Interstate Bank. It was more of a church or a shrine.

He looked around for Roarke and Chuck Sproule. He couldn't find either of the engineers, and a surge of adrenaline went through his body. He tensed in his anger, but still the straps held him prisoner to the forklift.

He glanced down at the floor. The dust there betrayed the tracks other forklifts had left—tracks which led only one way: down the long hall to the double glass doors and the Light beyond.

Trenton counted the tracks of *two* automated lifts.

At that moment, a voice sounded out behind him. "Your friends of your brotherhood have already gone on to the New Light. I wouldn't worry about them any longer, if I were you."

A man walked around into view and even in the twilight shadows of the former bank Trenton could see the depth of their mistake. The speaker was the sentry with whom Chuck Sproule had spoken when they had gained entry to the Hooverville. He was bald on the top of his head, with long flaxen hair hanging down over his ears, and he clutched a Bible to the vest of his floor-length white robe as if it were a talisman. But even in the vague light of the bank Trenton noticed how the man's beatific expression also bore the pained look of a man protective of his God and beliefs.

It's the same in every era, Trenton mused. *People feel that their experience with God is the only true experience. The problem becomes: What do you do with those who won't come around to your way of thinking?*

Trenton knew. If you're a warrior-cardinal and you've got the Pope— or the Light—behind you, and if you can find enough wood for a fire, you can probably think of something....

"What did you do with my men?" Trenton demanded.

The fanatic smiled thinly, and sadly. Two other individuals hove into view. These were not priests. They were black-uniformed men in no way affected by the alpha-rhythms beyond. More than likely, Trenton realized, they'd never gone in as far as the white-gowned priest. Otherwise, they wouldn't be Confederates. They'd be mendicants.

Both Confederates wore blue berets and both wore .357 Magnums at their waists. One, however, was an older, grizzled sort, and the other was much younger, perhaps the man's son. Certainly his protégé.

The micro-miniaturized assists in Trenton's Moonsuit whined as he tried once more to free himself. He didn't like the direction of the tracks on the floor.

"Won't work, hoofer," the older Confederate said. He took out a cigar and lit it, much to the disgust of the priest. Smoke curled from the man's nostrils as if he were a demon.

"Do you have any idea who I am?" Trenton said. "Do you know what's going on here?" He wasn't about to lay all of his cards on the table, just those to make them think differently. Or raise the ante.

The priest deferred to the older Confederate's authority. The Confederate stood brazenly close to Trenton.

He said: "You're from the government, *and* you're a hoofer. We always thought Scanlon would use you space guys to get back California." He stood back and blew a pungent cloud of vile smoke at Trenton's face. "Well, it won't work. We've got a nice arrangement here and it suits us just fine."

Trenton called upon his skills, both as a transpersonal psychologist and as a former Lunar President. He said, "Your nice arrangement contributes to the breakdown of society by allowing people to be pulled into the Seeds."

The priest balked, at the use of the word "Seed." Trenton could see already how much the man revered whatever it was speaking to him from the center of the Seed's light. The Confederates, though, had no such feelings.

The priest spoke up quickly, using his own authority. "The saints make their own choices. If it's God's will—"

"Or the effect of altered brain states in whoever is within three hundred yards," Trenton said loudly, trying to talk some sense into the man. "The Seeds are alien artifacts designed to cripple the minds of any intelligent species. They were sent here from another world."

The younger Confederate's eyes were poised upon Trenton as if hearing a story—a *scary* story—for the first time and quite possibly believing it.

Trenton knew this; he could see it. He went on. "And my associates have got proof that the invasion is on its way. That's why we're here."

"Bull," the older Confederate said above a specter of nasty cigar smoke.

The Confederate before him was as convinced as a hanging judge of Trenton's guilt. The priest, though, managed a condescending smile.

The man in white said, "Our angel will *tell* you differently, who-ever you are. You haven't felt the truth yet. The truth from the heart, not the mind."

The elderly priest's eyes were dark and familiar to him: they were almost like those of Mehmed II as he laid siege to the walls of Con-stantinople. Trenton, recalling the *sanskaric* image, could also see that expression in every one of the Islamic attackers of the city. They knew what they had to do, and they knew that they were right in doing it.

The priest said softly, "Friend, who's to say the form that God must take in this day and age? Has it never occurred to you that the Halo may have been his divine instrument? His manifestation in this age? Who are we to expect a simple carpenter's son to return? This *is* a blessing. You'll see."

Trenton didn't like the sound of that.

He didn't like the sound as well of the younger Confederate walk-ing determinedly down the hallway toward the double glass doors.

The older Confederate beneath his jaunty beret smiled. He said, "Fightin' Jack's network is tighter than you government people think. We knew *something* was up; we just didn't know what. But it's about time we fought back in spades."

The younger Confederate opened both of the doors to a width that would allow a robot forklift with a Moon Man strapped securely to it to pass through.

Trenton said slowly, "Do you think Fightin' Jack will be able to put off an invasion fleet? No one's been able to stop a Seed since they landed. All Jack Wheeler wants to do is run the country—any country. He doesn't care what kind of shape it's in!"

The cigar glowed angrily. The older man said, "You'd be surprised, hoofer, what Jack Wheeler can do. We got Air Force bases, naval bases, shit, we even got Vandenberg."

"And Vandenberg's got two Seeds all of its very own," Trenton pointed out. "It's a couple of Hoovervilles now, just like this place is."

"Perhaps," the white-robed priest began, "it's the way things were meant. Who knows?"

"*I* know that if *we* don't do something about it, then everyone'll suf-fer!" Trenton said in a shout.

The forklift suddenly moved, coming to life from a hidden com-mand. That command came from a remote-control box which the younger Confederate held in his thin hands.

Trenton turned around to face the priest. "You call yourself holy? You're going to let these men do this?"

"We work together to survive," the fanatic said, holding to the authority of the Bible at his chest and what he knew to lurk outside down the street.

And Trenton could see it: This was the way the Pope worked with his warrior-cardinals. *Someone* had to do the Lord's dirty work. No era was without its volunteers.

Trenton heaved and fought, his Moonsuit grating at the straps as the forklift bounced on small rubberized wheels out of the doors of the First Interstate and on into the street. The young Confederate smiled an executioner's smile and waved good-bye.

The alpha-waves flooded Trenton's body like a subtle intonation, the hidden vibrations of a Tibetan gong.

Everywhere in this part of the neighborhood was a foglike ambience, a diffuse thickness of white in the air. Not smoke or fog—but something *alive*.

The forklift went slowly, heading toward a softly burning Light at the far end of the street. Trenton gasped and struggled in his bonds. The street down which he was being escorted was far inside the confines of the Hooverville tents and run-down hovels. Here, cars and apartments, businesses and gas stations, were thoroughly abandoned. No one lived here.

No one except the saints.

Out ahead of him, as if frozen in time, caught in midstep, were dozens of people—and every one of them was enraptured by the *thing* which hung suspended in the skeletal framework of an office building that had been under construction in the autumn of a.d. 2033.

The event-horizon was directly ahead of him. The alpha-rhythms seemed to shake the alloy of his Moonsuit, but it was so gentle a sensation that Trenton suddenly found himself enjoying the ride.

Stop it! he shouted to his own mind. *Fight it! Don't let it happen!*

To the left of the avenue, pitched in the blue-white Light like an ice sculpture of itself, was the apartment complex where he and Annette once lived. Were those faces, framed in an instant of time, still watching from the windows above? He couldn't quite tell, for the Light was getting brighter by degrees, and on its own, in its mysterious way, seemed to demand more of his attention as he approached.

The Seed hung in the abandoned orange girders by the threads of its ensnared para-sail, several stories off the ground. It hung like a spider's egg sac, a wrinkled testicle, a bundle of white fibers clotting someone's lungs, choking off what's vital. *Yes!* he reminded himself. *It's all of those things! Yes, yes, yes!*

But from some inexplicable source behind the Light came Love, and it reached out to him and touched him. His heart began to glow. Literally.

He was becoming a saint.

His Stively-built heart pumped its regular rhythms, but Trenton could feel his heart chakra flower outward its many-petaled lotus of Divine Joy.

The forklift stopped at this point and the electronic locks which held him snapped apart, and he was free.

Trenton fell to the ground, but the gyros of his Moonsuit kept him from tumbling. He stood upright quickly as the forklift backed off.

But he no longer cared.

Ahead of him, fifty yards distant, he made out the forms of Basil Roarke and Chuck Sproule where their vehicles had deposited them. They both faced the angel, with Chuck Sproule several dozen yards closer to the skeleton of the half-built building than was Roarke. Sproule's arms were at his sides, but his long blond hair hung down behind his crimson-gold Moonsuit. Roarke's fists were clenched, but clearly he was headed right for the Light despite whatever impulses he was fighting.

Both men were caught in midstride, and neither acknowledged Trenton when he called out to them.

But somehow it didn't seem to matter now. The angel soothed him, spoke to him in a voice deeper and more ethereal than the voice in the Sheriar. It touched his center of loneliness; it spoke to his need to get his family back together, the need he had to hold the Moon Men together. Yancy City, Macondo, even America.

And the whisperings from the Light said: *Let go. It's all in God's hands now. You are only a man, and a man can only do so much....*

He started walking toward the angel, feeling himself becoming lighter and lighter in his step. Out ahead of him the other saints moved as well, if somewhat slowly. Trenton's eyes swelled with tears of love for the other saints for he knew the happiness which they must be feeling right now. The priest had been right. The Seeds *were* angels! He could feel it in his heart even as he passed the Toyota station wagon that once belonged to someone he knew quite a long time ago.

Forget, the angel's song sang to him. *It's all a burden from the past, and the past is gone.*

He could feel his quest for unity rise in him like a volcanic outbursting of empathic love for all things upon the earth. How many past lives had he spent in the Church or powerful governments trying to bring men and women together? And how many times had he tried and *failed*? Too many. The angel said: Relax. *It's not your job to do God's work. Be a man. Walk in the Light of the Lord.*

He was happy. Perhaps for the first time in his life he was happy. Tears streamed down the plasti-derm gauze on his cheek and neck, down into his Moonsuit. Poor foolish Man! Unable to find his own way in two thousand years, so God had to send a Halo, itself a symbol of all things transcendent.

And God blinked.

It appeared to Trenton as if a huge gray-black bird beat its wing for every step he took toward the angel. There was no wind, no sound of animals or insects, just the mental choir of the angel's song. And every devotional step he took toward the building within which the angel had taken up residence brought another blink in the eye of God overhead.

Then Trenton noticed how the leaves on the eucalyptus trees lining the streets seemed to blur as if each were vibrating at an unusually quick rate of speed. Overhead, the gray-black cloud passed once more. And again…and again.

And the saints far out ahead of him seemed to be slowing down. *Everything* seemed to be slowing down, the closer he found himself to the angel.

When he realized what was happening, he laughed with joy that such a thing was possible.

Time was speeding up as he entered the event-horizon. Here, the angel's celestial power slowed time for the saints, but on the outside, the days went by at their normal pace.

God blinked. And blinked again. And continued to blink.

Come to me, my child, the angel seemed to call. *Come and be comforted.*

And Trenton knew that only in the arms of the angel could true comfort be found.

23

The Trenton girls had not heard about their father in many days, but Robbie Rogers and Lisa Palazetti assured them both that he was doing just fine. He was busy trying to locate their mother down on the earth. The girls in the meantime kept to themselves, attending school only when they were supposed to, but spending all of their free time working on a new project which—unknown to them—Robbie had revealed to Dr. Palazetti in a spare moment. The girls' room was now a jungle of electronics, with schematics on one low table where toys and dolls used to sit. A new computer console was over in one corner and the room itself had a residue of solder and burnt wiring hovering about it. But both women didn't think it would come to much. It could also be a school project the little girls were working on. Lisa saw no harm in it; she also saw no reason to inform Emmett, who was watching over them as well.

One day went by, then another, then another. Finally Cheryl came to school with the most wonderfully precise photographs of Pluto and its lonely moon. Their teacher, Ms. Savard, a wonderfully enthusiastic woman, thought that they were special computer-enhancements of photographs taken by the early-twenty-first-century deep-probe, the *Horai Seeker*. Ms. Savard thought that the photographs were *so* good that the whole class spent the rest of the day talking about how far distant the outer planets actually were and how they were still unreachable even with the Shortjump. Cindy and Cheryl listened attentively to the discussions concerning the tremendous amounts of power it took for just one Shortjump to Mars or to the asteroids, and on occasion slipped each other a furtive smile.

Ms. Savard was so pleased with the girls' photographs that she wanted to run them over to the editor of the local newspaper, but the twins insisted that she didn't. It was more, they said, than just a fourth-grade project.

One evening, just when the computers were dimming Yancy City's hall lights for the onset of "night," Cindy and Cheryl crept out of their home and waylaid an electric getabout which they'd spotted idling in the park down the street from them. Robbie Rogers was in her own room back at their condo studying for exams and she had not seen the girls slip away, lugging duffel bags crammed full of special equipment.

In their flame-pink Moonsuits they ran for the electric tram followed by their robot companion, Anson McDonald.

They stopped the getabout and Cindy began throwing their bags and rolled up schematics inside.

Cheryl faced the little robot. "Anson."

"Yes, Cheryl," it said in a flat voice.

Cheryl began opening the chest cavity of their squat companion. "Remember, give the nodes to Gopal and Terry and Patty, first. Okay?"

"I understand, Cheryl."

Cheryl deposited several of the extra nodules in the cavity of the robot, looking to see if any grown-ups were nearby. None were.

She concluded, "Tell Gopal we call them Gemini nodes. He'll understand what we mean."

"Yes, Cheryl."

"Tell him to hold one in his hand and to *listen*. Just listen." Cheryl patted the robot on its stunted head.

Anson McDonald turned on its rubberized wheels and rolled along a computer stripe in the center of the outer hallway and headed for the nursery, where the other children lived.

Cheryl stood up and stared at her sister. "I hope Mr. Toquero doesn't get mad at us," she said, genuinely worried.

Cindy fingered her Gemini node. They had fashioned them onto necklaces of gold, and they resembled large gray-white pearls. Cindy's node was currently enlivening the cortical channels in her right brain hemisphere, while Cheryl's was dominating her left brain. They had named them Gemini because the nodules affected either side of the brain as if the brain were not one organ but a unified couplet. Twins, as it were. And each side of the brain had its own past-life recollections—the right side for artistic, holistic, creative urges, and the left for logical, linguistic, scientific thinking. Cindy had been one and Cheryl had been the other.

And it was also important that their other little friends in Yancy City get the remaining Gemini nodules.

But for the moment they themselves could not deliver them. They had work to do elsewhere.

Roderigo Xavier Toquero did not like authority. He knew that there were always certain rules to follow, but he itched all over just thinking about Lloyd Bramlett lurking in the halls of a city his family had helped to build. He knew damn well that Bramlett—and those of his ilk—down upon the earth wanted the moon back under their control. He could see it in Bramlett's eyes. They were eyes that said: *Once we stop the Seeds and once we stop the invasion—the House of Toquero is next.*

Toquero smiled beneath his neatly trimmed black goatee, a grin that became an elfin leer. His sessions with Trenton in the Sheriar, both before and after the fall of the *Jaguar Skies*, revealed to him the reason why he hated Bramlett and his kind so intensely.

He'd seen them before. His particular problems in this incarnation apparently revolved around former lives of abuse at the hands of tyrants and corrupt political leaders of all kinds. Much of his past-life pain was repaid in this life, as the Sheriar revealed, in the form of a handsome body, rugged physical spirit, and absolutely devilish good looks. Plus, the money his father provided through the Toquero mining and industrial interests gave him a wider range of freedom than any he had experienced in any life.

But as Ross had shown him with the Sheriar, they had all been together before in history during the fall of Constantinople, and it would be interesting to find out why. All Toquero hoped was that Lloyd Bramlett was among the Ottoman hordes of Mehmed II. Bramlett just *felt* wrong to him. Perhaps it was the cigarettes.

Toquero's musings helped him in his duties as he finished up preparing the *Lady Nelia Sealing* for its return back to the mother ship, the *Clark Savage, Jr.* He was plagued lately by a lot of unanswered questions, not the least of which were the drawings and schematics of Annette Sayles-Trenton's original diagrams for the projected Longjump engine which he had found a few days before in the *Lady Nelia*. The Trenton twins had been to visit the *Lady* several times in the past week, but as per Emmett's orders he'd had his technicians keep a very close eye upon them. They might be able to wander off in a sandcrawler, but taking up a whole research vessel like the *Lady Nelia Sealing* would be a little much. Still, the girls were worth watching closely, for, as Lisa Palazetti had pointed out, their behavior had changed perceptibly.

As Toquero stood in his purple Moonsuit in the lower bay of the *Lady Nelia*, he heard an electric getabout whistling into the huge hangar of the launch area. The tram came around to the extended ramp of the *Lady Nelia Sealing* and stopped.

Little footsteps could then be heard as they walked around in the launch area, as if whoever owned them was checking out the undersides of the research vessel. Tiny, birdlike voices of nine-year-old girls could then be made out as they discussed something quite serious with one another.

"Hello, mystery girls," Torque said, standing at the door of the ramp, looking down.

"Hi, Torque," Cindy said with a small smile of greeting.

In one of Toquero's Moongloved hands he held a rolled-up schematic of the *Lady*'s Shortjump engine which the girls had left the last time they were there.

"I found this," he said, holding it up for them to see. "You left it the other day."

Cheryl craned her head upward as Cindy mounted the ramp. Cheryl said, "Oh, that's an old one. You can keep it if you want."

Cindy walked past him into the hold. "We got a new one," she announced.

Cheryl came in, trundling her duffel bag, which bulged quite oddly, to Toquero's way of thinking. She also carried a toolbox, which she handed to her sister.

"Don't get mad or anything," Toquero started. "But just what are you guys doing?"

The tykes were like gremlins, going about their business with no telling what on their minds.

Cheryl's bright brown eyes shone innocently. She said, "We're doing a project for Ms. Savard about the *Lady Nelia*."

"Yes," Cindy chimed in as the tools came out one by one on the floor of the science bay of the vessel. "Everyone has to do a report on a ship. Gopal is doing one on the *Rikki Rafner* and Terry Thorpe's studying the big ship around Mars, the *Nora Elgin*."

Toquero nodded approvingly. "Both of those are my father's personal ships. Nice choice."

"Thank you," Cindy muttered.

Cheryl's schematics unrolled and the paper's curled ends found themselves held down by wrenches. Cheryl stood over them and perused them carefully. Torque watched.

Cheryl then turned to him. "Can you explain to us how the fusion differentials are contained by the Shortjump's flux chambers? We're trying to figure out why the deuterium bursts cannot be sustained or even magnified."

Torque's eyebrows went up.

"That's a pretty tall order, sweetheart. You're going to have to ask either Emmett or your mother about that one. I only program them and Jump with them."

"Oh," Cheryl said with a touch of disappointment.

But Toquero noticed how she clutched her pretty new necklace, and thought for a moment. A pencil then appeared in her little pink-gloved hand and scribbles wormed their way into mathematical symbols along one side of the unscrolled schematic.

"Just how long have you guys known calculus?" he then asked, watching them.

"Mr. Roarke taught us," Cindy said.

"Roarke, right," he mumbled. You could blame a lot on Roarke; but Toquero found himself wondering about what was being demonstrated before him. Roarke had to go to MIT to learn his physics.

Cheryl then stood back from her equations and began rummaging through her toolbox. It wasn't a child's box of play tools; these were the real McCoys.

Cheryl stood up with a wrench in one hand and an unguessable device in the other. With a loving smile she asked, "Can you show us the engine again, Torque?"

In his Watchtower, high above the lunar plain, Emmett Shea played with one of his alpha-wave yo-yos. But he was experiencing no joy in it. He knew that something somewhere was out of whack.

They had temporarily lost contact with Ross and Basil Roarke down in the Northridge Hooverville, and only that afternoon was he given word that a message had been tight-beamed up to Macondo and President Dubie that President Scanlon wanted the Moon Men out of town, as it were. Emmett didn't know just how much Dubie was telling Scanlon, but he did know that they were all on the brink of a devastating discovery that could change the way they all thought about the Halo and the Seeds and the upcoming invasion.

Over in the corner twinkled his hologram, and in it were cancerous blisters of light—as relayed from the Tsutsumida arrays on farside—that showed him just how "sick" their galactic quarter really was. He had made a few refinements in the system in the last few days, narrowing down the star systems of the most recent Seeding.

The pieces of the broken Seeds in the laboratories several levels below him yielded up little more than the fact that they'd been created long ago by a race of beings far and away their superiors. Perhaps this was what Ralph Scanlon, in his great-hearted cowardice, was afraid of. Perhaps Scanlon thought it better to live with their malaise than try to treat it. Emmett smiled. Only a psychotherapist such as Ross would think in those terms. All Ralph Scanlon wanted to do was get enough of America back so that he could golf on it.

Emmett put the yo-yo down. It was beginning to cloud his thoughts. He stared at the haze of stars in the hologram.

Pressing a button on the computer which was sustaining it, the laser system beamed in a series of connecting red lines, going from star to star to star.

One line left the bright yellow orb that was the sun and seemed destined for Eta Cassiopeiae. Even at twenty percent the speed of light, the Halo would take several hundred years to arrive there. Still, in several centuries any life forms living on the planets around Eta Cassiopeiae would have a chance to make significant alterations in their civilization to such a degree as to protect themselves.

Or not, Emmett suddenly thought. *We weren't ready. Why should they be?*

But then, he reasoned as he stood staring at the Halo's path of destruction through the sector, *why should it have to happen in the first place? Who gave the creators of the Halo the right to Seed us—or anyone else, for that matter?*

He knew. At least, he knew what Ross would say.

Karma. Punishments for past crimes. The Halo, in some bizarre way, was part of the *dharmic* function of Law in the universe. The earth was Seeded for a reason. Just what that reason was, Operation Cakewalk was supposed to find out. Perhaps a live Seed might offer a clue as to the broader purposes of their creators.

Emmett wasn't even sure he'd be able to fathom the Seed's mysteries. Each one contained so much power that its gradients defied what he knew about energy. For its size, each Seed seemed to draw upon the kind of power a star would use to sustain its own fusion reactions.

It was almost too much to think about. And now there was also a rumor that President Scanlon had nearly been killed scuba diving in the Sargasso Sea. He tried wrestling with a Portuguese man-of-war and almost lost. The world's fragile economies were barely holding together, and that fool Scanlon was out playing with jellyfish....

He glanced over at the Nerzhin sleep-couch where the Sheriar jack lay idle. He felt an overwhelming need for Ross right now, not just as a therapist but as a friend and ally to help with the burden of so many responsibilities. They all knew—and Ralph Scanlon knew—that if they could not stop the Seeds it was possible that the only communities which would survive another Seeding would be those already established on the moon and Mars. Already there was a contingency plan to begin evacuation into outer space. But that would require the use of the Shortjump—and as yet that wasn't allowed on the earth.

After all, the reasoning went, which nations should go first? The Russians? The Americans? What about those poor folks down in Africa or over in Korea? Didn't they have a right to survive as well?

Leave it to Ross to give it a college try. He always did think big.

Emmett walked over to the Sheriar jack. Perhaps it would explain why he was here at this particular juncture in history. It was as Ross had once told him: Everything happens for a reason. *Everything.*

Emmett lay down and plugged in. There were just some things he needed to know. And he needed to know them *now.*

The Sheriar sends through him calming alpha-rhythms and he drifts back.

An image appears and the computer locks onto it and magnifies it. He is a youth of fifteen. Around him are cries and the sounds of metal on metal as swords of Armenian steel clamor for attention in the fall of Constantinople. He has lost his herd of swine to a blown hole in the city's walls and dust is in his eyes and lungs. He fears for his life. He cannot find his family and he suspects that they've been killed already by inrushing hordes of Mehmed II who are flooding the city.

He runs to the rend in the wall. He wants to flee, for he does not have the armor or the skills of a Crusader. But even their power, their thousand-year-old empire, is failing them now.

Why is this happening? Whirlwinds of smoke and ash dance about him as he runs into a half-dozen Ottoman troops. Archers.

They are aiming upward to the ramparts at the Crusaders they've trapped there. Arrows fly skyward and bodies fall down, pincushioned with oaken arrow shafts.

One archer takes aim at a special Crusader on the wall. The boy Emmett Shea is in this lifetime recognizes him as a man who prayed for the unity of the city under the duress of the approaching horde.

Emmett cries out, "Stop!" and runs for the archer, but slips in mud made bloody by a Christian's uncivilized death. He slips before stopping the archer.

The Crusader above takes an arrow clean into his noble heart. He falls from the high rampart and lands broken in a gust of dust.

He gasps at the sight as an Ottoman irregular bludgeons him on the side of the head and he falls down across the Crusader.

The soldiers rush the rampart, leaving the boy and the older Crusader. Emmett stares feebly into the Christian's eyes.

Ross Trenton stares back.

And had the fifteen-year-old boy Emmett Shea not slipped in the bloodied mud, then this Crusader might have lived.

It was all his fault....

24

The Eye in the sky continued to blink above the former Lunar President, uncaringly swinging the passage of day and night around him like the flappings of a great omnivorous creature—the legendary Arabian roc, its feathers fanning the trees alongside the avenue with its unending flight.

That was just one of many associations—both from literature and from his own inventiveness—which came to Trenton as his Moonsuit walked his bulky frame toward the glowing warmth of the angel suspended in the abandoned construction ruin. God blinked and blinked and blinked. The roc flew, circling in its never-ending quest for food.

Then quite suddenly, in the midst of his slow walk toward the Light of God, the full weight of daylight fell down around him as if someone had upended a scaffold of bricks about his shoulders. His bliss ended, yanked from his heart like a vaudeville comedian being hooked offstage by a rude impresario.

And daylight appeared—and froze.

He had been in midstride and the miniature gyros of his bright gold Moonsuit kicked in suddenly, preventing him from toppling over.

The Light from the angel of God had disappeared and his artificial heart slammed furiously in his chest.

He had been set free. The nightmare was over!

All around him men and women in clothing styles almost a decade out-of-date stood hopelessly confused, their faces a gathering of haunted expressions. Several suddenly dropped to their knees gasping huge sobs of relief—or despair.

Trenton, held upright by the powerful stanchions of his Moonsuit, shuddered in the sudden withdrawal.

What happened?

Spinning around, he heard the barks of rifles and the subsequent screams of hundreds of pilgrims, mendicants, and white-robed priests back in the Hooverville so far behind where he stood.

"My God!" he breathed, dropping into a crouch.

A great shimmering of air in the avenue halfway down the street suddenly revealed the spheroid form of a lunar research vessel. The *Retta Kenn*, straight from the *Clark Savage, Jr.* high in earth-orbit overhead, Jumped right out of bent-space and the instant it appeared in the center of the deserted boulevard, its ramp crashed down with a rude *clang!* and Space Marines, led by an overanxious Lieutenant MacReadie, clambered out with a bulldog roar from each soldier.

Trenton whirled around to the lair of the Seed. Its Light was out; it just hung there.

It had been nullified!

The half-built complex of steel girders and concrete pillars revealed the true identity of the angel. Dull as an old tire, the Seed hung on an edge of the building's outer wall, snared by the glossy shroud of the para-glider which had, an eternity ago, entangled itself there.

All around the vicinity the saints were falling to their knees, those closest to the Seed going into a kind of catatonic shock.

The Seed was dead!

But something else was wrong. The light of the sun canted at a different angle, the shadows shorter by degrees.

It was now suddenly winter.

How long had he been trapped? How much time had gone by? His mind raced for answers.

"Roarke!" Trenton shouted, looking back into the pack of saints.

Basil Roarke, in his glossy brown Moonsuit, was one of the former saints down on his knees crying his heart out. He huddled next to a Nissan sedan, itself ten years out-of-date and virtually brand-new. The dealer's sticker was still on its window.

Trenton ran over to him as the Space Marines in assault vehicles popped out of nowhere throughout the former event-horizon of the Seed. And all of the vessels were from the *Clark Savage, Jr.* Citizens from the broken Hooverville scrambled in the panic of gunfire and shouts.

"Roarke, snap out of it! We made it!" Trenton grabbed the squat wrangler.

But Roarke, powered by the assists in his Moonsuit, suddenly rose up like the gorge caught in the molten, angry throat of a volcano.

"*God damn!*" he shouted, his eyes gone manic and red.

Trenton held him. "Easy boy! Down, Roarke, down!"

But the engineer didn't want *down*. He wanted blood. The blood of the angel…the blood of a priest or two….

Roarke wrenched himself away from Trenton as bullets sang and danced on the pavement where they stood. The Confederates were fighting the Marines, and they were now standing fully in the middle of the action.

He ducked behind the Nissan as green ribbons of laser light sliced through the air from the gun ports of the *Retta Kenn*. Overhead, khaki mushrooms were sprouting as Space Marines parachuted in from nowhere. Cargo jets were Shortjumping into the airspace above Northridge, then Shortjumping out before anti-aircraft guns in the sweaty hands of hidden Confederates could get a bead on them. Trenton had never seen *that* done before.

It was a full-fledged invasion, carefully planned and professionally executed.

And Western Confederates were running in retreat. The Hooverville citizenry stampeded in their hysteria and their cries of horror swelled around Trenton like the sound of ocean birds above a crashing surf.

Roarke bounded away, having spotted a Confederate's blue beret riding high above the crowd spilling through the building next to them.

"Roarke, wait!" Trenton shouted, grabbing for him, but missing. The enraged wrangler bolted off.

Roarke bullied his way through the innocent Hooverville inhabitants and dived for the Confederate who'd suddenly spied him.

The Confederate brought up his service revolver, but Roarke struck him like a freight train, with all the power of his Moonsuit behind him.

The two went down against the bricks of a building, making an ugly sound that spoke in very certain terms of many broken bones. Roarke powered up and looked around for other blue berets; the blue beret beneath him did not move. Roarke took off.

To Trenton's right he heard the growling of a stolen U.S. Army half-track appear around the corner, mounted on top by a large field gun and a vengeful Confederate sergeant.

The gun turned in his direction, but before he could plunge for cover, Trenton heard someone shout his name.

"Heads up, Ross!"

Trenton instantly rolled out onto the grass nearby and hid behind a thick eucalyptus trunk.

Torque Toquero in his purple Moonsuit appeared at a run from the *Retta Kenn*, firing his clapper rifle at the oncoming Army half-track.

"Jesus!" Trenton shouted as the air filled with will-o'-the-wisps of ball lightning, most of which found their way to the metal hull of the half-track. The Confederate sergeant on top shielded his eyes, but that didn't stop several thousand electron-volts of electricity from frying both him and the driver within. The half-track exploded when the blue-white faeries of death depleted themselves and vanished.

Toquero scurried to where Trenton lay behind the tree. The rogue's one exposed eye glittered with high excitement.

"Did you see Roarke?" Toquero asked, breathing excitedly. He quickly adjusted the charge on his clapper. "I swear that man's crazy."

"Where'd he go?" Trenton asked.

"Hell if I know," Toquero responded, looking around. He then stared at the former Lunar President. "Are you okay? We thought we'd lost you there for a while."

Trenton said sardonically, "I thought I was lost too."

A painful residue of bliss still tugged at his heart, but he knew now that it was nothing more than his brain's pleasure centers responding to the call of the intense alpha-waves. But now that he was returning to normal, his own natural beta-waves were taking over.

"What's happening?" he then asked. He waved his gauntleted hand at his former neighborhood. "What's all this?"

Marines and panicked citizens ran all around them where they crouched.

Toquero said, "We saved Northridge for last, but we think we've got them now."

"Got who?"

"The Western Confederates," Toquero said, lifting his clapper to take aim at a sniper's nest of Confederates on the second floor of an office building down the street.

"What?"

"We've been fighting them for the last *three* weeks, all up and down California. We saved the best for last."

"Sonofabitch," Trenton muttered.

Toquero fired off a round of electricity which shinnied all across the face of the building in which the Confederates were hiding. Lathing, bricks, and torrents of pulverized glass exploded in the fury of the Jovebolts. Toquero fired as if obsessed.

"That's what I say, too," Toquero added flatly.

Trenton then said, "Three weeks? Are you sure three weeks?"

Toquero stared down the street with his one good eye. "That's how long we've been fighting. *You've* been here four months. It's January 25th. Happy New Year, Ross." Toquero began firing again.

Trenton felt as if he'd just been struck with one of the clapper's charges. Could it have been *that* long? Were the Seeds *that* powerful?

He glanced down at the building with the dead Seed hanging like a black widow spider in her deceitful web. Standing quite close to the abandoned construction site was a Moon Man in his unique green Moonsuit. He was busy indicating where the Space Marines were to take up their guard around it so that no one would damage it.

The Moon Man was Glenn Thorpe, but to Ross's astonishment, Thorpe was shouldering what looked like a gun.

"Thorpe with a *gun?*" he said out loud above the whine of a stray Confederate bullet. Trenton was flabbergasted to see such a thing. He had been convinced that the inventor was a die-hard pacifist.

Thorpe waved a Moongloved hand at Trenton and Toquero. He heaved the heavy rifle on his shoulder and ran over.

Trenton stood and Toquero brought his own rifle to bear, constantly on the watch for blue berets. An explosion blew a building apart far behind them, but the Moon Men ignored it.

"What the hell is that?" Trenton pointed.

"It's a beta-gun," Glenn said happily.

The weapon was a convolution of wires, rods, power-source, all twisted around a rifle stock, complete with scope and trigger.

"It shorts out Seeds." Glenn's pale blue eyes sparkled. "It took me a while to figure it out, but I did it."

Trenton had never seen the small man so pleased with himself.

He then stared at the coven of saints and the mendicants who were helping them to their feet.

"Where's Chuck?" Trenton then asked.

The long-haired wrangler was nowhere in sight.

Thorpe squinted at the location where the most endangered saints had been. He pointed a green-metallic glove to the location. "Was he over there?"

"Right," Trenton nodded. "And Roarke was about forty yards behind him."

Toquero's one eye went gloomy and Glenn looked down at the ground as if suddenly saddened.

"It got him," Glenn Thorpe confessed. "If he was where you say, then the Seed pulled him in."

"Along with the others," Toquero added.

But Toquero's words were heavier with meaning. Losing Chuck Sproule to the Seed's pull was one thing…

"Annette—" Trenton began, his hand-crafted heart bumping loudly in his chest.

"A lot has happened in the last four months, Ross." He could barely get the words out.

Trenton was afraid to ask. But he had to. "Like what? Tell me."

Glenn sighed heavily. "The Seeds worm-hole space, only they seem to pull in living organisms. This one got Annette about two years ago."

"*What?*"

"Emmett worked out the power gradient and sent us all of the data. The Seeds bend space and suck people in. Annette was at the very edge of the event-horizon during the Seeding, so it took her about four years to get to the innermost point." Glenn's eyes sadly considered the location on the boulevard where all the saints finally joined hearts with the Light of God.

Trenton closed his eyes.

"I'm sorry, Ross," Toquero said.

Then Glenn and the one-eyed rogue exchanged knowing—and solemn—expressions. Trenton caught it all.

"That's not all of it, is it?" he said.

"No," Torque said slowly, as if testing the words. "Emmett's gone too. And so are your girls, Ross."

Trenton's Stively-built heart almost exploded. He grabbed Toquero, flushed with panic.

"*What?*"

"It's not what you think, Ross," Toquero said to their leader. "We'll fill you in later on, but your girls came across several dead Seeds near Copernicus and they were affected by them...."

"I don't understand," Trenton stammered.

"We don't either. Nobody does," Toquero said swiftly. "But they used Annette's final notes and modified the Shortjump engine in the *Lady Nelia Sealing*, and—"

"And what?"

"Longjumped," Glenn said, his voice like the hammer in a funeral bell.

" Longjumped ?"

"Last month," Toquero said. "They didn't come back, and with the notes they left, Emmett figured out what they had done."

"Not Emmett—" Trenton began, feeling all the unity he'd striven for in his life wholly disintegrating around him.

"Yes," Toquero said—but not without a little bit of anger. "And he took the *Roxanne Vail*. Right out of the *Savage*'s hangar. My daddy's real mad at what we're doing to his ships."

Trenton leaned against the weary eucalyptus, oblivious of the gunfire, screams, shouts, and general chaos transpiring around him.

"Two nine-year-old girls gone," he said. "Gone into nowhere."

Glenn jumped in, saying, "But, Ross, Ticia tells us it might not be so bad. The girls had a navigation system, and Emmett's note suggests that we might even be able to find out where the Seed sends the absorbed humans."

Trenton's heart and soul were black.

"Don't you see?" Thorpe said with enthusiasm. "Emmett thinks the Seeds interconnect in a network throughout the region. The girls might be following one of them, and Emmett might be too."

"But why did Emmett go? Why didn't he wait?"

The other two Moon Men traded looks. "He's been playing with your Sheriar, and evidently he thinks he's been screwing up your lifetimes. Then when your girls went looking for Annette in the *Lady Nelia*, Emmett took off as well."

"God, what strange people we are," Trenton said after a strained moment of silence.

Trenton stared up at the Seed, wanting to crush it with his bare hands. But he couldn't. It was a gateway; it was the secret to the higher purpose of the Halo and the Halo's creators.

Or *Creator*.

And he knew what the odds were when a man tried to fight God.

However, at the moment he had work to do there in Northridge. He pointed to the clapper in Toquero's holster.

"You using that?"

Toquero unsnapped it from his holster and tossed it to him. He then shouldered his rifle.

"All right," he said to his men. "First things first."

He started off back toward the Hooverville, ignoring the rainstorm of bullets snickering all around him.

"Hey!" Toquero shouted, running to catch up. "Just what comes first?"

"A priest," Trenton told him. "A priest, then an angel."

The Floating White House had finally found the balmy waters of the Gulf Stream and was slowly headed toward the middle Atlantic states.

Which was all right with James Guthrie as he stood in an open-windowed room in the White House itself. He could almost smell land and the changes it would bring once they got back to living in a real White House on real American soil.

However, they were all going to have to face the Russians first.

The conference room filled with a dozen Soviet dignitaries, most of whom weren't used to the pitch and yaw of ocean living. They stood stocky as bears and slightly green in color.

"Your President is an idiot and a scoundrel!" the interpreter shouted to Guthrie as the Soviet Premier himself stood by, a mound of indignation and seasickness. The man's eyebrows were two shaggy raccoons above eyes afloat in a vodka hangover and Dramamine. He sat down heavily.

The interpreter went on. "All Scanlon wishes to do is play games and avoid responsibilities! He has defied openly all treaties! He has kept to himself secrets of the Seeds! He acts like you Americans are the only people on the earth worth saving!"

Guthrie took it all in the face like a level-five hurricane, and kept thinking about Hurricane Rose one hundred miles to the southeast of them and quickly approaching. He didn't know which could be worse.

One of the Soviet advisers sitting around the conference table was holding an ominous black suitcase. Guthrie knew that within it were all the buttons necessary to make life uncomfortable for everyone on the planet for several thousand years. Soviet missile silos, like the American ones, were never Seeded.

The Premier continued his tirade as the interpreter quickly tried to catch up. At the end of it came: "Just give us one reason why we should not declare war! Just one!"

Suddenly a door at the far end of the conference room opened, and in strode Ralph Scanlon with a futuristic-looking rifle propped casually upon his shoulder. He was crisscrossed with bandages and scars from tentacle stings, but apparently didn't care.

The Soviets, to a man, jumped up, going pale catching sight of the gun.

Scanlon swaggered over to the Soviet Premier, who was choking on his anger.

Scanlon grinned. "Now, calm down, Serge! Just you calm yourself down!"

The President of the United States hefted the huge gun away from his shoulders and dropped it gently—revealing his tremendous strength as he did so—upon the conference table.

"Let's cut through the bullshit, Serge," he said with a smile that stretched from Oregon to Maine. "We got us a whole world to clean up, and we're gonna do it with these here beta-guns. Why don't you just let me and Guthrie show you how to *really* hunt bear!"

TWO

LONGJUMP

26

At the back of his feverous mind, Ross Trenton could hear his own overworked conscience mutter: *Physician, heal thyself.*

The nausea he felt within him came from his own self-loathing and the feeling that he ought to be doing more. But as he sat in his private quarters on board the *Clark Savage, Jr.*, he knew that for the moment other men and women had more important duties.

One of these was to keep the largest ship ever constructed by human hands from falling apart in outer space. The ship actually groaned, and Trenton, sitting in his therapist's chair—held in by the loving clutch of Velcro straps—didn't like the sound of what he heard.

Out in the corridors of the massive Longjump vessel, technicians of the Toquero empire—highly trained and *very* serious about their undertaking—scurried hither and yon, plugging up leaks, battening down the hatches. Even if he chose to ignore the nautical metaphor, Trenton could still hear the ship groan. The nausea that wrenched at him also tore at the *Savage*, and he had to keep reminding himself how much body chemistry affected human thinking.

He wanted his little girls back and he wanted his best friend. His anxieties and frustrations at not being able to accomplish their rescue *himself* curled like a clenched fist in the pit of his stomach. Then, having the *Clark Savage, Jr.* make a historic third-of-a-light-year Longjump didn't help matters either. He felt thoroughly helpless. His only option, he finally realized, was to ride it out. He might be their leader on this one, but other, more competent men and women had to run the ship.

A dark-haired, white-tunicked angel appeared in the outer doorway to his quarters. The angel looked a trifle green.

"I don't feel so good," Lisa Palazetti said as she paused in the doorway. She was headed for the bridge. "How about you?"

Trenton couldn't help the sour expression on his face.

The former Lunar President craned slowly around in his chair. "I thought you had something to counteract the Longjump effects."

They all had much to learn about the new Longjump process. Severe spacesickness was the first.

At that moment, another figure appeared in the doorway in a gray, almost pin-striped Moonsuit—which somehow seemed to suit him. He didn't seem the slightest bit taken by the Longjump's pull.

James Guthrie, now wearing contacts and a swift flat-top haircut, smiled. "She does, Dr. Trenton. But I recommend Dramamine. It seems to work the best."

Dr. Palazetti, enwrapped in her own anxieties about the lost and wandering Emmett Shea, gave the U.S. representative on Operation Hopscotch a very mean-spirited look. No one wanted anyone from the home-planet government there, but Ralph Scanlon—being the cagey cuss he was—had insisted on his closest aide to be present. But Guthrie was so innocuous as to be nearly invisible. However, she turned back to Trenton.

"Torque wants us up on the bridge for the next Jump. The big one. I thought I'd pass it along."

"Thanks, Lisa," Trenton said with a forced smile. "But I'm staying here, I think. They don't need me."

"Ross—" Her brown eyes darkened with concern.

"Look," he said evenly. "I'm all right."

Guthrie interrupted. "Mr. President, I think you should be with us when we come in sight of the invasion fleet."

Trenton growled. "Don't call me that, Guthrie. And I'm staying right where I am." And that was that.

Lisa Palazetti, one hand on her stomach and one hand waving good-bye, walked away wordlessly toward the elevator. Guthrie remained. In his hand was an aluminum clipboard. It glowed like a piece of kryptonite.

"But, sir, this *is* important."

"Guthrie," Trenton said, barely controlling himself. "I only allowed you on this expedition because it's a joint operation. I had to pull a *lot* of strings back in Macondo, and I do not like to pull strings. Do you understand me, Guthrie?"

"Yes, sir."

The representative walked on down the hallway, giving no indication that he'd taken offense. *Damn*, Trenton cursed at himself. *Why'd I get involved with this in the first place?*

He knew why: their work wasn't done. Not by a long shot. While the earth authorities were busy manufacturing beta-guns and attempting to resurrect civil order in the plagued cities of the world, the Moon Men—with the blessing of Lunar President Dubie and Roderigo Toquero's father—decided to grab the bull by the horns, as it were, and make a surprise raid on the incoming invasion with the only real weapon they had: the *Clark Savage, Jr.* armed with particle-beam weaponry and a Longjump engine powered by a captured Seed.

He sat in his chair brooding, listening to the Toquero technicians chatter back and forth over the ship's com-system. Their voices sounded almost frantic and Trenton could understand why. Over half of Toquero's crew had been on the ill-fated *Jaguar Skies*, and no one on board the *Clark Savage, Jr.* wanted a repeat performance of that historic catastrophe.

What made matters personally scary for Trenton was the fact that the dreadnought of the Toquero family wasn't under their control. A certain section of the ship had been walled off and sealed several weeks back by a handful of people who Trenton never anticipated would cause anybody any trouble whatsoever.

A voice crackled over the intercom, calling out for him. "Mr. President," James Guthrie hailed. "Captain Toquero requests your presence on the bridge."

Trenton fired back: "If Toquero wants me, he can ask me himself. Since when does he need you to—"

"Okay," Toquero's voice interjected. "Come on up, Ross. I was just giving Guthrie something to do."

"Tell him to go out and strip barnacles off the hull," Trenton snarled.

Toquero, too busy to indulge Trenton in his moods, said, "We're ready to make the Longjump into the invasion vicinity. The Marines are manning the beam turrets now. I'd like to have you up here for this one, Ross."

Toquero's voice was full of mature authority, which pleased Trenton. The young bachelor had always carried with him a certain residue of guilt over losing the *Jaguar Skies* and nearly bankrupting his father. But the *Clark Savage, Jr.*, though built along the same lines, was a completely different ship.

And *that* was because of the individuals sequestered in the nursery several doors down from Trenton's own quarters. They were the ones truly in control.

"All you need are those kids—and the Marines," Trenton said. "I'll stay here and watch."

"Suit yourself," Toquero said, switching off.

Whoever invented children, Trenton mused to himself, *didn't know what he was doing. Or she...*

As it turned out, while the Trenton twins had been modifying the smaller research vessel, the *Lady Nelia Sealing*, seven of Cindy and Cheryl's friends had made their way into the *Clark Savage, Jr.* on an outing to the ship, and with the help of the Gemini nodes given to them by Anson McDonald, had begun going to work.

All of this occurred at a time when the Moon Men were busy helping the American authorities fight for their cities back. The data which the children had come up with, under the leadership of nine-year-old Gopal Govinda, were sent down to Yancy City, and it was clear that the children were hard at work reconverting the Shortjump engine.

However, they had discovered that the long arrow-shaped rod in each Seed—dead or alive—was its source of power, and it seemed to draw upon energies straight from bent-space. Ticia Rhodes had theorized that much of the Big Bang's original pulse had curled in on itself, and the Longjump—as both Emmett Shea and Annette Sayles-Trenton theorized originally—could work if they could tap into that energy and "ride out" the pulse to various gravity wells, or star-suns, nearby.

The "arachnaes," as the children called them, pulled that same power for the Seeds. One such arachnae was currently running the *Clark Savage, Jr.* as well as the two missing research vessels, the *Lady Nelia Sealing* and the *Roxanne Vail*, which Emmett himself had absconded with.

Perhaps of more interest to Trenton was the rather cryptic information Gopal Govinda had provided him with about the Gemini nodes themselves. All the nine-year-old orphan revealed to him was that he believed that the nodes—themselves small computers of unspeakable potential—drew the Seeds to sources of intelligence. To be sure, as Glenn Thorpe himself discovered back in the San Fernando Valley when he had first "cracked" a Seed, the Gemini nodes didn't do anything when touched or handled by an adult human. Yet, as Gopal Govinda had informed them, the nodes worked only on younger minds whose bodies had yet to undergo the transformation into adulthood.

And what they did was to magnify, a thousandfold, the accumulated intelligences of each child who held one. It wasn't a question of making a child, such as Cindy or Cheryl, smarter. The nodes resurrected *all* the past lives of a child, thus making his or her mind something of a multi-functional computer. Trenton's Sheriar only skimmed vague, dreamlike impressions of former lives, delicately fleshing them out so that both therapist and patient could investigate where they came from and what they meant for the patient in this life.

The Gemini nodes, though, brought *all* past lives to bear, and Trenton didn't know whether to fear the children in the nursery or feel sorry for them. All he could do was think about his own twins and what they must have had in mind when—as they said in their last transmission—they wanted to go off and find their mother.

While he—along with President Scanlon and Lunar President Dubie—considered Operation Cakewalk a roaring success, he didn't much care. The unity returning to the earth had been traded across the board for the unity of his own family. Even if there was some evidence to believe that Annette had been "slung" along one of the gravity lines between the stars and could be found, their knowledge of the Longjump—and the hostile universe at large—was so meager as to be laughable.

But Ross Trenton wasn't laughing.

Technicians and Space Marines were running to their posts *as the Clark Savage, Jr.* prepared for the Longjump that would take it within striking range of the incoming invasion fleet.

Trenton, though, eased the door to his quarters shut and turned off the com-system's unceasing chatter.

The larger-model Sheriar stood peacefully over in the corner. This one was designed to service over a hundred minds at once, if he so chose, and he had felt he might have some use for it on board the *Savage*. Quite expensive and fragile, he'd debated bringing it in the first place, since he had lost his first Sheriar—the one he was given upon leaving his teachers at the Meher Baba Trust compound in India—*when the Jaguar Skies* fell. Since Operation Hopscotch was mostly military in design, he didn't know if he'd actually ever need it.

But if after the Hopscotch they could find both Emmett and the twins, he had every intention in the world of plugging all three of them in to find out what made them do what they did in the first place.

Still, he knew the logic of *karma*. What he was going through at the moment had, in some way, to be part of a punishment of some kind. The anguish was almost killing him. His whole family—except for a sister and a surviving mother on the earth—was gone. It was nearly unbearable.

He turned to the Sheriar for an answer. Not using the smaller mini-disc in his collar this time, he instead lay upon the Nerzhin sleep-couch. This particular Sheriar, for convenience's sake, was hooked up, ship-wide, to all of the sleep-couches so that his patients, whoever they may be, wouldn't have to come to his office if they so chose. But now, it was all his.

Trenton lay down and went looking for answers as Toquero's crew rattled around the massive dreadnought preparing for Jump—and battle.

He feels the need for comfort. To know why he is suffering so. He thinks of the figure of Jesus of Nazareth, a man like all the known Avatars, who radiated love and kindness. He envisions the time of Herod and the Sheriar goes back to glean the right sanskaric *image.*

As the Sheriar's alpha-rhythms drop him into the solacing sleep of his trance, it catches a two-thousand-year-old image.

And he sees himself suddenly surrounded by ice.

Ice!

A walrus-fur hood lines his round face, and primitive leather straps hold together thick-soled leggings that go up beyond his knees. Kamiks, skin boots, the Sheriar tells him with a soothing whisper. And he is in a slender boat. A kayak.

A kayak?

But I want the sands of Palestine, he complains loudly, but the Sheriar, like God, isn't listening. The fact of the matter is that in the time of Christ, Ross Trenton's atma was a seal-hunting Eskimo.

The image, though, entraps him and he watches the hunter he was in A.D. 41 ply the greenish waters of the Arctic.

The sky overhead is whale-hide gray as he hoists up his whale-bone spear. Something is moving in a shadow underneath the waters near an ice floe.

Bubbles beneath him churn as his family waits on shore. He raises his spear, poised for what is suddenly rising to the surface.

A row of teeth imbedded in a jaw black with streaming ocean water rises up to seize the kayak, and Trenton—in this life—gazes with horror into the heartless, cruel eye on the slick black-and-white-masked killer whale's head.

He cries out, dropping his spear, as this malevolent water-god breaks him in half with one merciless bite. He swirls down into the uncaring blue of the dark ocean's depths.

He tries to scream in the suffocating waters, but a voice inter-rupts the Sheriar vision.

"Dr. Trenton," a small child's vibrato enters. "You should not trouble yourself with these matters. It is only mind stuff, and stuff that happened a long time ago."

The waters off Baffin Bay vanish into the nothingness of death and Trenton sits bolt upright on the Nerzhin sleep-couch.

"Gopal!" he shouts.

The *Clark Savage, Jr.* floated out in the middle of nowhere, so far out in fact that the sun was barely the brightest star in the sky. All the rest was a scintillating luminescence.

The *Savage* stood like an upright skyscraper, its dozens of port lights alive with activity. The dreadnought—now no longer a research ship—resembled to the eye something like an unfolded umbrella or a toad-stool. Originally designed for Shortjumps, it possessed a wide circular "cap" atop a long structural column which ended at the Jumpship bays. The "cap" was three stories thick, and the ship was well over a hundred and fifty yards long. With a contingent of thirty Space Marines and a regular House of Toquero crew, the total population of the dreadnought came to eighty-eight.

And the thing was armed to the teeth.

The bridge of the *Clark Savage, Jr.* was an amphitheater of the best engineers and pilots the lunar colonies could enlist. Down in the Pit they were hard at work making sure the battleship wouldn't come apart in mid-Jump, while above them, curving inward all the way to the ceil-ing, was a single wall with several screens on it. Television scanners and computer screens gave them a welter of status reports and visuals, both inside the huge ship and outside.

At the top of the amphitheater, in his captain's chair, sat one-eyed Torque Toquero in his purple Moonsuit. To either side of him ran vari-ous consoles with chairs for the commanding Moon Men. In one of these sat Lloyd Bramlett in his military black Moonsuit and in another sat Ticia Rhodes in her own flesh-toned orange suit. Behind them, like a harmless watchdog, stood James Guthrie with his clipboard and ter-ribly important papers.

Toquero noticed his presence out of the corner of his unpatched eye and bent sideways to the lion-haired Ticia Rhodes. "How'd he get a Moonsuit with pinstripes? Do they make them with pinstripes?"

"Beats me," the physicist said, not lifting her eyes away from her gravity-wave monitors and the power indicators coming up from the Seed-containment room below. There, Glenn Thorpe was watching their power source: the "arachnae" which was contained in a beta-wave-bombarded magnetic field. It was seat-of-the-pants technology, but it seemed to be working.

Lloyd Bramlett, who headed his own private security team to keep the Moon Men in check, fidgeted nervously in his chair. He pointed to one of the television screens that was awash with brilliant multicolored stars.

"So why can't we see it?" he demanded. "I thought we'd come out close enough to see the invasion."

Toquero, one ear cocked to the various intership communications of the crew, turned to him and said, "It's because we're a few million miles behind them, that's why."

"Behind them?" Bramlett stared up at the velvet eye patch above the pointed roguish goatee. "But I thought—"

Ticia spoke out. "We're traveling the same gravity line between the sun and Delta Pavonis. The same one the invasion is using, except that it's traveling in normal space. We have to Longjump behind it so that we won't run the risk of colliding with it."

"Or them," Toquero added.

Bramlett made a disapproving noise and slouched in his chair helplessly. No one really wanted him there, and he knew it. And he got no support from Guthrie, which surprised everyone.

However, Toquero wasn't in a position to cater to anyone's whims, particularly when his console flashed a full line of green go-lights.

He looked down at Ticia. "I'm ready here," he told her. "What does your computer say?"

Ticia punched in several keys and within seconds the yellow "hold" lights turned green.

"All set here," she advised him.

Toquero pressed the intercom leading to the various particle-beam turrets spaced the length and width of the *Clark Savage, Jr.*

"Wait for my order," he said to the Space Marines. "They don't expect us, and if we can snap a few pictures and survey the situation first, that's exactly what we're going to do."

He paused for a moment, all eyes upon him in the Pit. He then leaned closer to the microphone. "Roarke, this means you too."

"*All right, all right!*" came an agitated voice from a particle-beam turret wherein he knew the stocky space engineer was nestled, his Moon-gloved hands sweating above a trigger.

Toquero sat upright. "I wish Ross was here."

Ticia said nothing, waiting for his signal.

Toquero then nodded to his second-in-command on the ship down in the Pit. "Let's Jump, Mr. Digeno."

"Yes, sir," came a voice from the darkened Pit below.

An alarm bell, warning them all that they were about to Jump, blared—then everything went suddenly out of focus as the Longjump engine distorted normal matter in normal space with the power of the arachnae.

Then almost as instantly, everyone was gripped with nausea. Down in the Pit, someone barfed into a doggie-bag provided just for the occasion.

Even Toquero felt it, but fought it back. Quickly he leaned to have a closer look at the screen.

"There!" someone down in the Pit shouted. "*We've got it!*"

Everyone gasped as the main television monitor brought into focus the invasion fleet.

Quickly Toquero slapped on the intercom to the waiting gunners in their armored turrets.

"Hold back your fire!" he shouted, standing. Then, to make sure, he added: "Roarke!"

"Okay! I get the picture," came the wrangler's reply.

Even Lloyd Bramlett stood as James Guthrie came up behind Captain Toquero to see better what the huge television screen portrayed.

"Ross has *got* to see this," Toquero mumbled to Ticia Rhodes.

On the screen, barely glimmering in the wan light from the sun so distant, was another Halo.

No invasion fleet, but another pregnant toroid forty miles in diameter and spinning at an unimaginable rate of speed. Excited whisperings from the Pit rose up about them.

Ticia quickly jumped to her instruments as the exterior probes of the dreadnought measured the toroid.

"My God," Bramlett breathed.

Mr. Digeno, down in the Pit, rattled off their immediate distance. "We're two hundred miles behind it, sir. We've matched speed."

Toquero scanned the indicators on his console to see how the ship—huge as it was—was holding up under the strain of the Longjump. He didn't like the occasional button flaring red. He'd have to let his officers tend to the duties they knew best.

Toquero said down into the Pit: "Get Dr. Trenton up here, Mr. Digeno."

"He doesn't answer, sir," the second-in-command responded.

"Damn," Toquero muttered.

"Will you look at that thing?" Ticia whispered.

The Halo seemed to hang like a golden wedding ring with a few million stars the size of dust particles as a backdrop. The Pit was absolutely silent as everyone stared. It was as if they were flies flirting with the dangerous presence of an enormous spider.

"Data coming up on screen two, sir," a female tech called out from the Pit.

Ticia Rhodes sat back, watching the information line itself out above them in huge, readable letters.

"That's what I thought," she said, thinking aloud. "Over fifty million tons and spinning at four revolutions per second. If I wasn't seeing it with my own eyes, I'd say that it was impossible."

"At least it's not an invasion fleet," Lloyd Bramlett responded, sitting back down.

"In a way it is, sir," the diminutive James Guthrie said from the shadows behind them. "It's clearly full of Seeds."

Ticia Rhodes began throwing switches and making sure that the members of her own staff down in the main research quarter of the *Savage* were getting all the information as quickly as it was coming in.

Bramlett looked once at Guthrie, then back to Toquero. "We've still got to stop it," he told them. "That's what we're here for, isn't it?"

"That and a few other things," Toquero told him distastefully. He knew how much Bramlett didn't care for the latter half of their mission: to find Annette Sayles-Trenton, her two daughters, and the missing mayor of Yancy City. Bramlett was all business, and he at least had James Guthrie as a living representative of President Ralph Scanlon to see that some of their military objectives were carried out.

Just then the intercom broke in with the frantic voice of a female technician. "Captain Toquero. We need you down in the nursery right away, sir."

Ticia Rhodes looked over at the one-eyed rogue as Toquero spoke. "What's going on?"

A tremendous clangor could be heard over the intercom speakers.

The female technician came back with: "It's Dr. Trenton, sir. He's trying to smash his way into the nursery."

Toquero was out of his captain's chair in one fluid motion.

"Mr. Digeno," he said, heading for the elevators. "The helm is yours."

oss Trenton, using the amplified assists of his mighty Moonsuit, swung his fists into the invincible Plexiglas wall which separated him from the rest of the nursery.

Four purple-Moonsuited security guards stood at a respectful distance, their clappers out just in case. But no one moved as the former Lunar President raged at the figures encased behind the transparent wall.

"God damn you, Gopal!" Trenton roared. The wall—put up by the children when the *Clark Savage, Jr.* had still been in lunar orbit—held with each crashing fist.

Behind the thick wall stood Robbie Rogers and Gopal Govinda. Ms. Rogers was the only adult the children apparently had any trust in, and Gopal Govinda, in his own pint-sized Moonsuit, leaned at her waist as the golden Moongloves beyond the acrylic wall came at them like angry comets.

"Robbie," Trenton said, catching his breath. "Tell them to keep their hands off my Sheriar! It's not a toy!"

Clearly Robbie was concerned—but mostly for the children.

"They didn't mean any harm, Dr. Trenton. Honest they didn't," she said, but the bemused expression on her face didn't speak well of her conviction.

From behind her, out of another room, a boy and a girl appeared. The girl, a curly redhead of five years of age, wore a headset and seemed overly puzzled by all the adult commotion. The smaller boy, a six-year-old, had a mechanical device in his hands of unusual design.

The redheaded girl turned to Gopal. "Gopal," she trilled in a bird-like voice, "make him stop. Tell him."

The six-year-old boy next to Gopal merely turned and walked out of the room, bored with the whole business.

Gopal said in a voice loud enough to be transmitted into the outer hallway: "Dr. Trenton, you are in no condition to use the Sheriar right now. We recommend against it."

Trenton's anger bore deeper within him; the look on the brown-skinned nine-year-old lunar orphan seemed wiser than the ages, but he nonetheless resented being told what to do by *anybody*.

"Who do you think you are to give *me* advice?" he shouted as the security guards of the House of Toquero raised their clappers. "You little—"

Gopal crossed his little matchstick arms defiantly. "Dr. Trenton, this is for the good of the whole ship. We're working on it."

The little redheaded girl nodded enthusiastically, as if the boy's cryptic words said everything.

The security team parted when the elevator ushered Glenn Thorpe from the engine room below.

"Problems?" he queried. Grease covered his Moongloved hands.

"*Lots* of problems," Trenton fairly snapped. "He's tinkering with the Sheriar. And I won't have it."

Thorpe nodded sagely, his mind off in the misty land of Seed technologies. Thorpe said, "He's tinkering with the whole ship. They've got everything wired and monitored from the nursery. Not much we can do about it, I'm afraid."

Glenn then smiled and wiggled his fingers in a playful wave at the little redhead behind the protective wall.

"Hi, baby!" he said, flirting.

"Hi, Daddy," little Terry Thorpe said.

Trenton snapped at his friend, "Don't encourage them. I don't care how smart they are, this is a dangerous operation."

"And we're trying to make it less dangerous," Gopal told the large man in the golden Moonsuit, "by making sure all the loose bolts are tightened down, so to speak."

Trenton choked on a growl. Thorpe intervened, whispering, "He doesn't mean you, man. Don't let him get to you."

"He's *already* gotten to me," Trenton argued.

From the elevator emerged Torque Toquero followed by a grim and edgy Lloyd Bramlett wheezing from too many clandestine cigarettes. Lisa Palazetti, recovered now from the nausea of the Jump, was right behind.

"What are you trying to do?" Lisa scolded, pushing her way through the guards. Her first concern was the children, and seeing Trenton— and all the scratches on the impenetrable wall—raised her professional, and maternal, hackles. "Answer me!"

Trenton heard his own mother's voice just then and backed off. He knew. Pushed just so far, and one individual could jeopardize the whole. Gopal had a reason for monitoring the Sheriar's use; he just couldn't fathom it.

"Gopal's interfering with my Sheriar," he told her.

The little nine-year-old fingered the golden chain with its Gemini node within the pendant. He said, "He was exploring a region of his guilt similar to Dr. Shea's. I cut him off."

Trenton watched how Lisa assimilated that bit of information, despite the fact that he disagreed with the boy. But then he had to keep reminding himself: this wasn't a "boy" with whom he was dealing. Was Jung one of Gopal's past lives? Piaget? How about Freud?

Toquero walked over to the wall and the former Lunar President. He'd lost some of his usual swagger. "Look, Ross, I don't know what's going on here, but I've got a ship to run." With a purple-gloved thumb he gestured over his shoulder into the anteroom of the nursery, where the children and Robbie Rogers stood. "We're here because of these kids. I don't like it any more than you do and my daddy doesn't like it." He stared at Trenton as hard as his one eye could. "You get the picture?"

Trenton got it, but didn't like it. Toquero was, by degrees, becoming serious about being shouldered with the responsibilities of running a ten-billion-dollar spaceship that *still* could rattle apart. And *everyone* on board remembered the *Jaguar Skies*.

Trenton breathed calmly, letting his artificial heart adjust the adrenaline flow in his body. However, he turned to Lisa Palazetti and spoke in a voice that everyone could hear. "All right. But the Sheriar is *mine*. Nobody fools with it from here on out." He then glanced sternly at the nine-year-old, trying to be a parent by doing so. "And I mean *nobody!*"

Gopal Govinda and little Terry Thorpe beside him both fingered their Gemini nodes, listening to the voices of their particular past lives.

Gopal said, "We are all here for a reason, Dr. Trenton. Don't separate yourself off. Just remember your friend Dr. Shea."

"And Cindy and Cheryl," little Terry said, her green eyes flashing with adult worry.

Toquero grabbed Trenton by the arm, his palm not even cupping it halfway around his bicep. "Let's go upstairs. We've got a problem of our own right now."

Trenton let himself be escorted to the elevator.

Mr. Digeno gave Toquero back his throne as Ticia Rhodes barely paused in her haste to see that their monitors were recording as much information as they could gather. James Guthrie hovered over everyone's shoulders, his bright eyes afire with the contagious excitement of the bridge—a rare display of enthusiasm for him.

Toquero, eyes on the overhead screen, said to Trenton in the semi-darkness, "There it is. A Halo, not an invasion."

Trenton's heart leapt. Against the stars of the television monitor it hung like a real angel's discarded halo, tossed aside in any old direction.

Instantly he thought of Annette. That Halo on the screen was meant to do it all over again—and somewhere down on the earth a woman would be caught getting out of her Nissan station wagon, home from a seminar at UCLA, or perhaps from grocery shopping. It didn't matter; its effects would invariably be the same, no matter whose wife it was.

Ticia Rhodes pushed back a graying lock of her hair from her face. She said, "I calculate that it's got over a billion Seeds in it. Maybe more."

Trenton concentrated on the Halo, forgetting about the little drama which had just transpired down below. He needed clues, more information.

"That's more Seeds than will be needed to take out the earth again," he said firmly.

"Maybe they're going to finish the job," Lloyd Bramlett added from the shadows.

"One Halo's enough," Trenton countered. "They know what their Seeds can do."

Ticia agreed. She then added, "It could also be using the sun's gravity well to sling it off in another direction. The first Halo's heading for Eta Cassiopeiae. We won't know where this one's bound until we rework its mass after it sheds its Seeds. *If* that's what it plans to do."

Ticia tabbed a few keys and down in front of them Emmett Shea's brilliant hologram of the galactic quarter twinkled into life.

Ticia continued, "Since the Halos are traveling at sublight-speeds, it takes them centuries to do their work. And there are dozens of sun-type stars around which life could evolve within forty light-years of us. It could be going anywhere."

Trenton stared at the golden toroid on the large television screen, then at the hologram which glistened out before them as if magically suspended in space for all to see.

He said, "Are there any other Halos behind this one?"

Ticia leaned her elbows on her desk-console and linked her fingers meditatively. "Emmett's gravity-wave detector shows us that no massive objects are on their way—other than this one." She leaned back. "The only significant perturbations are those we—I should say *I*—believe are the *Lady Nelia Sealing* and the *Roxanne Vail.*"

Trenton felt the silence of the bridge rush around him like flood-waters. When Emmett had gone off after the Trenton twins, he had left behind him a treasure chest of data, along with models of his gravity-wave detectors. Ticia and her own crew easily deciphered his notes, but much remained a mystery. There were other perturbations as well, which they rarely spoke about. It appeared that "something" or many such "somethings" were traveling along the gravity lines each single Seed generated. Ticia hadn't penetrated that particular mystery yet, but she was determined to. For they all believed that somewhere along one of those lines was Annette Sayles-Trenton, and if that was true, then they just might be able to rescue her. If not...

Trenton, taken by the nature of their historic encounter with the new Halo, said aloud, "Just who the hell is *making* these things?"

At that moment a row of red and yellow lights appeared on Toquero's main board. At the same time, Mr. Digeno, from his own console, shouted up, "Captain Toquero, I'm getting a program-lock from Mr. Roarke's bazooka. He's going to fire on it, sir."

Trenton stepped up to Toquero's chair.

Toquero quickly flashed on a video pickup of Roarke's perch in his gunner's blister on the top of the *Clark Savage, Jr.*

The wrangler, in full Moonsuit with environment helmet, clutched the trigger as he sat in a fetal position staring at the black void beyond the glass dome of the turret.

"It's mine," Roarke insisted, knowing he was now being visually monitored. "I want to do it!"

Trenton stared at Toquero, then at Ticia Rhodes.

"Do we want to do this thing?" he asked. "I mean, it won't be any-where near the earth for a full year."

Lloyd Bramlett, dark in his dark Moonsuit, rushed over. "It's not for you to change your mind, Trenton. We take it out *now*. That's the plan."

Ticia mused. "It would be a shame, Mr. Bramlett. We could spend a whole year analyzing it from a distance. Personally, I'd like to see how it Seeds. The thing's very massive and spinning at an impossible rate. I'd like to know how it's done myself."

"You know as well as I do," Bramlett insisted, "that we're here first as a military expedition, and second as anything else."

Trenton scowled at the Pentagon liaison. He stood his full height. But Bramlett apparently wasn't intimidated by the psychologist's size.

"You ask Guthrie here." Bramlett indicated the small man behind them, watching.

"Actually, sir," Guthrie said flatly, "I'm only a civilian observer."

Toquero smiled broadly behind his pointed goatee. "You're all alone, Bramlett. We've got a priceless opportunity to—"

Clappers clicked their safeties off behind them as Toquero became aware of Bramlett's own security team.

Trenton said, "He's right. The Halo has to go. We'll have more than enough to explore during the Hopscotch."

But the glare he leveled at the liaison officer suggested that the man's authority after this would be considerably diminished. Bramlett, though, seemed pleased.

It also didn't escape Trenton that James Guthrie was smiling off in his private corner.

The lights along Toquero's board shifted into green as Roarke's particle-beam bazooka took aim and came up to power.

Trenton mused out loud, "You think we can really destroy some-thing like that with a particle-beam weapon?" He turned to Ticia Rhodes. "What's the physics on that thing?"

"We won't know until we try," she said calmly. "But we've got Roarke's bazooka aimed so that it will at least force the Halo off course. That is, assuming the beam has any effect. These Halos are the most massive constructs I've ever seen." She shrugged, willing to give any-thing a try.

"Where will the Halo go?" Trenton queried.

Ticia punched in a program which led the hologram before them to trace out a projected path. If done just right, the Halo two hundred miles out ahead of them would find itself wandering at twenty percent light-speed upward out of the galactic plane. Clearly the alien toroid would encounter nothing along the way. Nothing but dust and random photons of light.

Trenton punched the intercom to Roarke's turret. "Okay, Roarke. We've got the computer locked, pull the trigger when we say so."

"Aw, Ross—"

Trenton glanced aside at Bramlett. "This okay with you, Lloyd?"

Bramlett's eyes were dark and troubled. "I'd rather we killed it. Plain and simple."

"It's too massive," Ticia said. "We didn't expect another Halo. The invasion was supposed to be a fleet of ships."

Bramlett acquiesced. "All right. Do what you want."

Trenton nodded to Toquero, who in turn pressed the ship-wide stations alert.

"Stand by for firing," Toquero called out on the intercom. Turning aside, he said to Trenton, "At least this is better than to come out blasting with all our guns drawn."

"Like shooting fish in a barrel," Basil Roarke said from within his earth-brown Moonsuit, having heard every word.

"We'll nudge it in the direction of its spin," Torque told them all. "We'll do a series of three blasts with the computer doing the tracking so we'll hit the same spot. How's that sound?"

"Fine," Trenton said, watching the television image of the alien artifact.

Toquero then said into the microphone, "Fire first series, Roarke. *Now!*"

What happened next came too fast to be perceived. Only the ship's computers, watched over by minds down in the nursery, made the proper adjustments.

Basil Roarke fired a deadly stream of highly charged particles, and they instantly leapt over the two hundred miles of emptiness.

The Halo became a supernova of tremendous light and soundless energy rushing right at them. All of the screens above the Pit went white with the rage of vindictive angels, and just as suddenly the ship's computers kicked in and every object around them went blurry.

Gut-wrenching nausea tore at Trenton's insides as the *Clark Savage, Jr.* took the full force of the impact and Shortjumped, not once but five times.

Trenton passed out—as did everyone else on the bridge before it was all over.

28

A red-and-yellow Donald Duck toy, forged from the best Taiwanese plastic, floated above the console of the *Roxanne Vail*, utterly unaware that another Longjump had been made.

Emmett watched the small bauble rotate in the zero gravity of the vessel's upper deck. Reaching out a gauntleted hand, he plucked it right out of the sky. *Distantly he wondered if Someone would come pluck *him* out of the sky.

However, there were a dozen toys on board the *Roxy Vail* and he took some comfort in that. A soulless God might play with his toy, but he certainly wouldn't be fool enough to destroy it. *Or would he?*

If he had a bunch of toys, he just might.

But Emmett quickly turned his mind away from such thoughts. God hadn't destroyed him yet; at least, he hadn't reached out his own gauntleted hand and crushed the *Roxanne Vail*. Emmett guessed that the universe was just plain filled up with toys. One little toy from the earth wouldn't matter much in the Big Picture.

He only hoped that another "toy" would go unharmed as well: the *Lady Nelia Sealing*.

The guilt which propelled him out of his life in Yancy City seemed to diminish for each magnificent Longjump. But each Jump—despite its attendant nausea and disorientation—seemed to yield up no trace of the twins, other than intriguing impulses set shimmering throughout his holoscan representation of the Halo's silent demesne.

The hologram, with its gentle "singing," portrayed the stellar community nearest the earth as being a ghetto, deracinated by the Halo's Seeding. How one Halo could effectively Seed so many star systems, he did not know. And even though he fully understood the principles of the Longjump—thanks to the mysterious transformations in the Trenton girls—he still did not comprehend why the Halo's creators didn't opt for the Longjump space-bending technique. It would have made the effort of Seeding much easier.

But the singing from the tiny stars in the hologram hypnotized him, like the automated computer toys his mother back in Boston had bought him when he was a child.

Perhaps it was his genuine desire to remain a child that had gotten him to abandon Yancy City. Perhaps that, coupled with the guilt over letting the Trenton girls evolve to an unmanageable state. But watching the holo, and thinking that it, too, was very much toylike, he tried to get himself to think like a nine-year-old would. *Two* nine-year-olds.

He knew now that he never again would be mayor. His true love was physics and his work on gravity-lines. But in order to accomplish that end, he would have to retrieve Cindy and Cheryl. He could not rest easy until then.

And where would the girls go first in their search for Annette? he had asked himself.

The Halo of '33 came from Alpha Centauri, and indeed the hologram—tied into his advanced gravity-wave detector—indicated that the planets around both Proxima and Alpha Centauri had been heavily Seeded. Their "songs" were plaintive and sorrowful. And very pronounced.

He had taken the *Roxanne Vail* into bent-space in three Longjumps, and the sight of entering a new star system had been staggering. But alone and afloat out in space, with so little to orient him, he made for the nearest earth-type planet. But in a double-star system, no world would be stable enough to be habitable, in human terms, because of conflicting gravities from the two neighboring suns, to say nothing of stellar radiation.

However, his hologram, interconnected by lines of gravity influences, seemed to shiver with the passage of a small ship. The *Lady Nelia Sealing* had passed this way as if a minuscule spider had skimmered ever so lightly along the interconnecting silken web between the linked worlds.

But the holo also revealed something more sinister than the lack of a Longjump vessel from the earth: all of the planets in the Proxima Centauri system had been effectively Seeded, and their "songs" were filling the gravity waves with their parasitic wail for something upon which to feed.

Fearing that the girls might have been trapped by a Seed down upon the surface of the fourth planet from Proxima Centauri, Emmett spent two days radioing from high orbit. The girls, however, were either captured by a Seed—or just plain gone.

Emmett opted for gone.

The next nearest stars in that galactic quarter were Zeta Tuscanae and Delta Pavonis. The hologram, once magnified, showed that both of those systems had also been heavily Seeded, their "songs" already familiar to him now.

However, what became more and more alarming to him was the notion that he was going to have to spend years searching out all of the quadrant's star systems, both Seeded and un-Seeded. The girls would not stop until they found their mother and he himself did not have the time or the equipment to fathom the Seeds' capacities to bend space and send individual humans along gravity lines—if, in fact, that is what they did. *Something* was wiggling up and down the gravity lines, but he didn't know what. Cindy and Cheryl had the time, equipment, and the will to conduct a search for Annette, and they had the understanding of the physics involved.

But he wanted the twins back. He couldn't live with the idea that he might have contributed to their accidental destruction.

So he Longjumped to the next likely candidate.

He knew that the incoming invasion was taking a direct route from Delta Pavonis to the earth, but that invasion fleet was behind him to the tune of nineteen light-years. He was also relatively certain that neither twin knew of the invasion; that had been part of the urgency behind Operation Cakewalk. He only hoped that if the twins had come this way they avoided whatever interplanetary military might be there waiting. *Waiting like the Hand of God....*

Toys orbited around him as he made small adjustments in the hologram hovering above its place on the command console. His stomach still queased as if a hand smaller than God's—but just as cruel—was yet holding onto it.

The computer revealed that Delta Pavonis was of the spectral class G7, having a solar mass of 0.98. It was a likely candidate for at least one habitable planet—and that would make sense if, as the Japanese scientists at Tsutsumida Station had discovered, the invasion fleet was coming from Delta Pavonis.

The computer also indicated that eight planets circled Delta Pavonis, with four inner planets, two massively ringed Jovians, and two dark gas giants the size of Uranus out where Pluto might belong.

Emmett stared at the computer and scratched his three-week-old beard. What he found most unusual about the computer's scan of the system was its startling lack of sheer planetary matter. The planets were intact, but there should have been *more* matter.

A closer examination revealed that what might have passed for an asteroid belt was thoroughly missing, as were the moons that should have orbited the ringed giants. He knew that over time, all planetary matter, including free-floating dust, gas, and ice, would eventually coalesce, falling into the gravity wells of nearby planets or the star itself. That was the fate of all planetary matter.

However, this was a mystery to him.

He reprogrammed the hologram to give him a three-dimensional view of the Delta Pavonis system. Within seconds, all of the planets flew into their laser-described orbits, and to give it some perspective, Emmett speeded it up.

An anomaly appeared and Emmett leaned back, amazed.

One particular asteroid, itself a small moon, was sailing in a dangerous parabola twenty-one degrees up from the elliptic. It passed in its awkward orbit just beyond the orbit of the third planet and betrayed the inevitability of its wandering: one of these days, relatively speaking, it was bound to collide with the fourth planet.

"If it hasn't done so already," he said out loud. "Which means *you* don't belong there."

It had moved.

The asteroid was a hundred and fifty-five miles in diameter, nearly oval-shaped, and stable in its own rotation.

It still did not belong there.

Emmett turned up the hologram's receiver and listened to the singing coming from Delta Pavonis' system. The fourth planet alone of all of the planets had been Seeded, although the third also seemed a candidate for possible life forms, since it was well in the life-zone out away from Delta Pavonis.

Yet, he wondered. There had been an invasion fleet sent *from* this place. Had they Seeded—or just destroyed—the fourth planet and moved on toward earth?

He stared out into the black maw of nothingness beyond the window of the *Roxanne Vail*. He had Longjumped into the system so far out that Delta Pavonis was little more than a bright gem in a background of gems.

But the asteroid was more of a showpiece, not a gem; a toy, he suddenly realized. The girls would have seen it, and perhaps they would have gone to investigate.

He programmed the *Roxanne Vail* for a Shortjump toward the asteroid. It was above the plane of the planets, and both the third and the fourth planets were on the opposite side of Delta Pavonis. His only real worry was the ability the Halo's makers might have to detect ships such as his. Gravity waves did resonate, revealing disturbances of all kinds, like dew-drops sliding down a spider's web.

He returned artificial gravity to the interior of the *Roxanne Vail*, for he didn't want to be at a disadvantage upon popping out into normal space. The floating toys rained about him, clacking and dancing upon the metal of the floor. He was careful to note that none had broken.

He swallowed, wishing for something to help with the nausea of the Jump process—and distantly he thought of Lisa. This would be right up her alley; she'd know what to use.

But he wouldn't allow himself any thoughts of her. He'd see her soon enough. He had work to do first.

He Jumped.

The console blurred and the lights of the planets in the holo bobbed ever so slightly. The hand of that minor god grabbed at his stomach and he thought that his lunch would come up.

But the *Vail* Jumped successfully, and the spherical research vessel leapt out into normal space.

And alarms shouted at him.

He sat up, face-to-face with red buttons blinking and loud indicators screaming for his attention.

Through the *Roxanne Vail*'s main window he could see the dull lump of the asteroid as it eclipsed its backdrop of pinpricked stars.

But that wasn't the source of the alarms.

The *Roxanne Vail* had come out into a field of objects that posed a potential threat to the ship, and all the alarms were flashing at him telling him so.

"Jesus!" he breathed as he quickly bent over, getting set for another Shortjump out of harm's way.

Radar showed literally hundreds of objects filling the space in the wake of the asteroid—none of which he could see through the window.

His face illuminated by the reds and yellows pulsing at him from the console, he looked up. A scraping could be heard as something bumped up against the outer hull of the ship. A rock? Ice?

The sudden fear of being sucked out into space through a fist-sized meteor hole raced through him with the speed of a lightning flash.

He jumped out of his chair when the object drifted into view outside his window. It was larger than he had anticipated.

"*Holy Christ!*" he shouted, the Donald Duck toy going *crunch!* accidentally underfoot.

What he saw was nearly human in shape, devoid of an environment suit, and quite, quite dead.

It also resembled a nine-year-old girl.

29

The five emergency Shortjumps skipped the *Clark Savage, Jr.* so far behind the hell-terror of the exploding Halo that by the time the first normal-space shock wave shuddered at them, it was nothing more than weak gamma rays and a lot of white light. The computers thought that a million miles from ground-zero might be safe enough.

However, no debris raced through space to pepper the super-alloyed hull of the dreadnought. The Halo had been vaporized instantly, and all that remained of it was a memory.

Trenton vaguely was aware that he was still alive when he heard two things: one was a cacophony of alarms sounding throughout the bridge, each demanding attention, and the other was a tapping sound on the shoulder of his Moonsuit and James Guthrie's voice.

"Sir?" he asked respectfully. "You can get up now, Dr. Trenton. We're out into normal space. We're safe."

Trenton opened one bleary eye, feeling his gorge rise from the punch of nausea the Jumps had delivered. The metallic sheen on Guthrie's peculiar Moonsuit rippled with greens and reds from the blinking lights on the various command consoles of the bridge.

How'd they get a pin-stripe effect? he wondered distantly, trying to focus on something.

Slowly he cranked himself up off the carpeted floor to see Torque Toquero—a little green himself—shouting orders down into the Pit at Mr. Digeno, and Ticia Rhodes trying to monitor her own computers. The screens overhead fuzzed and hissed. Ozone filled the air. Something somewhere was burning, or trying to burn.

The *Jaguar Skies!* he realized. *Not again....*

But James Guthrie was a pool of calm and helped him to his feet.

"It's okay, sir," Guthrie reported, his aluminum clipboard gripped in the crook of his arm. "Just some minor damage that Mr. Toquero is taking care of."

"What the hell happened?" he demanded, breathing raggedly.

"It's that pinhead Roarke's fault!" Lloyd Bramlett said, sunk down in his chair. His lunch was sprinkled in his lap and on the floor. "He overrode the computer and just shot at the goddamn thing!"

"I did not!" came a feeble, plaintive voice over the intercom from Basil Roarke. "You keep me out of this!"

Trenton staggered over to Ticia Rhodes. "Is that what happened, Ticia?"

She looked up—and very much looked her age this time. "Imagine firing a bolt of electrons at a pulsar forty miles across. It might do no damage whatsoever, or—"

Toquero spun around, anger and panic both taking turns on his face. "Or blow us to kingdom come!" He leveled a purple Moonglove at Lloyd Bramlett. "Bramlett, we should've let that Halo go! We had a whole year!"

Bramlett stood, obviously bound for his own quarters. He managed to say: "Orders are orders. We couldn't have known it was going to explode until we tried."

"I'm not going to endanger my ship again!" Toquero stared maliciously at Lloyd Bramlett. "Your authority ends now, Bramlett. You're out of a job. Get the hell *off* the bridge!"

Inwardly Trenton managed a smile. Toquero was the youngest of his Moon Men. He was growing up *real* fast, thanks to the Halo.

Bramlett, though, ignored the bearded Toquero and wobbled toward the elevators.

Trenton glanced at Toquero. "The ship. Is it holding up? I thought I smelled something burning…"

Toquero waved expressively at his console. "There's burning everywhere! We've got power leaks on all the floors, and one of the research Jump ships below got shook loose from her berth."

"Which one?"

"The *Lucille Copeland*," Toquero reported tersely. "That leaves us with two—and that's not a lot, Ross." He bent closer to the psychologist. "We don't have enough to evacuate. Just like the *Jaguar Skies*. This ship's jinxed. *I'm* jinxed!"

"Horseshit," Trenton grumbled. He indicated several of the green go-ready lights beginning to reappear on the captain's console. "We're just shaken up a bit. If it's very bad, then we can Longjump home. Assuming we can still do so." He turned to the physicist. "Ticia?"

She nodded. "None of the Jump engines or arachnaes were damaged. We can Jump. I can't guarantee the shape we'd be in if we had to do it *now*. But, yes, we could Jump."

Trenton stood back, with Guthrie filling his shadow. He shook his head with disgust. Toquero had been right in the first place. They didn't know what they were doing.

Babes in the woods, he thought. Just whose woods, he didn't want to think about.

Down in the nursery, three of the seven children were asleep in their Nerzhin sleep-couches, one was eating her lunch, and the three remaining were busy in their "workroom" watching the lights of the new hologram they had just built.

Robbie Rogers, going gray with worry, sat in a chair nearby, but did not interfere.

Gopal Govinda, still in his pinkish-orange Moonsuit, crouched on the floor, his gloves off so that he could work better. A small computer and keyboard played into the hologram, and before them rose the scintillating lights of Delta Pavonis' system.

Redheaded Terry Thorpe—out of her Moonsuit and into a pantsuit arrangement—clutched her Gemini nodule. To Gopal she said, "Maybe we should tell Mr. Toquero and Dr. Trenton who we are, Gopal."

Gopal managed a wistful smile on his wizened nine-year-old face. "We are who we are *now*." He didn't take his brown eyes from the hologram dancing before them in the half-light of their workroom. "Besides," he said softly, "they might take the ship away from us if they didn't believe us."

"Dr. Trenton and the Sheriar know—" she stated, but didn't finish her thought. Already her Gemini nodule was filtering a hundred more powerful minds into her own brain.

"No they don't," little five-year-old Patty Brown said from inside a device she was working on nearby. She stuck her head out, her auburn curls tied back in a cute ponytail. She said, "They don't know *anything*!" She smiled, then submerged into her device, which snaked with wires off toward their mainframe computer. She soldered away happily.

Gopal then said, "As long as the ship functions, we're safe. They won't stop us."

Terry Thorpe naturally allied herself with her father, who was part of the grown-ups. But her bond with Gopal and the other five children—including Cindy and Cheryl—went deeper.

"Dr. Trenton would understand," she insisted.

"But the others wouldn't," Gopal asserted quietly.

"Maybe," little Patty Brown said from inside her invention, "we should tell them we found Cindy and Cheryl."

At this revelation, Robbie Rogers leaned forward and turned her dark blue eyes on them. "What? You found them? How?"

Gopal was quick to answer. "We don't know if it's them yet."

"The computer says," little Patty protested.

"The computer says *something*," Gopal countered. His Gemini nodule dangled from his gold chain and seemed to glow in the amber light.

Terry Thorpe, who had been instrumental in redesigning Emmett Shea's special hologram, pointed into its three-dimensional disk of Delta Pavonis and its planets.

She said, "We know that someone has moved in toward the fourth planet. We picked it up."

"A ship?" Robbie asked. "The *Lady Nelia?*"

"We think so," Gopal confessed. "But there is something else."

His nine-year-old's voice resonated like that of a grown-up. Robbie Rogers found it scary; she'd been relaying her observations to Lisa Palazetti ever since she'd been allowed in to watch over them. No one knew this and at times it made her feel guilty. But it had to be done.

"What else do you see?" she then asked.

"The whole planet's hurt," Gopal announced. With a slight adjustment to the holo's program, the singing returned, but this time it did not appear melodious. It was more a feral growl, a painful static of disturbance that Robbie Rogers could literally feel.

"It's been Seeded," Terry said to her from the floor.

"With *lots* of Seeds," little Patty had to add.

Robbie couldn't conceal her concern. "And Cindy and Cheryl have gone there?"

Gopal looked away from the hologram. The computer had colored the fourth planet a baleful reddish orange to represent the "pain." He said, "There's a great deal of movement along the gravity lines leading to Delta Pavonis' planets. It could even be Dr. Shea."

Robbie stood up in the light of the hologram. "Don't you think this is important enough to tell Dr. Trenton?"

Patty Brown poked her head out of her project on the floor. She said, "We're sending all this up to Dr. Rhodes. They'll know soon."

"But what about Cindy and Cheryl?" Robbie insisted.

The three children looked at each other and clearly they had no answers. "It could be them," Gopal told her in a low voice; but then he added: "It could also be something else."

And as if, ostrichlike, to hide from the world of scary creatures, little Patty Brown tunneled back into her machine. But soon she was singing to herself, soldering away.

Terry Thorpe, picking up her own tools, reassured Robbie Rogers, whose horror and worry were written from left to right across her face. She said, "Everything will be fine when Mr. Toquero finds out who we are."

Robbie hesitated to ask it, but she managed to ask it nonetheless. "Who *are* you?"

Terry smiled. "That's a secret."

Little Patty Brown, from inside her box, giggled, and Gopal Govinda said nothing.

30

Sitting in a relaxing half-lotus position in the center of a leafy glade, Cindy Trenton meditated while her sister worked on the limping *Lady Nelia Sealing.*

Her Gemini nodule was a teardrop of pearlescent light on her chest, her Moonsuit pink against the lichenesque glade upon which she sat. In her mind, that which was "Cindy" corralled all the past lives she'd led so that the ones which could assist them would float to the surface more efficiently. Meditating helped.

From the left side of her brain, where all the mathematicians and scientists resided with their trainload of *sanskaras*, she kept envisioning conservatory halls, equation-filled blackboards. The echoes of students hurrying off to class filled the background of her recollection. *Paris*, she guessed through a silent voice. *1911. And outside it is a brisk fall day....*

From underneath the rotund *Lady Nelia Sealing*, where a metal plate hung from its double hinges, Cheryl Trenton backed off, grease covering her pink Moonsuit. She held an acetylene torch in her hands, and her Gemini nodule tapped at her alloyed chest with every movement.

"Who are you now?" she asked Cindy. "Can he help us?"

Cheryl wore welding goggles, taken from the *Lady Nelia's* equipment stores, but she did not appear to be worried by their predicament—even though they were twenty light-years from home and the first human beings to set foot on another world beyond the solar system. The *sanskaric* personality she was evoking was that of a life spent as a Scottish engineer from the late nineteenth century who knew everything there was to know about how engines worked and how the chassis which held them bore up. Right now they had a ship to fix, not a world to explore.

"I'm Louis Alverez Forcine," Cindy announced, sleepy-eyed from her trance. "I worked with Dr. Einstein."

She concentrated on the chalk scribblings on the blackboard where Dr. Forcine had just worked out a problem for an advanced physics seminar. Cindy gasped, feeling Dr. Forcine's enthusiasm; the past life was *that* real. She'd seen it before, several times in fact, but it always amazed her how the resurrected *Weltanschauung*, the worldview, of every particular life astounded her. It was all she could do to keep herself from going insane.

But the Gemini nodes would never allow for that. They were extremely simple intelligence-locators, computers of such advanced design that were the "homing" components to the Seeds. The arachnaes, as they discovered several months ago, tapped power from the forces of paranormal space, and the Gemini nodules piloted the Seeds toward clusters of intelligent beings.

However, the nodules—as powerful as they were—never swamped the children who held them. Neither Cindy nor Cheryl had yet found out why.

Cindy concentrated. The equations on the chalkboard in Louis Alverez Forcine's seminar room seemed so familiar to her that they were childishly simple; after all, she *was* Louis Alverez Forcine. But what Cindy was after was Dr. Forcine's particular *pattern* of thinking, his flights of intuition, his intellectual rigor. Those were the most useful traits the twins needed now.

Cindy stood up, leaving the vision, and opened her eyes. The *Lady Nelia Sealing* had Shortjumped down from a high orbit onto a grassy meadow, but the soft ground underneath the stubby vessel had given way, bending the landing gear on one side. They wouldn't be able to Shortjump away unless one of them could fix it.

Cheryl had already gone back to work, sizzling away at the strut brace which had caused all of their problems.

"Is it fixed yet?" Cindy asked.

Sparks from the torch rained down upon the soft grasslike creatures of the glade. They were tiny polyps of enormous families—not plants, quite—but used chloroplasts instead of blood and went absolutely nowhere all their lives. They also retained much moisture, so the sparks did no real damage to the glade. The twins had also discovered that Delta Pavonis Four had very low levels of atmospheric oxygen—only eighteen percent compared to earth's twenty-one. Fires were hard to start. But as the girls had discovered, the presence of so much nitrogen in the air—coupled with the rich biota of the planet—gave the new world a funny, almost giddy smell. They had spent a whole day analyzing the air for deadly spores or microorganisms, but they had found nothing of immediate concern. That didn't rule out harmful insectlike beings or mean-nasty dinosaurs, but none of these were in evidence on the glade. And the air *did* smell wonderful.

Cheryl paused and said, "I'm almost done, but we're going to need heavier tools to do a complete job."

"You mean a grown-up."

Cheryl slid her goggles back into place. "Yes."

Clearly she was having a difficult time hoisting up the torch and jockeying the tank of welding gas around. There were just so many things a nine-year-old girl could do, regardless of all the hearts and minds she had access to.

Cheryl had "called up" the past life she was currently using many times before this. Angus MacFarland, a husky flame-haired Scotsman, had spent most of his adult life building bridges for the Trans-India Railroad in the latter half of the nineteenth century. He had known all about structural stress. He was also hale and hearty, but in *this* incarnation his *atma* was locked for the time being inside the body of a precocious nine-year-old girl.

As Cheryl concentrated, Cindy spoke. She said, "Louis Alverez Forcine was quite close to predicting gravity-wave links between stellar masses. But he saw those links as being straight, not curved, as Riemann did."

Cheryl paused. The torch with its blue lip of flame was heavy in her hand. She said, "We need a computer, like Daddy's Sheriar. If Mommy is traveling along the gravity lines, then we need to find out where she's bound."

"There's the Yancy City mainframe computer," Cindy started.

But Cheryl shook her little head, her brown curls daubed with sweat from her labors. "Mommy came here. Our computer says so. If she isn't here, then we'll move on."

Cindy said nothing. Glancing around their landing zone, she felt secure somehow, knowing that if their mother had passed this way—or was indeed even there at the moment—then it wouldn't be a bad place in which to be marooned.

The meadow, carpeted in the flat-leafed polyps, stretched for several hundred yards to where a grove of willow or palmlike plants dozed quietly beneath the wan light of Delta Pavonis. The branches of the trees resembled cilia, like those of bottom-dwelling creatures of the earth's oceans. The leaves were as transparent as the fabulous Dacca gauzes of Bangladesh, almost the texture of woven air. Their leaves were out and gently swaying in their search for airborne food. There was a grace about them which Cindy liked as she watched them.

Still, in the back of her mind was the presence of their missing mother. The hologram in the *Lady Nelia Sealing* had drawn them to Delta Pavonis' fourth planet because of the intense gravity-wave perturbations that shouldn't have appeared. The planets they'd already visited in the Centauri system and even those in the strange Zeta Tuscanae system had been heavily Seeded—but evenly so, like the earth. Delta Pavonis Four seemed more like a magnet, showing an intensity they hadn't expected.

Using their combined past lives as navigators and pilots, the girls brought the *Lady Nelia* down to the surface of Delta Pavonis Four, onto a single continent that was presently in the grip of a hemisphere-wide cyclone, or rain system. A break in the clouds was their cue, and they Shortjumped to a glade, only to sink a foot and a half into the rain-soaked soil, bending a vital strut. They spent the night listening to the drum-dance of raindrops as their computers and atmospheric monitors checked the outside environment for unpleasant bugs and noxious gases.

What was more important to them, however, was the presence of intense alpha-rhythms coming from the western edge of the large continent upon which they'd landed. The hologram Dr. Shea had amplified had indicated that this "anomaly" was very significant. They had decided to investigate. Once they got their ship fixed. And once it stopped raining.

Cindy watched the clouds. They bulged and contorted in ways alien to her—but then, all clouds were alien to her. She was a Moon Baby. What she knew of clouds came from videos and films from school. Still, these were very unlike earth's clouds, somewhat thicker, more substantial because of the peculiar qualities of the very atmosphere. But the sky was a cerulean blue and the clouds themselves were a bright gray-white. In that respect, they were familiar.

But the clouds had mesmerized her. When she glanced out across the meadow, she noticed something.

The trees were disappearing.

"Cheryl!" she called out.

The palmlike trees ringing the meadow were drawing in their cilia pods, and the trees themselves went rigid with a kind of insensate fear. Then ever so slowly they began withdrawing down into their sturdy, leather-barked trunks.

Then she could feel it.

A slight vibration came up through the flexible alloy of her Moonsuit and the glade began to hum as if singing.

The clouds overhead began to thicken, as if speeded up in the eye of a camera's lens, and the air itself smelled of ocean brine.

"Cheryl!" She turned, shouting. "Something's happening!"

Cheryl shut off the acetylene torch, having finished jury-rigging the strut. "What?" she called out.

Cindy, assisted by the power units of her Moonsuit, bounded in the .9 gravity up to the *Lady Nelia Sealing.*

"Look what's happening to the trees," she said with alarm. "And the grasses. They're singing a little song."

Cheryl sniffed the air. "It's getting cold. Barometric pressure's dropped. A storm's coming in."

Cindy bent down to the grass blades, the tuneful polyps. She ran a Moonglove through them softly.

"They're *moving*, Cheryl," she breathed. "But why?"

Small, barely visible insectlike beings were in the process of scrambling for cover deep within the corridors of their meadow home, and Cindy could feel the vibrations climbing right up through the metal of her Moonsuit.

"I wish Daddy was here," she said aloud, holding onto her Gemini node with her other hand.

"We'd better go," Cheryl announced. The sky was shredding up its herd of buffalo-sized clouds. "That cyclone is coming back around. We're going to get it if we stay."

They ran into the *Lady Nelia Sealing*, pulling the automated gangplank behind them. It began to rain almost as soon as they made it inside.

In the command module above the research bay, the twins quickly brought the vessel up to Shortjump capacity. The lights on the console going from red to yellow to go-ready green.

"That's a fast storm," Cheryl commented, glancing out of the windows of the command center. "Storms don't build up this fast."

"Maybe on this planet they do," Cindy suggested.

The internal humming from the *Lady Nelia* brought both a sense of security as they prepared for the Jump. Still, they waited.

Cheryl pointed to the computer. "Look. The wind's already up to ninety knots."

The vessel, secured to the planet by a sturdy gravity anchor, could not be shaken loose or toppled by any natural storm. But the wind about the glade was uncommonly fierce.

Then the *Lady Nelia Sealing* shook and rose a few inches, and that sensation was accompanied by a sinister rumbling.

The girls traded perplexed looks. "An earthquake?" Cheryl wondered aloud. "An earthquake *too*?"

"What kind of place is this?" Cindy added.

All the lights were now green and the ship was ready.

Cheryl was about to prepare to lift off when her sister grabbed her arm. "Look! *What's that*?" Cindy cried.

A television screen facing the rain-swept glade ran with a curtain of sky-water, but through it they could make out an object moving across the alien meadow. It left a trail of mud and tortured grass behind it as it slogged toward them.

It was a large *Wheel*.

And behind it, clouds were a rolling, purling cascade of furious whites and grays unleashing sudden torrents of water unmercifully across the whole landscape.

Pink lightning suddenly veined the clouds gathered over the meadow, and it caught both girls by surprise. They screamed and sat back as if struck, for an instant becoming true nine-year-old girls.

The Wheel was twenty feet tall with a clear plastic hub in the center. The twin wheel tracks which surrounded the hub were of a uniform brown color—not quite metallic, but not quite organic either. But it was definitely an artifact.

Oblivious of the storm unfolding around it, the thing sloshed across the glade at a uniform speed.

Cheryl quickly prepared for a Shortjump; the *Lady Nelia* had begun to rock in the throes of the earthquake.

"It's not going to hold!" she said. "We have to Jump!"

Cindy protested, pointing to the television monitor. "But that thing out there—"

Just then a massive tremor heaved itself up through the entire meadow and they heard the metal in the landing struts groan. The Shortjump engines hummed loudly.

But the Wheel took a dangerous spin and Cindy held her sister's trigger finger back. They watched the screen with horror.

The object spun around, out of control, and pitched terribly like a wayward top. It slammed into the rain-pelted glade.

At that moment, the *Lady Nelia* seemed to rise, and the planet became a living being surging beneath them. Its roar assaulted them mightily.

"Jump!" Cindy shouted, releasing her sister's arm, and the pink-gloved hand shot for the go-ready console.

They Jumped.

The space around the *Roxanne Vail* seemed almost supernatural with its ghastly profusion of floating, alien bodies.

Emmett Shea stared at them through the thick command windows of the *Roxy* like a child at a circus freak show. The adult part of him did the mathematics for the bizarre drift-vector of the cloud of scaled gray-green bodies as they followed in the wake of the oblong asteroid. The results stunned him, horrified him, as he watched the asteroid mindlessly eclipse the stars behind it, all of an unknown zodiac.

Quickly Emmett routed the equations into his computer so that it could incorporate the data into his hologram of the system. He noted that the ship's own radar registered the presence of thirty-four thousand bodies, give or take a few dozen. Also within the cloud—though quite invisible in the eternal darkness—were indications of other debris. But the most striking characteristic of the aliens themselves was their rough human shape and the fact that they were about the size of nine-year-old girls.

He sat back, frightened and elated, and pondered the glowing lights of the hologram as the *Roxanne Vail* held to its position in normal space. Occasionally one of the bodies would scrape along the *Roxy*'s hull like a dead man clawing his way out of his crypt, but then it would gently tumble out into the stygian wilderness of interplanetary space.

This was a discovery of *vast* proportions—and the guilt that he was alone on a private, indulgent search struck him solidly. As mayor he'd had responsibilities. Someone *else* should be out here, he thought moodily. But who? He erased the thought from his mind. When he got back to Yancy City with the Trenton girls—and perhaps information about Annette Sayles-Trenton herself—he'd have the Moon Men mount an expedition.

He concentrated on the asteroid as represented in the glowing hologram. It seemed to be just your run-of-the-mill asteroid, composed of planetary nickel and iron, wandering, as all asteroids do, out in the middle of nowhere.

Were the aliens part of an attempt to establish a foothold on the orb? Had some cosmic catastrophe beset the effort, washing them off into space centuries ago? He thought of the *Jaguar Skies*; how he and Annette were working as a tight team on the evasive Longjump principle; how Ross Trenton was trying to keep everyone sane and organized—and how Toquero lost so many friends and acquaintances when the *Jaguar Skies*'s experimental Shortjump engines misfired—no one was sure exactly how—and made history by crumpling itself unhappily alongside one of Copernicus' outlying rills. Disasters in space, he knew, were not common—but when they occurred, they tended to be *disasters*.

The asteroid a thousand miles out ahead of the *Roxanne Vail* clearly had seen one such disaster. As he played idly with a small plastic robot toy, he wondered if these beings had been part of an effort to overcome in their own way the influence of the Halo. Had these creatures—like the Moon Men—barely gotten established in space when the Halo came sailing by?

He considered the hologram on the command console. None of the four inner planets had a moon or satellite of any kind. While that was rare, it wasn't impossible either. Upon which planet did these creatures evolve? Had they leapt out into space for the asteroid, the way the House of Toquero—along with a few wise Canadian and Japanese corporations—decided to do toward the moon?

Questions, questions, questions....

Then he thought of the Trenton girls. His own gravity-wave scanner, which could track movement along the nearby interstellar gravity lines, clearly indicated that *someone* had recently Longjumped into the system. But so far, all that his instruments betrayed was the presence of a massive cloud of bodies and debris—and one lone asteroid.

He decided that a closer inspection of the asteroid was worthwhile.

He programmed in a careful Shortjump within three hundred miles of the asteroid. At that range, he would be able to observe the huge rock more closely, and he would still be within sight of the cloud of the frozen alien bodies and other ejecta.

Holding onto his toy robot, he swallowed hard, preparing for the nausea of the Jump.

He Jumped.

The asteroid beyond the window blurred and became larger by two-thirds, as alarm bells clamored for attention once more.

But the *Roxanne Vail* didn't pop into normal space and coexist with any of the aliens drifting nearby. The ship's computers merely hammered home the notion that it had Jumped too close to solid objects for it to feel comfortable. Emmett switched off the alarms.

Here there were *more* aliens, and that surprised him. Over time, the bodies would have carelessly drifted further and further behind the asteroid—and off into the space between the planets.

Not so. And that led him to speculate that perhaps the catastrophe which had sent them off the asteroid was more recent—relatively speaking—in their peculiar history. Perhaps instead of a few million years, it might be whittled down to a few hundred thousand.

Now he was very curious.

Switching on the exterior lights of the *Roxanne Vail*, he examined the aliens up close—recording every moment on videotape for his files in Yancy City when he returned. The Moon Men were going to need this information.

As he had observed before, the aliens were vaguely humanoid—but only marginally so. They had helmet-shaped heads and no necks—as if their bodies were themselves environment suits. Their skulls, as well as their entire bodies, were plated with a greenish onyx chain mail, or perhaps scales. Their faces were expressionless, locked in death's rapture. They had no signs of either ears or noses, but they each possessed a slit for a mouth and two eyes—both of which were tightly closed. Larger plates ran up their spines, and to Emmett these almost resembled solar cells, as if their bodies were designed to draw power from their distant sun.

However, none wore backpacks or breathing tanks, and all were quite, quite dead.

He also noticed another unusual feature each of the aliens possessed: four arms.

They each had one set of arms, about the length of a nine-year-old's arms, but then underneath, pulled close to their rib cages in a rictus of death-pain, was another pair, perhaps used for their work in or on the asteroid.

Their utter novelty fascinated Emmett. They hypnotized him.

He had to have one.

Emmett slipped down into the research bay of the *Roxanne Vail* on the level below. The *Roxy*—as well as all of the other research vessels of the *Clark Savage, Jr.*—was equipped with grappling arms and a special port for receiving or transferring material in space.

He made his Moonsuit space-ready, attaching its environment helmet to its collar, just in case something went wrong.

The robot arm went out silently as Emmett gripped the deft waldo controls in his Moonglove. A beacon of white light dropped its cone of crystal luminescence down around the nearest alien, and Emmett reached for it. He was careful he didn't break it—in case it was so frozen as to be brittle—or bruise it or crush it. He'd need it intact.

He pulled it into the small port and began processing air into the lock. As he did this, he sealed off the lower research level from the upper command center. Germs in space could be just as mean as aliens with four arms, scales, and pointy teeth. The interior atmospheric monitors were also on and able to detect anything the body of the alien might emit, accidentally or otherwise.

A long metal gurney protruded and the alien slid into view.

Emmett's heart thudded loudly and for a long moment he wondered if he'd be able to go near the prone form of the alien. At first he had visions of the thing suddenly bursting to life and flying at him with all of its unearthly strength. But as he watched, it just lay there—a gray-green, withered, leathery *body*.

Not taking his eyes from the alien, he drew over a portable, medical-monitoring unit, unsealing it from its protective plastic.

As he attached leads to its head and feet and pulled over a small X-ray unit, he noted how the second pair of arms was in reality strangely evolved mandibles. The arms were themselves triple-jointed and the smallish mandibles seemed designed—or evolved—to grip bolts or nuts, even turn screws. *Incredible!* he thought. *Evolved for space work....*

He began the X-ray and he also prepared for a more thorough CAT scan of the creature. He turned to the console; he wanted the computer to know everything.

Just then a red light lit up on the board and a small, whining *beep!* sounded out in the confined science bay.

Emmett whirled around just in time to see the alien's fingers twitch.

He slammed back against the console in horror.

Then a foot moved. Slightly. The damn thing moved! *It was coming to life!*

Emmett dived into a compartment at the side of the room and brought out a clapper, falling against the lockers with a loud *clang!* of his Moonsuit.

Jesus! he shouted to himself. *How could it still be alive? That's damn near impossible!*

With both Moongloves gripping the clapper, he poised himself to fire at the creature.

He watched as the scales braiding the alien's body began fleshing out a more healthy green color.

The CAT scanner, or the electrodes, had done something to spark the creature back to life, and Emmett swiftly pounded the on-button *off*, almost smashing it. He backed away even further.

Suddenly the slit on the creature's face parted and the bay filled with a *hiss!* Short and quick, the alien took in enough air to expand its lungs.

Its chest heaved as its heart—or whatever suitable organ—came to life. Its legs jerked and its fingers moved more freely.

Its eyes opened, large and utterly round, staring up at the ceiling and CAT scanner overhead.

"Oh, my God," Emmett muttered, his right arm out with the clapper, shaking.

The creature, through its breathing, uttered a sound and slowly sat up. Its smaller pair of arms went back behind it, bracing it as it rose.

The creature's eyes were black and fathomless, but they searched the room and set upon Emmett.

Emmett froze.

Then the unexpected happened: the creature opened its narrow mouth, let out a terrified shriek, then fell right off the examining table, trailing wires and electrodes.

Ten minutes later, when Emmett found the courage to move, he discovered that he had scared it completely to death.

32

The *Lady Nelia Sealing*, nosing up like a blunt bullet, chose a high orbit above Delta Pavonis Four, popping out of bent-space effortlessly, with the precision of a surgeon's needle with a surgeon's deft touch.

However, on the inside, though fully protected, were two sick little girls.

Curlicues of cyclonic disturbances churned across the many monitoring screens on their console as the *Lady Nelia* righted herself and awaited the next command for either a Shortjump or another Longjump. The Trenton girls, meanwhile, fought back their discomfort, regaining their equilibrium. The ship's console lights were go-ready and green.

In the quiet of the ship—now that the danger had been surmounted—the twins turned their attention to the planet below them.

Delta Pavonis Four, despite its intensely focused alpha-waves on the landmass beneath them, was almost entirely a water world, a sculptured marble of earthly blues and whites. As the *Lady* arched in its safe orbit, the nightside edge of the planet approached, and there it was easier to see the snarls of lightning infecting hundreds of square miles of open sea.

An infrared scan of the single landmass beneath them through the veil of twisted weather revealed oddly weaving pathways, or perhaps rivers, which seemed to snake across the continent. There was nothing like them on earth and the computer's data store could not account for them.

"Earthquakes?" Cindy asked her sister. Even the dozens of scientific lives she'd led in her past could not explain to her what the orange-red lines might have been.

Only the eastern edge of the single continent seemed a safe harbor. Their instruments indicated that the continent was under a great deal of tectonic upheaval, all of which seemed to radiate from the western coast—not too far from where they had originally touched down.

The planet was a mess.

Both girls sat back and watched their monitors gather data. The hologram, showing the planet rotating in its computer simulation, kept revealing the source of the alpha-waves as a single red pustule on the western edge of the continent. However, the clouds had been persistently thick, and they weren't able to see from space what the trouble could possibly be.

Cheryl leaned over a small computer screen, eyebrows knitted in deep thought.

Then she announced: "The storms are caused by steam invection from subsurface lava beneath the oceans."

Cindy, however, was thinking about something else entirely. "But what about that wheel-thing we saw? Somebody made it. And how come we don't see any cities down there?"

"Maybe that's it," Cheryl pointed to the ghostly hologrammatic representation of Delta Pavonis Four turning slowly in miniature before them. The red pustule underneath the cloud cover came into view. "Maybe that's the city," she speculated.

Cindy shook her head. "We'd see the infrared of a city. That's not infrared, what the computer is giving us. It's alpha-waves."

"Then maybe it's Seeded," Cheryl countered, her face expressionless.

Cindy wasn't buying. "Then why would the wheel-thing be heading *toward* a massive Seeding?"

That shut them both up for several minutes.

Cheryl then rewound the videotape upon which they'd first captured sight of the Wheel. If their mother was indeed down upon the planet somewhere, the Wheel might give them a clue. Cheryl replayed the tape.

They watched as the Wheel once again showed itself upon the storm-graced glade, as it canted itself through its awful pirouette in the wind and rain, then finally teetered out of control.

Cindy sat up. "Magnify the focus! *Look!*" A pink-gloved finger went out.

Something, or some*one*, was definitely inside the glass hub of the Wheel, and his shadow could be made out even though the gray sheets of rain dappled both the Wheel itself and the lens-port of the camera which had been atop the *Lady Nelia Sealing*. The tape then filled with the sizzle of static as the vessel left normal space to escape the earthquake.

Both girls then examined the continent as seen through the clouds with radar and infrared scanning.

"But where'd it come from?" Cindy whispered. "People live in cities. There're no cities down there."

Cheryl's brown eyes flashed. "Maybe it's not a people, that guy in the Wheel. And who says they have to live in cities?"

Cindy countered: "It had to come from *somewhere*."

Only the slightly glowing "trails" on the continent indicated any sign of artifice. But it was also possible—as each girl knew—that those red trails might be entirely natural to the physics of the planet, a planet which already, despite its atmospheric congeniality, was very much unlike the earth.

The two girls conferred and decided for another Jump down to the planet, only this time they would locate themselves a mile to the east of their original glade. They wanted to check out the mysterious Wheel, but they also wanted to avoid whatever damage the quake might have done to the terrain itself. Cheryl was all too aware of how badly weakened the one landing strut was; they couldn't afford another mishap.

Standing on the lowered ramp of the *Lady Nelia Sealing*, they could see that they were a bit safer where they had landed—though perhaps not by much.

The research vessel had touched down in a more rugged area, though it, too, was carpeted with the same lime-green polyplike "grass" and here and there along the tops of the smallish hills were plants quite like palm trees. The trees—and this they took to be a good sign—were up out of their protective trunks and waving their cilia about in the stormy air, searching for airborne morsels.

Though the sun was shielded by clouds, a late-afternoon dolor had filled the air; it was almost a kind of cloying homesickness that the girls could feel. Neither child had seen sunsets before, or known of the tug that weather could have on the soul of a human being. Here they could feel it.

But the Gemini nodules kept the voices of exploration alive within them, and the girls wheeled out their four-wheeled, all-terrain craft, or ATC's, similar to those once used for recreation on the earth. Arming themselves with amplified binoculars and nonmagnetic direction finders, they soared down the metal ramp from the science bay of the *Lady Nelia Sealing*, out onto the soaked grasses of the meadow.

Cindy squealed with joy, feeling the wind in her face as her ATC bounced effortlessly along the glade. Cheryl caught up with her, feeling much the same kind of excitement. Riding the insulated halls of Yancy City was never like *this*.

Cindy turned toward a gully to the west. Into her pin-mike at her cheek she said, "I don't like those trees. Let's stay away from them."

"Okay," Cheryl acknowledged, following in her sister's soggy wake.

Another glade met them, and it, too, held a profusion of mirrorlike puddles of fresh rainwater. Only here, as both girls noted, was a kind of purple-colored bush that seemed to have tubes for leaves. Each bush was about as tall as a nine-year-old, and so the two nine-year-olds decided to bypass them as well.

"Look how eroded everything is!" Cheryl observed.

Cindy said nothing as they journeyed along at a modest pace to the west. Thunder grumbled in the herd of gray clouds overhead.

Cindy then said, "I think the Wheel's just over those hills."

"Me, too," Cheryl acknowledged.

They halted at the base of a smoothly carpeted hill that was crowned this time with boulders of peppered white granite.

The Trenton girls dismounted their electric ATC's and scurried up to the top of the hillock, their binoculars ready.

More grumbling came from the sky and Cindy looked up. "Is it going to rain again?"

Cheryl then said, "That sounded like funny thunder to me."

At the top of the hill the noises got louder and both girls dropped suddenly down behind the cover of the exposed rocks.

"*Look at them!*" Cindy gasped.

The glade upon which they had originally touched down was now full of creatures.

Cheryl brought up her binoculars and stared down at the creatures with absolutely uncontrollable joy. The Wheel still lay where it had first fallen, and several dozen humanlike beings were in the process of trying to set it in an upright position. And some of those creatures were on horseback.

"Are those horses?" Cindy whispered excitedly. "They *look* like horses to me."

There were no horses on the moon and both girls were in love with the gentle creatures of the earth's plains.

These, though, were a tad different. They were six-legged, with tails like whips, and were of a uniform gray color.

The people riding them were just as peculiar. They had the bearing of leaders or aristocrats, and waved their four arms about, commanding the lesser mortals on the muddy ground. Their speech was at once guttural and nasal. They had quite long hair, but neither girl was too sure if their hair was long, or if it was just growing directly down their spines. They all wore breechcloths to cover their private parts. The riders on horseback were of different skin colors, some white, some flesh-toned; there were even a couple of crimson-skinned beings among the cavalry. A very unusual crew indeed.

Their faces, though, seemed human and familiar. Two eyes, a mouth, and it also looked as if they had ears—their use of speech predicated as much anyway.

Cheryl lowered her binoculars and sat with her back to the boulder behind which she was hiding.

She looked at her sister. "So where did *they* come from?"

Cindy, still scanning the muddy glade and the heroic effort by the aliens to raise the Wheel, said, "Maybe they live underground. A big cave city like Yancy or Macondo."

Cheryl shook her head. "Too many earthquakes. And horses wouldn't like it."

"Those aren't horses," Cindy told her evenly. She then sat up, the powered stays of her Moonsuit keeping her balanced. "Look, Cheryl! They got it!"

Cheryl jumped up to see that the creatures slogging in the mud of the glade had finally righted the hapless Wheel, even though the being inside of the glass hub didn't appear to share his comrades' enthusiasm.

One horseback alien, with a crimson-purple skin color, pulled from its saddlebags something like a two-way radio. Barks and sneezes came from its mouth as he spoke into it to whoever was at the other end.

"Now, why are they doing *that?*" Cindy then said aloud.

"Doing what?" Cheryl asked.

"That." Cindy pointed carefully.

The creatures on the ground—all of the same caste and color—were presently staring, rather reverentially, off to the cloudy western horizon, where big-bellied clouds seemed eager to unload great gobs of rain.

The creature on the inside of the Wheel, dressed in a bright silky white gown of some kind, appeared to sit back down in a chair, disappearing from view. Then, within seconds, the Wheel's twin tracks began moving, and the strange machine lumbered off on its original course.

The creatures down on the glade watched it go with no sign of emotion, and their horse-bound masters prodded their mounts for the long journey home. The Wheel rose over a distant hill and vanished from view.

The Trenton twins looked at each other wordlessly.

Just at that moment they heard a commotion behind them and they both lurched about.

One of the white-maned creatures, whose skin was a bright crimson, came loping out of nowhere, evidently scouting the hills on its six-legged beast.

It cut them off from their ATC's hidden in the rocks below them.

Cindy screamed, dropping her binoculars. They had no weapons—and the creature on the strange beast very clearly did.

But what the white-maned alien did next startled them.

Its eyes went wide, its mouth opened to an almond shape, and it screamed bloody murder.

And when it screamed, something deep inside its chest cracked or popped, and the alien slid sideways off its saddle, falling to the grass with a sickening *thud*.

Its mount just stared at the girls stupidly with its multiple eyes, not knowing—or caring—what to do next.

The girls jumped up in alarm, but had forgotten that they were suddenly in total view of the army in the meadow fifty yards below them.

All of the creatures saw their pink Moonsuits glittering dully in the gray afternoon light.

And all of the creatures died.

Their eyes went wide and black, their mouths opened, and choked screams rasped from them instantly.

Only the leader with the long white hair and walkie-talkie in its hand remained in the saddle. However, within seconds the paralysis left, and it, too, lurched over into the mud of the glade.

The mounts seemed totally unaffected by the presence of the girls from the earth.

But neither Cindy nor Cheryl was thinking about the ugly mounts with the ratlike tails.

They were thinking about a hundred or so alien beings they'd just frightened to death.

33

"So what do you think about *this*?" Torque Toquero asked theatrically from his captain's chair, indicating the hologrammatic display before them.

The Moon Men, minus Basil Roarke and Dr. Palazetti, were assembled behind the scion of the House of Toquero, having just survived the Longjump into the Delta Pavonis planetary system. Even Lloyd Bramlett, in his ominous black Moonsuit, was present in the shadows.

Trenton leaned over Toquero's shoulder. "And Gopal says that something's there?"

"Right," Toquero muttered as they all watched the hologram spin its planets in a pale greenish light—with the fourth planet revealing a single pustule in villainous red. "But he doesn't know what. The red spot on the planet is just the computer's way of showing us that there is an anomaly."

Someone behind them diplomatically cleared his throat, and Trenton turned around to see the ever-present James Guthrie in his own peculiar Moonsuit.

"If I may say something," he began.

"Go ahead," Trenton advised.

"Since the second Halo bypassed the Centauri system and seems to have come directly from this planetary system, it might be wise to check it out—just to be on the safe side."

"Good thinking, Guthrie," Lloyd Bramlett croaked from his corner. His bitterness was obvious and his rancor at Toquero was almost histrionic.

"That's not what I meant," Guthrie said calmly, his small blue eyes reflecting his control and assurance.

"Well, what *did* you mean?" Bramlett snapped. "Or did you mean anything at all?"

"Okay, Lloyd—" Trenton started, but Guthrie held up his pinstriped, Moongloved hand.

"I meant that it's possible that the Halos might be coming from this star system, and the fourth planet in particular."

"That's just stupid, Guthrie..." Bramlett began with gnashed teeth and clenched fists.

"Actually, it's not," Ticia Rhodes said from her station. She drew a hand through her long mane of gray-blond hair and looked idly up at the men surrounding Toquero. "The odds are pretty good that no intelligent life exists around the stars of the Centauri group, if only because it's a multiple star system. Delta Pavonis has all the makings of a Sol-type system, and the Halos could be coming from there."

"They could be coming from *anywhere*, Dr. Rhodes." Bramlett's dark eyes got darker.

But Ticia wasn't intimidated. She responded: "That's true. But they don't have all the time in the world to Seed the galaxy. At sublight-speeds, the Halos have to know where they're going."

Trenton, following this, recalled the damage to both the city and the people of Los Angeles. He said, "The makers of the Halos *know* that there is life on the earth this time. That's why they sent the second one."

James Guthrie then added: "And perhaps there's life on the fourth planet of this system." Here he pointed to the hologram. "Perhaps there are people who could use our help."

"This isn't a mission of mercy, Guthrie," Bramlett interjected. "The directives of Operation Hopscotch distinctly say that we're to stop the invasion—or Halo, as it turned out to be—and investigate the possible source of the invasion fleet, *then* return and report our findings."

Trenton turned slowly, his huge frame moving with authority in his golden Moonsuit. All eyes were upon him. He stared at the dethroned Pentagon liaison officer.

"*And* we're to investigate the disappearance of Dr. Shea and a couple of other people I hold dear, including a certain physicist, whom we still need, by the way."

Trenton stepped down from the captain's chair and seemed prepared to crumple up Bramlett's Moonsuit like a beer can. He had in mind just then the occasion he'd gone sailing with Annette on the waters of Lake Tahoe, where later that night his two little babies had been conceived. He wasn't about to let this *bureaucrat* hinder his efforts at unifying his family.

Guthrie held out his arm gently, halting Dr. Trenton. "Sir," he said calmly, "don't let him goad you."

Trenton pondered the little aide with a touch of wry wonder. Bramlett *had* been goading him and he hadn't quite recognized it. *Good for you, Guthrie*, he said to himself.

"Moreover," Ticia Rhodes said, now leaning back in her chair, her hands behind her head. "My guess is that the equipment Emmett has is the same as the little girls have in the *Lady Nelia Sealing*, and both ships are going to come to this system sooner or later." She glanced up at the eye-patched Toquero. "At least, it's better than Longjumping one place and another looking for them. I'm for Hopscotching into the system further and seeing what we can see."

"I like that," Toquero said, looking at them all. "The voice of authority." He then leveled a challenging glare at Lloyd Bramlett. He said, "And besides that, it's my ship and I happen to like our missing Moon Men. Mr. Digeno!"

From down in the Pit: "Yes, sir."

"Prepare for Longjump. One Jump to the fourth planet and two Shortjumps into orbit at the elliptic."

"Yes, sir."

"Gentlemen," Toquero said, leaning back, feeling a bit more in control. "Man your Dramamine."

The first Longjump into the Delta Pavonis system sent ripples of nausea through not only the passengers of the *Clark Savage, Jr.* but also the ship itself.

Toquero, green to the gills, shouted orders into his console microphone, directing commands to the men and women responsible for red and yellow lights blossoming upon his board. The ship continued to vibrate and groan even as it leapt into normal space.

Trenton had taken Bramlett's chair when Bramlett elected to join his own security crew on the lower deck. Guthrie, sitting beside Trenton, was a noiseless ghost, hardly present at all. He made Trenton's skin crawl.

But as soon as Trenton's stomach settled and he could focus his eyes clearly, he felt an inward rush of panic as he heard crewmen running about, doing what they could to keep the dreadnought from falling apart.

"Are we going to make it, or what?" he asked Toquero.

The one-eyed, bearded rogue, turned aside. "Damned if I know, Ross. Just between you and me, I'd rather go home and let someone else do this."

"There's no one but us," James Guthrie said, completely unscathed.

"You aren't a Moon Man, Guthrie," Toquero said, returning to his board and its urgent parade of lights.

"Yes, sir," Guthrie said, humbling himself.

Just then a tiny voice came from all of their consoles. Gopal Govinda was on the air.

"Could I direct your attention to the midlatitudes of Delta Pavonis Four on the main screen overhead?"

Even the crew in the Pit hadn't seen the new images now being thrown on the large screens above them—so busy had they been with the dangerous Longjumping.

"My God," Ticia Rhodes said, standing up from her chair.

Trenton himself felt his Stively-built heart slam in his chest as the screen came alive with the blue-white water world beneath them. The *Clark Savage, Jr.* in high orbit turned all of its cameras and monitors planetward.

"Christ," Trenton muttered. "Look at the size of that thing!"

A single continent lay beneath them, but at the western edge, just slightly out to sea, was a very, very large object thrusting way beyond the tops of the clouds of the storm now shredding itself over land.

It was an arch.

Gold-tinted and glittering brightly in the light of Delta Pavonis, the *thing* arched up into the high stratosphere and sank back down into the waters of the ocean.

"It's a *Halo*," Ross Trenton said for them all.

In all its surreal glory, like a discarded brass ring, a Halo had lodged itself just offshore and the clouds of the latest hurricane were just leaving the vicinity, exposing it clearly for their cameras.

Toquero was on his feet. "Mr. Digeno! Ms. Jolly! Are you down there?"

Penny Jolly, their aerial photographic expert, a bright woman of twenty-four, shouted back up: "I'm here, sir!"

"I want a high resolution scan on that object," Toquero ordered even as the reds and yellows of all sorts of emergencies screamed at him from his board. He ignored them. He said to Trenton, as their alarmed eyes met, "Man, those bastards meant business on this planet!"

As Trenton's heart hammered away, a sheen of sweat broke out over his body. *This* wasn't what they had expected at all.

The Halo had crashed right into Delta Pavonis Four. It was a *major* planetary disaster.

In the conference room, the Moon Men gathered once the captain had attended to the various crises the Longjump had invested them with. Glenn Thorpe came up from his laboratory, and James Guthrie, minus his aluminum clipboard, attended as well. Lloyd Bramlett had been refused admission.

Toquero, his head in his hands at the far end of the table where the hologram danced in the middle, groaned, "We're showing some structural stress now. We can't take too much more of this."

Trenton took the initiative. He said, "Torque, this is a very significant discovery. It's bound to tell us something about the makers of the Halos."

"*If* we get back to tell about it."

"We'll get back," Trenton said calmly.

"My daddy's going to kill me," one-eyed Toquero said, sitting back heavily.

Glenn Thorpe and Ticia Rhodes had been going over the computer printouts and considering the various television monitors on the walls. Thorpe turned to Trenton. "Ross, I don't get it. There aren't *any* cities down there. Why the hell'd they send a Halo *there*?"

Ticia Rhodes looked at the hologram. "We're not picking up anything in orbit, no satellites, no debris of any kind. If there's intelligent life down there, it's not much above the rock-throwing stage."

Toquero turned a weary eye to the television screen as the giant Halo rose through the clouds of the planet beneath them. "Well, they sure got a rock thrown at *them*. Look at the size of that sonofabitch."

Trenton speculated: "Maybe it wiped out all of the cities. Look at the way the western coastline is fractured."

"Volcanoes and earthquakes," Ticia said, nodding. "We're going to need a geologist."

Toquero, thinking she referred to his incompetence for not bringing along one of his father's mining experts, looked over at the woman. "Well, *excuse me* for not anticipating something like this!"

"She meant," Trenton jumped in quickly, "that it'd be a nice idea next time to have a Moon Man who's a geologist. This has nothing to do with you."

"God, I hope not," Toquero said flatly. "This is starting to get out of hand."

"We're twenty light-years from the earth, Mr. Toquero," James Guthrie piped in.

"What does *that* mean?" Toquero said angrily.

"It means," Trenton said, "that we're going to have to pull together and stay together. It's a long swim home if we don't."

Glenn Thorpe, who loved problems of a technical kind, as opposed to those of an emotional kind that Ross liked, pointed to the hologram. "Listen, what *I* want to know is why the devil the Halo didn't break up when it crashed. *Look* what it did to the nearby continent. Tidal waves and earthquakes have destroyed much of that end of the landmass."

Ticia said, "*I* want to know what it's made out of. That's the key."

Trenton gazed at the enlarged planet on the rotating hologram; he then pondered the television image that Ms. Jolly in the Pit was magnifying for them.

He said, "It looks as if the Halo sustained a great deal of damage when it did hit."

On the screen—when they could get a glimpse of it through the clouds—the Halo resembled a gigantic metallic arch, sunken halfway down into the ocean depths, its whole lower part crumpled and distorted beneath the waves. It appeared to Trenton as if there might have been a very strong superstructure within it, but that its outer shell had sustained considerable damage. However, as their instruments measured it for them, the Halo's arch was over eighteen miles high, just skimming the outer edges of Delta Pavonis Four's atmosphere.

Ticia leaned back and put her hands on her lap, folded. She began thinking out loud. "There are some things we can assume. The first is that this Halo did *not* strike the planet at twenty percent the speed of light. We'd have seen a big spotlight in our southern skies if it had."

Trenton nodded, following her train of thought. He said, "So it must have drifted, edge on. But then…that would mean that the Halo had been traveling for a *very* long time to reach this system." His heart almost sank out of sight in the blood-horizon of his chest. It would take them millennia to find his little girls, to say nothing of Emmett or his wife. This was just another planet which had been attacked by the makers of the Halo.

Glenn Thorpe turned in his pale-green Moonsuit to face Trenton. "Then how long has it been here? That's another crucial question."

Trenton realized what had to follow next. "The only way we're going to know is by going down there and looking for ourselves. Samples of plant life and an examination of soil erosion would tell us."

Toquero thought they were still talking about their lack of a geologist. "All right. We go down and dig a bunch of holes and take the dirt back to Macondo. I know just the guy you'll need—"

"We might not even need to do that, Torque," Trenton told him. "Aerial scans should provide us with all the data to determine how long vulcanism has been going on. *I'd* like to see the reason why this place was singled out."

"*I* want to see the alpha-globes," Glenn Thorpe then said.

Everyone looked at him as the thin inventor pointed a pale-green Moonglove at the hologram. "Remember that Gopal's program indicates alpha-waves. It looks to me as if they're so strong here because the Halo dropped its whole load."

Trenton didn't relish the idea of walking into another Hooverville trap—even though they now had several of Glenn's new beta-guns on hand. What were a few beta-guns compared to a few million loose Seeds?

But the evidence was clear: the Halo, now a massive arch in the sea, had spilled much of its cargo where the two pillars of the arch had grounded themselves. Both of those locations would no doubt be tremendous sources of alpha-rhythms.

"We're only going to be able to get so close, if that's what you want to do," Thorpe stated.

Trenton was thinking—strangely—of Emmett just then. This was a phenomenon Emmett would be attracted to, another toy, something to ponder and amuse himself with.

The door to the conference room wheezed open just then and Lisa Palazetti came in and stood before them; however, her words were directed more at Trenton.

"There's something going on in the nursery," she began tersely. In her white physician's tunic she seemed like an angel of mercy, but the aura of Emmett's disappearance was all too obvious around her.

"What?" Toquero looked up, panicked. "What *now?*"

She turned to Trenton and walked over carefully. "It's little Patty Brown. She and Gopal have had an argument and Robbie sent word to me what it was about."

"What *was* it about?" Trenton asked.

Lisa took in a deep breath—part out of anxiety and part, clearly, out of restrained hope. "Patty Brown's been working on something to do with gravity lines. She seems to think that Cindy and Cheryl are here, on the planet, but Gopal isn't so sure."

The words were like a stone tossed into a mirror. Trenton sat up, not wanting to believe the words he was hearing.

"Is Robbie sure?" he asked almost too quickly, flooded with sudden hope. "I don't trust those kids. I don't know what's transformed them."

Lisa's brown eyes were filled with constant thoughts of Emmett and his whereabouts, and this Trenton could plainly see.

"The children are worried about a lot of things," the doctor said. "But Patty's the one working on the gravity lines and she thinks your girls have traveled here recently."

"Like how recently?"

"Robbie didn't catch that, but the children know. Their computers are telling them all sorts of things. We may have to get into the nursery to find out." Obviously she didn't like saying that, but it was an option the adults knew they were going to have to exercise one of these days. Robbie Rogers would be able to do only so much on her own before the children suspected.

Glenn Thorpe looked at Ticia Rhodes, then considered Torque Toquero. He said, "Well, it looks like we're going down whether we want to or not."

Trenton sat back, feeling the *Clark Savage, Jr.* thrum underneath him as it plied the waves of space. *It's like the fall of Constantinople*, he thought suddenly. *Everything happening at once and all I can do is go along with it.*

It was a feeling—despite its prospects—he didn't like.

As the *Retta Kenn* warmed herself for a Shortjump down to the planet, Trenton prepared himself as Toquero punched in the necessary sequences for the computer. Glenn Thorpe sat beside him in the command center.

Trenton said, "I don't like the idea of your coming along, Torque."

Torque, totally out of humor, said, "It's my ship. And it's my ass if anything goes wrong. Mr. Digeno has the helm, and my men are watching Bramlett and *his* men. Guthrie too."

"Guthrie's harmless," Trenton added.

"I don't trust anybody from the earth," Toquero said as he punched buttons.

Glenn smiled thinly. "You really have it in for Bramlett, don't you?"

No one had known of Toquero's altercation with the Pentagon liaison officer back in Yancy City. Bramlett hadn't reported it; Toquero hadn't mentioned it.

"It's in my blood," Toquero said. "My family's off the earth now. We probably will be moving away entirely. At least now that we've got the Longjump. And *we* intend to get as far away from Ralph Scanlon and his band of idiots as possible. That includes Lloyd Bramlett."

The lights on the console came up go-ready green.

"When we get back," Thorpe said, strapping himself in, "maybe we can feed Bramlett to Roarke."

"*You guys keep me out of this!*" shouted Basil Roarke from his station in the science bay below.

Trenton also strapped himself in. He said, "Right now, we're Moon Men. Forget about Bramlett. We've got work to do."

Remembering both the *Jaguar Skies* and the fall of Constantinople, the former President of the Moon braced himself.

They Jumped.

The late-afternoon thunderstorm had abated and the air was filled with a clean, oddly perfumed smell which Trenton couldn't quite place. *Alien* came to mind. Even blindfolded, he'd know that he was *somewhere else*.

They let air from the outside into the lower science bay, first to examine it, then to acclimatize themselves to it as they finished their systems checks. Roarke rushed around attaching his guns to his belt and preparing his Moonsuit for the foray. Glenn Thorpe busied himself with his alpha-wave detectors.

Trenton stood at the open door where the ramp had been extended down into the soft, wet grasses of the peninsula upon which the *Retta Kenn* had landed.

He turned to Glenn, who was pondering a small detector.

"What does it say?"

Glenn shrugged with amazement. "I'm picking up alpha-waves all right, but they're…different."

"Different how?"

Thorpe looked out over the plain and the violently building clouds to the southwest. "They're not meant for us, it seems. We shouldn't be affected by the globes dumped by the Halo."

Toquero came down from the command center above. "So it means that it's meant for the people who *are* here. Swell." He was attaching a powerful clapper pistol to his utility belt at the waist of his purple Moonsuit.

"You mean there are *people* here?" Basil Roarke's little beads for eyes flashed with childlike excitement. "Great. Let's go find them!"

He pushed his way through his companions and thundered loudly down the metal ramp, armed to the teeth, ready for anything.

Roarke pounced upon the planet, landing with a splash in the sodden grass.

"Moon Guys!" he shouted gleefully. "And I'm first on another planet!"

Toquero came down after him and walked on around him. "Except for Hummer on Mars and Shurtliff on Mercury, I guess you're the first, Basil. Out of the way."

Roarke in his shining brown Moonsuit raced out onto the peninsula's grasses as a distant thunder drummed out over the ocean.

Then Roarke froze and stared back at the other three Moon Men by the *Retta Kenn*.

"What's the matter, Roarke?" Glenn Thorpe said from the ramp where he was still pondering his alpha-wave device.

"Hey." Roarke pointed behind the *Retta Kenn* where the small ship's television monitors hadn't seen. "What are *those* things?"

"What things?" Trenton said with a sudden rush of anxiety which his handmade heart tried to quash.

Roarke ran back toward them, passing underneath the ship and on out the other side, leaving muddy footprints from his Moonsuit as he went.

"*These* things!" he shouted with moronic joy.

Trenton quickly followed him as Toquero and Thorpe came around the ship.

Their unpredictable wrangler was running through a playground of a kind.

It was a playground littered with the hulks, lichen-draped and rusting, of several dozen Wheels.

34

Within the space of two hours, Emmett Shea had converted the science bay of the *Roxanne Vail* into something resembling a morgue. Wrapped in the gray-black of plastic body bags over in a corner were the bodies of fifteen aliens he'd managed to snare with the waldo grappling arms and draw in. Fifteen *dead* aliens.

Like a beaten monarch, a forlorn Lear, he sat in his chair winding the spring of a toy robot, thinking. He had done everything he could to figure out just why the creatures awoke, then suddenly died on him—but he couldn't understand it at all. They just simply died.

The revival pattern had been identical in all cases, and all of the aliens seemed structurally the same. Some peculiar biological mechanism responded to even the slightest electrical stimulation within the creatures' bodies. They seemed to be hibernating; on the other hand, they might have gone into a kind of systemic shock when they were expunged from the asteroid in the distance. That they could come alive at all in the first place was a paramount mystery to him.

It was definitely the worst case of xenophobia he'd ever seen. These creatures seemed to be absolutely paralyzed with fear of human beings—or *aliens*, to them.

He set the toy robot down on the console and watched it walk along stupidly and fall off in the modest gravity of the science bay. It bounced once and came to rest next to a motionless body bag.

He needed the Moon Men for this one, he realized.

He wasn't a biologist or a psychologist. Plainly, the aliens could endure years—centuries? millennia?—in outer space, but something in their minds, perhaps culturally induced, compelled them to self-destruct.

Which, he thought, was a pity. To live for so long, albeit in a dormant state, in outer space, only to reawaken in time to die officially. It was the crudest irony he could imagine.

Emmett picked up another toy—a pink-and-red plastic airplane for a two-year-old child. Idly he spun its stubby propeller and thought about *culture*.

Xenophobia implies a strong sense of one's own culture. The aliens who'd boarded the asteroid *had* to have some kind of culture; they couldn't have leapt off their home planet without it in the first place. Unless, of course, they had evolved on or in the asteroid originally.

But he didn't think that too likely. These beings were highly evolved and highly adapted. No doubt they came from either the third or fourth planet of this system.

Yet what were they doing out here?

He knew he was going to have to investigate the asteroid closer, as well as make a protracted sojourn down to the third and fourth planets.

But first things first. He had an intriguing problem on his hands and he wanted to solve it—particularly since it seemed that he had caused the deaths of several alien beings whom he had no reason to harm in the first place.

He needed Ross. Ross would know what to do.

Not that a human would have any greater access to the psychology of an alien mind. But Ross, as a transpersonal psychologist, knew how to use the Sheriar in such a fashion as to find the deeper reasons why a person does what he or she does in this life.

Emmett sat up suddenly.

"Now, why didn't *I* think of that?" he said aloud, setting the little toy plane on the console.

As part of the original *Jaguar Skies* charter years ago, Ross Trenton had the huge vessel and the five smaller research craft stocked with Sheriars. Ross kept the larger Sheriar models for his office in Yancy City and for the big Toquero ship itself.

But in a storage locker on each Jumpship was a shoe-box-size Sheriar. Ross knew—as did everyone on the moon—that one day the Toqueros would lead colonies to Mars and beyond for permanent settlement. Ross wanted each ship to have a Sheriar, because he knew that he would be accompanying them.

Emmett, however, wasn't interested in probing the aliens for past lives to help them with their problems of loneliness and space solitude. The Sheriar could be used as a modest, impressionistic telepathic link, if the alpha-rhythms could be programmed just right.

Besides, he didn't even know if an alien would *have* a past life. Perhaps this was their first time around.

But he wanted to know what mechanism was aroused in their waking minds which frightened them to death.

The Sheriar might provide an answer.

The sixteenth alien lies upon the metal table, this time facing away from him. Emmett drifts into the gentle rhythms of the Sheriar as one lead, attached behind his ear, goes down into the computer and on into a lead which is attached to the alien's skull. He breathes deeply and waits....

Blackness.

Not the blackness of death harking back to a past life and time, but the blackness of the Great Unknowing.

There is pleasure here. The Sheriar whispers *fana*, and Emmett's fading consciousness knows that it is the Mind-empty region of Nirvana or pure Void.

But this is not the Sheriar evoking this pleasant state. It is slowly, ever so slowly coming from the waking alien.

The alien, he suddenly realizes, has a name. *X'yn*. He knows this because he is now the alien—and in this vast blackness X'yn is happy.

X'yn is happy because to be afloat in the dark of the Great Unknowing is the promised outcome of his life on Vradha. *Vradha*....

The asteroid is called Vradha in X'yn's language, which comes easily to Emmett through the present-consciousness level of the Sheriar. He gasps at the *alienness*. X'yn is coming alive, but doesn't know that he has an *alien* eavesdropper.

To Emmett come the images, *sanskara*like, of the rugged asteroid-world, and for an instant Emmett feels what it's like to be born in space and to live in space.

The images come through the Sheriar and the computer sorts them, filters them, makes them palatable for the mind of a human. Much of it Emmett doesn't understand and those images haze and fade away. Other images become more concrete, though, and these Emmett's own mind holds onto.

He reels in his semiconscious state as an image—very stark and very bold—comes to him.

X'yn, he discovers, is of a race that long ago left its home planet, the fourth planet of this system, and took the asteroid Vradha as its new home.

The reason for this was to build Halos.

Through the Sheriar, Emmett gets a clear image of the asteroid—or better yet, an image of the *interior* of the asteroid. Through the alien's awakening memory, he sees Halos being constructed. They are called *xotls*. And the aliens are specifically evolved as workers to serve the construction purposes of the leadership faction that has demanded that *xotls* be built.

The image he gets next is of the whole interior of the asteroid, Vradha. It is like a blast furnace, alive with yellows and golds and reds as matter is converted at one end of the asteroid and reworked and formed into usable alloys at the other. Vradha is a factory, whose interior is eighty miles wide, room enough for one Halo every ten years, in human terms. It is almost too much for Emmett to believe.

As X'yn remembers it—and as Emmett is seeing it for the first time—the process of building a divine *xotl* is almost magical. Matter appears out of nowhere, coming from the opposite end of the asteroid, translated into existence from planetary matter gleaned from debris orbiting Delta Pavonis.

Emmett recalls the wide eccentric orbit of the asteroid. Vradha, he suddenly realizes, goes *looking* for material to build *xotls*.

As the alien approaches the equivalent of REM sleep on the table, the Sheriar—still on its lowest setting—filters in more images to Emmett's startled mind.

The *xotls* are built of impossible alloys, their superstructure a skeletal toroid of rigid hexagons within which millions of Seeds are ferried. Emmett watches through the alien's memory, hazy as it is. X'yn is merely a drone, stationed at a control platform within the interior walls of Vradha itself, and ferry-ships lure behind them enormous clouds of Seeds bundled together by massive magnetic tractor beams. Other workers, adapted for the free-fall of space, work to place the alpha-globes within the hexagons. There seem to be ten thousand alien beings at work on the lone *xotl* in X'yn's memory. Not quite like insects, but not quite like malicious warriors, they each approach their duties with nothing less than a genetically derived zeal.

And the *xotls* get built. One right after another.

Emmett cannot get a time frame for the whole process, but it seems as if X'yn has seen the construction of several *xotls*.

He watches through the alien's memory as the Halos are then thrown into powerful spins—the acceleration process itself taking months to get the *xotls* up to proper speeds of rotation.

Then Emmett gets an image of Vradha turning in its position in orbit, then being aimed at a particular star in the heavens.

And out it goes without celebration, so fast that X'yn never remembers seeing one of them depart. One moment the *xotls* are spinning magnificently, then the next moment they are simply *gone*. Bound for another star, never to return.

But Emmett's mind reflexively asks: *Why?* Why are the Halos built in the first place? What's it all about?

But the alien, X'yn, is slowly awakening, and other, more relevant recollections rise to the surface of his unfolding memories.

Emmett sees the last Halo X'yn worked on. It is almost ready to go, having begun its spin-for-launch only a few sleep periods ago. Its hum can be felt throughout Vradha's many hidden halls and nesting chambers.

X'yn is present with others of his caste at a prelaunch ceremony. The images are tinged with anxiety and dread. X'yn is troubled. *The ceremonies which accompany the launch of a *xotl* are normally staid occasions of little pomp but much reverence for the appeasement the Halos are designed. *Out there*, somewhere beyond their system, is the Great Unknowing, which must be acknowledged in some ineffable manner. Each Halo is an act toward such appeasement, each ceremony a reminder of their duties in life.

However, X'yn finds himself caught in an insurrection. Workers elsewhere in the circular halls of Vradha are revolting for reasons which X'yn has never been informed. X'yn is a devotee, a worker, not a revolutionary soldier.

Screams and shouts fill the Sheriar images as X'yn recalls being hustled aboard a special ferry along with several hundred others.

Emmett hears through the X'yn that Pollinators, their special caste of breeders, are being held hostage to the demands of the insurrectionists.

X'yn, in his awakening state, feels a bolt of remembered panic. His mate, his Pollinator, is in the area under siege.

Then Emmett receives a shock. Through X'yn's eyes he sees it and feels it: the Pollinators are universally male and X'yn is *female*.

Moreover, all Pollinators are to perish at the time of their pollinating—and X'yn, though having chosen a male to pollinate her eggs, has not yet become fertile. And her Pollinator is being held captive.

The golden toroid of the *xotl* spins and spins inside Vradha as the escaping ferry drifts out. But something is wrong! Spears of green laser light slice out at them and the ferry is knifed in half, spilling the workers out into the space around the newest *xotl*.

X'yn watches with panic, shutting her biosystem down, preparing for emergency space-sleep, as she tumbles helplessly toward the toroid and its dangerously spinning mass.

Then suddenly the vast ejection doors part at the other end of the asteroid. The revolutionists have taken control of Vradha's machinery and have begun sending the *xotl* out before its time!

But the Halo merely drifts out beyond the doors with its feeble spin.

However, in the starfield beyond, before her body's defenses shut down entirely, X'yn sees that the *xotl* is accidentally aimed at their birth-world. Emmett catches the name of Delta Pavonis Four: *Cirran*. The *xotl* has no programmable direction controls, and is drifting, drifting, drifting....

It is drifting toward Cirran.

X'yn wants to cry out to the heartless Great Unknowing, but knows it is futile. She is being pulled along in the massive gravity-wake of the toroid, but not enough to be dragged along with it all the way to Cirran. Just enough to pass outside of the asteroid, along with several hundred, perhaps thousands, of her fellow workers.

She weeps for her birth-world. The home world. The *xotl* will destroy it for certain. But there is nothing she can do about it. Nothing.

This is fate. She forgets *xotls*. She forgets the Great Unknowing. She forgets her Pollinator. She simply forgets.

And closes up. Shuts down. And drifts.

The Sheriar whispers into Emmett's semiconscious mind the time, relative to human understanding, when all of this happened. The revolution occurred more than two hundred years ago.

X'yn had been in space, hibernating, for all that time.

Then quite suddenly, just when Emmett thinks that X'yn has fallen back into the arms of its instinctive space-sleep, the alien blinks its thick-lensed eyes and awakens upon the table, still connected to the Sheriar.

And just as it does, Emmett gets a partial answer to one of his unspoken questions.

In the back of X'yn's mind is the knowledge that long, long ago in their past, the Cirrans were told by the Great Unknowing that they were to be the *only* race of beings in their stretch of the galactic wilderness to explore space. Not the beings surrounding a dim yellow star twenty light-years away who called themselves *human*. Nor any other race within forty light-years. All star systems must be Seeded. Quieted. Put to rest. And only when this is done will the Great Unknowing let the Cirrans themselves go into the galactic reaches.

This is their Covenant.

And *this* is what's on the alien's mind as it fleshes itself out on the table as it comes awake.

Emmett, still sleepy and caught up in the amazing world which has just been revealed to him, is too stunned to move.

The alien sits up, using its tool-designed lower arms, and slowly swings its spindly legs around. It sees Emmett coming fully awake in his chair, surrounded by strange multicolored objects fashioned of durable polymers called *toys*.

X'yn comes awake and sees Emmett in his sturdy Moonsuit with the Sheriar lead in its jack behind his ear.

And opens its mouth.

And yawns—sort of.

The one thing it does *not* do, however, is scream and fall over.

35

On the hilltop with its clutch of white granite boulders, Cindy started crying.

Even as she held her Gemini nodule in her Moongloved hand, the power it contained wasn't enough to allay the fear that it had been their presence which had killed all of the alien beings on the swampy glade. Her sensitivity, coupled with the stress of the realization of what they had done, overrode the nodule's ability to maintain contact with her inner resources of former lives.

Her sister, normally the staid one among them, was also stunned by the phenomenon, as she watched the gray clouds overhead obscure the sun even more, like the closing curtain of a particularly unhappy play.

"They saw us and died," Cindy said, looking down at the quiet meadow, sniffling.

Only the lazy and stupid mounts had survived, and they were currently involved with snipping at the grasslike turf of the meadow with their bizarre teeth. They had no idea whatsoever what had just transpired.

Cheryl stood up in her pink Moonsuit, holding tight to her Gemini node, thinking. After a moment of thought, she managed to ask, "But why did they do that? We're not scary."

"They were afraid," her sister reported.

Cheryl turned to the west, where the storm seemed to be building most of its new strength. The ocean wasn't too far away—if their map had been correct—and a wide set of tracks headed off in that direction over the mossy hills.

"The Wheel," she said, lost in thought.

"What?" Cindy asked.

"There was a man inside the wheel-thing," Cheryl mused.

"He didn't see us."

"Maybe."

Cindy fingered her Gemini stone and a glimmer of resolve and courage appeared back in her brown eyes. She breathed deeply. Then: "Let's leave here. This has nothing to do with Mommy. I don't like it here, anyway." She stood up.

Cheryl, still pondering the westerly building clouds, said, "Maybe they know about Mommy." She turned to her sister. "Uncle Emmett's hologram said she passed this way. There's something out there, and maybe these people know about it."

Small patters of rain made the terrain a lonely place. The sky seemed to be lowering itself slowly to the land, as if weighted with more than it could carry. Without the thousands of past lives in each Gemini node to fill them with bravado and curiosity, the girls knew they would be lost now. *Very* lost.

Cheryl, resurrecting a biologist out of her dim past, said suddenly, "Maybe they have some kind of organ that breaks down and makes them panic and die like that."

"Maybe," Cindy admitted.

"If that's true," Cheryl continued excitedly, "then it was just an accident. Anything could have done it."

"Okay."

Still, Cindy didn't feel convinced, and Cheryl knew it.

"And that man in the wheel-thing," Cheryl began.

"He's not a man," Cindy reminded her.

"If we're very careful, maybe we can follow the Wheel and see where it leads. He might know about Mom."

A philosopher in Cindy's remote past was also pondering the *whys* and *wherefores*, and none of it made any sense—other than the prospect that the more they learned about their situation, the closer they would get to understanding what happened to their mother.

Cheryl began striding downhill toward her waiting ATC, wary of the six-legged mount which watched her with a bunch of frightening eyes. Cindy quickly followed.

The Wheel had several minutes of a head start on them, and they were going to have to hustle to catch up with it, particularly if they were going to reach it before the storm struck. And neither girl liked the size of the storm coming.

In the dark of the nursery it would normally have been storytime, had the *Clark Savage, Jr.* still been in the earth or Lunar orbit and had the nursery been full of the children of miners and engineers on their way to their jobs.

However, storytime was, for Robbie Rogers, naptime, and as the children tiptoed around her toward the main ventilation grid, she snored happily away. Little Patty Brown, who was staying behind on this occasion, closed the door so they wouldn't wake their baby-sitter.

She said in a hushed whisper: "Mr. Toquero will be real mad, Gopal."

Gopal Govinda's Moonsuit was presently coiled with several dozen yards of optical fiber, and beside him Terry Thorpe—her bulging red hair tied back in a frizzy ponytail—stood with an equipment pack on her back. Gopal was busy unscrewing the ventilator grid.

He said, "It's *our* ship."

Little Patty said, "You should tell him that. Mr. Bramlett needs to know too."

In the semidarkness of the nursery, their Gemini nodules almost glowed.

"Mr. Toquero doesn't like Mr. Bramlett," Gopal said softly. "It's not our fight. We've got the ship to worry about."

"And Cindy and Cheryl," Terry Thorpe said.

The grid came off gently and Gopal set it down. Terry took off her pack and handed it to him. Gopal placed it inside and crawled in after it. Terry prepared to follow.

Little Patty bent over. "Gopal, Mr. Digeno will be watching our movements."

Gopal stuck his head out, his black hair shining. "Mr. Digeno is currently visiting Midshipman Evelyn Tanita. I've rerouted the vent-sensors so we can move freely. The *Savage* should never have left lunar orbit when it did. It still isn't ready."

"Maybe if you tell Mr. Toquero who we are—" Little Patty Brown started.

"He would never believe us. We have to prove it first."

Gopal disappeared from sight. Terry Thorpe gave little Patty a hug, then followed Gopal down into the depths of the orbiting battleship.

Patty Brown was quick to replace the grid.

The trail the Wheel made across the death-glade was slowly filling with mud which the strange grasses had absorbed from earlier storms. The ATC's silently hissed along at a cautious speed, since the girls didn't want to surprise the alien being inside of the Wheel's hub and have him die as well. They needed answers now.

Cindy had recovered. A smile was dwelling on her face, and her eyes were open wide with joy as they bounced along in their four-wheeled vehicles.

Into her pin-mike at her cheek, she said to her sister, "I can smell the ocean! Can you smell it?"

Cheryl nodded. "I think the Wheel is headed for the ocean. It's that way." She indicated a point low on the horizon that seemed to be busy manufacturing clouds.

They were on a thick peninsula, which was a low-lying accumulation of hills that seemed to have been eroded heavily at some time in the distant past. There were no jagged rocks, and what subsurface rock that was exposed was all rounded and curved.

There was, however, a growing population of trees and bushes. The grasses also appeared greener, but in some spots flourished as a bright yellow color. The Wheel made a convenient path through all of it, and clearly was avoiding any of the larger obstacles in its way.

The rain came down at them in sprinkles as the bigger storm threatened them. Thunder cleared its throat in the distance.

But the girls were not frightened, merely curious. The Wheel was far out ahead of them, lost over the low hills.

"Do you feel anything?" Cheryl suddenly asked.

Cindy was to the left of the single track, Cheryl to the right. The track was now frothy with the mud of recent passage.

"Yes," Cindy acknowledged.

A calm sensation had surrounded the girls. It was almost pleasant and invigorating, and it appeared to increase the more they headed directly to the west.

Cindy looked at her sister. "The computer showed an anomaly off-shore. Maybe—"

"The clouds were too thick," Cheryl reminded her.

"The Wheel's headed there, I bet," Cindy affirmed.

Cheryl agreed.

Then suddenly she leveled a Moonglove at an object which lay dead center of the Wheel's track, dropped in the mud.

"What's that?" she cried out.

Cheryl stopped her ATC in the gentle rain and reached down to pick it up.

It was a spheroid, the color of turquoise, more blue than green, about the size of a softball.

"Wow," Cheryl said. "Look how pretty it is!"

Cindy drove her ATC into the track itself and stopped. "What is it?"

Cheryl turned it over, examining it, then tossed it to her sister.

"It's a rock, I think. Tap it. It's real hard," Cheryl instructed.

Cindy tapped it with a Moongloved finger and it indeed seemed as hard as a newly polished gemstone.

Cheryl was looking down at the Wheel's trail. She then said, "The wheel-thing didn't crush it."

Cindy looked up. "Were there any others? I don't remember seeing any."

Cheryl shrugged within her pink Moonsuit.

Cindy dropped the rock beside the track into the sodden grass. "I'll leave this here. We'll get it on the way back."

"Okay," Cheryl said, pulling her ATC around.

A few minutes later, going slower and looking for them, they found another polished rock. Only this stone was of a rich purple color. It was very shiny and the girls liked it even better than the first one.

Cheryl decided to keep this one rather than leave it, and Cindy let her.

They raced out, looking for more.

As they followed the Wheel's track, the feelings of unusual calm descended about them with increasing power. It was as if someone were humming a lullaby through the clouds and rainy landscape. It didn't seem like an alien world at all, but rather like a dream world where only pleasant things could happen.

"Alpha-waves," Cheryl finally said into her pin-mike as they approached a hill, following the soggy trail.

"I was thinking that," Cindy announced. Then suddenly she pointed. "There! Another one!"

"No," Cheryl corrected her. "Two of them!"

They raced up to where the stones lay in the mud and jumped off their ATC's.

One of the objects was a jet black, unflawed. The other a pretty fire-engine red.

"They're beautiful," Cindy cooed.

The girls were back on their ATC's and pursuing the Wheel. Cindy kept the black stone, and Cheryl had added the crimson stone to the pouch with the purple one.

They suddenly came into sight of the Wheel. The Wheel had come out onto a level stretch of the peninsula and was heading due west, toward the storm clouds, at a speed no greater than ten miles an hour.

At first the girls were reluctant to approach the Wheel directly, remembering their effect upon the group of aliens a mile or so behind them. However, the subtle alpha-waves gave them strength by diminishing their fears, and so they plunged down into the small valley after the Wheel.

And as they went, they found five more stones, each one a startling color, with one being a calico mix of browns, whites, and shiny blacks.

Finally they caught up with the huge, lumbering Wheel that squished its way over the meadow grasses.

They kept just behind it, but were still unable to see the alien being within it.

This close to the Wheel, they could see for the first time how the Wheel moved. It was really two tracks with a space of about ten inches between them. It seemed to be made of a very soft metal or perhaps even a chitinous exoskeleton material. They couldn't hear any kind of engine running it; but then, it could have been electric, for all they knew, just like their ATC's.

The Wheel absolutely mesmerized them.

And just as they were watching it, they noticed that between the two tracks at the rear of the Wheel was a hole about three feet from the surface.

From the hole a small round object plopped suddenly onto the muddy trail. The object was round and pearl white.

Cheryl screamed, stopping her ATC. So did Cindy.

They both began unloading their treasures and throwing them to the ground.

"*They're eggs!*" Cheryl shouted.

"*Yuk!*" Cindy added.

The Wheel disappeared up over a rise, leaving another egg in its wake.

As the powerful gyros hidden in the hip units of Basil Roarke's Moonsuit groaned to help him maintain balance, the space engineer walked along the narrow ledge of a capsized Wheel like a glossy-skinned god striding the rings of Saturn.

Trenton—not as foolish or as daring—stood underneath the alien artifact, watching Roarke monkey around on top.

Roarke said, with more jubilance than scientific curiosity, "What *are* these things, anyway?"

Toquero, his one unpatched eye staring intently, said, "Whatever it is, it's decomposing. It looks like it's been here for years. Look at all this gunk."

The "gunk," more specifically, seemed like a kind of Spanish moss, though much of it was rust-colored and adhering only in spots.

With a careful touch of his golden Moonglove, Trenton noticed how soft the crystal hub of the Wheel had become because of the moss-like substance.

"The Wheel looks like a living thing," he said to his Moon Men. "Or at least was. This stuff isn't rusting away. It's being eaten."

The plain of the peninsula was littered with the peculiar Wheels, and each one was in its own decisive state of decomposition, with some appearing to be newer than others. Then there were a few Wheels which had disintegrated to such a condition as to be nothing more than a large jumble of peninsula grasses and moss.

The wind whipped around them as they explored the Wheels, with the roar of the ocean's surf quite nearby. The restless fog which seemed to occupy most of the distant ocean's surface had begun to dissipate, perhaps tormented by the winds high above in the building storm clouds.

Roarke, teetering on the wheel-track of his dead Wheel, looked out over the ocean. "You guys hear that sound?"

Glenn Thorpe, who was betraying no interest in the plain of Wheels, had been staring off toward the ocean. He nodded. "It's the Halo. It's closer than we thought. That sound's probably the wind blowing through it or around it."

Thorpe began setting up his alpha-wave detector, aiming a parabolic receiving dish to the woolly gray fog to the west of them.

Trenton stood beside him. "It's alpha-rhythms, all right. They're coming from the Halo out there."

Thorpe adjusted a few dials, fine-tuning his receiver. "I just don't get why we're not affected."

Trenton squinted into the distance, feeling—perhaps because of the alpha-waves—a pleasant nostalgia for Annette's love of sailing, and one afternoon in particular off the coast of Catalina Island.

He snapped out of it.

"Maybe we're too far away," he told the engineer. "We're going to have to be very careful, Glenn." He would never forget his walk toward the "angel" in the center of Northridge.

From behind him, Roarke shouted out, "Hey, Ross! You gotta see this, man. There's something *in* here!"

The wrangler had found a newer Wheel several yards away, and was up on its tilted wheel-track peering intently through the crystal of the hub.

Trenton jogged over, followed by Toquero, who kept his right hand on his clapper.

"I think it's a chair," Roarke announced, happy as a child on Christmas morning.

The crystal itself was already turning milky white in its decay, but something clearly was lodged inside.

"I can't tell," Trenton admitted.

The sea wind sighed across the grasses of the plain as Trenton bent down underneath the newer Wheel. A rend or a large wound in the glass had, over time, appeared.

"Might be a door here," Trenton observed.

Roarke scampered noisily down along the chitinous surface of the wheel-track and jumped to the ground. Toquero stood back, letting the eager wrangler through.

"It *is* a door," Roarke announced, heading right for it as if he'd had an invitation.

"Be careful," Trenton cautioned, allowing him in.

Roarke got down on his knees and with his amplified arms pulled the door open further. It was like a plastic window or blister in the crystal hub's wall, and it came apart silently. He wormed his way inside.

Toquero, on the opposite side, asked, "What do you see, Roarke?"

The interior of the hub might have been eight feet or so in diameter—maybe larger. As Roarke stood up inside, he indeed found a chair. He also found an old, fragile cloth of some kind. He picked it up from the floor and handed it out to Trenton.

"Take a gander at this," he said. "Somebody was wearing it once."

Toquero rushed around as Ross held up the strange garment.

"He's right," Torque admitted, pointing.

Trenton held it out at arm's length. It appeared to be a drape for a being about four and a half feet high—and one with at least two sets of arms.

Toquero laughed suddenly, finding it funny. "*Four* arms? You've got to be kidding. I thought four-armed aliens went out with comic books."

Trenton knew better. "Comic books are still with us, and so, evidently, are four-armed aliens."

Roarke came out of the hub on his hands and knees, mud-splattered like any six-year-old kid. In his hands, however, were two rounded objects, both a dull basalt gray.

"Found these underneath the chair," Roarke said. "Rocks, I guess. They seem kinda light for rocks, though."

He handed one to Trenton and one to Toquero.

"I don't think they're rocks," Trenton suddenly realized. The assists of his Moonglove whined ever so slightly and the "rock" cracked. Quickly his other hand came underneath it and caught the debris as the object fell apart in his right hand.

Into his left hand appeared a curled-up, raisin-skinned alien.

"God!" Roarke choked, backing off, making an unpleasant face.

Trenton held it up so Toquero could see. "There's your four-armed, two-legged alien, Torque. We got us a couple of eggs here."

Trenton shook his golden Moonglove to rid itself of the debris of the pulverized egg and took the other, surviving one from Toquero, who was only too happy to give it up.

As Trenton slipped both the dead fetus and the other egg into a plastic bag for safekeeping, Toquero pondered the Wheels themselves.

He said, "But what were they doing inside of the Wheels? How come the eggs weren't full of little Wheels?"

Trenton said, "That's what our team will have to find out one of these days."

Then he looked at Toquero directly.

The young rogue was staring up into the sky behind the former Lunar President with his mouth wide open.

Then he heard Glenn Thorpe cry out: "Holy Mother of God! Look at the size of that thing!"

Trenton whirled around and faced west.

His Stively-built heart almost shut down, for far out to sea the clouds were parting swiftly and there it was: the Halo.

Even Roarke was taken aback.

The four Moon Men stood alone on the peninsula as the wind howled through the exposed superstructure of the ruined Halo—which was now an enormous artificial arch reaching high into the sky, so high that its apex stretched up beyond the storm clouds, out of sight.

"My God," Toquero breathed. "I don't believe it."

"Believe it," Glenn Thorpe said, now rushing to set up his automatic cameras. He stared at Trenton. "Ross, look at these readings. The alpha-waves."

Trenton held up Thorpe's instrument and aimed it at the "island" where the first leg of the arch rose up into the sky.

"That island out there is nothing but a big pile of Seeds!" Thorpe said excitedly. "Just take a look at the readings!"

Roarke stood like a dumbfounded gibbon, especially one who'd just been tapped between the eyes with a ball peen hammer.

The sounds the wind made as it ghosted through the torn alloy of the outer hull of the Halo's arch came at them now like the moanings of a church organ in a vast cathedral.

Torque whipped out his binoculars, as did Trenton. They pondered the misty, distant island of Seeds.

Toquero said, "All of the Seeds just spilled out upon impact."

"Not all of them," Trenton was quick to observe. "Just those at that end of the Halo. That island's about nine hundred feet high. Just look at it!"

Thorpe, who wasn't using binoculars, pointed further out beyond the island of Seeds and the spectacularly rising golden leg of the arch.

"Ross, way out there. Look. The rest of the Halo's just under the water. Barely."

Trenton turned his glasses out to sea. The waves there, violent and gray-green, seemed to hustle themselves into a froth above the makings of a coral reef: tiny underwater creatures were accreting themselves on the metal hulk of the crumpled Halo.

Trenton announced: "We're going to need an oceanographer *and* a geologist for this one."

Toquero lowered his binoculars. "What's *that* supposed to mean?"

Trenton said, "It means that this is too big for just our bunch of Moon Men. We've got to consult your father on this, that's all."

The moaning goblin-cries the Halo made spooked around them, borne on the very wind itself. Trenton looked over at their wrangler in his shining brown Moonsuit.

"Roarke?"

Basil Roarke—tiny drops of ocean mist in the bristles of his Marine haircut—turned to Trenton. "That thing gives me the creeps, Ross."

They all could feel it. The arch resembled the leg of a Norse god standing high above them, ankle-deep in the sea.

Suddenly Glenn Thorpe shouted out, "There's the other end of it! See?" Thorpe leveled a glossy arm to the west, where the clouds parted thirty or more miles away. Barely, *just* barely, they could make out the other leg of the arch as it thrust down into the sea and no doubt into a massive mountain of Seeds, girded by the braces and crumpled skeleton of the Halo's superstructure.

"It must have made one *hell* of a noise when it landed," Toquero muttered.

"And a big splash," Glenn pointed out. "My guess is that it destroyed this part of the continent. It's a wonder it didn't bust up completely when it struck."

Trenton himself was thoroughly stunned—and impressed. It had been one thing to have seen it on their screens on board the *Clark Savage, Jr.*, and it was something entirely different to be faced with it directly in all its surreal glory. And, like Roarke, he felt eerie in its presence.

And that set off little alarm bells in Trenton's mind.

"Roarke?" he called out.

The engineer turned to Trenton, looking pale and deflated somehow. He said, "Remember that preacher? Remember what he did to us back in L.A.?"

Toquero said, "He wasn't a preacher. He was a fanatic. The Seed made him crazy."

Roarke scowled at Toquero, bunching up his Moongloved fists. He faced Trenton. "I mean what he did to us on the forklifts!"

"I remember," Trenton said. "I remember the whole thing."

"Well, *I* was closer," the wrangler said, thumping his chest for emphasis. He then gestured to the island of Seeds and the banshee choir of wind sounds from the broken hull of the giant arch. "I'm feeling it now. The same thing. It's coming from out there!"

Trenton lifted up the plastic sample bag containing the wrinkled fetus of the alien and the whole, though thoroughly dead, egg. He then recalled being strapped to the forklift and slowly sent toward the light of the angel, feeling the transformation of spirit within him.

Roarke was thinking the same thing. The engineer looked at the plain of Wheels. He said, "I don't like it here. I *hate* it! There were pregnant women inside those Wheels and they were sent to be killed. *Poof!* And they're gone!"

Trenton hadn't looked at it quite like that.

37

Emmett wasn't as afraid of the alien before him as he thought he might have been.

Perhaps it was due to the soft rhythms of the alpha-waves the Sheriar had sent through him, or perhaps it had been the careful expedition into the waking alien's mind and the images absorbed from X'yn's consciousness.

But when the alien propped herself upright on the table and the Sheriar shut down, Emmett instinctively felt as if he had nothing to fear.

The corneas of her eyes were large and brown, with a thick, filmy substance that was now coming alive as she turned to him. Her plated skin seemed to ripple as her veins and organs pumped life back into her, and her many-fingered hands flexed slowly in the light of the science bay.

The Sheriar remained connected even though the initial program had shut itself off. Now the computer was filtering beta-waves and the images which both of their minds were conjuring. It was through the computer that Emmett could feel a sense of the creature's awe at being rescued by another space-going being. The sensation was wordless, coming to Emmett instead as a series of inchoate feelings, followed by an occasional nonassociational image or two.

X'yn tried speaking in her own language. A sound filled with a flutelike quality resonated throughout the science bay, at the same time a tiny diamondlike bead between the alien's widely set eyes began flashing to the syllabic chitterings from deep within her throat. Instantly Emmett got an image of the manner in which her species communicated in space without the use of direct-beam radio: dots and dashes of light, in Morse-code fashion. The blinking bead followed X'yn's talk, down to the syllable.

But she wasn't speaking English.

Over the Sheriar came the meaning of her vocalizations.

—*You are of the Great Unknowing. Come to rescue X'yn.*

His only understanding of the Great Unknowing had come through the dream-image of her waking consciousness. He shook his head and said out loud: "I don't think so."

X'yn blinked as if the sound grated on her ears, and for a moment Emmett wondered if she had understood, if the Sheriar was working as a two-way communicator.

He was also wondering if or when she would scream and fall over like her comrades.

But the alien's eyes began to scan the small bay compartment, pausing on the scattering of particolored toys, then eventually spotting the body bags on the floor in the corner.

"Why did they perish?" Emmett suddenly asked, holding in his mind the vivid image of each one of her friends waking, then falling over dead. He hoped that the Sheriar would be able to transfer it.

—You are of the Great Unknowing.

She had repeated it. And Emmett still didn't understand to what she was referring.

The Sheriar instantly picked up on an image.

The Great Unknowing was something mysterious to the alien, part of the blackness of space; intelligent, unreachable, undefinable. But out there, nonetheless. And clearly her recognition of Emmett in his Moonsuit, and of the fact that she was inside a space ferry of some kind, allowed her to make a connection. Emmett and the Great Unknowing were part of the same thing. They had to be.

—The voice of the Great Unknowing no longer speaks to us. It spoke to them when they saw you.

"I didn't mean to kill them," he told her quickly.

For a long moment X'yn was very quiet.

—You reminded them of what is to be feared. Your...machine...got me beyond the shock threshold.

All the while, as her thoughts and images filtered through the Sheriar, she spoke aloud with her guttural clicks and flutelike melodies. It gave her speech depth.

At first Emmett thought that the alien was referring to a xenophobic reaction in her fellow creatures which caused them to die of fright. But there was more to it than that, for the alien seemed so indifferent.

An image—lifted from a sudden memory in the alien—came to him over the Sheriar quite involuntarily. Once, many, many cycles ago, the *xotl* factory—the asteroid, Vradha—had constructed a Halo to be sent toward a specific star system. Emmett caught an impression of a contorted constellation and one bright star, and knew instantly that even though the star was not the earth's sun, it *was* the sun of a system in which the Cirrans had suspected an intelligent, potentially spacefaring species dwelled. Was it Beta Hydri? Zeta Tuscanae? He couldn't tell, for the constellations as seen from Delta Pavonis Four were completely different.

However, he instantly recalled the "charter" imposed upon the Cirrans, which was the reason why Vradha had been built. It had been their job to quiet down this region. So the new Halo was constructed and sent out, and the Cirrans seemed content that the Great Unknowing had been appeased in this way.

—*It is our act of petitioning.*

X'yn had gingerly climbed down from the steel table and was trying to stand on her own. Her extra set of arms attached themselves easily and efficiently to the edges of the table. She appeared to adjust quickly.

"I don't understand," Emmett told her out loud, letting his ignorance flow over the Sheriar wires.

—*The Great Unknowing no longer speaks to us. It is what we must do to bring it back. We believe there are—*

Here the alien paused for the right verbal context before proceeding.

—*People such as yourselves who keep the Great Unknowing from speaking to us.*

Immediately Emmett thought back to the moment when he and Ross had brainstormed the idea of Operation Cakewalk. No one had known exactly why the invasion fleet was taking so long to reach the earth. The Halo of '33 had done its work so well that civilization had been crippled within *hours* of the Seeding.

This was why. There was no invasion fleet—only a fleet of Halos. And it had all been done so that the Cirrans could get back into favor with their missing God.

Then Emmett received some bad news. X'yn's fellow workers *had* died of a xenophobic reaction, but there was more to it than that. They had also died of guilt. For if an alien being—a *human* being—had made it into their system, then the Cirrans had failed in their duties. They weren't afraid of human beings; they were just afraid of what their presence *meant* in their quest for the favor of their Great Unknowing.

Emmett sat back. It was almost like the Tower of Babel story. They were building *xotls* instead of ziggurats to become closer to God.

Just how evolved are *these people, anyway?* he wondered.

Suddenly the *Roxanne Vail* heaved as if caught up in the swell of a mighty wave.

X'yn fell to the floor as several of Emmett's loose toys followed her. Emmett grabbed the edges of his chair and held on as alarms sounded throughout the small vessel.

Swiftly he unplugged from the Sheriar and bolted for the ladder. X'yn, still not used to standing just yet on her own, floundered where she lay.

In the command center, a pale yellow light filled all of the television screens on the console, as well as the narrow windows in the side of the ship itself.

Vradha.

"Oh, my God!" Emmett shouted out.

The asteroid wasn't dead after all and had somehow turned in their direction. It was presently coming for them.

The *Roxanne Vail* swelled once more in the pull of some kind of tractor beam and Emmett fought for control of the ship.

Out ahead of them, a hundred miles away, the asteroid loomed at them, its front end glowing an angry orange-yellow, an eye of fire. The eye of a very unhappy deity.

38

Trenton stood knee-deep in the blithely churning waters of a blue tidal pool as Torque Toquero, in his purple Moonsuit, wrestled adroitly with an inflatable raft. Trenton cradled the small electric outboard motor in his right arm, leaving his left one free for balance. All the while, the figure of the Brobdingnagian pillar of the ruined Halo loomed over them in the distance, its spectral choir of sea winds haunting them with each shift of the approaching storm.

Trenton craned around as Glenn Thorpe splashed down into the shallow water with his pack of alpha-wave equipment.

Thorpe knew of the power of the Seeds all too well, and didn't much like what the Moon Men were about to do. He was extremely uneasy. "This might not be a bright idea, Ross," he stated. "Those alpha-waves are very powerful, even if they aren't gauged to our brain rhythms."

Trenton nodded. "But if Gopal is right, we might find out something about Emmett and those kids of mine."

Thorpe said nothing as he handed his equipment over to Toquero, who carefully nestled it into the bottom of the raft. The alpha-rhythms troubled him as well.

Only a short time ago the *Clark Savage, Jr.* had tight-beamed a message from Ticia Rhodes reporting that Gopal and the other children had discovered evidence of a nearby Shortjump—nearby, that is, to the vicinity of the downed Halo. They weren't sure yet if it had been either the *Roxanne Vail* or the *Lady Nelia Sealing* or some other phenomenon, but Gopal was of the opinion that it might be worth looking into. Thorpe thought it dangerous, and Trenton didn't trust Gopal. But Toquero said, "What the hell. Let's do it anyway," so they did.

All except Roarke.

Roarke simply went back to exploring the Wheels, absolutely resolved not to go anywhere near the giant arch in the ocean. He just shook his thick head and walked back through the playground of dead Wheels. Since they weren't going to be out at sea that long, Trenton let the volatile engineer go, knowing full well that *someday* he was going to harness that boy into the Sheriar and find out what made him tick.

Glenn gestured over to Trenton. "Ross, take a look at these tidal pools. They're similar to the waters back at Gordon's Cove."

Toquero, bobbing now in the stern of the rubberized raft, noticed it as well. "There's no life here," he commented. "You'd expect crabs or something. Fish, at least."

Trenton stared out at the massive arch and its mountain of discarded Seeds. "We're in the middle of a Hooverville as big as can be. Everything but plant life has vanished."

"And those Wheels," Thorpe pointed out, climbing into the raft.

Trenton steered the raft into position before jumping in himself. "Maybe Roarke will find out why those Wheels stayed and the people within them disappeared."

Trenton rolled into the raft, which dipped with his weight. Toquero, though, turned the outboard in the opposite direction to counterbalance Trenton's mass, and they were off.

Basil Roarke didn't need a Sheriar to tell him what he was feeling, or why.

Using the amplified motors of his hips, knees, and ankles, he began running like a schoolboy happy to be out of class for the day. And *class* was the Halo. Or more specifically, the alpha-waves coming from the isle of Seeds.

And the farther he got from the shore, the better he felt. His heart soared; his feet were like antelope's hooves. He bounded and skipped through the playground of Wheels.

There were so many of them!

They reminded him of the old junkyards back in Philadelphia that his mother insisted he avoid and in which he persistently found himself. He was in paradise.

Until Ross called out over the radio jack in his ear.

"Basil!" Trenton's voice boomed. In the background, the cough and churl of ocean waves could be perceived. "Are you there?" Trenton called.

Roarke halted, breathing deeply in the sea air. "Present and accounted for."

"What's your location?"

"About five hundred yards from the *Retta Kenn*. Don't worry about me. I'm not going anywhere."

Trenton paused for a moment, then said, "The sea's rougher than we thought. We're going to see if we can circle the island and take some readings, and determine if there's anything to Gopal's discovery."

So go, he said to himself. They were grown-ups, and grown-ups always would rather work than play.

"We'll be out here for at least half an hour. Stay close to the ship," Trenton ordered. "Understand?"

"Sure."

"And stay out of trouble."

"Right."

But overhead was a building gray herd of wonderful cumulus clouds and the wind filled his heart with exuberance. He was alone! All alone!

And within minutes of running as far from the *Retta Kenn* as he could get, he found a nice new Wheel stuck in a gully to explore.

Mr. Leonard Digeno sat at the helm with the ever-present James Guthrie by his side. Digeno didn't like him there, but Captain Toquero said that the government observer had a free run of the ship. Overhead, the various screens of the Pit gave them a wide assortment of views of the planet as the *Clark Savage, Jr.* hung in high orbit.

Digeno, broad, square, and powerful, hove around, ignoring Guthrie's pin-striped presence. Instead, he spoke to Ticia Rhodes, who was in the midst of having her dinner on the bridge.

"So you think those things are highways?" he asked.

Ticia, mouth full of chicken-salad sandwich, muffled: "Yep." She swallowed as James Guthrie stood erect, staring at the screen, now magnified, of an exposed area of the large continent beneath them.

Digeno, Italian as they come, sat back. "They look like fettuccine to me."

The infrared scanners heightened in glowing crimson the twisting "highways" that crisscrossed the continent in a seemingly random pattern.

Dr. Rhodes nodded. "They're clearly artificial."

James Guthrie noted something on his aluminum clipboard. He said, "But there are no cities."

The wild-haired physicist again nodded. "The Halo easily destroyed what might have existed down there by way of cities or towns or hives or anthills, or whatever it was they lived in. Yet some of those highways are newer than the others. That's what I don't understand."

Indeed, some of them were glowing ever so slightly, as if having seen recent use. The infrared scanners clearly indicated this.

Guthrie turned to her. "And Mr. Toquero set the *Retta Kenn* quite close to one, it seems. Was that wise?"

Digeno folded his thick hands. "They're about thirty miles from the nearest…highway. If Captain Toquero needs us, he'll let us know. Lieutenant MacReadie is ready with his Marines, just in case."

James Guthrie felt horribly uneasy. All of the authority of Operation Hopscotch was presently down on the surface of Delta Pavonis Four, and that didn't make any sense to him.

But then, the Moon Men were an odd lot, he recalled to himself. They were remarkably independent of one another—the so-called "lunar-solitude" effect—yet they functioned well as a team when they had to.

"Perhaps we should inform Mr. Bramlett and his security personnel that—"

But Mr. Digeno cut Guthrie off. "Captain Toquero said that Lloyd Bramlett is to mind his own business." Mr. Digeno's dark countenance frowned in Guthrie's direction and Guthrie took the hint.

Ticia Rhodes, meanwhile, had gone over another infrared scan on the terrain, specifically, where the *Retta Kenn* currently resided—even though an approaching storm veiled the visual monitors.

She suddenly leaned closer. A sudden gust of chatter rose up from the Pit as the other officers saw it as well.

"Mr. Digeno," she said, sandwich in hand, "I think we just found our first city."

Mr. Digeno cranked forward. "*That's* a city? It looks like a blood clot to me."

The screen showed a glowing continent interwoven with the crimson trails, one of which ended at a location that burned red on the screen above them.

"I don't get it," Ticia suddenly said as the Pit crew began rerouting their monitors toward it. "It seems to be moving."

James Guthrie's pencil scratched on the pad of his aluminum clipboard.

Toquero's black hair rippled like the fur on a seal in the chill ocean air. He kept one hand on the tiller and with the other grasped the side as best he could.

"It's getting rougher," he said to the other two Moon Men. "I don't like it."

Trenton nodded toward the island and the rising leg of the mighty arch. "It's the combined effect of the alpha-waves."

Toquero's seriousness was infectious. Glenn looked away from his receiver. "The sound's enough to scare anybody for miles around."

A ghost of a vast shipwreck seemed to haunt the skies above the white-capped waves. It was a sound reminiscent of grief, of heartbreak, of the loneliness they all had felt as Moon Men at one time or another. It called to them plaintively in whistles and moans. It was everything *alien* to Trenton as he gazed helplessly upon it. It drew them, called out to them, as it might have to his own baby girls, as it might have to Emmett.

Glenn Thorpe shot him.

He almost fell out of the boat as he grappled for balance. Salt tears had swelled beneath his eyes as the alpha-rhythms sang to him of his loss.

"Sorry, Ross," Glenn said, lowering his beta-gun. "I thought you had your generator on."

Toquero was laughing now. He pointed to the minuscule device that Thorpe had attached to all of their Moonsuits, which Trenton had neglected to engage.

"The alpha-waves almost got to you," Toquero said. "You're slipping."

Thorpe, being closest, leaned over and switched the small beta-wave generator on and Trenton could feel the alpha-rhythms in his brain recede.

"Sorry," he mumbled, retaining an image of Annette in his mind.

"Nothing to be sorry about," Glenn commented. "I was feeling it too."

Trenton faced his men. "What we're going to need next time is a *full* expedition. This is just too big for us."

To that they all agreed.

But nothing was too big for Basil Roarke.

The Wheel he'd found lodged in a hidden gully did not speak of the civilization which might have designed and built it, but instead spoke of its novelty.

The Wheel, in its westward journey, had apparently slipped into the rills of an eroding gully and trapped itself. It glistened silvery and new as Roarke approached it with a caution the whole planet deserved.

The wheel-track that led up to it was littered here and there with an occasional egg. Roarke ignored them. He was more interested in the Wheel itself. It would give him something to do until the other Moon Men got back from their fishing trip.

This particular Wheel, unlike the others of the peninsula, had not fallen into disrepair. No lichen or mosses tugged it earthward. It obviously had not been stuck in its narrow gully for long.

A very gentle rain began misting around him as Roarke clambered down into the gully to get a better view of it underneath.

Through the glass he could make out the usual chair, or "throne," stuck in the bottom of the crystal hub, and another odd-looking garment lay there as well. *Gone toward Mother Angelica*, he thought to himself. The island of Seeds was as good as the "angel" of any Hooverville back on the earth.

And Mother Angelica back at St. Botolph's in Connecticut was just as good as any "angel." He shivered as he recalled her—and the many thrashings her rod had given him.

He'd rather face a Seed than Mother Angelica again.

He found the circular door underneath the hub and struggled with it. It came open with a *snap!* Its hinges had been made somewhat brittle by time.

He squirmed inside to look around.

Outside it had begun to rain a bit harder, and it was just as good an excuse to be inside as standing out in the gully or on the peninsula.

The Wheel had wrenched itself in the gully in an upright position, so the chair within was in its normal place. Normal, that is, for humans. Roarke swept off the garment and sat down.

It was a tight squeeze, but the chair was made of a greenish substance that could have been plastic or some other resilient material, and he slipped in comfortably.

The storm thrummed a cascade of rain about the hull of the crystal hub, and a drumming of thunder shook the Wheel.

Perhaps it wasn't a bright idea, after all, he started thinking. Maybe...

Then the Wheel shook again with thunder and he suddenly broke out in a sweat.

Then glancing down at the porthole on the floor where he had made his entry, he noticed something happening which he didn't like.

The opening was puckering shut.

He jumped out of the chair and dived for it just as it pulled itself tight like the sphincter of a great crystalline anus.

"*Whoa!*" he shouted, pounding his powered Moongloves down at it. Thunder crashed above him everywhere.

Then the Wheel lurched and he tumbled over.

It wasn't thunder he'd been hearing. The Wheel was coming alive and the wheel-tracks had somehow, in some inexplicable fashion, restarted themselves. The Wheel moved.

"*Hey!*" he shouted, jumping up, throwing himself against the crystal of the hub.

The Wheel came alive and its track dug into the dirt of the gully and flung itself up out of its nesting place.

It rose up onto the grassy plain of the peninsula, and turned around, facing the east. *Now* the thunder came down at him, along with several forks of pink lightning.

"*Ross!*" he screamed into his pin-mike at his cheek. "It's got me! It's got me! *Help!*"

The Wheel took off and there was nothing the engineer could do about it.

39

To the west of the nine-year-old girls, the wheel they'd been following disappeared over a lichen-carpeted rise in the peninsula. Storm clouds parted like curtains, it seemed, to let it through, then closed up. The rain began in earnest.

The twins had dumped their eggs back onto the Wheel's mud-puddled track and were both exasperated.

"But there *was* someone inside it," Cindy protested as pearl-drops of rain battered her invincible Moonsuit. "Maybe it was laying the eggs."

Cheryl, who was filtering in further ruminations of the men and women she had once been, said, "Maybe they use the Wheels to help them lay eggs."

"But how?"

"I don't know," Cheryl confessed as she fingered the necklace of her Gemini nodule. She then gripped the handlebars of her ATC and twisted them for acceleration. "Let's go and find out," she then said.

"Okay," her sister chimed.

Speckled gobs of mud and shorn tubers of the strange "grass" flipped up behind their all-terrain craft as the girls sought to parallel their Wheel's path. The rainstorm gave no indication that it was increasing; it was just a lot of fuss and bluster. Voices deep within each girl suggested to them that this might be the normal weather pattern for this part of the continent, so the girls ignored the storm's threat even though any kind of weather was new to them.

The pink-suited twins swept up over the gentle rise in the green-loamed plain and down into the cup of a small, flatiron valley. Thunder grumbled distantly.

"Oh!" Cindy breathed into her pin-mike, pointing. "Oh, my! Look at all of them!"

Like fallen tombstones, several dozen Wheels lay scattered about the green valley, most of which had long since decayed into almost unrecognizable forms. But they *were* Wheels.

The storm beat its death-drums above them.

The Wheel, though, continued its mindless journey, threading its way in and around the dead machines—or whatever they were. The twins had no idea.

The girls stopped momentarily to gaze upon the lifeless hulks as the rain dappled the landscape.

"The sea air erodes them," Cheryl speculated.

"Or something," Cindy said. "They've been here a long time, it looks like."

Their particular Wheel had gone on out ahead, dropping a colorful egg just about every fifty yards, some of which lost themselves entirely in the mud of the track itself.

Then the Wheel sought to mount another rise, but began to slow down as they watched.

"It's dying," Cheryl said. "It's going to stop over there."

The Wheel had located a spot halfway up a gentle slope where some boulders and a stretch of lavender grass had made themselves at home.

The girls dug in at their ATC's and raced through the graveyard of Wheels, splattering mud behind them.

*The Wheel's twin tracks gouged the grass of the hill, trying to make it up, but seemed somehow to be spent of its strength, its duty done.

Cindy was the first to see the alien inside. She whipped around the left side and slid to a halt, waiting for it to catch up with her.

Inside of the glass prison sat a wan, beaten entity shrouded in a white funeral garment. Its face, wholly unhuman, was pulled back in a tight death mask of agony. With all four of its arms, it grasped the throne inside as if it were accelerating toward death at an amazing speed. Yet it was still alive. It blinked, and ripples shuddered throughout its body as both girls carefully watched. The alien showed no interest in them at this point, and it was evident the Wheel was slowing.

"What's happening to it?" Cindy whispered in her pin-mike to Cheryl on the other side of the Wheel.

"I don't know," she whispered back.

Suddenly the creature's eyes turned reverentially to the west, and both girls were reminded of the soothing alpha-waves coming from that direction. The creature seemed to have accepted its death with a kind of ecstasy of dissolution.

And as it did, it shuddered once more, and out of the rear of the Wheel plopped another egg. A final one. Out it fell, but this time it was of an unpleasant gray color, like a stone, an ordinary rock. The Wheel painfully began to slow.

The Wheel made the top of the rise, but stopped. The girls stopped as well and stared inside.

Laced across the chair were the remains of the white garment and nothing more. Here the alpha-rhythms were almost palpable, as if something in the storm clouds themselves magnified them and focused them upon anything exposed on the hillside.

Clearly the Wheel had now joined its friends on the long gravestone peninsula.

The Trenton twins merely exchanged perplexed glances and listened to the electric hum of their ATC's and the beat of the rain, which was just now on the increase.

"So where are they now?" Lisa Palazetti asked, sloe-eyed, having just been woken from a deep sleep by First Officer Digeno, who had called her to the Pit.

Lisa stepped onto the bridge where Mr. Digeno and James Guthrie were watching one particular screen. Guthrie stepped back to let the doctor by, and as a consequence, became virtually invisible. The man never seemed to sleep; but Lisa had much else on her mind.

"There." Mr. Digeno pointed. "We've been following them for quite a while. I wouldn't have woken you if I didn't think it was important."

One special screen showed a diagram of the *Clark Savage, Jr.* The umbrella-shaped ship was a lacework of super-alloyed girders and small service tunnels, running both horizontally throughout the main levels of the ship and vertically down through the "stem" to where the research vessels were docked.

Down very near the base of the *Clark Savage, Jr.* on the schematic of the ship there appeared a greenish blip, a dot indicating movement of some kind where movement should not have been.

"Someone's there?" Lisa asked, rubbing the sleep out of her eyes. "Someone's down in one of the tunnels?"

Mr. Digeno's dark eyebrows came together with worry. "The children are down there. Right where we can't get at them too."

But also on the schematic, though at a much higher level, was another green blip.

"Who's that?" Lisa wanted to know. "More of the children?" She'd begun wondering just which of the kids was where.

"No," Digeno said ominously. "That one is Bramlett. *And* about three of his security team."

James Guthrie stepped forth at this point. "Might I suggest that we confine Mr. Bramlett to quarters, sir? We are in a holding pattern, and most of the crew is asleep at the moment. Which is where Lloyd is supposed to be."

Digeno held up a thick, muscled hand. "Not yet. I want to see what he's up to."

But Lisa came awake with alarm. "Is he going to hurt the children? I don't want him anywhere near those kids, Mr. Digeno!"

Digeno's eyes never left the blips on the computer schematic of the *Clark Savage, Jr.* He said, "No one's going to hurt the children. Bramlett is only doing what we're doing, that's all."

"And what *are* we doing?" Lisa demanded, flushed with frustration.

"Watching the children rework the ship," Digeno stated evenly.

"What?"

Digeno nodded and faced her. "They've been rebuilding the ship ever since they came on board before we left lunar orbit. But now they're fine-tuning their work. They've replaced much of the wiring, down to the launch bay, and their own computers are augmenting ours. They're up to something and I think Bramlett knows this and he doesn't like it."

Lisa glanced from the schematic back to Mr. Digeno. "What does Dr. Trenton have to say about this? Does Torque know?"

"We can't reach them just yet," Digeno said, leaning back, watching the other screens above the Pit. "There's some atmospheric interference down there, but as soon as we break through, we'll let them know. I was told to keep you informed on the whereabouts of the children."

"But what about Robbie? Doesn't she know they're missing from the nursery?"

Digeno shrugged. "She's asleep. Either they've gassed her or she's just taking a nap. She doesn't know they're gone. I just picked up their presence in the vents half an hour ago."

As Mr. Digeno kept a hawk's eye on the blip that seemed to represent an unsuspecting Lloyd Bramlett and his security team, Lisa watched the blip that must have been Gopal Govinda and one of the little girls.

"I don't get it," Lisa said out loud. "Just who *are* those kids, anyway?"

Cindy hugged herself for warmth as the sea winds brought with them a sudden chill. She knew that it was only her imagination, for the Moonsuits were totally environmental; the temperature always perfect.

No, she thought. This is something else.

"I don't like it here," she announced to her sister.

Cheryl had been looking around, both out ahead of them down into another Wheel-littered valley, and behind them where more Wheels lay rotting in the rain.

As if thoughts long buried during the pursuit of the Wheel had now risen to the surface of her mind, she blinked her eyes and looked at her sister with recognition. She said, "I don't think Mommy came this way. The computer must be wrong."

Cindy, holding to her Gemini nodule, listened and thought deeply. "The computer says that the anomaly to the west out in the ocean is so powerful that it's acting like a magnet. She might have been pulled way out there."

But there was an ocean *out there*, and neither girl liked the thought that their mother along with millions of other human beings might have been sucked along the gravity line between the earth and Delta Pavonis Four, only to appear out of nowhere in the middle of an alien ocean.

On the other hand, as Uncle Emmett's own computations had also suggested, the humans drawn down into a Seed's event-horizon might have gone anywhere. Anywhere to where the gravity lines led.

Cindy didn't know; it needed more work.

Cheryl then suggested: "Let's Jump the *Lady* closer to the ocean. Maybe there's a city there."

Cindy said, "Okay."

She just wanted to get away from the plain of dead Wheels. Besides, it was beginning to rain heavier and heavier, and the gray sky mixed with the subtle alpha-rhythms caused a slight depression to form in her mind. Only the Gemini nodule seemed to be staving off the gloom.

Both girls simultaneously wheeled their ATC's about and retraced their original path. They ignored the pretty eggs which lay in the Wheel's puddled track, and concentrated on their next plan of attack.

And the further they got across the plain, away from the alpha-rhythms out to sea, the better, and more adventurous, they felt.

They even reached a point where they started racing each other, bending down over the control handles like motorcycle racers plowing through the mud of an obstacle course.

Naturally, they were surprised when they ran into more aliens.

They rammed their ATC's up through some harmless-looking bushes at the top of a particular hill, and the moment they did, they came into full view of a team of cream-skinned aliens picking up the eggs the Wheel had laid behind it.

Cheryl shouted something Cindy didn't catch. She was busy braking her bike, and fighting for balance—which she lost. Cindy tumbled over the top of her ATC, and sprawled down the slope in the mud and rain.

There were four alien beings, all astride slothful six-legged mounts. They were wearing very strange helmets which completely covered their heads. They were also energized by small packs on the backs of their necks.

In their four hands, each alien gripped a long metal pole with a scoop on the end, and they were in the process of retrieving the eggs.

Cheryl, upright on her stalled ATC, waited for the four aliens to scream and fall over—and for Cindy to hurry up and get on her feet.

But that didn't happen.

The aliens didn't scream, for the helmets were doing something powerful to their brains which stifled the self-destruct mechanism with intense beta-waves.

The creature in the lead hefted a gun and did not hesitate to fire upon Cindy as she slopped through the mud, trying to get to her feet.

An invisible stream of light shut down the power in Cindy's Moon-suit and the nine-year-old found herself lying helplessly rigid in the mud. She screamed.

Cheryl only had time to gasp, not even to scream. For the lead alien with his faceless iron helmet blasted her as well.

Both girls were locked inside the indestructible shells of their pink Moonsuits. And as the four alien beings slowly moved toward them, the Trenton twins started screaming in earnest.

——— 40 ———

Emmett sat at the control console of the *Roxanne Vail*, clutching it tightly as the ship shuddered in the asteroid's unyielding pull.

How the planetoid had turned and approached so quickly was beyond him. His main concern was its intention, and the glowing orange eye of the vast transformation plate in front of it.

As he reprogrammed the computer for a thousand-mile Shortjump back toward the planetary elliptic, he watched with horror as tiny sparkles appeared miles out in front of the transforming plate. They were the bodies of the cast-out Cirrans—X'yn's comrades—which were being scooped up, probably as an accident of merely being in the way. Emmett was dead sure that the *Roxanne Vail* was a more delicious target. Vradha had seen it and Vradha was on its way.

Emmett suddenly heard the clickings and guttural throat-poppings of the alien down in the science bay. Perhaps she was calling out to him; perhaps she was panicking. However, given the monstrous visage of the asteroid out in the starry distance, X'yn was now an ally. They were both in the same metaphorical boat.

He was going to need input on this maneuver.

He held the *Roxy* on a stable course as he raced back down to the science bay. There, the alien was leaning against the curving interior wall, perched at a small porthole, watching as her former home-away-from-home approached. The leads to the Sheriar were still attached.

Emmett quickly reprogrammed the computer in the bay to transfer the Sheriar's images to the computer above. All the while, X'yn was trying her best to communicate to him something of the dire nature of their circumstances. Emmett didn't need a Sheriar for that.

"Don't worry!" he said aloud, trying to calm her as he made for the ladder. "We'll be out of here before you know it!"

The alien's wide eyes watched him race back up to the command module above.

Swiftly reworking the Sheriar's program, Emmett took out another package containing leads, and these he plugged in. At the same time, the *Roxanne Vail* began vibrating in a way he hadn't noticed before.

It was as if every bolt and rivet was being meticulously examined and gently pried apart by invisible fingers reaching out across the vastness of space—the space between the asteroid Vradha and the *Roxanne Vail.*

It took the Sheriar several seconds to sort out the images, since Emmett's own brain could not afford to calm down to a total alpha-wave rhythm, given the crisis. However, X'yn's mind seemed committed to the inevitability of her situation and viewed the approach of Vradha with a kind of indifference which Emmett didn't know how to take at first.

Until he got a keener impression of what had become of Delta Pavonis' loose planetary matter, including the single moon which for billions of years loomed large in the sky above Cirran. Everything became clear to him now.

X'yn's ancestors had long since swept up all of the free-floating planetary matter in the system in order to build their vital *xotls.* Halos, along with the Seeds they bore, required immense energies and incredible tonnages of raw material. As Emmett picked up vaguely from the alien down below, Vradha—or the computers guiding it from within—would think nothing of consuming a small craft from another star system. If it would help the Cirrans get back in touch with the voices of the Great Unknowing, then any sacrifice was worth it.

—*But if you had ever heard the voice of...God...you would know its importance.*

X'yn's thoughts over the Sheriar channels were clear, but without emotion. A soldier for God, he realized. And when God spoke to you, then you became Chosen.

And you could then do anything you wanted because God allowed it. You could even give your life.

"Ross has got to know this," Emmett suddenly announced to himself. Trenton was deeply interested in history, and these aliens were no different in the ways they justified their actions. No different at all.

The lights on the console before him went go-ready green for an emergency Shortjump.

But Emmett hesitated.

Vradha was still a hundred miles or more away and he knew he could slip out of normal space at any time, like an insect dropping free from a spider's web, much to the surprise of the spider.

There was more he wanted to know from the alien. *Much* more. Emmett absorbed all that the alien could send.

The Cirrans, for all their advances, had reworked their whole star system just to get back the voices of the Great Unknowing. They didn't care how their *xotls* affected other star systems—only that by silencing them, could they get back to God.

Why? he demanded over the Sheriar. *Who gave you the right?*

The rumbling of the approaching asteroid's awesome power seemed to take her back. Its cadence, its rhythm, its familiarity took her to a place which was comforting.

Emmett *saw* their mission. Though he had no earthly time frame for it, he knew that the Cirrans were space travelers long before mankind had gotten the courage to wander westward across the Atlantic to unknown lands. The Cirrans by then were taking their own bold steps into space, never once meeting with disaster.

Their ships were strangely organic, almost living beings. They resembled the long spiral shells of Mesozoic gastropods back on the earth, and seemed to tunnel their way through outer space. Their expeditions took them to the inner planets, then heroically out to the stars nearest Delta Pavonis.

But then they began hearing the voices of the Great Unknowing. Emmett wasn't sure how much of what he was getting from X'yn was mere belief or historic truth, since it had all happened centuries before her birth.

However, two expeditions to nearby stars—lasting for decades— never established contact with their home world, and "voices" began talking to them, perhaps from guilty consciences. Not only did leaders and technologists hear the voices, but so did the average Cirran on the home world and the space stations above. It was racial, species-wide.

Emmett recalled a theory Ross himself had been keen on, handed down from a Princeton psychologist, Julian Jaynes, now long since dead. Jaynes believed that early man, up to the end of the Bronze Age, also heard "voices," sometimes in burning bushes, sometimes in the thunder of the clouds in Norwegian fjords.

In any case, the voices went away as man developed language and memory and civilization.

X'yn had no use for Emmett's mental wanderings; she was only devoted to Vradha's task of building *xotls* to cast out into the galactic arm. Much in the same way, Emmett realized, that men invented mantras and prayer and Sheriars in order to get back to the whisperings of the Holy Spirit.

The *Roxanne Vail* heaved.

Emmett bent forward, holding on as the tractor beam angled the research craft dead-center of the enormous transforming plate of the asteroid. The go-ready lights were still green and waiting.

"And the Seeds," Emmett blurted out. He felt suddenly like a cop grilling a suspect under the focused light of the Law dangling overhead.

But X'yn had nothing to hide. The Cirrans, as a race, were an honest lot. Or so it seemed.

—*Merely to quieten, to calm.*

And, the thought came over the Sheriar, to wait out the possible rise to intelligence of any race who might evolve on a prospective planet. The Cirrans were told to cover all bets.

"Do you know how *powerful* the Seeds are? Do you?" he fairly shouted out where he sat alone in the command center. He sent to her images of the "saints" or trapped humans; concepts of bent-space and event-horizons; of the millions of human beings flung out in all directions, somehow, following the gravity lines the Seeds mysteriously tapped into.

—*Consequences. We are not responsible for them. We do not care. The... pacifiers...must be powerful if we are to hear the Great Unknowing again. To know of the fates of our space explorers....*

Aghast, Emmett finally felt the absolute *alienness* of the creature in the bay below him. They were true Nazis. They knew what they *had* to do. If anyone they trampled didn't like it, it was *their* problem.

And the voices of the Great Unknowing would not return to the Cirrans unless the *xotls* did their job. It might take them centuries before they knew for sure, but they would wait. In the meantime, they would build as many of the Halos as possible and send them wherever life might spring up into the flower of intelligence. *Getting their house in order....*

The asteroid miles out in front of the *Roxanne Vail* seemed to have disappeared but for the round, glowing maw of the transformation plate. It could barely be perceived as moving; yet Emmett's instruments indicated that it indeed was moving at them, the plate getting larger and larger like an approaching sun.

"I've got some friends I want you to meet, X'yn," he said aloud, hoping the Sheriar would translate only so much—and no more.

Then the ship jerked violently. Vradha's transforming plate became suddenly blue.

And all the go-ready green lights went instantly yellow and red, all up and down the console.

"Shit!" Emmett shouted, as several plastic toys tumbled onto the floor. *"What's this?"*

He slammed a fist onto the Shortjump button, but nothing happened. Alarms sounded and lights flashed.

His heart almost exploded and he sent a desperate thought wave over the Sheriar lead down to the alien underneath him in the science bay. And X'yn responded:—*Vradha wishes to know us. We are being transferred. But we are not to worry. I am told it is an easy death. The ship is now in Vradha's hands.*

41

"Just whose idea was this, anyway?" Trenton called out from the fore of the rubberized raft as it slammed into the green waves lapping the island of mesmerizing Seeds.

"Yours," Toquero said grimly, his one eye intent on keeping them afloat.

Glenn Thorpe, in the chitin of his protective Moonsuit, sat in the center of the boat with his head down in his instruments. Trenton, when he could, snapped photographs. A squall had boiled up above them and much of the tall pillar of the broken arch was becoming obscured. Still, they gathered what they could.

But if any earth ship had passed this way, drawn by the power of the space-bending Seeds, there was no sign of one. Trenton knew that now.

The golden arch looked as if it was an armored leg of a sky god thrust deep into the ocean floor. When the Halo had crashed, Trenton mused to himself, it must have sounded like Thor striding the earth. Very little would have survived the shock of impact, and the Seeds themselves, geared to the intelligences nearby, would have removed the possibility of any survivors. The Wheels were proof of that.

The waves leapt up into foam, and salt began to work its way into the narrow creases of their Moonsuits.

"How close do we want to get, Ross?" Torque asked above the roar of the wind and the waves.

Trenton looked back to Glenn Thorpe. "How much more do we need?"

Thorpe stared blankly at the huge accumulation of dumped Seeds that had become an island. "Couldn't hurt," he began slowly, "to have one of the Seeds. They're so unlike any of the ones we've brought from the earth." He nodded his head enthusiastically. "Let's steal us a Seed. What the hell."

The island, as they approached, was more than twenty miles in diameter, a flattened cone of dull-gray Seeds piled like buckshot around the tattered structure of the arch. A kind of chalk-white lichen or sea growth of some kind had, over the years, worked its way up out of the cratered sea bed and in between the rounded hulls of the individual Seeds, cementing them further in place. If anything more evolved was growing there, or living there, Trenton couldn't determine offhand.

A narrow inlet allowed the boat to moor up against a convenient cobbled pier, and Trenton and Toquero both reached out to stabilize the craft.

Thorpe stared upward through the swiftly building clouds as raindrops swirled around them.

"You know, Ross, the physics of the thing are just right."

"What are you talking about?" Trenton said, jumping ashore onto the vibrating Seeds.

"I think it's possible that you could actually climb the Halo up into outer space," Glenn said, making his way out of the raft.

Toquero stayed put, grim lines of worry and doubt inhabiting his youthful countenance.

The Seeds sent their casual vibrations up through the alloy of their Moonsuits, and to Trenton it almost felt like a Sheriar session, for it was quite relaxing and rather pleasant. But he knew that for *others*, the Seeds were monstrous space-bending demons.

Glenn bent over and snapped a Seed up from the white spongelike substance that gripped it. Glenn brushed a residue from the Seed as he gently held it.

"Two months ago on the earth," he said with a wry smile, "this would have been suicide."

"You couldn't even have done it," Trenton reminded him.

Thorpe then scanned the island. "What about finding a piece of the Halo itself?" He leveled an arm up at the arch, which bent upward into the gray-white clouds.

"Good idea," Trenton acknowledged. With a Moonglove, he slicked water from his black hair and perused the globes scattered aimlessly about. "This place reminds me of a gutted salmon. These Seeds are like eggs."

It wasn't a pleasant image.

Suddenly from the boat where he waited by the electric motor, Toquero called out, "Ross, did you hear that?"

"Hear what?"

Toquero clapped a hand to his ear when he had thought he'd heard a cry coming over the radio.

Trenton did the same. "I don't hear anything." Thorpe stood with his alpha-globe and waited.

A shrill, high-pitched string of obscenities filled the airwaves like black flak.

"It's Roarke," Trenton breathed, recognizing it, his Stively-built jumping a notch in his chest. The combined metal structures of the arch and the island of Seeds were causing a great deal of interference, but Roarke's pleas for help came through nevertheless.

Glenn Thorpe danced down the hill of Seeds and tossed his prize into the boat. "If Roarke's talking to us for any reason, it can only mean he's in trouble."

"Right," Trenton agreed.

Toquero, dark with disgust, pushed away from the Seeded pier. He said, "Some outfit *we* are. Not only do we need a biologist and a geologist, we also need a baby-sitter."

Trenton smiled slightly. "We have one. She's up in the nursery with the children."

Toquero drove the raft out into the building waves and the fall of new rain. "Well, Robbie ought to be down here with *us*."

The ventilation shafts of the *Clark Savage, Jr.* were barely big enough for adult human beings, but the children of the nursery found them no trouble at all, even with their Moonsuits.

Lisa Palazetti had just discovered this on her own, even though Mr. Digeno's schematic in the Pit a few levels above had already shown her that was true.

Sitting in Ross Trenton's quarters, with the Sheriar nearby, Lisa had been thinking about Emmett, not the children.

However, she soon began thinking of the mysterious kids when the ventilator grid which led to Trenton's quarters began to work its way out of its place on the wall into the darkened apartment unit of the former Lunar President.

Lisa sat at the computer of the Sheriar, in the dark, and watched incredulously as the grille popped open and a little person crawled out.

Patty Brown, wearing a bright pink pair of overalls, tennis shoes, and lugging some machinery, made her awkward way into Dr. Trenton's quarters. In the fine strands of her auburn hair, Patty wore a com-set as if it were a tiara.

Lisa rose from the chair like a white specter, very concerned. Only minutes before had she passed several of Lloyd Bramlett's private security team in the outer hallway.

She didn't want to frighten the little five-year-old girl.

Gopal Govinda, in his Moonsuit, followed little Patty. He brought with him a toolkit, and as soon as he stood up, they both made for Dr. Trenton's Sheriar.

"Hi, Lisa!" little Patty sang, seeing the physician standing in the luminescent shadows.

The two children walked past her with complete impunity, their Gemini nodules dangling like captive stars on their chests.

"What are you children doing here?" Lisa asked in a cautious whisper.

Gopal set his tools down on the edge of the console. He said in a grown-up's voice: "We're helping Dr. Trenton with his Sheriar."

"I thought Dr. Trenton told you not to play with the Sheriar, Gopal."

"We're not *playing* with it," little Patty said, fussing with a panel beneath. "We're *fixing* it!"

"I don't think it's broken, Patty."

Gopal faced the beautiful physician. He said solemnly, "We're improving the whole ship. Dr. Trenton's Sheriar is a vital part of the ship's function. If he is to do his work right in the future, he'll need it to work more efficiently. We have even modified your own computers, Dr. Palazetti."

From underneath the computer, in the dark, a tiny light came on, and little Patty's voice chimed out: "Yes! I made it better!"

The five-year-old began working away, singing to herself, lost in thought.

Lisa sat back down and folded her hands in her lap. *Such serious little people*, she thought to herself. *Why can't they just be the children they are?*

And that got her off thinking about Emmett and the true child *he* was. His decision to run for mayor of Yancy City had been a political necessity if the House of Toquero's influence would continue to matter, especially against the desperate earthbound corporations and governments trying to find a way to overcome their fall into the widespread ruin of Hoovervilles. When Emmett had run successfully for mayor, nobody had foreseen that the Seeds would ultimately be neutralized.

Had Emmett simply jumped ship too soon? she wondered. His heart was always in his work—and in his play. Perhaps he'd been forced into a situation he knew he couldn't endure.

She asked herself a dozen questions as she sat in the dark, watching the strange children behave like strange adults. Which was what Emmett was: a child masquerading as an adult. And one that was just as strange.

Just then, as the two children were both at work underneath the main console of Trenton's Sheriar, a loud commotion filled the outer hallway.

Lisa sat up suddenly as the door burst open and in rushed Lloyd Bramlett, in his military black Moonsuit, followed by an entourage of heavily armed security personnel.

"All right!" he shouted, punching the lights on. "Everybody stop where you are!"

He meant the children.

Lisa jumped up, enraged. "Lloyd. Just what the hell—"

Bramlett held out his hand as if he were directing traffic at a crosswalk. The little kids crawled back out onto the floor and looked up.

"This is a ship-wide security matter, Doctor. You have nothing to do with this."

"Like hell I don't!" She stamped. "These children are under *my* supervision."

Lloyd brought an evil sneer to his face. "Then you're under arrest too." He waved his hand down at the little boy and girl and said, "They've been systematically undermining this vessel, and the *Clark Savage, Jr.*, despite what you might think, is still operating under the auspices of the United States government and NASA."

One of the security men came around and grabbed the Gemini nodule in its weir of soft gold from around little Patty Brown's neck and snatched it away. Little Patty's eyes went wide with sudden horror, and then she began crying.

Lisa Palazetti punched Bramlett in the side of the head—awkwardly, but enough to knock him off balance.

"You coward!" she shouted, her fist clenched.

Bramlett regained his balance and stifled an urge, a *mighty* urge, to flatten her on the spot. He rubbed the place on his upper jaw where Lisa's bony knuckles had impacted rather clumsily.

He said, "You don't know who you're messing with, *Doctor* Palazetti."

His eyes were full of frustration and hatred. *This* was no Moon Man, she realized.

Bramlett turned away from her suddenly and reached for Gopal's Gemini nodule.

But the skinny nine-year-old went spread-eagled on the floor. Instantly little Patty did the same.

Then just as suddenly, Lisa felt herself tranquil, calm—even sleepy. Yes, very sleepy.

The room filled with soothing vibrations and everyone was feeling them.

The security guards began to teeter and Lloyd Bramlett was the first to fall to his knees. He fell face-flat to the carpeted floor and cloaked himself with a rasping series of snores. The security team instantly did the same, piling one on top of another.

Alpha-waves, Lisa suddenly—if peacefully—realized. *Tight-beamed directly at the adults. They had expected this to happen....*

Lisa had fallen back into her chair, but was too helpless to get up. The men on the floor were, universally, conked.

"I'm sorry, Lisa," came a birdlike voice from the cranny of the ventilator shaft.

The stubby snout of a modified beta-gun, one her father had built, protruded from the arms of Terry Thorpe, who had remained hidden for just such a contingency as this. The girl had modified the beta-gun to send out stultifying alpha-waves as well.

Unfortunately, in order to stop Mr. Bramlett and his meanies, she had to blast Lisa as well. And though Dr. Palazetti had gotten only a slight bit of it, the ray was effective enough to hammer her back into Dr. Trenton's comfy chair.

Gopal got up and helped little Patty Brown recover from her tears, as well as helped her tie the Gemini nodule back around her neck, returning her to her previous state.

He then touched his ear-link and spoke into the pin-mike at his cheek. "Peggy?" he called out in a low voice.

246

Lisa watched as the small boy called to Peggy Howe, one of the other children in the nursery. When he got a reply, he said, "Mr. Bramlett and his men have attacked us, but they have been neutralized. You'd better pass along the new coordinates to Mr. Digeno. I think now would be a good time." At the other end, Peggy Howe seemed to understand.

He switched off and began helping little Patty replace the computer panel as Terry Thorpe withdrew back into the vent. Lisa didn't understand any of this.

"What coordinates? What are you talking about?" she asked—but just barely. She was slowly fading into the dreamy halls of sleep.

"Peggy found where Cindy and Cheryl are," little Patty said happily.

"And Dr. Shea, too," Gopal added, but Lisa had just then slipped away into unconsciousness.

"Let's go," Gopal Govinda said.

They went.

42

The rain of the burdened clouds over the peninsula sizzled around the Trenton twins as the aliens slowly approached them where they lay.

Cindy screamed as three of the four multi-armed beings stood over her gazing through the thick lenses of their protective helmets.

"I can't move!" she cried out to her sister in a shrill voice. "*Cheryl!*"

The fourth alien on its mount hugged its sack of retrieved eggs to its small chest. The aliens had no faces to be seen through their helmets; they seemed like machines walking menacingly through the thunderous rain crashing around them.

Cheryl tried gunning her ATC to life where she sat, but even the powered assists at her wrists were frozen and locked. Her hip assists wouldn't move, nor would any of her leg assists. Her Moonsuit had been thoroughly neutralized.

"Call the ship, Cheryl! *Call the ship!*" Cindy cried through her panic.

"I can't!" Cheryl shouted as the aliens came closer. "I can't do anything!"

The one creature on its mount spoke chatteringly into a mouth-piece that must have been a radio as the other three conversed among one another. Spidery antennae rose up above the helmets of the aliens, spearing the rain as it fell.

One of the creatures then walked over to Cindy and bent down, examining her.

She screamed in a high-pitched voice that did not frighten the alien. Instead, a long upper arm came down at her and its narrow, bony fingers snatched her Gemini nodule completely away.

"No!" she shouted. "Don't! Cheryl! *Cheryl!*"

With the Gemini nodule taken from her, all the courage of her thousands of heroic lives drained away, and there she was: a nine-year-old girl, locked piteously in a Moonsuit, twenty light-years away from her home on the earth's moon. She responded as any frightened nine-year-old would: she began crying.

The aliens chattered among themselves, ignoring Cindy for the moment, each taking a turn examining the nodule itself. They had recognized it, but seemingly could not understand what it was doing in Cindy's possession.

That was when they turned on Cheryl.

"Oh no!" Cheryl screamed.

She struggled where she sat on her idle ATC, but only managed to fall completely off.

Her Gemini nodule, on its own gold chain, dangled out onto the rain-soaked grasses, as a cream-colored alien arm, riddled with warts and veins and strangely coiled hairs, came down and plucked it away.

The courage of her courageous captains instantly disappeared from her *sanskaric* memory, and she was just as helpless as her sister.

"Radio the ship!" Cindy cried from where she lay spread out on the green tubes of the peninsula grass.

But Cheryl, now just another nine-year-old in heart and mind, did not know what good that would do. They were far, far away from home. And there was no one nearby to help them.

Basil Roarke felt much the same way as he bounded around the inside of the Wheel's crystal hub like a bee in a bell jar.

In the process, he had thoroughly demolished the "throne," or chair, and pieces of it constantly got underfoot as he tried to escape.

"*Ross!*" he shouted into his radio pin-mike at his cheek. "*Toquero! Anybody!*" He sent out his call on all channels, but static and the blood-rush of sheer panic were all that filled his ears in return.

So he pounded.

Fists clenched, shoulders flexed, he pounded. And pounded mightily until alarms went off in his utility belt, telling him that his Moonsuit would soon run out of power.

The glass of the hub was completely resistant to any kind of force or pressure he could exert. And like an obedient idiot, he had left his clappers back at the *Retta Kenn* at Ross's suggestion. Ross never did like the idea that mankind's first alien planetfall should be one of military bearing. So Roarke was presently weaponless.

And *that* he didn't like.

He fell against the glass and slid down to the floor. The alarms at his belt stopped as he rested. He toggled his radio link, gasping for air. "You guys! Can you peckerheads hear me?"

He then transferred to the link to the *Retta Kenn*, which would tight-beam his calls up to the *Clark Savage, Jr.* "Digeno! Are you up there? Officer Jolly! Is *anybody* up there? I need help and I need it *now!*"

The Wheel continued on its way back across the peninsula containing the hulks of its fellow creatures. The thunder clamored outside in the sky as rain braided down the curved wall of the crystal hub. The Wheel, for all Roarke could tell, seemed to know what it was doing and where it was going. It moved in and around the smooth granite boulders on the peninsula and avoided certain clusters of frilly trees.

But no one was responding to his calls. Lightning and electromagnetic disturbances were interfering with his Moonsuit's transmission—and he felt utterly trapped.

Then the Wheel noiselessly climbed up over a hill crowned with red-feathered bushes. On its way down the other side it passed a hooded alien astride a six-legged horse.

Roarke jumped up.

"Hey!" he shouted. "What the hell is *that*?" His radio channels were open, and if anyone was listening, they'd heard.

The alien, protected by its alpha-wave helmet, had also seen Roarke. It was in the midst of spooning up an egg of a harsh crimson color with a long, flexible pole when the Wheel passed him. It couldn't help but see the huge Moonsuited figure within.

"Ross?" he stammered, eyes latched on the apparition of the cream-skinned alien receding in the distance. "Ross, we got us some aliens here! Real aliens!"

The alien being suddenly reared its mount around and began following the Wheel, having apparently taken a few seconds to come to its senses.

"Oh, no," Roarke gulped, seeing this shift of events. "Don't do this to me."

Roarke backed away from the crystal wall of the hub as the creature galloped by in the rain. It gave Roarke a sideways glance, as if to make sure that it had seen what it *thought* it had seen, and disappeared well out ahead of the slow-going Wheel.

Roarke lost sight of the rider, who disappeared up over another hill, toward which the Wheel seemed destined.

The stocky engineer bunched his fists and crouched as the Wheel's twin wheel-tracks dug into the sodden ground and toiled their way up the next hill. The six-legged "horse" had left a whole series of crescent-shaped tracks in the ground and the Wheel was paralleling them. They were both headed in the same direction.

The Wheel reached the top of the hill as the wind of the rainstorm swept chaos around him.

And there they were. A whole *bunch* of aliens. The guy had gone and run back to his friends.

Then Roarke jumped up, seeing something he hadn't quite expected to see.

On the backs of two of the large six-legged creatures were the forms of pink Moonsuits, strapped and secured for the ride back.

"*Hey!*" Roarke shouted, falling up against the crystal hub. He jumped and pounded furiously. "Cindy! Cheryl! It's me! Basil!"

His voice went nowhere and neither of the girls was in a position to see him inside the Wheel. One seemed stretched out as flat as a board and the other was curled in an awkward fetal position. Their captors didn't seem to care what shape they were in.

Until the Wheel with Roarke inside drove on by.

He clapped his hand to his pin-mike and shouted, "Ross, they're here! I found them! I found your girls! Ross, are you there? *Hey!*"

The first alien which Roarke had initially passed gesticulated wildly at his comrades and they all pointed to the two captive girls and then to the Wheel. They then pulled their mounts around and started frantically after Roarke's Wheel.

Before too long, the Wheel took a turn in its passage across the gently hilled peninsula, and came in sight of the *Lady Nelia Sealing*. Roarke's heart virtually leapt with boundless joy.

Until he saw what a bunch of helmeted aliens were doing to it: they were picking it apart like ants on a dead grasshopper.

They now had carts and more horses, and one of them appeared to be operating a kind of crane. They appeared to be quite serious about their task.

"Oh, shit," Roarke said to himself, swallowing hard. "They'll get the Jump engines. Ross!" he shouted into his pin-mike. "*Ross!*"

The Wheel proceeded beyond the glade as the storm overhead gathered force. The aliens with Cindy and Cheryl were swift behind his Wheel, but he couldn't see them now.

That was when he started picking up transmissions from Trenton.

For a moment during the storm, the static relaxed and Trenton could be heard calling to him.

Quickly he responded. "Ross, I found your kids. And you'd better get your ass over here. We're in a hell of a lot of trouble!" He spoke loud and fast; he didn't know how much time they all had.

He then added: "And I'm inside a Wheel and I can't get out. It's moving east. *The damn thing's alive!*"

"*You idiot!*" shouted Toquero.

Trenton's voice interrupted. "We're coming. Just hold on. Engage your homing signal now!"

Then the static growled and garbled, and over Trenton's channel Roarke could hear the organ-pipe hootings of the storm through the ruined arch's tortured metal. Trenton, still talking, was cut off entirely.

Roarke danced and ricocheted, screamed and yelled.

The Wheel continued on through the wild storm.

Toquero had one hand on the tiller of the engine and had one eye—his *only* eye—on the shore.

"I knew we shouldn't have left him behind," the rogue shouted above the rain. "I just *knew* it."

Trenton, though, was holding onto the words the wrangler had left him with: *I found your kids.* It rose like a chant even above the cries of the wind through the arch behind them. The shoreline approached as if it were the edge of heaven, a place of salvation.

He then looked down at Glenn Thorpe in the middle of the boat. The inventor sat with one hand on the borrowed Seed from the island and he stared at it like Rembrandt's *Aristotle Contemplating the Bust of Homer.*

Then Glenn's eyes caught Trenton's. "I'm picking up the *Savage.* They've found Emmett." He'd also been listening to the big ship's transmissions.

Trenton's heart hammered in his chest. "*What?*"

Thorpe had one ear focused on the ship's tight-beamed transmission. "I barely got it, but I think Mr. Digeno said that the children in the nursery have located the *Roxanne Vail.*"

Trenton wouldn't even allow himself the luxury of a smile. *Not yet, not yet!* a voice cried out within him.

"Emmett can wait," he said.

"I don't think so," Thorpe reported. Toquero was also listening to the frantic calls from the *Clark Savage, Jr.,* which were being distorted by the storm's electrical chaos. The waves of the shore crashed loudly before them.

Thorpe prepared his equipment; they were going to land at a run. He said, "It seems that Emmett's in trouble. The *Savage* can't wait."

"Oh, swell," Toquero moaned. "What next?"

They hit the beach like Marines and jumped out, scrambling into action. They left the boat bobbing in the surge of the tides as their Moonsuits whined and propelled them up the granite crags of the peninsula.

Roarke was running out of air.

Inside the Wheel it had gotten hot and muggy and it was clear to him now that the Wheel *was* something of an execution vehicle, for the creatures who went in the direction of the Halo in the ocean were meant to perish once they got there—whatever their condition.

Roarke fell to his knees, conserving his strength. Hope buoyed his spirit, as well as the knowledge that the homing signal emanating from his belt would be picked up by the *Clark Savage, Jr.*—assuming, of course, that it could make it up through the gargantuan storm swirling around them. Lightning scissored the clouds everywhere.

As he stared down at the terrain below the hub, Roarke suddenly noticed that they were no longer on the tubers of the grasslike plain. It seemed filmy, smooth, even slimy.

"Oh, no," he started.

He was on his feet in a flash of power from his Moonsuit. "Oh, no…"

The Wheel seemed now to be traversing a strip of slimy, mucoid substance that was about a hundred yards wide. Puddles from the storm dotted it like mirrors—but whatever it was, it was nothing *natural*.

The Wheel followed it, and clearly it was a highway of some kind. Nothing else was on it, and as the sun came out through a quiet moment in the storm, Roarke could see that it was bound for a small valley out ahead of him.

That was when he saw the city.

He squinted through the clear glass of the hub, trying to make out the structure. The highway seemed destined directly for it.

Then, as the Wheel got closer, Roarke revolted in an unutterable, choking panic.

The strip of slime upon which the Wheel was making its way was actually coming *from* the city.

"Ross!" Roarke shouted into his pin-mike. *"Ross, you gotta get me out of here!"*

The pathway of slime was a trail left by the city, which was a giant snaillike creature. It was heading east at a very slow crawl, and out of its hull came smoke from the dwellers inside. Various antennae protruded above it, and windows could be seen lining its sides. Other, smaller creatures of a bovine sort were slowly following the city, grazing on the greenish tubers of the plain to either side of the backwash trail of slime.

And the Wheel was clearly bound for the rear of the city.

It gaped at Roarke like a huge, open anus. Which was exactly what it was. And there, alien beings, all in protective helmets, waited for the Wheel's arrival.

The "city" was a bioengineered construct, just like the Wheel, and it seemed to be capable of sustaining several hundred of the four-armed creatures. Behind it a flesh-colored "foot" trailed like a tongue, leaving in its wake the long "highway" of mucilage.

Roarke absolutely *hated* snails. He thought he was going to die.

43

Quite suddenly, the helm of the *Clark Savage, Jr.* lit up like a Christmas tree.

Mr. Digeno, the second-in-command, was sipping his third cup of coffee when the specially designed hologram of Delta Pavonis Four became something other than the planet it had been programmed to resemble.

Instead it became a sidelong view of the entire Delta Pavonis system.

"What's this?" Mr. Digeno said, sitting up. He set his coffee cup down. "What's happening to the computers?"

Ticia Rhodes, who had just stepped from the elevators, came around to Mr. Digeno's side. Digeno turned to the physicist. He pointed to the hologram.

"Why is the computer doing this?" he demanded.

James Guthrie, who was sitting nearby in a chair vacated by a com-officer, cranked himself around and looked up. He intervened for the physicist.

"It appears to be a program override from one of the computers down in the nursery, sir," the bureaucrat reported.

Digeno, who didn't know that Guthrie had been down below in the Pit, leaned over—then considered the hologram which hovered in plain view.

"What do *you* know about this, Dr. Rhodes?"

Ticia, taken aback by the sudden override, seemed momentarily embarrassed. She had something else on her mind. "Mr. Digeno," she said, "there's been an altercation in Dr. Trenton's quarters."

Digeno's dark Italian eyes went darker just then. "What *kind* of an altercation?"

James Guthrie climbed up out of the well of the Pit as the other technicians raced to maintain some control over their computers. Everything, it seemed, was happening because of the nursery.

However, Ticia, seeing Guthrie, appeared reluctant to speak fully.

"Don't worry about him," Digeno said. "He leaves this room and I break his legs. Captain's orders."

Ticia took a deep breath. She said, "I found Lisa unconscious in Dr. Trenton's office. I guess she'd been in there using the Sheriar." Digeno's eyes were impatient coals burning slowly. Ticia continued, saying, "And there were a few of Lloyd Bramlett's men as well."

"What about Mr. Bramlett?" Digeno asked.

"He was there too."

Digeno swiveled around in his chair, flooded with disgust. "Oh, great. Torque's going to love this one. I can just see it."

Ticia, now spying the new hologram of the Delta Pavonis system, walked to her chair. She wasn't through. She then said, "That's not all. I think that the rest of Lloyd's men are going to break into the nursery."

Digeno, one hand on the intercom, ready to summon Toquero's own guard, said, "You *think?*"

"I thought that the children might be in danger, but Lloyd's squad is crawling all over the place and they're carrying acetylene torches." Ticia found her chair and pointed to the new hologram. "Where the hell did *this* come from?"

"That's what I asked you when you came in," Digeno said disgustedly. He leaned into the intercom. "Sergeant Eaves," he called out to the security team. "You are to proceed to Level One and arrest anyone trying to break into the nursery."

Guthrie mounted the bridge and stood beside Dr. Rhodes. "Evidently," he began, "the children have been tying in their gravity-wave scanners with our computers up here while we've been busy."

Dr. Rhodes tried ignoring him. However, he held out his ever-present aluminum clipboard and from it he removed a printout. He handed it to her.

"These are the coordinates of Dr. Shea's ship, the *Roxanne Vail*. They came across Ms. Jolly's computer and I took the liberty of taking them down for you."

Ticia snatched the printout from Guthrie's hand and glanced at it. She then considered the hovering lights in the hologram.

She leveled an arm at the hologram. "Mr. Digeno, if this schematic is correct, Dr. Shea is somewhere in the vicinity of that asteroid."

There was a tiny speck of light, swinging high out of the elliptic of the other planets. If the *Roxanne Vail* was there, the holo was too small to represent it.

"Are you sure?" Digeno asked. He glared at Guthrie. "Did one of the children send this here, or did you make this up all by yourself?"

Guthrie shrugged from within his Moonsuit. "You might want to contact Gopal, or perhaps Terry Thorpe."

Ticia announced: "They aren't in the nursery. At least Gopal isn't."

"Then where is all this coming from?" Digeno demanded. "Have Robbie Rogers find out which kid has made contact with Dr. Shea's ship. I want this verified."

His irritability seemed contagious and the men and women down in the Pit began rechecking their data.

Moments later, in the frenzy, Penny Jolly called out, "Sir, it's a distress signal. It's coming in over a gravity line, a direct route to the asteroid."

Digeno began thinking, and thinking fast, and Ticia Rhodes was pondering their options as well.

Guthrie cleared his throat and bent over Digeno's chair. "Might I suggest two things, sir?"

"Very fast," Digeno said, snapping his fingers.

"First of all, have Sergeant Eaves clear up the mess in the nursery, then second, let Dr. Trenton and Mr. Toquero know that we've Short-jumped to check out the distress signal from the *Roxanne Vail*."

Digeno scowled at Guthrie, clenching both of his powerful fists. "Give the man a cigar," he said to no one especially.

Penny Jolly, looking harried and harassed, stood up at her communications console. "Mr. Digeno, I still can't get a clear channel to them. There's a very bad storm down there—"

Digeno slapped his hand to the console. "Then tight-beam the message to the *Retta Kenn*, then have it relay the message when the storm clears."

"Is that possible?" Guthrie queried.

"We do it all the time," Digeno grated.

"But what about Mr. Bramlett's men?" he then asked. "They should be secured if we're going to Shortjump, sir. There could be some damage."

At that moment a call came over the intercom directly to the captain's chair. It was the voice of Robbie Rogers.

"Mr. Digeno?" she asked hesitantly.

Digeno snapped on the intercom button. "I'm here, Ms. Rogers. What's wrong?"

"Well, I'm not too sure," she began haltingly. "I was wondering why there is a bunch of Mr. Bramlett's men asleep out in the hallway."

Digeno looked blankly at James Guthrie, who in turn glanced down at Ticia Rhodes.

Mr. Digeno switched off the intercom and shouted down into the Pit, "Shortjump in three minutes. Mr. Guthrie has the coordinates."

The computers on board the *Roxanne Vail* were going unaccountably haywire. Everything had been shut down but the vital environmentals which kept Emmett and the alien being alive. It was as if the tractor beam knew which parts of the *Roxanne Vail* to shut down and which to keep functioning. Its invisible fingers probed everywhere.

Vradha *knew* what the *Roxanne Vail* was. It fingered and fondled it; tasted it inside and out with an insatiable tongue. The ship's alarms would not shut themselves off.

Up from the Sheriar leads came X'yn's thoughts—calm and uncaring.

—*Vradha needs to know.*

Emmett clutched the console as the *Roxy* heaved once more uncontrollably.

"Wants to know what?" he shouted out, instantly realizing that within the *Roxanne Vail* was both a Longjump engine and a Shortjump engine. And clearly the Cirrans, for whatever reason, had never developed faster-than-light travel.

The alien's silence was that of a convict emotionally committed to her own inevitable execution.

"Answer me!" he demanded. "You owe me that!"

The image coming over the Sheriar veiled the alien's arrogance. The Cirrans didn't owe anybody anything, for God—or the Great Unknowing—spoke to them only.

—*Vradha has its own store of basic elements. It wishes to rebuild us. Know us for what we are....*

"What?"

Emmett stared aghast at the glowing lights of Vradha's transformation grid. A weave of crisscrossing beams revealed the interior of the asteroid itself.

And just beyond the grid inside Vradha, an exact replica of the *Roxanne Vail* was being formed.

The Cirrans may not have FTL travel, he suddenly realized, but they've got a whole hell of a lot that we don't have, and this asteroid is one of them.

The alien continued.

—*Vradha will structure your craft and ourselves as well from the materials they have. But the final transformation will be instantaneous.*

One big gulp, Emmett realized.

And the *Roxanne Vail* was helpless, caught in the spider's web that Vradha had slung about itself to gather space debris. There was nothing he could do.

Except for one thing.

He unplugged himself from the Sheriar and made for the science bay below him.

Upon seeing the gigantic snail—or whatever it was—that masqueraded as a bioengineered city, Basil Roarke did everything he could to get out of the Wheel, including kicking and clawing.

But the Wheel, evidently under partial control by the aliens at the rear-end of the city, rolled up onto the "foot" of the snail itself and into the rear hangar.

And into utter, utter darkness.

"*Ross!*" he screamed into his radio, feeling his world close in on him.

He fell and scampered backward as far as he could go inside the hub as his eyes adjusted to the gastrointestinal darkness of the strange, mobile city.

To either side of him were cantilevered dwelling units rising up the interior of the massive shell which hovered over him like an old-time dirigible hangar, and from these a bioluminescent light could be seen. Odd, pendulous lamps hung down from the ceiling of the shell and these provided most of the interior lighting for the aliens.

The aliens themselves were each helmeted with the same kind of protective covers that Roarke had seen on the others who'd captured Cindy and Cheryl. And they had been waiting for his arrival.

The Wheel came to an uneasy halt in the middle of the city, stopping before a larger sphincterlike set of doors. The aliens, some bearing weapons, other carrying tools, escorted Roarke's Wheel gently through the sphincter when it opened, leading him toward a factory area. The smoke of furnace fires—or cooking fires!—flowed around the Wheel like the specters of the alien dead, filling the air with oranges and reds.

Roarke bounded to his feet as the Wheel came to its final stop. Glancing behind him, to check on whether or not the sphincter to the factory had closed, he saw the horseback aliens bring in Cindy and Cheryl. Vaguely, through the crystal walls of the hub, he could hear the girls blubbering through their tears from where they'd been strapped onto the beasts.

To his left, through the glass, he then noticed other Wheels, and these were being grown. They dangled from calciferous stalactites, and they seemed to be in various stages of evolution. Wires and bony stays surrounded each Wheel as if each were a bonsai tree being shaped just right.

However, to Roarke's horror a different group of aliens—all helmeted and all glancing occasionally in his direction—was assisting *another* alien into the hub of a brand-new Wheel.

This individual seemed fat and bulky and was draped in a special white robe. He wore no helmet, but seemed nonetheless transfixed.

Roarke realized that the individual was full of eggs and was on its way to the Halo to be "executed," in exactly the same way that he and Ross and Chuck Sproule had been fed to the angel of Northridge. Whatever disaster the fall of the Halo had created for this planet, these creatures were taking advantage of it. The alien being helped into the Wheel bore a committed expression on his unshielded face, neither happy nor sad.

When the creature had been seated and the hub sealed, the new Wheel dropped clumsily away from its stalactite berth and began heading toward the rear of the small city.

The alien within was a sacrificial lamb, a *kamikaze* pilot borne on a divine wind.

"Mr. Roarke!" shouted one of the twins. *"It's Mr. Roarke!"* That galvanized him and he lurched about, searching for a hole, a crack, a tear he hadn't seen before.

Cindy cried out pitifully as two of the helmeted aliens untied her and threw her to the floor. She'd been hurt, and Roarke watched as the little girl's head struck the floor violently.

"Hey!" he shouted, pounding on the glass. "Leave her alone! Stop!" The rage that rose within him came from a deep, dark place that wasn't human—or was just *barely* human. It blinded him and filled his ears with a ringing that seemed to be half voices and half energy out of control.

Suddenly his Wheel sagged, as if depleted, and the sphincter in the base of the crystal hub itself eased open with a sigh, letting the bad air out and the good air in.

He almost gagged, for the air wasn't good at all. It smelled like flatulence from the bowels of a dead walrus. And while Cindy had been treated roughly, Cheryl had fallen into spasms of vomiting. She was now crying and choking where the aliens had thrown her savagely to the floor.

Roarke jumped down to the opening in the hub and wormed his way out of the Wheel with his Moonsuit assisting his unspeakable anger.

The aliens backed off and held out their weapons, ready.

They seemed so confident. But they didn't know that they had Basil Roarke in their midst—and he tore into them, swinging.

The aliens shouted and barked to one another from within their unwieldy helmets, knocking into each other, scrambling to safety.

Roarke raced into their midst and picked one up, squeezing it. The creature's arms came off unexpectedly. It screamed as its helmet also came away, and died.

Another creature came at him with something that might have been a rifle. He didn't care what it was. He grabbed and broke the gun right in half before their shielded eyes. They staggered backward unbelievingly.

He tossed the pieces of the rifle aside, bunched up a Moonfisted glove, and caved in the helmet of the individual who'd held it. The creature was dead before it hit the ground.

Then Roarke was struck with a lightning bolt.

Or something quite like it.

He fell to one side and rolled over, feeling as if someone had kicked him fully in the chest.

One of the creatures waddled up with a rifle about as big as he was and aimed it at him. He fired, and Roarke didn't feel a thing this time.

But it was a different gun entirely. His Moonsuit now was suddenly locked in place. He tried to get up and plaster the alien into the next world, but he couldn't move.

He snarled and raged—and another alien came up with a simple metal bar. Which he whacked across Roarke's face, sending the wrangler rolling up against the base of a new Wheel hanging from the ceiling.

He was almost blinded with pain, and blood flowed freely down into the collar of his metallic brown Moonsuit.

The girls screamed now, for both could see the aliens falling upon him.

Indeed, a whole gathering of the creatures suddenly rushed at the Trenton twins with metal rods, and as Roarke's vision cleared, he could see the creatures begin to beat the twins to death.

The aliens, in their own xenophobic frenzy, screamed and wailed and pummeled the girls—as another group beset themselves on Roarke.

Then quite unexpectedly, as blood filled his mouth, his eyes, and ears, a terrific rush of wind soared in from the outer section of the city. The shouts and barks of the aliens ceased as the bioengineered city filled with a familiar humming—the humming, the song, the choir of a gathering of angels.

The aliens standing around the sobbing twins with their sticks, weapons, and hammers, went absolutely rigid. Their hands unlimbered and everything clattered loudly to the floor.

The whole interior filled with sudden individual implosions of air as the aliens, one by one and in whole groups, popped out of existence.

They left behind them little thunderclaps of inrushing air and the instant the *Retta Kenn* appeared in the strange city, all of the aliens vanished entirely.

The Moon Men had brought with them a Seed.

The living city came apart right under their feet.

The *Retta Kenn* snapped into existence with a swirl of Shortjump energies that electrified the air. Inside, the alpha-globe, attuned to the brain waves of the aliens, glowed like a vengeful wraith.

Ross Trenton was down the ramp of the *Retta Kenn* almost as soon as it had Jumped out into normal space, and in his hand he held a clapper, fully charged and ready to fire.

Toquero was right behind him with his own rifle as Glenn Thorpe, homing in on Roarke's signal, tried to keep the ship stationary.

But the gigantic shell which housed the city began shifting with a cacophonous crashing and cracking of the brittle chitin which composed the husk, now that the living organism that was a snail had vanished. It, too, had been evolved enough to be sucked into the bent-spaces of the Seed's peculiar event-horizon.

"Daddy!" Cheryl screamed from where she lay. The *Retta Kenn* was in plain view, and the golden Moonsuited figure of her father brought out the lonely cry of a nine-year-old.

Both girls were beaten and bloody from countless contusions and cuts, but the aliens had not hurt them badly: they had spent their energies trying to crush the uncrushable Moonsuits with their bars and wrenches.

The city reeled as Trenton ran over to his girls.

Toquero, falling off balance, switched on the overhead beam of the Moonsuit helmet which he had donned. He darted the beam around the murky interior of the shell as the shell settled to the earth with a horrible-sounding racket which shook everyone.

"Roarke!" he shouted. "Where the hell are you?"

Bioluminescent fluids which filled the dangling lamps of the interior flowed like greenish blood under their feet as Toquero raced deeper into the city. Trenton splashed through the glowing fluid over to where his girls lay helpless.

All around them the city started to disintegrate, now that its host organism had been thrust into bent-space. Large chitinous plates dropped down about Trenton from the ceiling, and he had to whisk Cheryl away from one plate which came crashing at them with a shriek as the membrane which held it tore apart.

"Daddy!" Cindy cried. Both girls were awash with tears and blood as Trenton swept them up in his powerful arms, holstering his clapper.

"Torque!" Trenton shouted, feeling the whole city shake.

Toquero had found Roarke underneath a Wheel which had just fallen loose from its stalactite growth-hook. The stalactites themselves had also shriveled and broken loose, as well as a whole bank of dwelling units, now empty of inhabitants.

"The place is coming apart!" Trenton shouted, hoisting up his girls under both arms.

Toquero, using the assists of his purple Moonsuit, hefted the Wheel off to one side, the light of his helmet stabbing wildly about.

"*I can't move!*" Roarke shouted. It was more of an outraged growl than a shout, and both Trenton and Toquero were astonished by its fierce timbre. Even for Roarke it sounded inhuman.

Then behind them, when they had least expected it, the *Retta Kenn* suddenly rolled over. The shell of the city had settled to the ground underneath them awkwardly and couldn't support it. The extended ramp of the ship flipped upward and a small fire broke out from the engines underneath.

"We've got to get out of here!" Trenton shouted to his team. Then he turned to Glenn Thorpe. "*Glenn, move! It's going to blow!*"

Trenton's artificial heart, roaring with apprehension and fright, pumped mightily as he bounded for the huge back entrance to the city, blinded by the light of Delta Pavonis as it briefly pierced the storm clouds outside. The boots of his Moonsuit were brightly daubed in the blue-green colors of the bioluminescent fluid and he found the going slippery.

Bring them all together! was the chorus in his mind. *Get them back!* It had been a risk to Shortjump so close to Roarke's signal, but they had run out of options. He jumped down off the edge of the rear entrance and stumbled to the slime-trail the snail creature had left in its wake.

Behind him appeared Toquero, lugging a snarling Basil Roarke, who was frozen in his Moonsuit in exactly the same fashion as Trenton's daughters had been.

"Glenn!" Trenton shouted back into the city through the crashes and explosions. Furnace fires and electrical conduits had burst out of control in the various dwelling units, and a bilious black smoke had begun coiling out of the rear of the small city like a living thing.

Glenn Thorpe suddenly appeared, staggering through the smoke, coughing.

"I couldn't save it," he called down to them, jumping. "The ship's lost. The landing strut broke loose and rammed the engines from underneath. We'd better move."

"What about the Seed?" Trenton asked.

"Lost." Thorpe started running out with Toquero away from the burning city.

Trenton, carrying a nine-year-old under each arm, ran as well, if a bit awkwardly.

"*Those sonsabitches!*" snarled Basil Roarke, bleeding from his wound across his eyes. "*I'll kill every one of them!*"

"They beat us!" cried Cindy.

Trenton didn't say anything, knowing that it could have been worse—*much* worse.

The Moon Men got well off the snail's mucilaginous trail and began running out onto the glade. The city then exploded, taking the *Retta Kenn* with it.

Toquero, smudged from top to bottom by all the soot and still hefting Basil Roarke, groaned. "My father will kill me. Another twenty-million-dollar ship gone."

"Don't worry about your father," Trenton said, watching the strange city collapse. "I'll talk to him."

Just at that moment, a whirlwind spun itself furiously into existence a hundred yards away, scattering several of the multilegged bovine creatures in panic. The *Lucille Copeland* appeared, settling easily onto the green meadow.

"Look!" Glenn Thorpe pointed. "It's MacReadie!"

The lower ramp slammed onto the glade and several of Lieutenant MacReadie's Space Marines came trundling out, armed and armored and just looking for trouble.

"*MacReadie!*" Trenton shouted out, waving his arm. Both girls were on the ground, quiet now.

"Forget those guys!" Roarke shouted, still enraged. "There's aliens all over this place!"

"Forget the aliens, Basil," Toquero said. "One thing at a time."

MacReadie, laser rifle in hand, ran all the way across the glade. Trenton picked his girls back up and the Moon Men jogged to meet him and his contingent.

"Dr. Trenton!" he began excitedly. "The *Savage* has picked up a distress signal from the *Roxanne Vail*."

"That's Emmett," Toquero said suddenly. "They found him."

MacReadie said, "Yes, sir. But they've gone on ahead. It'll take several Shortjumps to reach them, but we've got to go now, if we're going to catch up."

Roarke, curled in his awkward position, shouted, "Hey, you guys! Listen to me! There's a bunch of them taking apart the *Lady Nelia!*"

MacReadie took one of the Trenton twins, shouldering his rifle. They began running back to the ship. He said, "We stopped there first. It took about two minutes."

"Two minutes to do what?"

"Watch them all fall over and die," MacReadie said flatly. "Except for the ones wearing helmets. They took a couple of shots at us, and we took a couple of shots back."

Roderigo Toquero then asked, "What about the ship?"

"Sorry, sir," MacReadie said. "It looked pretty bad."

"Swell," Toquero groaned. His one eye had gone dark and disgusted. "That's just swell."

The *Lucille Copeland* Shortjumped three times to meet the motion-vectors of the *Clark Savage, Jr.*, and as soon as the smaller vessel had docked safely, Mr. Digeno let it be known that they were going to Shortjump even closer to the asteroid.

Which they did.

Trenton and his Moon Men were thoroughly nauseous from all of the combined Jumps, but they could not indulge themselves in the luxury of being sick. Trenton gave his girls over to Lisa Palazetti and several technicians, who proceeded to diamond-drill them out of their ruined Moonsuits, and then followed Toquero back up the long main shaft of the huge dreadnought to the bridge.

On all of the color-hued screens above the Pit were different versions of the same thing: the asteroid.

Toquero slipped into his captain's chair as Mr. Digeno returned to his console in the Pit. Trenton sat beside Toquero, noticing that James Guthrie, looking bland and intractable, was standing behind Ticia Rhodes.

Toquero looked at the screen. "How far out are we?"

"Three hundred miles and closing, sir," someone down in the Pit cried out.

Trenton suddenly felt all wrong. He could feel it through his Moonsuit. "Torque," he said in a low voice. "Do you feel that vibration? Is it the *Savage*, or what?"

"It's the asteroid," Ticia called out from her station. "I'm picking up a massive tractor field stretching out for hundreds of miles in front of the asteroid."

The *Clark Savage, Jr.* pulled around before the asteroid, and when its burning mouth seemingly opened just for them, everyone in the Pit went quiet.

"There's Dr. Shea!" Penny Jolly, the harried com-officer, hailed.

On their screens, a tiny beleaguered star floated out before the translucent screen.

"Jesus Christ," Toquero breathed, bending over slightly. "That asteroid's a whole city!"

"And it's got Emmett," Trenton said quickly. "Ms. Jolly, see if you can raise him, and fast. He's too close to that thing."

Trenton's Stively-built heart hammered away in his chest. *We're so close*, he thought to himself. *Just bring the boy in!*

Seconds later, Penny Jolly turned her head around; she was riven with fear. "Sir, I can't raise him at all. His computers are shut down and all I'm getting is a distress signal locked on repeat."

Roderigo turned to Trenton. "We're going to need the Marines for this."

"Right," Trenton agreed. With MacReadie's men manning their particle-beam bazookas in the ball turrets ringing the upper half of the *Clark Savage, Jr.*, they'd be able to do what they were trained to do. Emmett was in danger and they had to get him out. They'd have time later to examine the asteroid closer.

"Mr. Digeno," Toquero said. "Jump the *Savage* forty miles from the *Roxanne Vail*." And on another com-link to another part of the ship, he ordered, "Lieutenant MacReadie, I need all seven bazookas manned. Shortjump in two minutes. *Go!*"

The face of Vradha grew larger and larger. Emmett could now feel the very molecules of his body being searched, examined, and clutched by invisible tentacles of highly focused energy. It was beyond anything he'd ever known.

A sudden lethargy had gripped him, as if Vradha was already withdrawing, molecule by molecule, the iron from his blood, the potassium from his brain, thus shutting down his entire system.

Over in a clustered corner, X'yn had found her comrades and sat staring at him as he fell into the science bay.

She chattered dully at him in her strange language, the light between her eyes blinking its unfathomable Morse.

"This is terrible," Emmett said out loud. Sweat trickled down the creases of his Moonsuit.

But he found what he had been looking for.

There was a bomb bay nestled underneath the science station. And in it was a fifty-megaton bomb. He had no choice now but to use it. It was for the Hopscotch.

Perhaps it had been the fatigue sucking strength from him, but he no longer felt panic. Or it could've been another form of resignation. He didn't care now.

The transformation screen of the asteroid approached with its tractor beam drawing the *Roxanne Vail* nearer and nearer. The vibrations of the screen shook every atom of Emmett's body as sleep—the sleep of death—began to fall about him.

If he survived the process, if the *Roxy* made it intact, there just might be time to defuse the bomb.

His last vision through the portholes of the vessel had shown him that the reconstructed version of the *Roxanne Vail* on the other side, deep within the asteroid, was almost complete.

Was there a pile of Cirrans being reconstructed as well? Was there a live, but resigned alien in the science bay? And was there a human being desperately punching in a timing sequence for a hydrogen bomb, lying flat on the floor, arms dangling down into a bomb bay?

And, he wondered as the environmentals shut down, casting the *Roxanne Vail* into darkness, *are there a dozen toy rockets and boats being materialized there as well?*

The molecules that used to be Emmett Shea disbanded and went hither.

The instant the *Clark Savage, Jr.* winked into existence, it was yanked violently by the tractor beam. Everywhere alarms went off, pipes burst, and crew members were thrown from their Jump chairs. Some decks lost power and several screens above the Pit went blank.

"All stations report!" shouted Toquero over a ship-wide com. Toquero then leaned over to Ms. Jolly. "Penny, get Emmett fast! We're going to dock him on our own if we have to!"

Mr. Digeno, at his chair, saw a row of red lights appear before him. They also appeared on Trenton's console, and on the captain's.

"We can't move, Captain," Digeno called out. "We're locked into their beam."

"Sir!" another technician shouted, jumping up, pointing to one of the surviving screens. "The *Roxanne Vail* has released its nuclear device, sir. There, see it?"

"Oh, shit," Toquero breathed.

Trenton grabbed Toquero by the arm. "Wait! Watch! Look where it's going!"

The vast shimmering transformation grid seemed to slowly draw the nuclear bomb into invisibility.

Then Trenton noticed what was happening on the *other side* of the grid. "Holy Mother of God. I don't believe it. It can't be possible..."

Just beyond the grid they could see not only the *Roxanne Vail* taking on form—but just a bit further in they could see the *Clark Savage, Jr.* being rebuilt, bolt by bolt, molecule by molecule.

"What's it doing?" James Guthrie queried from his shadow behind Ticia Rhodes.

"It's duplicating us," Ticia said in a low voice, hardly audible to anyone but herself. "And Emmett's ship as well."

She turned to Ross with a wholly desperate look. "And it's going to happen to us too."

The nuclear bomb simply disappeared several miles out in front of the grid. The *Roxanne Vail* began to fade. As it did, its replica began to become more substantial, look more incandescently real.

As did the mushroom-shaped dreadnought behind it in the cavernous asteroid.

Trenton felt tired, exhausted by all the worry and activity. "This is just too much. We're about to lose Emmett." He found himself standing and leaning heavily on the console—thinking distantly of Emmett, Annette, and his baby girls now ensconced in the nursery with Lisa Palazetti. *Too many people to think about, just too many responsibilities....*

James Guthrie said, "I think I'm going to lie down. You men don't need me for this." And the sleepy-eyed bureaucrat slowly left.

A voice grated from Toquero's helm. "This is MacReadie. None of the bazookas are working, Captain. My men are also feeling very, very tired. Can you or Dr. Trenton advise us?"

It was very quiet in the Pit. Some of the technicians had already gotten up and filed out—not deserting their duties. They were merely redundant personnel and had decided to let the others work their problems out.

But that's not the way Trenton saw it, nor did Ticia Rhodes.

"Ticia," he said heavily. "Are you feeling...?"

She stood up slowly, hesitantly. "Yes. I think it has something to do with the duplication process. I'm beginning to feel...rather light-headed."

Toquero, who was fighting to keep his ship under control, faced his friends. "You aren't going to leave me, are you?" The alarm was sharp in his voice, but he, too, was already beginning to feel the death-calm surrounding them. The desperate lights on the console blinked madly.

"Fifteen minutes before impact," someone down below called out in a lackadaisical voice.

"Fifteen minutes," Trenton said. "That's not much time."

"The *Roxanne Vail* is gone, sir," Penny Jolly announced calmly.

Indeed, there was nothing but space between the asteroid and the *Clark Savage, Jr.* However, deep inside the asteroid itself a fuller version of the *Roxanne Vail* was suspended all alone—as the new copy of the *Clark Savage, Jr.* slowly took form.

Trenton said to Toquero, "We've got a few minutes yet. Let me think this over."

Torque Toquero sat on his throne and stared at the screens above the Pit, looking like a man in a gas chamber waiting for the cyanide pellet to shuttle into the bucket of acid underneath.

As Trenton made his way down to his quarters, he could only think of his girls. But he also noticed what was happening to him as well.

Everything seemed insubstantial, as if the walls of the ship were transforming themselves into glass. The subtle vibrations of the tractor beam seemed to disconnect muscle from bone, electron from proton, but he swore to himself that it was just his imagination.

What it *truly* felt like was his memory—the *sanskara*—of the shouting hordes of Mehmed II as his army laid siege to the fortress of Constantinople. In the Sheriar he had returned to that moment many times, and always it felt the same: the sea of voices encompassing him, the helplessness, the inevitability of death.

He bumped into Lisa Palazetti, who had just come from the nursery, which the children had long since opened to the adults—now that Mr. Bramlett's men had been neutralized.

"Lisa," he began slowly, gauging his words carefully, "Emmett's been—" But he couldn't finish it.

However, Lisa's own mind swirled with activity, even though she also looked exhausted. "I've put Cindy and Cheryl into their Nerzhins. All of the children are down as well. I've been thinking of doing the same myself."

"Good idea," he said with a reassuring smile.

He touched her on the shoulder and she haltingly walked down the hall to her own quarters.

That's when he thought of the sleep-couches—and the Sheriar. It almost knocked him over.

He quickly made his way to the console in his own quarters, where his Sheriar lay waiting, the main Sheriar computer, the one, he knew, which was linked to every single Nerzhin sleep-couch on board the ship.

It could work, he thought suddenly, trying to fight the onrush of sleep, the hordes of Mehmed II. "Torque," he called out over the com.

"What?"

"Is it possible that you can get the whole crew down into their sleep-couches?"

After a moment: "Are you crazy?"

"No," Trenton said, punching the Sheriar alive, starting it up. "I want you in your Nerzhin as well."

"I'd love to catch some sleep, Ross, but I'm about to lose my ship and about eighty of my friends, except for Bramlett, of course. He doesn't count."

"Do me a favor."

"Okay."

Neither man's voice was full of enthusiasm. But Trenton knew that they had one chance and one chance only.

"Aim the tight-beam antenna at the antenna on the other *Savage*."

"Right."

"I'm serious," Trenton said sternly. Morpheus, the god of sleep, seemed to have weighted his eyelids with twenty-pound irons. "Then set up the computer to receive what we're going to send."

He heard Toquero dutifully carrying out the request on his own. Clearly Ms. Jolly had also left the Pit.

He then switched over to ship-wide communication. And took a very deep breath. "This is Ross Trenton. I want all crew members, including the captain, to return to their quarters and plug in to their Nerzhin sleep-couches. If you are not near your own couch, then use the nearest available one. This is *very* important. Trust me on this." He then added: "And this means you, too, Roarke. No arguments!"

From Toquero came: "You'd better be right on this one, Ross. Or I'm going to tell my father."

The rogue was tired and he switched off.

Trenton hurriedly scrambled over to his own sleep-couch and watched the names appear on the computer console. One by one, the crew members, from MacReadie's Marines to Lisa Palazetti to his own girls—who were already fast asleep—had plugged in.

The computer then showed that the main exterior antenna was ready. The Sheriar, singing in its alpha-rhythms, began drawing each crew member into its memory-function. Trenton had conducted group sessions in the Sheriar before, but never on a scale such as this.

And he had *never* done what he was about to do. But it was theoretically possible, and it just might work....

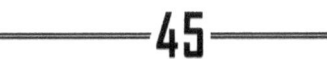

45

The secret of the Sheriar lay in the process of the incarnation of souls itself. Bodies were mere garments, like coats, which each *atma* donned from lifetime to lifetime. Belief in any specific religion didn't matter; only conduct, only the actions both good and evil of the man or woman involved. Those actions, or *karma*, determined the "texture" of the next coat the *atma* would put on in the new life to come.

So said the man buried in the marble tomb at Ahmednagar, India, the man who had designed the Sheriar and outlined the wisdom of its use.

But Ross Trenton now understood it differently. As his own master had said: *Everything that happens to you is a lesson, everyone you meet is a teacher.* No exceptions. And it never stops.

As he sat, ready at his own Nerzhin sleep-couch, he waited for Torque to vacate his captain's chair and make his lethargic way to his own quarters. The ship, now on automatic, could hold itself until the transformation was complete.

But he *had* to have everyone.

When Toquero's name appeared on the Sheriar screen, he was ready.

It had been the vibrations of the tractor beam which had changed him—literally and physically. It was quite similar to the alpha-rhythms generated by the powerful Seed of Northridge, but with one exception: it went deep. It went down to his soul, his *atma*, and suggested something of *change*.

No *atma* could survive the disintegration of the body. And he assumed that that was what was happening as objects filtered through the asteroid's screen.

But as he slowly lowered himself into the Sheriar's alpha-sleep, letting himself relax, he prepared for a different kind of reincarnation.

One always went from death to birth, to a new body when the old one could no longer be used.

But why couldn't an atma, absorbed by the engrams of the Sheriar, held in abeyance electronically, go from one body to its duplicate?

The Sheriar being reconstructed in the new *Savage, Jr.* would be exactly like the one in his quarters, and so would be the people plugged into it. Except for one aspect. If he understood the transformation process properly, those bodies would be devoid of *atmas*, mere empty husks—for no body could withstand disintegration.

But those bodies would be linked to the Sheriar by way of the Nerzhin sleep-couches, and the Sheriar would be tied in to the *Clark Savage, Jr.*'s main computer.

He was going to play "hopscotch" with the aliens and tight-beam the Sheriar's eighty-plus engrams of human souls through the transformation grid.

For he wasn't about to let the troops of Mehmed II take Constantinople this time.

Going down, he saw his Moon Men, most of whom he had worked with in Sheriar therapy before. As the *Clark Savage, Jr.* shuddered in the pull of the tractor beam radiating from the asteroid, Trenton felt his own exuberance, the flight of his own soul as it was borne up on wings of revelation.

And the Moon Men were with him.

The fall of Constantinople had been just one of many lessons for him. Even then, as John Jerome Marcarius, emissary from Rome, he had known that the Pope and Christianity had no further business in the Middle East. Islam was its own great religion, and it had only been utter arrogance on Rome's part to think that the world needed one true religion to soothe every man's soul. He knew it then, seeing the anxious faces of the Ottoman troops in 1453. *It had been wrong.*

And the Moon Men, in one way or another, in one form or another, had been there. As each engram became firmly distinct within the Sheriar, he saw them all. But this time there was a difference: it was *right.* The travail, the struggles of the Moon Men to reverse the historical impact of the Halo, was *exactly* the crucible he was to experience with them. And he was their leader. To have passed on the lunar presidency to Norman Dubie back on the moon might have been politically expedient, but it might not have been vital. It had caused Emmett to prematurely accept the mayoral position in Yancy—and that had caused him to run away. And his own search for Annette had subsequently distorted his thinking.

But the Halo had been the catalyst. And the people who ran this asteroid were also in the wrong. The failure of the fall of Constantinople could be rectified by accepting one's weaknesses and strengths. *That* was the key.

Then came several images as the *atmas* of the children became ingrained within the Sheriar. Why had Cindy and Cheryl gone after their missing mother? Certainly the odds were against them that they could find her. *No*, he suddenly realized, *it goes deeper, much deeper.* He saw *all* of the children and who they had been before they had come into this life. Gently he peeled back the layer of their last *sanskaras* and he saw it: all of the children, including his own, had been crew members on board the *Jaguar Skies*, and they all had been killed when it slammed into Copernicus. Gopal Govinda had been Torque Toquero's cousin and chief engineer; Terry Thorpe, a navigator straight out of MIT on the earth; little Patty Brown had been an elderly banking executive, close to Toquero's father. Little Peggy Howe had been a poet fleeing earth and a bad marriage which fell apart through no fault of her own.

Their desire to take over the *Clark Savage, Jr.* in *this* life had been part of a hidden impulse not to let the *Jaguar Skies* tragedy repeat itself. And Cindy and Cheryl both had been yeomen assigned to young Roderigo Toquero himself—they, too, had perished.

What goes around, comes around, he realized.

Then he heard the Sheriar's voice whisper to him: *Prepare for transition...*and he braced himself mentally. This might not work, he knew, but it was their only chance.

Then came one final image, slowly and *very* reluctantly settling into the Sheriar—which had been waiting for the new *atma* to arrive. Basil Roarke's consciousness dropped down into the alpha-wave state and Trenton eased into the space engineer's strange mind-set, his *Weltanschauung*, and envisioned the man's former life.

Trenton's heart roared with delight. Basil Roarke had been a whale out in the Pacific Ocean, rising in the soft swells of lazy waves, waiting out his last evolutionary stage, waiting to be born, for the first time *ever*, as a human being. And Basil Roarke's life here and now had been nothing but the troubled adjustment to the human condition.

And for Ross Trenton, that revelation came to him on an oceanic swell of ecstatic joy. Everything now made sense.

Then suddenly they Leapt.

For an instant everything went blank as the Sheriar, with the help of the computer at the helm and the tight-beam antenna, shot its engrammatic code across the thirty miles of space through the transformation grid of the asteroid.

The *Clark Savage, Jr.* disappeared entirely, eaten away in one final, instantaneous gulp—its duplicate already formed deep within the asteroid.

With one difference.

The humans came awake suddenly as the Sheriar shut down upon their arrival, all placed in their newly fleshed bodies carefully and precisely by the Sheriar's discreet programming.

Trenton sat up to the sound of footfalls in the outer corridor as Toquero's technicians and crew scrambled to their stations, fully awake and energized by their sudden survival. The lethargy had gone.

Trenton raced down the corridor himself, but not to the elevator to the bridge just yet.

In the nursery, Robbie Rogers had risen from her Nerzhin sleepcouch and was attending the children. Gopal Govinda, still in his brown Moonsuit, sat calmly on a chair that was between the beds of Cindy and Cheryl. And they all had survived the transition.

"You should have told me who you were," he said to Gopal Govinda.

The little boy, still in possession of his Gemini nodule, which was just as powerful as ever, said, "Would you have believed me?"

Trenton shook his head. "No. I guess not."

His girls, though, were asleep and safe. Bandages covered their heads and faces—but they were safe.

Just as he met Lisa Palazetti coming hurriedly to the nursery, alarms sounded out overhead.

"What about Emmett—?" she started.

He held her tight for a brief moment. "I'm going to find out now. You stay down here with the children."

He ran for the elevator.

Gaining the bridge, he found the Pit in a tornado of activity as Toquero's men and women checked on the condition of their magnificent ship.

Torque turned to him, both relieved and a bit pissed off. He said, "That was very risky, Ross. Had I known—"

Trenton sat down in the chair normally reserved for Lloyd Bramlett. "Had *I* known it wasn't going to work, I would have done it anyway." He looked around. "By the way, just where is Bramlett?"

The elevator wheezed open behind them as James Guthrie and Ticia Rhodes appeared.

Toquero said, "I haven't seen him."

Trenton frowned. "I want a body count. Fast."

"We've got a few things to do first," Toquero said. He pointed to the screens above the Pit, which were just now coming to life. "I think we found the guys who made our Halos."

They were inside the asteroid, surrounded by the golden glow of the lights of transformation which helped in the creation of the Halos.

And out before them was another Halo nearly three-fourths completed.

"Oh, my God," Ticia Rhodes said. "Look at it! And there, on the other side! There are *people* looking at us!"

Indeed, as the new *Clark Savage, Jr.* hovered silently in its space several miles from the Halo, it might have been dead, for all the aliens knew. Indeed, that was what the aliens no doubt *were* thinking.

"Torque," Trenton said suddenly. "They don't know we made it."

James Guthrie came over behind Trenton. "Sir, what about the *Roxanne Vail?*"

The screens showed them the smaller vessel also intact. Toquero shouted down to Penny Jolly, who was just now putting her console in order.

"Penny, get us interior video with the *Roxy*. Get *any* kind of communication you can, but tight-beam it. I don't want our friends getting any ideas."

"Yes, sir!"

Trenton stared at the screens as they fizzed and hissed. Jolly was doing her best.

Then suddenly a light burst bright red down on Mr. Digeno's console and the stocky Italian officer shouted up: "Captain! We've got someone firing a bazooka!"

Trenton was on his feet. "Who? Find out! Get MacReadie. We can't blow it now! We just can't!"

Over a newly opened line to the stern bazooka blister came a shrill, angry voice, no doubt originating from the man at the bazooka. Or the wrangler at the bazooka.

Basil Roarke shouted: "*Sonsabitches!*"

At the very bottom of the mushroom-shaped dreadnought a small line of highly charged particles, invisible to the naked eye, sizzled toward the Halo itself. On their screens they could see a trail of furious explosions suddenly appearing along one side of the Halo. Then just as suddenly, explosions appeared all along the inner wall of the asteroid itself. Roarke was firing at anything that seemed reasonable.

"We've got to stop him," Toquero shouted.

"No!" Trenton stated. "It's too late. This is what we're supposed to do anyway."

"Here they come, Mr. Toquero!" shouted an officer down in the Pit.

Dozens of small ships leapt away from the interior walls of the huge asteroid and sped directly at the *Clark Savage, Jr.*

Toquero didn't have to be told. He slammed on the intercom. "Lieutenant MacReadie! Get your men to all of the bazookas! We've got company!"

Then from the Pit came Penny Jolly's voice. "Captain Toquero, I've got visual contact with the *Vail.*"

They all stood to see the fate of their best friend.

They saw the science bay littered with the bagged bodies of the aliens that Emmett had snared in space, along with the lifeless body of one alien in particular who was staring blankly at Emmett.

And Emmett himself was down on the floor. Nor was he moving. If there was any life in his body—his *atma*—nothing showed. His eyes, though, were open, caught in his body's last rapture as he seemed to be pondering an object on the floor which the camera could barely see. But it was enough. A green plastic toy boat, with a smiling face on its prow, lay on its side, just out of Emmett's reach.

"Shut it off," Trenton said heavily.

For an instant they were all silent on the bridge as Marines and crew members elsewhere gained their stations.

Then Mr. Digeno broke the solemnity with the reality of their situation. "Captain Toquero, sir, I'm picking up readings from the nuclear device."

"What device?" Toquero queried. The eye-patched rogue had forgotten.

But several miles between the Halo and the approaching horde of attackers drifted the nuclear device which Emmett had released from the *Roxanne Vail*. It had been duplicated as well.

"It's going to go off in sixty seconds!" Digeno then announced.

"We've got to Jump!" Trenton said to Toquero.

"What about Emmett?" Toquero asked, standing at his console.

"Emmett's where we can't reach him," Trenton stated.

"Ships closing, sir," another technician shouted out.

From all around them came the smaller vessels crewed by vengeful aliens. MacReadie's Space Marines were already firing at them as well as at the Halo itself, which had sustained permanent damage.

Toquero sat down and said, "Prepare for Jump. Mr. Digeno, get us out of here. You pick the coordinates. Just get us far enough away from that hydrogen bomb."

Chair belts clacked into place as crew members got ready. James Guthrie leaned against the wall and watched.

The *Clark Savage, Jr.* removed itself from the interior of the asteroid.

It came back into normal space a thousand miles away, just in time to see the asteroid vomit a long trail of ugly yellow light, all the fires of hell unleashed in the silence of space.

The asteroid itself remained intact, but now—even at their distance—they could see that the explosion had completely destroyed its interior and everything within it.

Trenton swallowed his nausea from the Jump as cheers rose from the Pit. The asteroid, the place where the Halos were made, was now on its way toward Delta Pavonis, having been blasted out of orbit with enough force to bury it rather effectively in the surface of the star several years from now.

Trenton leaned back, saying good-bye to Emmett Shea, his best friend, with a silent prayer. Torque Toquero was busy shouting orders down to Leonard Digeno and Penny Jolly, busy trying to hold his father's ship together. And behind them, James Guthrie was busy scribbling something down on his stupid cribsheet.

Trenton shook his head. His job was done. For now.

Then suddenly over the intercom they could hear Basil Roarke shouting: "*Sonsabitches! Take that! And that!*"

Roarke was still at his bazooka and still firing away at the burned-out shell of the asteroid as it tumbled slowly through the background of crystal stars.

Toquero grabbed the intercom. "Will somebody down there turn that guy's bazooka off?"

Somebody did.

EPILOGUE

The *Clark Savage, Jr.* drifted in its orbit for two days before they decided to return home. It had taken them that long to repair the damage that all the Jumps had caused in the massive ship. In the meantime, Lieutenant MacReadie and his men returned to Delta Pavonis Four to make sure that the *Lady Nelia Sealing* was thoroughly destroyed where it had been partially disassembled on the rainswept glade. The *Retta Kenn* had burned along with the shell of the living city, and nothing remained of it which the aliens might have had use for.

No other aliens were spotted by MacReadie's team, but three more of the strange mobile cities were sighted from low orbit, but these the Moon Men decided to leave for another expedition to examine. At least the secrets of Jump technology were safe.

As it turned out, they had taken a few casualties themselves. Three Marines had not made it to their Nerzhin sleep-couches in time, and when their bodies were found they confirmed Trenton's initial intuition. They were perfectly alive—but their souls were not present.

There was one other casualty that he knew they would have to pay for one way or another. Lloyd Bramlett, probably out of spite, had refused to put himself in Trenton's hands through the Sheriar. Bramlett instead was found in one of the armory chambers, in a specially armored Moonsuit, evidently intent upon gaining control of the ship through some kind of force. The transition had caught him unprepared. His body, now in a vegetative state, was in sick bay along with the three Marines.

This bothered Trenton. He never had liked the man, but he didn't think Bramlett so totally evil as to "die" the way he had. The consequences, though, were political. As Trenton sat in his quarters on their last day in orbit about Delta Pavonis, he thought about Lloyd Bramlett and the government back in the United States, which was recovering from the destruction of the Halo and the Hoovervilles.

However, he wasn't thinking *that* hard on the subject, for he was playing with one of Emmett's alpha-wave yo-yos. Apparently the children had brought it with them, and little Peggy Howe had given it to him on one of his visits to the nursery to see Cindy and Cheryl. He walked slowly around.

He stood in his golden Moonsuit and flung the yo-yo down and reeled it back up. Its motion generated the subtle alpha-waves and they calmed him; they allowed him to think less and less of the tension Lloyd Bramlett's death would cause the House of Toquero and the Moon Men. It also allowed him finally to let Annette go, and that was the hardest of all.

A knock at the door revealed James Guthrie in the outer hallway. Not ceasing his play with the yo-yo, he called out to the bureaucrat to enter.

"We're Longjumping in three hours, Dr. Trenton," Guthrie said. The adventure clearly had aged the little man, but not as much as some of the others. He seemed practically invincible, as if shielded from the realities of the world behind his paperwork and duties.

"Thank you, James," Trenton said. "I'll be up to the bridge soon."

Guthrie, though, did not move, perhaps entranced by the yo-yo as well. An awkward moment of silence appeared.

"Was there something else, James?"

Guthrie cleared his throat. "I was thinking."

"Yes?"

"You might be able to get some mileage from all of this, sir."

"Mileage. What do you mean?" Down the yo-yo went, then up it came, alpha-waves surrounding them like lassos.

"Mr. Bramlett had connections at the Pentagon and with Mr. Scanlon."

Trenton stopped. "And...?"

Guthrie was clearly uneasy to broach the subject. He did anyway. "Ralph Scanlon will be up for election a year from this November, sir."

The two men eyed each other. More silence.

Guthrie continued. "When the world knows what you and the Moon Men have done, you might be able to—"

"Beat Ralph Scanlon?"

"Yes, sir."

Everything seemed to freeze around Ross Trenton just then. And he thought he could hear the tiny motors in his Stively-built heart humming happily away.

This was something he hadn't thought about before.

Or maybe he had, and it had taken him this long to realize it. He suddenly recalled his walk into Tahoe City and how he had felt at seeing the gradual decline of small-town America. After all, he had come from a small town himself.

Perhaps it was time for a change.

He almost blushed in front of the small man, as if his thoughts were too transparent. He fingered the yo-yo idly. *Yes, perhaps it was time....*

He then looked at James Guthrie in his peculiar pinstriped Moonsuit. "When will you be seeing the President?"

"I will deliver my whole report as soon as we return to lunar orbit."

Trenton then recalled Ralph Scanlon's penchant for playing around when there was always work to be done.

He smiled wryly and handed Guthrie the yo-yo.

"Give this to him as a gift. Tell him it's from me. I think he'll like it."

Guthrie smiled. "Yes, sir. Is there anything else I can do for you?"

Trenton stood, his hands on his hips, like a man who suddenly knew what he wanted out of life.

"I'll let you know."

www.ingramcontent.com/pod-product-compliance
Lightning Source LLC
Chambersburg PA
CBHW020440270626
47155CB00022B/789